One family

Westmoreland Desires

Three passionate and enticing love stories
from one beloved Mills & Boon author!

Westmoreland Desires

BRENDA JACKSON

First published in Great Britain 2011
Harlequin Mills & Boon Limited,
Eton House, 18-24 Paradise Road, Richmond, Surrey TW9 1SR

WESTMORELAND DESIRES
© by Harlequin Enterprises II B.V./S.à.r.l 2011

Riding the Storm, Jared's Counterfeit Fiancée and *The Chase is On* were first published in Great Britain by Harlequin Mills & Boon Limited in separate, single volumes.

Riding the Storm © Brenda Jackson 2004
Jared's Counterfeit Fiancée © Brenda Jackson 2005
The Chase is On © Brenda Jackson 2005

ISBN: 978 0 263 88337 4

05-0111

Printed and bound in Spain
by Litografia Rosés S.A., Barcelona

Brenda Jackson is a die "heart" romantic who married her childhood sweetheart and still proudly wears the "going steady" ring he gave her when she was fifteen. Because she's always believed in the power of love, Brenda's stories always have happy endings. In her real-life love story, Brenda and her husband of thirty-three years live in Jacksonville, Florida, and have two sons. A *USA TODAY* bestselling author, Brenda divides her time between family, writing and working in management at a major insurance company. You may write Brenda at PO Box 28267, Jacksonville, Florida 32226, USA, by e-mail at WriterBJackson@aol.com, or visit her website at www.brendajackson.net.

RIDING THE STORM

To my family and friends.
And to Jayla Ti'ona Hall. This one is for you
when you are old enough to read it.

****

Through wisdom a house is builded,
And by understanding it is established.
—*Proverbs 24:3*

One

"Jayla? What are you doing in New Orleans?"

A gasp of surprise and recognition slipped from Jayla Cole's lips when she quickly turned around. Her gaze immediately connected with that of the tall, dark and dangerously handsome man towering over her as they stood in the lobby of the Sheraton Hotel in the beautiful French Quarter.

There stood Storm Westmoreland. The man had the reputation of being able to talk the panties off any woman who caught his interest. According to what she'd heard, even though Storm sported a clean-cut, all-American-kind-of-a-guy image, he was a master at providing pleasure without promises of forever. The word was that he had the uncanny ability to turn any female's fantasy into reality and had created many memories that were too incredible to forget. Many women considered him the "Perfect Storm."

He was also a man who, for ten years, had avoided her like the plague.

"I arrived in town a couple of days ago to attend the International Organization for Business Communicators convention," she heard herself saying, while trying not to be captivated by the deep darkness of his eyes, the sensual fullness of his lips or the diamond stud he wore in his left ear. And if all that weren't bad enough, there was his skin tone that was the color of semi-sweet chocolate, hair that was cut low and neatly trimmed on his head and the sexiest pair of dimples.

He was dressed in a pair of khakis and a pullover shirt that accentuated his solid frame. His chest was broad and his butt was as tight as she remembered. He always looked good in anything he wore. Her heart accelerated at the memory of her mischievous teenage years when she'd once caught him off guard by boldly brushing up against him. She had thought she'd died and gone to heaven that day. And just like then, Storm was still more than just handsome—he was drop-dead, make-you-want-to-scream, gorgeous.

"What about you?" she decided to ask. "What are you doing in New Orleans?"

"I was here for the International Association of Fire Captains meeting."

She nodded, doing a remarkable job of switching her attention from his strong male features to his words. "I read about your promotion in the newspapers. Dad would have been proud of you, Storm."

"Thanks."

She saw the sadness that immediately appeared in his eyes and understood why. He hadn't gotten over her father's death, either. In fact, the last time she had seen Storm had been at her father's funeral six months ago. He did, however, on occasion call to see how she was doing. Adam Cole had been Storm's first fire captain when he had joined the squad at twenty, over twelve years ago. Her father always thought of Storm as the son he'd never had.

She would never forget the first time her dad had brought him to dinner when she was sixteen. Storm had made quite an impression on her. Not caring that there was a six-year difference in their ages, she'd had a big-time crush on him and would never forget how she had gone out of her way to make him notice her. But no matter how much she'd tried, he never did. And now as she thought back, some of her tactics had been rather outrageous as well as embarrassing. Thank goodness Storm had taken all of her antics in stride and had rebuffed her advances in a genteel way. Now, at twenty-six, she was ten years older and wiser, and she could admit something she had refused to admit then. The man was not her type and was totally out of her league.

"So, how long will you be in The Big Easy?" he asked, breaking once again into her thoughts.

"I'll be here for the rest of the week. The conference ended today, but I've made plans to stick around until Sunday to take in the sights. I haven't been to New Orleans in over five years."

He smiled and it was a smile that made her insides feel jittery. "I was here a couple of years ago and totally enjoyed myself," he said.

She couldn't help wondering if he'd come with a woman or if he'd made the trip with his brothers. Everyone who'd lived in the Atlanta area for an extended period of time was familiar with the Westmoreland brothers—

Dare, Thorn, Stone, Chase and Storm. Their only sister, Delaney, who was the youngest of the siblings, had made news a couple years ago when she married a desert sheikh from the Middle East.

Dare Westmoreland was a sheriff in a suburb of Atlanta called College Park; Thorn was well-known nationally for the motorcycles he raced and built; Stone, who wrote under the pen name of Rock Mason, was a national bestselling author of action-thriller novels and Chase, Storm's fraternal twin, owned a soul-food restaurant in downtown Atlanta.

"So how long do you plan on staying?" she asked.

"My meeting ended today. Like you, I plan on staying until Sunday to take in the sights and to eat my fill of Cajun food."

His words had sounded so husky and sexy she could actually feel her throat tighten.

"How would you like to join me for dinner?"

Jayla blinked, not sure she had heard him correctly. "Excuse me?"

He gave her what had to be his Perfect Storm sexy smile. "I said how would you like to join me for dinner? I haven't seen you since Adam's funeral, and although we've talked briefly on the phone a couple of times since then, I'd love to sit and chat with you to see how you've been doing."

A part of her flinched inside. His words reminded her of the promise he had made to her father before he'd died—that if she ever needed anything, he would be there for her. She didn't relish the thought of another domineering man in her life, especially one who reminded her so much of her father. The reason Storm and Adam Cole had gotten along so well was because they'd thought a lot alike.

"Thanks for the offer, but I've already made plans for later," she said, lying through her teeth.

It seemed that turning down his offer didn't faze him one bit. He merely shrugged his shoulders before checking his watch. "All right, but if you change your mind give me a call. I'm in Room 536."

"Thanks, I'll do that."

He looked at her and smiled. "It was good seeing you again, Jayla, and if you ever need anything don't hesitate to call me."

If he really believed she would call him, then he didn't know her at all, Jayla quickly thought. Her father may have thought of Storm as a son, but she'd never considered him a brother. In her mind, he had been the guy who could make her all hot and bothered; the guy who was the perfect figment of a teenage girl's imagination. He had been real, bigger than life and for two solid years before leaving Atlanta to attend college, he had been the one person who had consumed all of her thoughts.

When she returned home four years ago, she had still found him totally irresistible, but it didn't take long to realize that he still wouldn't give her the time of day.

"And it was good seeing you again, too, Storm. Just in case we don't run into each other again while we're here, I hope you have a safe trip back to Atlanta," she said, hoping she sounded a lot more excited than she actually felt.

"And I ditto that for you," he said. He surprised her when he grasped her fingers and held them firmly. She'd shivered for a second before she could stop herself. His touch had been like a shock. She couldn't help noticing how strong his hand was, and his gaze was deep and intent.

She remembered another time their gazes had connected

in such a way. It had been last year, when the men at the fire station had given her father a surprise birthday party. She distinctively remembered Storm standing across the room talking to someone and then suddenly turning, locking his gaze with hers as if he were actually seeing her for the first time. The episode had been brief, but earth-tilting for her nonetheless.

"Your father was a very special man, Jayla, and he meant a lot to me," he said softly before releasing his grip and taking a step back.

She nodded, putting how intense Storm's nearness made her feel to the back of her mind while holding back the tears that always flooded her eyes whenever she thought of losing her father to pancreatic cancer. He had died within three months of the condition being diagnosed.

Although while growing up she had thought he was too authoritative at times, he had been a loving father. "And you meant a lot to him, as well, Storm," she said, through the tightness in her throat. "You were the son he never had."

She watched him inhale deeply and knew that her words had touched him.

"Promise that if you ever need anything that you'll call me."

She sighed, knowing she would have to lie to him for a second time that day. "I will, Storm."

Evidently satisfied with her answer, he turned and walked away. She watched, transfixed, trying to ignore how the solid muscles of his body yielded beneath the material of his shirt and pants. The last thought that came into her mind before he stepped into the elevator was that he certainly did have a great-looking butt.

* * *

When the elevator door swooshed shut, Storm leaned back against the back wall to get his bearings. Seeing Jayla Cole had had one hell of an effect on him. She had been cute and adorable at sixteen, but over the years she had grown into the most breathtaking creature he'd ever set his eyes on.

"Jayla." He said her name softly, drawing out the sound with a deep, husky sigh. He would never forget the time Adam had invited him to dinner to celebrate Jayla's return to Atlanta from college. It was supposed to have been a very simple and quiet affair and had ended up being far from it. He had walked into the house and felt as if someone had punched him in the stomach. The air had miraculously been sucked from his lungs.

Jayla had become a woman, a very beautiful and desirable woman, and the only thing that had kept him from adding her to his To Do list was the deep respect he'd had for her father. But that hadn't kept her from occasionally creeping into his dreams at night or from being the lone person on his Would Definitely Do If I Could list.

He sighed deeply. She had the most luscious pair of whiskey-colored eyes he'd ever seen, medium brown hair that shimmered with strands of golden highlights and skin the color of creamy cocoa. He thought the entire combination went far beyond classic beauty. And he hadn't been able to ignore just how good her body looked in the shorts and tank top she'd been wearing and how great she'd smelled. He hadn't recognized the fragrance and he'd thought he knew them all.

She had actually trembled when he'd reached out and touched her hand. He'd felt it and her responsiveness to his

touch had given his body a jump-start. It had taken everything within him to pretend he wasn't affected by her.
Since he was thirty-two, he calculated that Jayla was now
twenty-six. She was now a full-grown woman. All woman.
But still there was something about her that radiated an innocence he'd seldom found in women her age. It was her
innocence that confused him most. He was an ace at fig-
uring out women, but there was something about her that
left him a bit mystified and he couldn't shake the feeling.
But one thing he was certain about—as far as he was concerned, Jayla was still off-limits.

Maybe it had been a blessing that she'd turned down his
invitation to dinner. The last thing he needed was to share
a meal with her. In fact, spending any amount of time with
her would only be asking for trouble, considering his attraction to her. He released a moan, a deep throaty sound,
and realized that the only thing that had changed with the
situation was that Adam was no longer alive to serve as a
buffer and a constant reminder of the one woman he could
not have.

"Damn."

Just thinking about Jayla sent a jolt of desire straight
from the bottom of his feet to the top of his head, leaving
an aching throb in his midsection. Storm rubbed a hand
down his face. Nothing had changed. The woman was still
too much temptation. She'd been a handful while growing
up; Adam had been faced with the challenge of raising his
daughter alone after his wife died, when Jayla was ten.

Adam had been a strict father, too strict at times, Storm
thought, but he'd wanted to keep his daughter safe and not
allow her to get into the kind of trouble other teenagers
were getting into. But Adam had also been a loving and

caring father and had always placed Jayla first in his life. Storm had always admired the man for that.

Storm's thoughts went back to Jayla and the outfit she was wearing. It hadn't been blatantly sexy, but it had definitely captured his interest. But that was as far as he would allow it to go, he thought with a resigned sigh. Jayla was definitely not his type.

He enjoyed his freedom-loving ways too much and no matter what anyone thought, he knew the main reason he lived a stress-free life was because of his active sex life. In his line of business, you needed an outlet when things got too overbearing. And as long as he was responsible and made sure all his encounters didn't involve any health risks, he would continue to engage in the pleasures of sex.

Okay, so he would admit that he was a man with commitment issues, thanks to Nicole Brown. So what if it had been fifteen years, there were some things a man didn't forget and rejection was one of them.

He and Nicole had dated during his senior year in high school and had even talked about getting married when he finished college. He would never forget the night he had told Nicole that his future plans had changed. He decided that, unlike his brothers, he didn't want to go to college. Instead, he wanted to stay in Atlanta and attend the Firefighters Academy. Nicole hadn't wasted any time in telling him what she thought about his plans. A man without a college education could not provide adequately for a family, she'd told him, and had broken up with him that same night.

He had loved her and her rejection had hurt. It had also taught him a very valuable lesson. Keep your heart to yourself. You could have sex for sex's sake, but love and marriage would never be part of the mix. So what if his uncle Corey, who had pledged to remain a bachelor for life, as well as his older brothers Dare, Thorn and Stone, had all gotten married in less than a year? That didn't mean he or his twin Chase would follow in their footsteps.

His thoughts shifted back to Nicole. He had seen her at a class reunion a few years back and had been grateful things had ended between them when they had. After three marriages, she was still looking for what she considered the perfect man with a good education and plenty of money. She had been surprised to learn that because firefighters made it a point to constantly study to improve their job performance and prepare for promotional exams, he had eventually gone to college, taking classes at night to earn a bachelor's degree in fire science and later a master's degree in public administration.

His thoughts left Nicole and went back to Jayla. He remembered when she had left Atlanta to attend a college in the north. Adam had wanted her to stay closer to home, but had relented and let her go. Adam would keep him updated on how well she was doing in school. He'd always been the proud father and when she had graduated at the top of her class, Adam had taken all the men in his squad out to celebrate. That had been four years ago....

The chiming of the elevator interrupted his reverie. The elevator opened on his floor and Storm stepped out. He had reached the conclusion that, incredible-looking or not, the last woman he would want to become involved with was Jayla Cole. But once again he thought about how she looked downstairs in the lobby. Incredible. Simply incredible...

The next morning, Jayla leaned back in her chair at the hotel restaurant, sipped her orange juice and smiled brightly. The call she had received before leaving her hotel room had made her very happy. Ecstatic was more like it.

The fertility clinic had called to let her know that everything had checked out and they had found a sperm donor whose profile met all of her requirements. There was a possibility they could schedule the procedure in less than a month.

She felt downright giddy at the thought of having a child. Her mother had died when she was ten, and her father's recent death had left her suffering with occasional bouts of loneliness. She had been an only child; she never had a sibling to share that special closeness with and now more than ever she wanted a child to love and to add special meaning to her life.

At first, she had looked at the pool of guys she had dated over the past couple of years, but for the most part they left a lot to be desired—they'd been either too overbearing or too overboring. So she'd decided to try a fertility clinic. After doing a load of research she had moved ahead with the preliminary paper work. Now in less than two months, she would take the first steps in becoming a new mother. A huge smile touched her lips. She couldn't wait to hold her baby in her arms. Her precious little one would have chocolate-colored skin, dark eyes, curvy full lips, cute dimples and...

"Good morning, Jayla. You seem to be in a rather good mood this morning."

Jayla looked up and met Storm's gaze. Although she had decided to avoid him for the remainder of her time in New Orleans, she wasn't upset that they had run into each other again so soon. She was too elated with life to let anything or anyone dampen her spirits today.

"I *am* in a good mood, Storm. I just received some wonderful news," she said smiling brightly. She saw the curiosity in his eyes, but knew he was too well-mannered to ask her for any details. And she had no intention of sharing her plans with him. Her decision to venture into single parenthood was personal and private. She hadn't shared it with anyone, not even Lisa, her best friend from work.

"Mind if I join you?"

Her smile widened. "Yes, have a seat."

She watched as he sat down and noticed his outfit complemented his physique just as it had the day before. He definitely looked good in a pair of cutoff jeans and a T-shirt that said Firefighters Are Hot.

"So what are you having this morning?" he asked, glancing over at her plate.

"Buffet. And everything is delicious."

He nodded. "Umm, I think I'll try it myself."

No sooner had he said the last word, a waiter appeared and Storm informed the man that he would be having the buffet. "I'll be back in a minute," he said standing.

Jayla watched as he made his way across the room to where the buffet was set up. She couldn't help but watch him. She knew there was no way she could feel guilty about being drawn to him, since she had always been attracted to him. And at least she wasn't the only one, she thought, glancing around and seeing that a number of admiring women had turned to check him out. However, it appeared he was more interested in filling his plate than in all the attention he was getting.

Jayla blinked when she suddenly realized something. Storm's features were identical to those she had requested when she'd filled out the questionnaire for the fertility clinic. If the clinic filled her request to the letter, the donor whose sperm she would receive would favor Storm and her baby would almost be his clone.

She shook her head, not believing what she'd subconsciously done. When she blinked again, she noticed that Storm had caught her staring at him, lifted his brow in question and then stared back at her.

Jayla's heart thudded in her chest as she watched as he crossed the room back to her with a plate filled to capacity. "Okay, what'd I do?" he asked sitting down. "You were staring at me like I'd suddenly grown an extra nose or something."

This time, Jayla had to force herself to smile. "No, you're fine. I just couldn't help but notice how much food you were piling on your plate," she said instead of telling him the real reason she'd been staring.

He chuckled. "Hey, I'm a growing boy. All my brothers and I eat like this."

Jayla took another sip of orange juice. She had met his brothers a while back and remembered all four of them being in excellent shape. If they routinely ate that much food, they must also work out…a lot. "Your parents must have had one heck of a grocery bill."

"They did, and while we were growing up my mom didn't work outside of the home, so it was up to my dad to bring home the bacon. And not once did he complain about the amount of money being spent on food. That's the way I want it in my household *if* I ever marry."

Jayla lifted a brow after taking another sip of orange juice. "What?"

"I don't want my wife to work outside of the home."

Jayla gazed at him as she set down her glass. She had

heard that very thing from several people who knew him. It was no secret that when Storm Westmoreland married, he would select a domestic diva.

"I have deep admiration and respect for any woman who works inside the home raising her family," she said truthfully.

His features showed signs of surprise. "You do?"

"Yes, raising a family is a full-time job."

He leaned back in his chair and studied her for a moment before asking, "So you would do it? You would be a stay-at-home-mom?"

"No."

He sat up straight. "But you just said that you—"

"Admired women who did it, but that doesn't necessarily mean that I would do it. I believe I can handle a career and motherhood and chose to have both."

"It won't be easy."

Jayla chuckled as she pushed aside her plate. "Nothing about being a parent is easy, Storm, whether you work in the home or outside the home. The most important thing is making sure the child is loved and well taken care of. Now if you will excuse me, I think I will try some of that fruit."

Storm watched as she stood and crossed the room. Wasn't it just yesterday that he had decided to stay away from her because she was too much of a temptation? When he had walked into the restaurant, he had sensed her presence even before he had actually seen her. Then he had glanced around and his gaze had locked in on her sitting alone at a table, drinking her orange juice with a huge smile on her face, completely oblivious to anyone and anything around her. Even now, he couldn't help but wonder what had put her in such a good mood.

He took a sip of his coffee, thinking she evidently didn't want him to know since she hadn't shared whatever it was with him. Electricity shot through him as he continued to watch as she put an assortment of fruit into a bowl. He liked the outfit she was wearing, a fuchsia sundress with spaghetti straps and a pair of flat sandals on her feet. She had gorgeous legs, and her hair flowed around her shoulders, emphasizing her beauty from every angle. She looked the very image of sexiness and at the same time she looked comfortable and ready for the New Orleans heat that was normal for a September day.

"The food in this place is good," she said returning to the table and digging into the different fruits she had brought back with her.

He lifted his dark head and his stomach tightened as he watched her slip a slice of pineapple into her mouth and relish it as if it were the best thing she'd ever eaten. She chewed very slowly while his gaze stayed glued to her mouth, finding the entire ordeal fascinating as well as arousing.

"So, what are you plans for today?"

Her question reeled him back in. He set his fork down and leaned back in his chair. He met her gaze, or at least tried to, without lowering it to her mouth again. "Take in the sights. I checked with the person at the concierge's desk and he suggested I do the Gray Line bus tour."

Jayla smiled brightly. "Hey, he gave me the same suggestion. Do you want to do it together?"

Innocent as it was, he wished she hadn't invited him to join her sightseeing expedition in precisely those words. *Do it together.* A totally different scenario than what she was proposing popped into his head and he was having a hard time getting it out of there. "You sure you don't mind the company?" he asked searching her face. Although he got very few, he recognized a brush-off when he got one and yesterday, after asking her to dinner, she had definitely given him the brush-off.

"No, I'd love the company."

He wondered what had changed her mood. Evidently the news she'd received had turned the snotty Jayla of last night into Miss Congeniality this morning.

"So what do you say, Mr. Fireman? Shall we hit the streets?"

Hitting the sheets was more to his liking, but he immediately reminded himself just who she was and that she was still off-limits. "Sure. I think it would be fun." *As long as we keep things simple,* he wanted to add but didn't.

She chuckled, a low, sexy sound, as she leaned forward. "And that's what I need, Storm, some honest-to-goodness fun."

He looked at her for a moment, then suddenly understood. The past six months had to have been hard. She and her father had been extremely close, so no doubt the loneliness was finally getting to her.

A jolt of protectiveness shot through him. Hadn't he promised Adam that he would look after her? Besides, if anyone could show her how to have fun, he could. Because of his attraction to her, over the years he had basically tried to avoid her. Now it seemed that doing so had robbed him of the chance to get to know her better. Maybe it was time that he took the first step to rectify the situation so that a relationship, one of friendship only, could develop between them.

Having fun with a woman without the involvement of

sex would be something new for him, but he was willing to try it. Since there was no way the two of them could ever be serious, he saw nothing wrong with letting his guard down and having a good time. "Then I will give you a day of fun, Jayla Cole," he said and meaning every word.

A smile touched the corners of his mouth. "And who knows? You just might surprise yourself and have so much fun, you may not ever want to get serious again."

Two

A rush of excitement shot through Jayla's bloodstream when the bus made another stop on its tour. This time to board the *Steamboat Natchez* for a cruise along the Mississippi River. So far, she and Storm had taken a carriage ride through the French Quarter, a tour of the swamps and visited a number of magnificently restored mansions and courtyards.

The *Natchez* was a beautiful replica of the steamboats that once cruised the Mississippi. Jayla stood at the railing appreciating the majestic beauty of the river and all the historical landmarks as they navigated its muddy waters. She was very much aware of the man standing beside her. During the boat ride, Storm had kept her amused by telling her interesting tidbits of information about riverboats.

As he talked, she tipped her head and studied him, letting eyes that were hidden behind the dark lenses of her sunglasses roam over him. She enjoyed looking at him as much as she enjoyed listening to him. Soft jazz was flowing through several speakers that were located on the lower deck and the sound of the boat gliding through the water had a relaxing effect on Jayla.

When Storm fell silent for a few moments, Jayla figured she needed to say something to assure him that he had her full attention, which he definitely did. "How do you know so much about riverboats?" she asked, genuinely curious. She watched his lips curve into a smile and a flutter went through her stomach.

"Mainly because of my cousin Ian," he replied as he absently flicked a strand of hair away from her face. "A few years ago, he and some investor friends of his decided to buy a beauty of a riverboat. It's over four hundred feet long and ninety feet high, and equipped with enough staterooms to hold over four hundred passengers."

"Wow! Where does it go?"

Storm leaned back against the rail and placed his hands in the pockets of his shorts. "Ian's riverboat, *The Delta Princess,* departs from Memphis on ten-day excursions along the Mississippi with stops in New Orleans, Baton Rouge, Vicksburg and Natchez. His crew provides first-class service and the food he serves on board is excellent. In the beginning, business was slow, but now he has reservations booked well over a year in advance. It didn't take him long to figure out what would be a drawing card."

Jayla lifted a brow. "What?"

"Gambling. You'd be surprised how many people have money they figure is worth losing if there's a chance that they might win more."

Jayla could believe that. A couple of years ago, she and

Lisa had taken a trip to Vegas and had seen first hand just how hungry to win some people were.

When there was another lull in the conversation, she turned away from him to look out over the river once more. It was peaceful, nothing like the tempest that was raging through her at the moment. Storm had kept his word. She'd had more fun today with him than she'd had in a long time. He possessed a fun-loving attitude that had spilled over to her. There were times when he had shared a joke with her that had her laughing so hard she actually thought something inside her body would break. It had felt good to laugh, and she was glad she'd been able to laugh with him.

She tried to think of the last time she had laughed with a man and recalled that it had been with her father. Even during his final days, when she'd known that pain had racked his body, he'd been able to tell a good joke every now and then. She heaved a small sigh. She missed her father so much. Because he had kept such a tight rein on her, she had been a rebellious teen while growing up. It was only when she'd returned from college that she had allowed herself to form that special father-daughter relationship with him.

After his death, at the encouragement of the officials at the hospice facility, she had gone through grief counseling and was glad she had. It had helped to let go and move on. One of the biggest decisions she'd been forced to make was whether to sell her parents' home and move into a smaller place. After much soul-searching, she had made a decision to move. She loved her new home and knew once she had her baby, it wouldn't be as lonely as it was now. She was getting excited again just thinking about it.

"So what are your plans for later?"

Storm's question invaded her thoughts and she tipped her head to look over at him. "My plans for later?"

"Yes. Yesterday, I invited you to join me for dinner and you turned me down, saying you'd already made plans. Today, I'm hoping to ask early enough so that I'll catch you before you make other arrangements."

Jayla sighed. She knew her mind needed a reality check, but she wasn't ready to give it one. Spending the day with Storm had been nice; it had been fun and definitely what she'd needed. But she didn't need to spend her evening with him as well. The only thing the two of them had in common was the fact they both loved and respected her father. That would be the common link they would always share. But spending more time with Storm would only reawaken all those old feelings of attraction she had always had for him.

She took off her sunglasses, met his gaze directly and immediately wished she hadn't. His eyes were dark, so dark you could barely see the pupils. The jolt that passed through her was so startling she had to remind herself to breathe.

"I was wondering when you were going to stop hiding behind these," he said, taking the sunglasses out of her hand when she was about to put them back on. He gave her a cocky smile. "But I didn't mind you checking me out."

Jayla couldn't hide the blush that darkened her cheeks. Nor could she resist easing her lips into a smile. So he'd known she had been looking him over. "I guess it probably gets rather annoying to you after a while, doesn't it?"

He arched a brow. "What?"

"Women constantly checking you out."

He smiled again. "Not really. Usually I beat them to the

punch and check them out, so by the time they decide they're interested, I know whether or not I am."

A grin tilted the corners of Jayla's lips. "Umm, such arrogance." She took her sunglasses from him and put them back on, preferring her shield.

"Instead of arrogance, I see it as not wasting time," he said simply. "I guess you can say I weed out those who won't make the cut."

Jayla sighed deeply and struggled with good judgment as to whether to ask her next question. Although she may have struggled with it, curiosity got the best of her. She couldn't help but ask, "So, did I make the cut?"

For a moment, she thought he would not answer. Then he leaned forward, pulled off her sunglasses and met her gaze. "With flying colors, Jayla Cole. I'm a hot-blooded man and would be telling a lie if I said I didn't find you attractive. But then, on the other hand, I have to respect who you'll always be to me."

"Adam's daughter?"

"Yes."

Jayla had to resist grinding her teeth in frustration. She doubted he realized that he'd hit a sore spot with her. Not because she was Adam Cole's daughter, but because being her father's daughter had been the reason Storm had always kept his distance from her. A part of her had gotten over his rejection years ago, but still, it downright infuriated her that he had labeled her as "hands off" because of his relationship with her father.

She watched as he pointedly checked his watch, as if to signal their topic of conversation was now over. "You never did say whether or not you had plans for later."

Jayla almost reached out to snatch her sunglasses from

his hand again, then changed her mind. Instead, she decided to have a little fun with him. She stepped close to him, reached out and took hold of the front of his shirt. "Why, Storm? What do you have in mind for later?" she asked, in a very suggestive tone of voice.

She watched as he studied her features with a well-practiced eye before he said, "Dinner."

She pressed a little closer to him. "Dinner? That's it?"

He glanced around. There were only a handful of people about. Most had gone up on deck to listen to the live jazz band that was performing. His gaze returned to hers. "Yes, that's it. Unless…"

She lifted a brow. "Unless what?" she asked, then watched as his mouth curved into a smile. A very sexy smile.

"Unless you want me to toss you into the river to cool off."

Jayla blinked. His smile was gone and the dark eyes staring at her were serious. She stared back, willing him to get the message she was sending with her eyes. His words had ticked her off. "Do you think I need to cool off, Storm?"

The smile that returned to his lips came slow, but it came nonetheless. "I think you need to behave, brat," he said, playfully tweaking her nose.

She frowned. Those were the same words he had spoken to her ten years earlier when she had made that pass at him. She knew he'd been as right then as he was now, but, dammit, it really annoyed her that he was still using her father as an excuse to keep her at arm's length. A part of her knew it was ludicrous for her to be upset, especially when she should probably be grateful, considering his "wham, bam, thank you, ma'am" reputation.

His Don Juan exploits were legendary. Even so, a part

of her hated his refusal to acknowledge she was not a child any longer. She was a full-grown woman and it was up to her to decide whom she was interested in and whom she wanted a relationship with. After all, pretty soon she would be a woman with the responsibility of raising a child alone.

"So, what about dinner, Jayla?"

Time seemed to stop as Jayla considered her options. On the one hand, having dinner with him was a really bad idea. She sure didn't need someone like Storm in her life, especially with her plans with the fertility clinic and her future as a single mom a definite go. That's what the rational part of her brain was trying to get through to her. On the other hand, there was that irrational part, the one that resented him for being all knowing and too damn caring. That part of her head said that one little dinner would do no harm. She knew she should leave well enough alone, but part of her just couldn't.

She met his gaze. "I'll think about it." And without saying anything else, she took her sunglasses from his hand and walked away.

Storm shook his head as he watched Jayla stroll across the deck. She'd had a lot of nerve asking if she made the cut, as if she hadn't felt the sparks that had flown between them yesterday as well as most of the morning. Fortunately for him, it was an attraction that he could control. But he had to admit that when she had pretended to come on to him a few moments ago, he had almost broken out in a sweat.

He remembered her teen years. During that time Adam had described her as headstrong, free-spirited and an independent thinker. It seemed not much about her had changed.

Storm watched as she moved around the tables that were filled to capacity with an assortment of food and knew he had to rethink his relationship with her. A lot about Jayla *had* changed and he was looking his fill, taking all those changes in at that very moment.

He couldn't remember the last time any woman had gotten his attention the way Jayla had. She didn't know how close she'd come to getting a kiss from him when she had molded her body to his. His gaze had latched on to her lips. They had looked so soft that he'd wanted to find out for himself just how soft and kissable they were.

He sighed. Her ploy had been no more than teasing, but his body was still reeling from the effects. However, no matter what, he had to keep her best interests at heart, even if she didn't know what her best interests were and even if it killed him.

Why couldn't he keep his eyes off her? Hadn't he decided she was off-limits? He glanced away and tried to focus on the beauty of the river as the riverboat continued to move through it. It was a beautiful September day and he had to admit he was enjoying Jayla's company. She had a knack for making him want to see her smile, hear her laugh; he could honestly say he had relished his time with her more than he had any woman in a long time.

He wondered if she was romantically involved with anyone. He recalled Adam mentioning once that he felt she was too nitpicky when it came to men and that she would never meet the "perfect man" that met her satisfaction. That conversation has taken place years ago and Storm couldn't help wondering if her attitude had changed. Had she found someone? Something or someone had definitely had her smiling when he'd first seen her at breakfast that morning. All she'd said was that she had just received some wonderful news, news she hadn't bothered sharing with him. Did the news have anything to do with a lover?

"Storm, don't you want something to eat?"

The sound of her voice grabbed his attention and he glanced back over to her, met her gaze and had to swallow. The hue of her eyes seemed to pull him to her. And he didn't want to think about her mouth, a mouth that now contained a pulse-stopping smile. It seems the feathers he had ruffled earlier were now all smoothed. When he didn't answer quickly enough, she quirked a brow and asked, "Well, do you?"

He fought the urge to tell her yes, that he was hungry, but what he wanted had nothing to do with food. Instead of saying anything, he strolled over to join her at the table and took the plate she offered him. "Yes. Thanks."

"You're welcome. You might want to try these, they're good," she said popping a Cajun cheese ball into her mouth.

Storm's breath hitched. He watched her chew, seeing her mouth barely moving. He quickly decided it wouldn't be that way if they were to kiss. He definitely intended to get a lot of movement out of that mouth. He continued to stare at her mouth for a moment and then sighed. Thinking about kissing her was not the way to go. He needed to concentrate on sharing a platonic relationship with her and nothing more,

"If you eat enough of these, there might not have to be a *later*."

Her words reclaimed his attention. "Excuse me?"

She smiled. "I said if you eat enough of these you might be able to forgo dinner later. They're so delicious."

His first instinct was to tell her that to him, food was like sex—he rarely got enough of it. But he decided telling her that wasn't a good idea. After they had both filled their plates, they walked up the steps to the upper deck where tables and chairs were located.

His attention shifted to claiming a table close to the rails so they could continue to enjoy the view of the river while they ate. When they were both seated, he turned his attention back to her. Her hair was blowing in the midday breeze and he stared at the magnitude of her beauty once again. While his attention was on her, her attention was on her food. Most people who came to New Orleans appreciated its culinary excellence and he could tell by the way she was enjoying her bowl of seafood gumbo that she was enjoying the cuisine, too.

Instead of concentrating on his food, Storm was becoming obsessed with a question. When he realized that he wasn't going to be able to eat before he got an answer, he decided to come out and ask her the one question that was gnawing at him.

"So, are you seeing anyone seriously, Jayla?"

He watched her lift her head and met his gaze. She smiled. "No, I've given up on men."

Storm frowned. Her answer was not what he had expected. "Why?"

She leaned back in her chair. "Because there're too many out there like you."

He leaned forward, lifting a dark brow. "And how am I?"

"The 'love them and leave them' type."

He couldn't dispute her words since he was definitely that. But still, there was something about hearing it from her that just didn't sit well with him. "Not all men are like me. I'm sure there are some who'd love to get serious with one woman and make a commitment."

She tipped her head back and grinned. "Really? Any recommendations?"

His frown deepened. There was no way he would ever introduce her to any of his friends. Most of them were players, just like him, and his only unmarried brother was too involved with his restaurant to indulge in a serious relationship. His thoughts then fell on his six male cousins, eight now if you counted the most recent additions to the Westmoreland family—the two sons his uncle Corey hadn't known about until recently. But still, he wouldn't dare introduce her to any of them either. If she was off-limits to him, then she was off-limits to them, as well.

"No," he decided to answer. "There aren't any I can recommend. Where have you been looking?"

She chuckled as she went back to her gumbo. "Nowhere lately, since I'm no longer interested. But when I was interested I tried everywhere—bars, clubs, blind dates and I even used the Internet."

Storm's mouth fell open. "The Internet?"

She smiled at the look of shock on his face. "Yes, the Internet and I have to admit that I thought I had gotten a very promising prospect...until I actually met him. He was at least fifteen years older than the picture he had on the Web site made him seem and instead of having two hands, it seemed he had a dozen. I had to almost deck him a few times for trying to touch me in places that he shouldn't."

Storm's hands trembled in anger at the thought that she had done something so foolish as to place herself in that situation. No wonder Adam had asked him to look out for her. Now he regretted that he hadn't done a better job at it. He could imagine any man wanting to touch her body, since it was so tempting, but wanting to touch her and actually doing it were two different things. "Don't ever date anyone off the Internet again," he all but snarled.

Jayla grinned. "Why, Storm, if I didn't know better, I'd think you were jealous," she said playfully.

Storm wasn't in a playful mood. "Jealous, hell. I'm just trying to look out for you. What if that guy would have placed you in a situation you couldn't get out of?"

Jayla raised her gaze upward. "Jeez, give me the benefit of having common sense, Storm. We met in a public place and—"

"He was groping you in a public place?"

She took a sip of her drink and then said, "We were dancing."

Storm took a deep, calming breath as he tried reeling in his anger. "I hope you learned a lesson."

"I did, and there's another reason I've given up on men."

He raised a brow. "Yeah, what's that?"

Her eyes turned serious. "Most are too controlling, which is something I definitely don't need after having Adam Cole for a father. I didn't start dating until I was seventeen, and I wasn't allowed to do sleepovers at my friends' homes."

Storm frowned. "There was nothing wrong with your father wanting to protect you, Jayla. I'm sure it wasn't easy for a single man to raise a daughter, especially one as spirited and defiant as I'd heard you could be at times."

Jayla shrugged. "Well, whatever. You wanted to know the reasons I'd given up on men and I've just told you why I don't date anymore. I figured what the hell, why bother. Men are too much trouble."

The eyes that were gazing up at him were big, round, sexy and serious. He shook his head. To tell the truth, he'd often thought women were too much trouble, too, but at no time had he considered giving them up. "I don't think you should write men off completely."

The jazz band that had taken a break earlier started back up again and conversation between him and Jayla ended. While she became absorbed in the musicians, he sat back and studied her for a long time. Being concerned about his late mentor's bratty daughter meant he was a good friend and not a jealous suitor as she'd claimed. He never cared enough about a woman to become jealous and Jayla Cole was no exception...or was she?

Jayla sipped her drink and half listened to the musicians who were performing a very jazzy tune. Of course she had recognized Storm's concern as a protective gesture but still, she couldn't resist ribbing him about being jealous.

He was so easy to tease. Charming, gorgeous and sexy as sin. But what she'd told him had been the truth. She had basically written men off. That's why she had decided to use the fertility clinic instead of a live donor.

She had made up in her mind that marriage wasn't for her. She enjoyed her independence too much to have to answer to anyone, and men had a way looking at their wives as possessions instead of partners, a lover for life, his other half and his soul mate. Her time and concentration would be focused on having her baby and raising it. Then later, if she did meet someone who met her qualifications, he would have to take the total package—her and her child.

She glanced over at Storm and saw his full attention was focused on the musicians. There was a dark scowl on his face and she wondered if he was still thinking about her and the Internet man.

Running into him in New Orleans was definitely an unexpected treat. She decided to enjoy the opportunity while it lasted. So far, their day together had been so much fun…at least for half the time. The other half of their time together she'd been too busy fighting her attraction to him to really enjoy herself. He was no different from the other men she had dated—possibly even worse—but that didn't stop that slow sizzle from moving through her body whenever he looked at her.

A part of her couldn't help but wonder if all the things she'd heard about him were fact or myth.

"The riverboat has returned to dock, Jayla."

His words, spoken low and in a husky tone, intruded into her thoughts. She glanced around and saw that the riverboat had returned to the Toulouse Street Wharf. "We returned sooner than I thought we would," she said, forcing down the lump of disappointment that suddenly appeared in her throat.

"We've been cruising the Mississippi for over three hours," he said, returning the irrepressible smile that had recently vanished from his lips. "Don't you think it's time we got back?"

She shrugged, wondering if he'd gotten bored with her already. Without saying a word, she stood and began gathering up the debris from their meal. He reached out and stopped her. She looked up and met his gaze.

"I'm not one of those men who expects a woman to clean up after him."

She opened her mouth to speak, but the words wouldn't come out. His hand was still on hers, holding it immobile, and she could feel the sensuous heat from his touch all the way down to her toes. She pressed her lips together to fight back the moan that threatened to escape. How could he overpower her senses in such a way that she couldn't think straight?

Frowning, she blew out an aggravated breath as she pulled her hand from his and resumed what she was doing. "I don't consider it as cleaning up after you, Storm. It's an old habit. Whenever Dad and I ate together, I always cleared the table afterward. We had a deal. He cooked and I cleaned."

"Really?" he asked, studying her intently as his lips quirked into a smile. "And why was that? Can't you cook?"

She glanced up at him and the deep dimples in his cheeks did things to her insides that were totally beyond her comprehension. She figured it would have been a lot easier for her to understand if she wasn't a twenty-six year old virgin. While in college she'd *almost* gone all the way with a senior guy by the name of Tyrone Pembrooke. But his roommate had returned unexpectedly, interrupting things. For her, it had been fortunate since she'd later discovered he had made a bet with his fraternity brothers that he would get into her panties in a week's time. She had almost learned too late that the name the senior guys had given the freshman girls was *fresh meat*.

"Yes, I can cook," she finally answered Storm. "Dad loved home cooking. He thought food wasn't worth eating if it wasn't made from scratch. He just couldn't get into those little microwave dinners that I was an expert at preparing."

Storm chuckled as he helped her gather up the remaining items off the table. "Hey, I can understand your father's pain since I like home-cooked food, too."

They walked over to the garbage container and tossed in their trash. "You cook for yourself every day?" Jayla asked as they headed toward the lower deck to depart.

"No. Since my shifts run twenty-four on and forty-eight off, I eat at the station when I'm working and the days I'm off I eat at Chase's Place, my brother's restaurant."

She nodded, remembering that his twin brother, Chase Westmoreland, owned a restaurant in downtown Atlanta. It was a really popular place; she had been to it several times and always found the food delicious. She glanced down at her watch. "When we get back to the hotel, it will be nap time for me."

"Umm, not for me. There's still more for me to see. I think I'll go check out that club on Bourbon Street that's located right next to the drugstore. I hear they have good entertainment."

Jayla lifted a brow. She knew exactly what club he was referring to, since a group of the guys who'd also attended the convention had visited there. And if what she'd heard about it was true, its only entertainment was of the strip-tease kind. She frowned wondering why the thought of Storm watching women bare all bothered her. Why did men fail to realize that there was more to a woman than what was underneath her clothes?

"Well, I hope you enjoy yourself," she said. Her tone had been more curt than she had intended.

"Oh, trust me, I will."

And she knew, just as clearly as he'd said it, that he would.

Three

Storm was having a lousy time, but when he glanced over at his cousin Ian, it was evident that he was enjoying himself. Ian had contacted him last night and told him that *The Delta Princess* would be making a stop in New Orleans and suggested they meet for drinks at this club.

A few seconds later, Ian must have felt him staring and looked over at him. "What's the matter with you, Storm?"

Storm decided to be honest. "I'm bored."

Ian lifted a brow. "How can you be bored looking at women take off their clothes?"

He shrugged. "It all looks basically the same."

A smile curved the corners of Ian's lips. "Well, yeah, I would hope so."

Storm couldn't help but return the smile. He and Ian were first cousins—their fathers were brothers. While growing up, they had always been close. They were the same age and one thing they'd always had in common was their appreciation of the opposite sex. Storm wasn't surprised that his cousin thought the fact that his lack of interest in women stripping naked was strange.

"Okay, who is she?"

Storm looked confused. "Who's who?"

"The woman who's ruined your interest in other women."

Storm frowned. He glared at Ian. "Where on earth did you get a crazy idea like that from? No one has ruined my interest in other women."

Ian met his glare. "And I say you're lying."

Storm released a frustrated sigh. Ian was damn lucky he hadn't hauled off and hit him. But that was his brother Thorn's style. Thorn was known for his moody, ready-to-knock-the-hell-out-of-you temperament. At least, that had been his attitude until he'd gotten married. Now Tara had unruffled Thorn's feathers and the last few times he'd seen him, Thorn had actually been easygoing. Marriage had certainly made a happy man out of Thorn, as well as his brothers Dare and Stone. Storm found it downright sickening. He'd also been curious as to why his brothers were smiling all the time. As far as he was concerned, they weren't getting anything at home that he wasn't getting out there in the streets.

Or were they?

"I can't believe you just sat there calmly after I called you a liar, so it must be true," Ian said, taking another sip of his beer.

Storm rolled his eyes. "I just don't feel like knocking the hell out of you right now Ian, so back off." What he preferred not to let his cousin know was that he had pretty much hit on the truth. For the time being, Jayla *had* ruined him for other women and he couldn't understand why. He certainly hadn't ever been intimate with her and he never ever intended to be. And yet, here he was bored to death at the sight of these half-clad dancers, while the thought of Jayla taking off her clothes made him break into a sweat.

"Want another drink, cuz?"

He glanced over at Ian. What he wanted was to go back to the hotel and call Jayla to see what she was doing. "No, I'll pass. When will you be back in Atlanta?"

Ian leaned back in his chair and smiled. "In a few weeks. I promised Tara I'd be in town for that charity ball she's working on. Why?"

"I'll check you out then." Storm stood and tossed a couple of bills on the table. "I'll let Uncle James and Aunt Sarah know you're doing okay."

Ian nodded. "And for heaven's sake if Mom asks if I was with a woman when you saw me, please say yes. With your brothers getting married, she's starting to look at us kind of funny."

Storm grinned. His mother was beginning to look at him and Chase kind of funny, too. He glanced around the room before turning his attention back to Ian. "I guess I can tell her that and not feel guilty about lying, since this place is full of women. I'll just leave out the part that the woman you were seeing was naked."

Ian chuckled. "Thanks, I'd appreciate that."

Storm turned to leave.

"Hey, Storm?"

Storm turned back around. "Yeah?"

Ian met his gaze directly. "I know it's just a temporary thing, man, but whomever she is I hope she's worth all the hell you're going through."

Storm frowned, opened his mouth to give his cousin a blazing retort that no woman was putting him through hell, changed his mind and turned and walked out of the club.

Jayla heard the phone ring when she had finished toweling herself off and slipped into the plush hotel bathrobe. She quickly left the bathroom and picked up the phone on the fourth ring. "Hello?"

"How was your nap?"

Jayla frowned. The last thing Storm needed to know was that she hadn't been able to sleep, thanks to thoughts of him being surrounded by naked women. Each time she'd tried closing her eyes, she saw women, taking off their clothes, heaving their breasts in his face, skimming panties down their legs and giving him an eyeful of all their treasures. She'd even heard there were some women who were bold enough to sit naked in a man's lap if he tipped her well enough.

"My nap was fantastic," she lied. "How was the entertainment at the club?" she asked then wished that she hadn't.

"It was definitely interesting."

Jayla's frown deepened. A part of her wanted to slam the phone down, but she had too much pride to do so. Besides, she took great care of herself and thought she looked rather decent, in or out of her clothes. As far as she was concerned, there was nothing those women who'd stripped off their clothes had on her other than that none of them was Adam Cole's daughter.

"I called to see if you're free later."

She rolled her eyes upward. So they were back to that again. "Dinner, you mean?"

"Yes."

In her present frame of mind, he was the last person she wanted to see. It was on the tip of her tongue to suggest he invite one of the "ladies" from the club to dine with him. But she thought better of making the suggestion, since he might very well do it. "I think I'll pass on dinner. I'm not hungry."

"Well, I am, so how about keeping me company?"

She lifted a brow. "Keep you company?"

"Yeah, I enjoy being with you."

Jayla dropped down on the bed, feeling ridiculously pleased by his admission. Although she knew that she shouldn't read too much into his words, she suddenly felt confident, cocky and in control. "Well, I hope you know that my company is going to cost you," she said, breaking the silence between them.

"In what way?"

She rubbed her fingers over the smooth wood-grain texture of the nightstand next to the bed. "I'm not hungry for anything heavy, but I'd love to have a slice of K-Paul's mouthwatering strawberry cheesecake."

She could hear him chuckle on the other end. "K-Paul's Louisiana Kitchen? I've heard of the place, but have never eaten there. I'm going to take your word that I won't be disappointed," he said.

She grinned. "Trust me, you won't be."

"How long will it take for you to get ready?"

"I just got out of the shower so it won't take me long to slip into something."

It was close to forty-five minutes before Jayla appeared in the lobby.

But the moment she walked off the elevator, Storm

knew she had been well worth the wait. His chest grew tight as he watched her walk toward him, thinking she looked absolutely incredible.

He'd known he was in trouble when she had mentioned on the phone that she had just gotten out of the shower. Immediately, visions of her naked had swam his mind, which was a lot better than any live scene he had witnessed at that club earlier.

Common sense told him to pull himself together and remember who she was. But at the moment, all his senses, common or otherwise, were being shot to hell with every step she took toward him. He stood practically unmoving as he watched her, enraptured, while hot desire surged through his bloodstream.

She was dressed in a short dress that totally flowed over her figure, emphasizing the gorgeous shape of her body as well as her long beautiful legs. His gaze lowered slightly to those legs. It had been hard to keep his eyes off them this morning, and it seemed this evening wouldn't be any different. She had the kind of legs any man would just love to caress and have wrapped around him.

He drew in a deep breath, not wanting to think such thoughts but discovering he was hard-pressed to stop them from coming. Whether he liked it or not, he was undeniably attracted to Jayla Cole.

"Sorry I kept you waiting," Jayla said when she came to a stop in front of Storm.

"You were worth the wait. Ready to go?"

"Yes."

They took a cab over to the restaurant and Storm was glad he'd gotten the hotel to make reservations for him. The place was packed. "Something smells delicious," he whispered to Jayla as a waiter showed them to their table.

"Everything in here is delicious," she said smiling.

Including you, Storm was tempted to say. He wondered how he could assume that when he'd never tasted her, but he just knew that she would taste delicious.

The waiter presented them with menus. "Just coffee for me now and I'll wait for later to order dessert," she said handing the menu back to their waiter.

Storm glanced over at her. "Since you're familiar with this place, what do you suggest?"

Jayla caressed her upper lip with the tip of her tongue as if in deep thought. "Umm, I'll have to recommend Chef Paul's Duck & Shrimp Dulac. I had it the last time I was here and it was totally magnificent."

Storm nodded and returned the menu to the waiter. "Then that's what I'll have and I'd like a bottle of sparkling mineral water."

"Great choice, sir," the waiter said before walking off.

Storm leaned back in his chair. "So, do you return to work on Monday?"

Jayla shook her head. "No, I won't officially return to work until a week from Monday. Then on Tuesday of that same week, I have a meeting with a Dr. Tara Westmoreland. Is she a family member of yours?"

Storm smiled. "Yes, Tara is my sister-in-law. She and my brother Thorn tied the knot a few months back. Why would you need to meet with Tara? She's a pediatrician and you don't have a child."

Not yet, Jayla thought to herself. "The reason I'm meeting with Dr. Westmoreland is for business reasons—in fact, we're doing lunch. The company I work for, Sala

Industries, is picking up the tab for the caterers the night that the Kids' World calendar is unveiled at a charity ball, and Dr. Westmoreland is on the committee. It will be a huge event, and we expect well over a thousand people to attend."

"I understand the ball will be next month," he said, after the waiter had returned with their drinks.

"Yes, the second weekend in October, in fact. And I understand your brother Thorn is Mr. July."

"Yes, he is." Storm couldn't forget how Tara had been given the unlucky task of persuading Thorn to pose as Mr. July. Doing so hadn't been easy, but things had worked out in the end, including Thorn's realizing that he loved Tara and the two of them getting married. Kids' World was a foundation that gave terminally ill children the chance to make their ultimate dream—a visit to any place in the world—come true. All proceeds for the foundation came from money raised through numerous charity events.

"I understand the calendar turned out wonderfully and the sale of them will be a huge success," Jayla said smiling, interrupting his thoughts. She gazed across the table at him for a second, then said. "Tell me about your family."

Storm raised a brow after taking a sip of his water. "Why?"

She smiled. "Because I was an only child and whenever you mention your siblings or your cousins I can tell you all share a special closeness. It was lonely growing up without sisters or brothers and I've already made up my mind to have a large family."

Storm chuckled. "How large?"

"At least two, possibly three, maybe even four."

Storm nodded. He wanted a large family as well. "The

Westmoreland family is a big one and we're all very close. It started out with my grandparents who had three sons, one of which was my father. My parents had six kids, all boys until Delaney came along. Dare is the oldest, then Thorn, Stone, Chase and me. As you know, Chase is my twin brother. My father's twin brother's name is James and he and his wife Sarah also had six kids, but all of them were boys—Jared, Spencer, Durango, Ian, Quade and Reggie. My father's youngest brother, Uncle Corey, never married, so it was assumed he'd never fathered any kids, but we discovered differently a few months ago."

Jayla placed her coffee cup down, curious. "Really?"

"His sons, who never knew he was their father, just like he never knew he had sons, had an investigator track him down. Uncle Corey is a retired park ranger in Montana and that's where they found him."

Jayla was fascinated with the story Storm was sharing with her. "But how did he not know that he was a father?"

"It seems a former girlfriend found out she was pregnant after they'd broken up and never bothered telling him. Unknown to Uncle Corey, the woman gave birth to triplets."

"Triplets?"

"Yes, triplets. Multiple births are common in our family. Like me and Chase, Ian and Quade, and my father and Uncle James are fraternal twins."

Jayla inhaled, trying to absorb all this. "And your uncle's former girlfriend had triplets?"

"Yes, the first in the Westmoreland family. It seems that she told them their father had died when they were born and only revealed the truth on her deathbed. Although

Uncle Corey never married the woman, she had moved out west to Texas and had taken his last name, so fortunately, her kids were born as Westmorelands."

"So your Uncle Corey has three sons he didn't know a thing about?"

"No, two sons and one daughter." He shook his head, chuckling. "And all this time we all thought Delaney was the only girl in the Westmoreland family in two generations. Last month Uncle Corey suprised us and got married!"

They suspended conversation when the waiter brought out Storm's food. Storm surprised Jayla when he handed her a fork. "There's too much here for one person. Share it with me."

She glanced at his plate. He did have a lot and it looked delicious. "Umm, maybe, I'll just take a few bites," she said taking the fork from him.

"Help yourself."

And she did. The picture of them sharing a meal played out a rather cozy and intimate scene in her mind, one she tried to ignore. She licked her lips after they had finished. The food had tasted great. "Now you're going to have to help me eat that cheesecake."

"Hey, I can handle it."

His words triggered a flutter in the pit of her stomach. There was no doubt in her mind that Storm Westmoreland could handle anything. And he did. They finished off the strawberry cheesecake in no time.

Storm checked his watch after he signed the check for their bill. "It's still early. How would you like to go dancing?"

His words echoed through Jayla's mind. She knew the smart thing to do would be to tell him, no, but for some reason, she didn't want to think smart. She didn't want to

think at all. She was in the company of a very handsome
man and she was in no hurry for them to part ways.

She met his gaze. "I'd love going dancing with you,
Storm."

The club that had come highly recommend from one of
the waiters at K-Paul's was dark, rather small, and
crowded. Storm and Jayla were lucky to find an empty
table inside Café Basil, which had a reputation of being the
undisputed king of nightlife in the French Quarter.

Storm doubted that another couple could fit on the dance
floor. Already, the place was jam-packed, but he was determined that they would squeeze in somehow. There was
no way he would leave this place tonight without molding
Jayla's body to his and holding her in his arms.

He glanced across the table at her, barely able to make
out her features in the dimly lit room. Her body was sway-
ing to the sound of the jazz band that was playing and as
he watched her, he had to restrain the emotions that were
pulsing inside of him.

He had been with numerous women before and each one
had met his specific qualifications—whatever they'd been
at the time. And every single one of them had known the
score. He promised nothing other than a good time in bed.
He wasn't interested in satisfying emotional needs, just
physical ones. But there was something about Jayla that
was pulling at him. The pull was definitely sexual, but
there was something about it that was emotional, too.

And Storm Westmoreland didn't do anything with
women that hinted of the emotional so why was he here,
bursting at the seams to take Jayla into his arms on that
dance floor?

Before he could ponder that question, the tune that was playing stopped and another started. Some of the dancers went back to their seats, clearing the way for others to take their turn. "This is our number," he said to Jayla, standing and reaching out for her hand.

She smiled and placed her hand in his. Immediately, he felt a tug in his gut that he tried ignoring as he led her onto the dance floor. He took a deep breath, then exhaled slowly the moment she came into his arms and molded her body to his.

"I like holding you," he said truthfully into her ear moments later, wanting her to hear his words over the sound of the band.

She leaned back and searched his face a moment before asking, "Do you?"

"Hmm…"

She smiled and he thought it was the most beautiful smile he'd ever seen on a woman and felt good that his words had brought a smile to her lips. Speaking of lips…

His gaze shifted to her mouth and he couldn't help but take in their proximity to his. All he had to do was inch a little closer and—

"You smell good, Storm."

He inhaled deeply and slowly shook his head. She could say the damnedest things at times. They should be concentrating on small talk that was socially acceptable for platonic friends and not the sultry murmurings of lovers. "Thanks, but you shouldn't say that to me."

"Why not? If you can tell me that you like holding me, then I should be able to tell you that I think you smell good."

His hands were around her waist, holding her tight, and her arms were draped about his neck. The music playing was slow and their bodies were barely moving. He knew it and she knew it, as well. He was also certain that she was aware that he was aroused. With her body so close to his, there was no way that she didn't know it.

He wanted her to feel all of him and pulled her closer into his arms. Automatically, she placed her head against his chest and he closed his eyes as they swayed to the sound of the music. If she thought he smelled good, then he thought likewise about her. The scent of her perfume was intoxicating, seductive and a total turn-on. Moments later, the music faded and they stopped dancing, but he refused to release her. He needed to continue to hold her in his arms.

Jayla lifted her face and met Storm's gaze. The look in his eyes was intense and purely sexual. "I should try and continue to fight this," he said as if the words were being forced from him. She could clearly understand what he meant.

She did. "Don't fight it," she said softly.

He narrowed his eyes at her. "You're not helping matters, Jayla." His words were a low growl in her ear.

She narrowed her eyes right back at him. "Why should I?"

He stared at her for a long time. Then he glanced around. It seemed they were the center of attention. He looked back at her. "But you deserve more than just—"

"A one-night stand? Shouldn't I be the one to make that decision, Storm? I'm twenty-six-years old. I work and pay my own bills. I'm a woman, not a child, and it's time you realized that."

He stared at her for a long moment, then said, "I just did." He tightened his hand on hers and tugged her along with him out of the club.

* * *

"Where are we going?" Jayla asked, almost out of breath as she tried keeping up with Storm's long strides as he tried hailing a cab.

"Back to the hotel."

A few moments later, Storm cursed. There were few cabs around and the ones he saw were already occupied. He glanced across the street and saw a parked horse-drawn coach. Evidently, someone had used it for a wedding and it reminded him of the coach that might be used as a prop in *Cinderella*. "Come on," he said, keeping a firm hold on Jayla's hand.

They quickly crossed the street and approached the driver, who was holding the reins to keep the horses from prancing. "We need a ride back to the Sheraton Hotel on Canal," Storm said, nearly out of breath.

The old man raised a bushy brow. "My rates are by the hour."

"Fine, just get us there quick and in one piece."

The driver nodded his head, indicating that he understood. Storm then turned and opened the carriage door. When Jayla lifted her leg to climb inside, Storm swept her into his arms and placed her inside on the seat. He then climbed in and shut the door.

As the coach lurched forward, anticipation and sexual desire the likes he had never known before gripped him and he could think of only one thing that could relax him.

He paused, wondering if he had lost his mind and then quickly decided that he had. There wasn't a damn thing he could do about it. He would worry about the consequences of his actions tomorrow. He was too far gone tonight.

He glanced over at Jayla where she sat on the other side of the seat. The interior lighting provided him with barely enough illumination to see her features, but he heard her breathing and it was coming out as erratic as his own.

"Come here, Jayla."

She met his gaze before sliding across the seat to him. He curved his hand about her neck and drew her to him. Leaning forward, he captured the lips he had been dying to taste for over ten years. He took possession and staked his claim. He couldn't help himself.

He felt the shiver that flowed from her body to his when she surrendered her tongue to his. He took his time to savor what she offered, relentlessly mating his mouth with hers as he tried to satisfy what seemed to be an endless hunger. Her taste was like a drug and he felt himself getting addicted to it as his controls were pushed to the limit, wanting more and determined to get it. He lapped up every moan she made while glorying in the feel of her kissing him back.

He deepened the kiss and she proved that she could handle him, tongue for tongue, lick for lick, stroke for stroke. It seemed that he had also tapped a hunger inside of her that she hadn't fed in a while. He intensified the kiss, knowing she wanted him as much as he wanted her.

They felt a jolt when the coach came to a stop and they broke off the kiss, pulling apart. He glanced out the window, then glanced back at her. They were at the hotel. Would she change her mind or would they finish what they'd started?

Knowing the decision was hers, he leaned over and placed a kiss on her lips. "What do you want, Jayla?" he asked, his breath hot and ragged against her ear. He hoped and prayed that she wanted the same thing that he did.

He watched as a smile touched her lips. She then reached out to run her hand down his chest, past his waist to settle firmly on his arousal that was pressing hard through his pants.

He swallowed hard, almost forgetting to breathe. His mind was suddenly filled with scenes of all the things he wanted to do to her.

She met his gaze and in a soft voice whispered, "I want you to make love to me, Storm."

Four

Storm's knuckles gently brushed across Jayla's cheeks just moments before his mouth descended on hers. The words she'd just spoken were what he wanted to hear, and at that moment he needed to taste her again.

He was swamped with conflicting emotions. A part of him wanted to pull back, unable to forget she was Adam's daughter, but then another part of him accepted and acknowledged what she'd said was true. She was old enough to make her own decisions. Even Adam had pretty much conceded that before he'd died.

He slowly, reluctantly, broke off the kiss and took a deep breath. Her eyes glinted with intense desire and he was suddenly filled with a dangerously high degree of anticipation to give her everything she wanted and needed. Without saying a word, he took her hand. Together, they got out of the coach and went into the hotel. The walk across the lobby to the elevator seemed endless, and all Storm could think about was what he would do to her once they were alone. That short dress she was wearing had driven him crazy all night. More than once, his gaze had been drawn to her bare legs, legs he wanted wrapped around him while they made love.

"My room or yours," he asked, moments before the elevator door swooshed open before them.

Their eyes met and held. "Whichever one is closest," she said as desire continued to flicker in her eyes.

"That would be yours."

They stepped into the elevator and after the door closed behind them, he leaned against the wall. They were alone and he tightened his hands by his side. The temptation to pull her into his arms and devour her mouth again was unbearable, and when she swept the tip of her tongue nervously across her top lip, his stomach clenched and he swore beneath his breath.

"I want you so damn much," he had to say. The scent of her perfume was soft and seductive.

"And I want you, too, Storm."

That statement didn't help matters, either. He had wanted to pull her into his arms the moment the elevator came to a stop on her floor, but taking a deep breath, he held the door as she stepped out off the car before him. Holding hands, they walked silently down the corridor to her hotel room. Intense sexual need was closing in on him. He had to admit he'd never wanted a woman this badly.

When they reached her room, he leaned against the wall as Jayla opened her purse, pulled out her key and inserted it into the lock. She opened the door with ease and walked into the room. He didn't waste any time following and closing the door behind them. She flipped a switch that brought a soft glow of light to the room, then turned slowly to him, meeting his gaze.

They didn't say anything for a brief moment; then he reached out and pulled her into his arms. His mind told him to take things slowly but the moment he touched her and desire swept through his body, he threw the thought of taking things slowly out the window. The only thing he could think of was lifting her short dress and becoming enfolded in her feminine heat.

He tightened his arms around her as his mouth greedily devoured hers and his chest expanded with the solid feel of her breasts pressing against it. His tongue again made a claim on her mouth while his hands skimmed across her backside, making him intensely aware of just how shapely she was. He deepened the kiss and a hoarse sound of pleasure erupted from his throat. Moments later, he broke off the kiss and pulled back. He wanted her with an intensity that bordered on desperation.

"You sure?" he asked, wanting to make certain she knew exactly what she was getting into.

"I'm positive," she said, drawing up close to him.

"Hell, I hope so." He pulled her back to him and his mouth came down on hers with a ferociousness that he didn't know he possessed. Fed by the raging storm that had erupted within him, his mouth plundered hers, sweeping her breath away and tasting the sweet, deep and delicious taste that was distinctively hers. He felt the tremor that passed through her and it increased his need to make love to her to the point where his veins throbbed.

Storm lifted his head just long enough to reach out and whip the short dress over Jayla's head, leaving her standing before him clad in a silky black camisole. He suddenly became dizzy with the sight of her standing before him, lush and sexy. Her scent was seductive and the pale lighting in the room traced a faint glow across her dark skin. His temperature went up another notch and he knew at that moment what he was about to share with Jayla went way beyond his regular routine of "wham-bam, thank you, ma'am." And for a mere second, that thought bothered him. But like everything else that was out of the norm for him tonight, he placed it on the back burner. He'd deal with his confusing thoughts tomorrow.

He reached out and pulled her back to him, capturing her mouth at the same time he picked her up in his arms and walked toward the bed. He placed her in the center of it and tumbled down beside her, his hands immediately going to her camisole to remove it from her body.

He sucked in air through clenched teeth when he pulled back and looked down at her, completely naked. At that moment he felt an unbearable desire to feel his mouth on her skin. Leaning toward her, his tongue traced a path down her neck to her breasts, where it stopped and drew a hard, budding nipple into his mouth and feasted, licking, sucking.

He felt her tremble again and heard the purring sound that came from deep within her throat. She wanted more and was letting him know it. He took his hand and ran it across the flat of her stomach, moving lower until he found the moist heat of her. He touched her there, glorying in her dampness. Deftly, expertly, his fingers went to work.

Jayla felt her breath rushing in and out of her lungs. Although there was light in the room and her eyes were open, she felt her world was on the edge of blackness. She felt light-headed, dizzy, dazed, and she was feeling things that she'd never felt before. Storm's fingers were driving her out of her mind, and what his mouth was doing to her breasts was pure torture. Her body felt hot, on fire, in need of something it had never had before, but something it desperately needed.

She groaned deep in her throat. It was either that or scream out loud. So she clamped her mouth shut, but couldn't stop from releasing a sound that was alien to her ears. At the moment, nothing mattered but the feel of Storm's mouth and hands on her.

"I can't wait any longer," she heard him say, as he eased away from her. She watched as he stood next to the bed and quickly removed his shirt, almost tearing off the buttons in the process. Then he wasted no time in removing his pants and briefs. She continued to watch him when, with the expertise of a man who had done it many times before, he ripped the condom from the packet he had taken from his pant pockets and slid it over his erection.

She blinked at the size of him and before she could form the words to let him know of her virginal state, he had returned to the bed, pulled her into his arms and captured her mouth with his, once again giving in to the thirst of her desire; a desire that only he could quench. Want and need spiraled through her, making blood pump fast and furious through her veins. It seemed his mouth and hands were everywhere. Her insides were churning, her stomach was spinning and her brain had turn to mush. She didn't know what was driving him, but whatever the source, it was driving her, too. She felt the tip of his erection pressing against the entrance to her feminine mound in such a way that beckoned her to part her legs for him.

Then he kissed her again, long, hard, as his tongue plowed hers in breath-stealing strokes. She savored all the things he was doing to her, all the ways he was making her feel and wondered if the feelings would ever end, hoping and praying that they wouldn't, yet at the same thing knowing there was something else she needed, something she had to have.

She felt him place his body over hers, felt the strength of his thighs entwining with hers and relished the strong beat of his heart against her breasts. He lifted her hips into his hands.

He broke off their kiss and met her gaze, looked down at her the moment he pushed himself inside of her, with one deep, hard thrust. Her body stiffened and she gasped as a surge of pain ripped through her.

He immediately went still as total disbelief lined his features. "Jayla?"

Her name was a low rumble from deep within his throat. She saw the shock that flared in his eyes and felt the tension coiling within him. A spurt of panic swept through her at the thought that he wouldn't finish what he'd started, so she decided to take action.

"Don't ask," she said, then leaned upward and recaptured his mouth with hers. Her hands clutched at his shoulders and her legs wrapped solidly around him, locking him in place. She felt his resistance and began kissing him in all the ways he had kissed her that night, letting her tongue tangle relentlessly with his. He slowly began moving, easing in and out her, claiming her, taking her, making love to her in a way she always dreamed that lovemaking was supposed to be. The only thought on her mind was the strength of him driving back and forth, rocking her world and sending her over the edge. She knew she would remember every moment of this night for as long as she lived.

A groan eased from Storm's lips as Jayla's body met his, stroke for stroke. His hand reached down and lifted her hips to him for a closer fit, as if they weren't already close enough. She was tight, sensuously so, and his body surged in and out of hers, back and forth, massaging her insides the same way and with the same rhythm that her breasts were massaging his chest.

He had recovered from shock at discovering she'd been a virgin and decided since he was the one initiating her into lovemaking, that he would do it right. And the little whimpering sounds coming from her lips told him that he was definitely making an impact.

"Storm…"

He felt her body jerk at the same time she pressed her head into his shoulder to stifle a scream. The intensity of her climax jolted him, nearly stealing his breath before he followed her in his own release, yanked into the strongest and most mindless orgasm he had ever experienced in his entire life. And it was destined to be the longest…or perhaps he was having multiples, back to back. There was no way to tell since the earth-shattering sensations were hitting him all at once in every form and from every possible angle. The feeling was unique, incredible, out of this world and once in a lifetime. He hadn't expected this and was caught off guard by the magnitude of what was happening to him. He was being hurled into something he had never before experienced.

"Jayla!"

Her name was torn from his lips and he threw his head back as he continued to pump rapidly into her when he felt another climax claim him—his third, possibly a fourth. With a growl that came low from deep within his throat, he leaned down and pressed a kiss to her mouth as his body continued to tumble into oblivion, and he knew what they had shared was nothing short of heaven.

"I did as you requested and didn't ask then, but I'm asking now, Jayla."

Storm's words gave her pause. She let out a deep breath and wondered why he couldn't be one of those men who just accepted things as they were?

She looked up at him and saw the intensity in the depth of his dark eyes. She also saw the impressive shape of his lips and his well-toned, broad chest that was sprinkled with dark curly hair. And it wasn't helping matters that they were both naked in bed, with him leaning on his elbow and looming over her. She closed her eyes and shook her head. The man was too handsome for his own good…or for hers.

"Tell me," he whispered, then leaned down and placed a soft kiss on her bare shoulder. "Tell me why, in this day and age, a twenty-six year old woman would still be a virgin."

She met his gaze. "Because women in this day and age have choices," she said slowly, then asked. "Have you ever taken a love compatibility quiz?"

Storm arched his brow. "A what?"

She smiled at the confused look on his face. "A love compatibility quiz. There's a site on the Internet where you can go and take this quiz if you're looking for Mr. or Miss Right. Well, after a few dates with losers—men who lacked confidence but had plenty of arrogance and who also acted as if it was a foregone conclusion that our date would end in my bed—I decided to take the quiz and my results indicated that my Mr. Right didn't exist."

Storm frowned down at her. Would he ever understand women? "You've been avoiding a serious relationship because of some quiz?"

"Pretty much…yes. I discovered like oil and water, me and relationships don't mix because I have a low tolerance when it comes to men who expect too much too soon."

It took Storm a minute to analyze everything she'd said. "What about those guys you dated off the Internet?"

Jayla released a single, self-deprecating chuckle. "That was my way of trying to prove the quiz wrong. From then on, I never wasted my time going on a guy hunt."

"But…but didn't you date in college?" Storm sputtered. Why hadn't her going off to college assured her returning to town with her hymen no longer intact?

She smiled again, a bit sadly this time. "Yes, but unfortunately, not long after I got there I met a guy name Tyrone Pembroke."

"What happened? He broke your heart?"

She chuckled derisively. "On the contrary. Actually he did me a favor by showing me just what jerks some guys were. He opened my eyes to the games they played, games I wasn't interested in. After Ty, I made it a point not to get serious about any one guy since I wasn't into casual sex, I never felt pressured into sleeping with anyone."

Storm nodded. "So why now and why with me?

To Jayla's way of thinking, that was an easy question. "Because of timing. I know you and I like you. I also know your position on relationships. I'm not looking for anything beyond what we shared tonight and neither are you, right?"

Storm held her gaze. "Right." The last thing he needed

was a clingy woman who wanted to occupy his time. Still, although he didn't want to feel it, he felt a special connection to Jayla since he had been her first. He couldn't recall ever taking a woman's virginity before.

"Now that I've answered your question, do you think I can get some sleep? I'm exhausted." Jayla asked softly.

Storm glanced down at her. Was she dismissing him? "Do you want me to leave?"

She smiled. "Actually…" she began, as she snuggled closer to him. "I was hoping you'd want to stay all night."

A grin spread across Storm's lips. Hell, yeah, he wanted to stay all night. "I think that can be arranged," he told her as he leaned down and placed a kiss on her lips. "Excuse me for a second while I go into the bathroom to take care of something. I'll be right back."

"All right."

There was just enough light in the darkened room to let Jayla admire Storm's nude form as he crossed the room to the bathroom. She inhaled deeply as heated sensations shot through her. He'd been the perfect lover. He was confident, secure in who he was, but not arrogant. She felt tired and yet exhilarated at the same time. Slightly sore, but still smoldering from his lovemaking. Funny how things worked out. Storm was the man she'd been trying to get to notice her since the time she had started noticing boys. She was beginning to believe the cliché that good things came to those who wait. Now timing had not only finally worked for them, it was working against them as well. At any other time, she would have loved to take what she'd shared with Storm tonight to a whole other level, but not now. What she had needed was him out of her system so she could focus on the baby.

Her baby.

"I'm back."

Her nipples peaked in instant response to his words. She watched as he made a casual stroll over to the bed, totally at ease with his naked state. Seeing him that way stirred up desires within her again and she no longer felt as tired as she had earlier.

"Do you want me to prepare you some bath water to soak in for a while before you go off to sleep?" he asked coming to sit on the side of the bed next to where she lay. "If you don't, you might wake up feeling a lot sorer than you probably do now."

Jayla leaned back against her pillow, seriously doubting that most men were as considerate as Storm was being. She pressed her lips together, liking his suggestion. "You're right, a soak in the tub sounds wonderful."

He smiled as he stood up. "I'll be back when your bath is ready."

"All right."

Again she watched him cross the room, finding it hard to tear her gaze from the sight of him, especially his tight behind. She smiled, feeling downright giddy at the thought that he'd agreed to spend the night with her. She might as well stretch this out for as far as she could because when they returned to Atlanta, things would be different. She would go her way and he would go his. They would both resume a life that had nothing to do with each other. He would go back to being a hero by fighting his fires and saving lives and she would eagerly prepare for the most life-altering experience she'd ever encountered—pregnancy.

"Ready?"

Hearing the sound of his voice, she glanced across the

room. A thick surge of desire shot through her veins at the sight of him leaning in the doorway, naked and aroused. If she wasn't ready, he certainly was.

"Yes, I'm ready," she said, barely able to voice the words. She moved to get out of bed and then he was there, sweeping her up into his arms. The heat of his skin seeped through the heat of hers and the feeling was electrifying. She immediately knew the meaning of the words *raging hormones*. Hers were totally out of control. She quickly decided that she needed to get back in control of things.

"I can walk, Storm."

"Yes, but I want to carry you. That's the least I can do."

She clamped her lips tight, deciding not to tell him that he had done quite a lot. He had turned their night into more than a one-night stand. It had become a romantic interlude, one she would remember for the rest of her life.

As he carried her into the bathroom, her breasts tingled from the contact with his skin. And when he leaned down, shifting her in his arms to place her into the bubbly water, sliding her body down his, the sensations that rocketed through her almost took her breath away.

"The water might be a little warmer than what you're used to, but it will be good for your muscles," he said, in a voice that let her know he, too, had been affected by the contact of their bare skin touching.

She nodded as he placed her in the water. He was right. The water was warm, but it immediately felt good to her body. She glanced up at him as he stood beside the tub looking down at her. She tried to keep her attention on the top part of his body and not the lower part. "You seem to be good at this, Westmoreland. Is this how you treat all your virgins?"

He chuckled and his gaze captured hers. "Believe it or not, I've never done a virgin before."

She lifted a brow. "Never?"

His smile widened. "No. never. You're my first, just like I was your first."

Jayla watched as his features shifted into a serious expression as if he had to really think about what he'd just said for a moment. "Do you need my help?" he asked her.

She shook her head. "No, I can manage. Thanks."

He nodded. "Call me when you're ready to get out."

She smiled. "Storm, really, I can manage things."

"Yeah, I know you can but I want you to call me anyway." Then he left, closing the door behind him.

Storm poured himself a glass of ice water and tipped it to his mouth, wishing it was something stronger but appreciating the cool liquid as it soothed his dry throat.

He had sworn off having anything to do with Jayla years ago; yet now, after finally making love to her, he was aching so badly for her again that it actually hurt. To make matters worse, the taste of her was still strong on his tongue and, before he could contain himself, he groaned, which was followed by a growl that erupted from deep within his throat. Jayla Cole had no idea just what a desirable and sexy woman she was. Even being a novice at making love, she was every man's fantasy. He could see her attracting the wrong kind of men and felt a heartfelt sense of pride, as well as relief, that she had kept her head on straight and had not been taken in by any of them.

But was he any better? His no-commitment, hands-on-but-hearts-off, no-strings-attached policy left a lot to be desired, but he and Jayla had been struck by that unique kind of passion that had sent her straight into his arms and had propelled him unerringly into her bed.

And he had no regrets.

Frowning, Storm took another huge swallow of water. No woman had ever gotten to him like this. It was time for him to start building a defense to the passion she aroused in him. He pulled on his pants and did his best to reorder his chaotic thoughts and unruly emotions.

He heard a sound and turned around. Jayla was standing in the doorway wearing one of the hotel's complimentary bathrobes. His heart fluttered as he assessed her from head to toe. She looked refreshed. She looked incredible, blatantly sexy. With a steadying breath, he asked, "Why didn't you call me when you were ready to get out of the tub?"

She smiled and his pulse kicked up a notch. "Because although I was tempted, it wouldn't be a good idea to start becoming dependent on you."

For him, it wasn't an issue of dependency. He'd known she could manage on her own but he had wanted to be there to help her anyway. There was something about her that pulled at his protective instincts…among other things. "Do you feel better?"

"Yes," Jayla said, blowing out a ragged breath as her gaze roamed over him, noticing that he had put his pants back on. What a shame. She was beginning to get used to seeing him naked.

She met his gaze again and couldn't help but notice that his eyes were dark, very dark, and her body's reaction to it was spontaneous. "I, ah, need to get a nightgown out the drawer," she said in a voice that sounded soft and husky even to her ears. She swallowed deeply when he slowly crossed the room to her.

"Have you ever slept in the nude?" he said, reaching out, opening her robe and sliding his hands over her bare skin, beginning with her waist, moving to her hips and then reaching around to cup her bottom.

"Ah, no," she said, barely getting the words out.

He gave her that killer smile. "Would you like to try it? I can't think of anything I'd like better than to have your naked body next to mine all night."

A small purring sound left Jayla's throat when he leaned forward and his tongue licked the area underneath her right ear, then the left. A sensuous shudder ran all through her, and she thought that a woman could definitely become dependent on his kind of treatment. And then she ceased to think at all when he stopped messing around with her ears and shifted his focus, opening his mouth hotly over hers.

Images of how intimate they'd been less than an hour ago flooded her mind. They had been together in bed with him on top of her, their legs entwined, their bodies connected while making love the same way they had done numerous times in her dreams. But this was no dream; it was reality. And the scent of his body heat and the sound of his breathing while he was kissing her did more than stir up her desire; it was stroking her with an intensity that shook her to the core, forging past those emotions she kept tightly guarded.

The thought that Storm was seeping through the barriers she'd set around her emotions disturbed Jayla, but she was too absorbed in the way his tongue was stroking the insides of her mouth to worry about it. This kiss was so full of greed and sensuality that she could feel the air crackling around them, and she was returning with equal vigor everything he was putting into their kiss.

And then slowly, reluctantly, he pulled back and his gaze locked to hers. "So, do we get naked?"

She swallowed. The huskiness in his voice made her want to do a lot more than get naked. "Yes," she managed to get out in a shaky breath.

"Good," he murmured, then reached up and pushed the robe off her shoulders, letting it fall in a heap at her feet. "Let's go back to bed."

Taking her hand into his, he lifted it to his lips and placed a warm kiss against the center of her palm. And then he picked her up in his arms and carried her to the bed. He placed her in the middle and then stood back to remove his pants.

Jayla watched him while thinking that nothing, other than a fire alarm going off, could distract her at that moment. She wanted to see every inch of him again, especially that part that had given her so much pleasure. He kept his gaze on her as he slowly eased down his pants. Then she watched as he pulled a condom packet out of his pants and went through the process of sheathing himself.

When he had finished, he glanced over at her and smiled. "Although I don't plan for us to do anything but sleep, there's nothing wrong with playing it safe."

She sighed and it took a lot of effort to concentrate on his words and not on him. "Umm, yes, that's smart thinking."

He quickly got into the bed, pulled her into his arms and felt her shiver. "You're cold?" he asked in a low, husky voice.

She shook her head. "No, quite the contrary. I'm hot."

He smiled. "I know a way to cool you off," he said, shifting his position to reach down between her legs to slide his fingers back and forth through her feminine curls.

She closed her eyes and moaned as he slowly but thoroughly began stroking a fire within her. "I—I don't think that's helping, Storm," she murmured, barely able to get the words out.

"Sure it is," he whispered close to her ear. "Just relax, feel and enjoy."

And she did.

His fingers literally drove her crazy. The sensation of his fingertips as they intimately skimmed her feminine folds at a sensuously maddening and erratic pace had her purring and moaning.

She made the mistake of opening her eyes and meeting his gaze. Something she saw in the depths of his eyes took her breath away. Her senses suddenly became filled with an emotion that caused a tightening in her chest at the same time that her body lost control, exploded. The sensations that shot through her made her cry out, call his name and then he was capturing her mouth with his, kissing her deeply while he continued to skim the tip of his fingers between her legs.

Moments later, she felt her body become weak and she could barely reclaim her breath as he cuddled her limp body next to his, holding her tightly. She knew if she wasn't careful, that she was going to fall—

No! She couldn't go there. She couldn't even think such a thing. The only thing she wanted to focus on was how he was making her feel. She had made plans for her future and Storm Westmoreland wasn't a part of those plans. But here, now, at this very moment, he was part of her present and was giving her undiluted pleasure. She could not refuse what he was offering and when they parted in two days, she would always have these memories.

Five

Storm drew in a long breath as he looked down at the woman asleep in his arms. His chest tightened and he forced back the surge of desire that swept through him. She was an unbelievably beautiful woman.

Bathed in the rays of predawn light that spilled through the hotel's window, Jayla's hair, a glossy medium brown with strands of golden highlight, was spread across the pillow and shone luxuriously against the darkness of her creamy skin.

Sharing a bed with her hadn't been easy. In fact, he doubted that he'd gotten any sleep. While trying to find that perfect sleeping position, she had twisted and turned most of the night. And he had been tormented with each and every move she'd made. At one time, she had lain facing him, with her leg thrown over his, with his arousal pressing against her center.

Then there had been that time when she had shifted around, placing her back to his chest, her sweet delectable backside right smack up against his groin. More than once during the course of the night he had been tempted to just say, "To hell with it," and ease inside of her. His mind had been filled with numerous possibilities. Instead, he had fought the urge and had wrapped his arms around her waist, pulled her close and thought about the time when he *had* been inside of her.

He would never forget how it felt, the moment he'd realized that she was a virgin. At first he'd been shocked, stunned and then panic had set in. But the notion of ending their lovemaking session had fled his mind when she pulled his mouth down to hers and kissed him with a hunger that he had quickly reciprocated.

And now he wanted her again. If truth were told, he hadn't stopped wanting her but had held back to give her body time to adjust to him. Now he was driven with an undeniable need to bury himself deep within her welcoming warmth again. He glanced over at the clock. It was just past six. He wanted to let her sleep but couldn't. He had to have her. Now.

He leaned over, close to her lips. "Jayla?" he whispered. A few moments later, she purred his name and slowly lifted one drowsy eye. Then she opened the other eye and blinked, as if to bring his face into focus.

"Storm," she murmured in a voice that was muffled with sleep, but to his way of thinking sounded sensuous as hell. Little tendrils of hair had drifted onto her face and graced one of her cheeks. He pushed the hair back from her face before sliding that same hand down the length of her body. Shifting slightly, he wanted her to feel his arousal pressing against the curve of her pelvis.

"I want you," he whispered and wondered if she could hear the urgency in his tone. The need. The desperation. She must have because she inched her lips closer to his for him to take control of her mouth, mate with it.

And he did.

His every muscle, his every nerve, felt sensitized as their tongues tangled with a hunger that was driving him crazy. The sweet, honeyed taste of her consumed his mind, sent a flame through his body and made him quickly lose touch with reality.

"Storm," she said softly, breaking off their kiss as her hands reached down, tentatively searching for him. When she captured him in the warmth of her hands, he thought he had died and gone to heaven. "I want this."

He definitely knew what she was asking for and didn't waste any time rolling her beneath him. He reached down and touched her, finding her hot, wet and ready. Lowering his head he needed to taste her breasts and drew one hardened nipple into his mouth, gently pulling it with his tongue, glorying in the shivers he felt going through her.

And then with her hands still holding him, she placed him at her opening and, slanting her hips upward, began easing him inside her. At this stage of the game, his arousal didn't know the meaning of slow and he pushed deep inside, finding her body still tight, but not as tight as it had been the night before. He stopped to give her time to adjust to him, but her soft moans and the rotation of her hips let him know she didn't want him to stop.

He thrust harder, buried himself to the depth they both wanted, and then he kissed her again, needing the contact to her mouth. And then he began to move inside of her as intense, dizzying, mind-boggling desire consumed him, sending him on a voyage that was out of this world. And Jayla was right there, taking the trip with him, as they flew higher and higher to the place where passion was taking them. A place that was a potent blend of exultation and euphoria, a place where he wanted to think that few people went—at least not to this degree and certainly not this level.

"Wow," he whispered huskily, for lack of a better word, and then he increased his pace, established their rhythm and like finely tuned musical instruments they played together in absolute harmony. Each movement added sensation and increased their pleasure. He dragged in a deep breath, feeling as if he were seconds from toppling over the edge, moments from exploding.

He clamped his hands down on her hips while he mated relentlessly with her. Her feminine muscles began gripping, clutching him with every thrust he took. And when he heard the sharp cry that was torn from her lips and felt her body jolt at the same time she arched her back, then shattered in his arms, he let go and began drowning in his own release.

"Jayla!"

He threw his head back, as something, everything, inside him broke free. If he thought he'd experienced pure, unadulterated ecstasy inside her body before, then this was a pleasure so raw and primitive that he doubted he would ever be able to recover from it. It was as if this was where he belonged, where he was supposed to be.

He quickly banished those thoughts from his mind as they continued to move together. He felt as if every cell within him was electrified, energized as they were propelled even deeper into the sensuous clutches that held them.

And then, before they could recover, it happened again,

just as fast and just as potent. They were hurled into another orgasm so powerful that he actually felt the room spin and wondered if he would ever regain his equilibrium. A cry tore from his throat, only to be drowned out by the sound of hers as once again they were plunged into the throes of pure ecstasy.

With a shuddered sigh, he pulled her closer to him, felt himself getting hard all over again and knew this woman was doing more than draining his body. She was draining his very soul and at the moment, he couldn't do a damn thing to stop her.

Jayla couldn't move, so she lay still, feeling sated, exhausted and caught up in the aftereffects of remarkable sex. She stared up at the ceiling as she tried to calm the rhythm of her breathing. She smiled as she forced herself onto her side and faced Storm. He was lying flat on his back with his eyes closed. He, too, took long, deep, steadying breaths. When she saw he was once again aroused, the sight of him sent her senses into a mindless sensuous rush all over again. He was as hard as a rock, seemingly ready for another round. How on earth was that possible?

She sighed deeply. "Everything I've heard about you is true, Storm." She watched as he slowly lifted his eyes, slightly turned his head and looked over at her.

"What have you heard about me?"

Every bone in her body felt as if it had melted, so she chuckled huskily. "That you're perfect in bed. Did you know some women call you, The Perfect Storm?"

Storm frowned. For some reason he didn't want her to think about the other women he'd been with. And he didn't want to think about them, either. The only woman he wanted to think about was her. Instead of answering her question, he leaned over and kissed her deeply, thoroughly, and moments later, when he pulled back, he reached down and touched her intimately. "I didn't mean to be rough."

A huge smile touched the corners of her lips. "You weren't. I got everything I asked for and then some."

"Yeah, but you're new at this."

"And enjoying every minute." She studied him for a moment, then said. "I was curious about you when I was sixteen. You were the first guy I was really interested in."

"Was I?"

"Yes."

Storm held her gaze. He could vividly recall how, whenever he dropped by to visit Adam, her whiskey-colored eyes would seek him out and convey her every youthful emotion. She'd had a crush on him. He had been aware of it and he had a feeling that Adam had been aware of it as well. Storm had known that around her he would have to tread lightly, because she was the boss's daughter who was noticing boys for the first time; but unfortunately, instead of a boy, she had set her sights and budding desires on a man. To make matters worse, she fully intended for him to notice her and he had tried like hell not to.

"Do we stay in bed for the rest of the day or do we get up and do something else?" she asked, interrupting his stroll down memory lane. "Just to let you know, the thought of staying in bed all day doesn't bother me."

Storm couldn't help but laugh. "What have I created here, a monster?"

She lifted a brow. "Like you can talk. I'd say you're up for it," she said, pointing out his aroused state.

"Well, yeah, but some things can't be rushed. Just give me some time, will you."

"Sure, if you think you need it, but from what I understand most men need time to get it up, not down."

One corner of Storm's mouth lifted. He was enjoying this turn in their conversation, but he knew if they didn't get out of bed really soon, their conversation might turn into something else. Forcing himself to move, he slowly sat up. "I guess I need to go back to my room and take a shower." He glanced over at the clock. "Do you want to meet me downstairs for breakfast?"

"Yeah, I'm starving."

He nodded knowingly. "And after breakfast, how about if we do some more sightseeing today?" *Anything to keep them out of their hotel rooms.* "When does your flight leave tomorrow?" he asked. Suddenly, reality of how short their time together would be began to seep in. From the expression on her face he could tell that she felt it, too.

"In the morning, around eight. What about yours?"

"Tomorrow evening, around three."

She nodded. "Too bad we aren't on the same flight," she said quietly.

He'd been thinking the same thing. "Yeah, it's too bad." But then, maybe it was for the best. Too much more of Jayla Cole would go to his head and right to a place he wasn't quite ready for.

He sighed deeply. So much had happened between them in the last forty-eight hours. "Nothing has changed, right Jayla? Neither of us is looking for a serious relationship."

Jayla glanced at him, understanding his need to reestablish ground rules. "Yeah, right, nothing has changed. Trust me, a serious relationship with anyone is the last thing I want or need right now. I'm going to be so busy over the next few months that an involvement of any kind will be the furthest thing from my mind."

He lifted a brow as he slid out of bed. "Oh? What will you be doing?"

Jayla nervously licked her lips. There was no way she could tell him that she would be preparing for motherhood. "There's this project that I'm going to start working on."

"Oh, and what kind of project is it?"

She sighed deeply; he would ask. She decided to brush off his question and forced out a chuckle, saying, "Nothing you'd be interested in, trust me."

He smiled as he studied her for a long moment, then said. "I might surprise you. If you ever need my help, don't hesitate to call."

She smiled. "Thanks for the offer, but I have everything under control."

"All right. I'll be back in a second."

She watched as he walked into the bathroom and closed the door. She rolled over on her stomach and buried her face in his pillow, enjoying his lingering scent. Had she been dreaming or had Storm just offered to help with her project? She felt it was pretty safe to assume that the last thing Storm Westmoreland would want was to be a daddy. Besides, she had no regrets in going solo. A man like him as the father of her child would definitely cramp her style. He'd already stated his belief that a woman couldn't work outside the home *and* raise a family. She didn't envy the woman he would end up marrying, since it was evident that he would be a controlling husband.

She got out of bed, slipped into her robe, walked over to the window and glanced out to watch the impending sunrise. Tomorrow, she and Storm would bring an end to their short affair and she hoped when they returned to Atlanta that they didn't run into each other anytime soon. It would be difficult to see him and not think about the intimacy they had shared here in The Big Easy. There definitely wouldn't be anything easy about that.

Storm slid his hands around Jayla's waist and pulled her snugly against him. "An hour?" he asked with a puzzled lift of his brow. "Are you saying it will take you an entire hour to pick out an outfit for tonight?"

She smiled up at him. "Yes. Already I see a number of things in this dress shop that I want to try on. It has to be just perfect."

"Jayla," he began, but she cut him off.

"Please, Storm. I want a new outfit for tonight."

He studied the excitement in Jayla's face, thinking she was even more beautiful than before, if that were possible. When he had met her for breakfast, he'd told her of the phone call he had received from his cousin Ian. Ian, a good friend of New Orleans's mayor, had been invited to a huge gala being given in the man's honor. Ian had invited Storm as his guest and Storm had gotten the okay to bring Jayla as his date. Instead of going sightseeing as they had originally planned, Jayla had insisted that the first thing she needed to do was go shopping for something to wear that night.

"All right, I guess I can find something to kill time while you shop," he said releasing her. "But I'll be back in a hour, Jayla."

She grinned, nodding. "And I'll have everything I need by then."

A short while later, Storm took his time as he strolled

around Jackson Square. It was a beautiful day and a lot of tourists were out and about. He smiled when he thought of how excited Jayla had been when he'd mentioned tonight's affair. He had enjoyed seeing her happy. He was also enjoying her company…almost a little too much. She was definitely someone he liked being with, both in and out of bed. More than once he had to remind himself not to make more of what they were sharing than there was.

It was no big deal that over the past few days, they'd discovered that they enjoyed many of the same things. She liked jazz, and so did he; she enjoyed watching bone-chilling thriller movies and so did he. She was one of the few people who lived in Atlanta whose favorite football team *wasn't* the Atlanta Falcons. His favorite team was the Dallas Cowboys and she was a fan of the Philadelphia Eagles.

It seemed the only thing they didn't agree on was his belief that a woman's place was at home raising her kids and not in an office all day. Jayla insisted that a man who held such traditional views would be too controlling in a marriage. He didn't see himself as wanting to control, but rather he saw himself as someone who wanted to be the sole provider for his family in the purest sense of the word.

He glanced at his watch. He still had over forty-five minutes to go before he went back to that dress shop for Jayla. Damn, but he missed her already. A warning bell suddenly went off in his head. He'd never admitted to missing a woman before, so why was he doing it now? He sighed deeply, deciding to be honest with himself. The honest truth was he liked having Jayla around and for him that didn't bode well.

He frowned as he continued to walk around Jackson Square, wondering what was there about her that was getting to him and playing games with his mind? They were games he had no desire to play. She knew the score and so did he. Neither of them wanted anything beyond what they were sharing here in New Orleans. Getting together and developing some sort of relationship when they returned to Atlanta was unacceptable, totally out of the question, a definite bad idea.

Then why was he allowing such thoughts to invade his mind?

"You're confused, aren't you?"

Storm turned to the sound of the craggy voice and saw an old woman sitting on the bench less than five feet from where he stood. He lifted a brow. "Excuse me. Did you say something?"

The old woman smiled serenely. "Yes. I said you're confused. Nothing like this has ever happened to you before has it?"

Storm tilted his head to the side as he studied the woman, wondering if she was operating with a full deck. She was talking as if she knew him. "I think you might have me mixed up with someone else."

"No, I don't," she muttered with a shake of her head. "And I'm not crazy," she said, as if reading his mind. "I'd tell you more if you let me look into your future."

Storm nodded as understanding dawned. The old woman was a fortune-teller. New Orleans was full of them. He crossed his arms over his chest amused. "And what do you think you can tell me that I don't already know?"

"Oh, you'd be surprised."

Storm didn't think so but decided to humor the old woman. "Okay, then surprise me. What do you have to work with? Tarot cards or a crystal ball?"

The older woman met his gaze and looked at him with a scrutiny that Storm found unnerving. Finally, she responded. "Neither. I'm a palm reader."

Storm nodded. *That figured.* "Okay, how much to read my palm?"

"Twenty dollars."

He sighed as he reached into his pocket and pulled a twenty-dollar bill while wondering why he was wasting his time. He glanced at his watch. He still had a good thirty minutes left before Jayla was ready and having his palm read was just as good as anything else to pass the time away.

He sat down next to the woman on the bench and stretched out his hand to her. "Okay, what does my palm say?"

He watched as the woman took his hand into her frail one and studied his palm. Moments later, when she lifted her gaze, the intensity in the depth of her dark eyes almost startled him. She smiled sympathetically. "I can see why you're confused."

He frowned. "Meaning what?"

"You are about to make unexpected changes in your life and although you yearn for peace, turbulence is in your future. Keep your sights high, be patient and let destiny take its course."

Storm's frown deepened. He had just gotten a promotion three months ago, so what changes was the woman talking about? He had thought about moving out of his present house and buying a larger one, but what problems could a decision like that bring on? There had to be more.

He lifted his brow. "Is that it?"

She stared at him and sighed deeply. "Trust me, son. That will be enough."

He shook his head, a part of him found the entire thing outright amusing. "Ahh, can you be a little more specific?"

"No, I've told you everything you need to know."

He slowly stood. He couldn't wait until he and his brothers had their next card game so he could tell them about this experience. Knowing them, they would probably find the whole thing hilarious. "Well, it was nice getting my palm read," he said, not knowing what else to say.

She shook her head slowly. "I wish you the best of luck."

Storm looked at the woman. She'd said it like she had truly meant it. "Thanks," he said before walking off, not sure just what he was thanking her for.

"Tell her you like the red one."

He turned back around and lifted a brow. "Excuse me?"

The old woman smiled. "Tell her you like the red one the best."

Storm frowned, not understanding what she meant. He decided it would be best not to ask, so he nodded, turned back around and kept walking. Moments later, when he returned to the dress shop, he saw Jayla standing at the checkout counter waiting for him. His face lit into a smile as he walked over to her. "Did you find anything?"

"Yes," she answered excitedly. "I found two really nice outfits and they're both beautiful. I want you to pick out the one you like the best."

He watched as she turned and grabbed two dresses off the counter, one blue and the other red. Storm blinked twice and his throat suddenly went dry when he remembered what the old woman had said. *Tell her you like the red one.* He stared at the two outfits that Jayla was holding up in front of her.

"Well, which do you like the best, Storm?" she asked, looking from one dress to the other.

"The red one," he replied promptly, feeling somewhat dazed, like he was a participant in *The Twilight Zone*.

Jayla didn't notice his consternation as she handed the red dress to the smiling saleswoman behind the counter. A huge grin touched her lips. "I like the red one best, too."

Later that night, Storm had to admit that he definitely liked the red dress, especially on Jayla. His tongue had nearly fallen out of his mouth the moment she had stepped off the elevator to meet him in the lobby.

Instantaneous. Immediate. A jolt of mind-wrenching desire had shot straight to his groin. There was nothing like an eye-catching, incredulously sexy, tight-fitting dress on a woman who definitely had sleek and delectable curves. Her silver accessories made her look sophisticated, elegant and hot, all at the same time. The dress was short, really short, but then she had legs that transformed the dress from provocative to mind-blowing. Her breasts sat high and looked full, lush and ready to tumble out of the low-cut neckline at any given moment.

"I had a lot of fun tonight, Storm, and I like your cousin Ian."

He glanced at her. They were sitting in the back of a cab on their way back to the hotel. It was dark, but the moonlight, as well as the bright lights from the buildings they passed, provided sufficient light for them to see each other's features clearly. But even if he hadn't been able to see her, he would have definitely been able to smell her. The perfume she was wearing was a luscious, blatantly sensual scent and it was doing downright crazy things to his libido.

"Yeah, and I could tell he liked you," he responded huskily. *Almost a little too much,* he thought. He smiled when he remembered the look on his cousin's face the moment he and Jayla had walked into the party. Ian's expression of appreciation was also shared by most of the other men present. His heart had swelled with pride that she was with him.

And he couldn't forget how Ian had pulled Jayla to him and planted a kiss on her lips when they'd been leaving. He grinned, knowing Ian had intended to give him a dose of his own medicine. Ian had wanted to get a rise out of him, the same way he enjoyed getting a rise out of his brothers whenever he kissed their wives. Now he knew how it felt.

"I can't wait to get to the hotel to get out of these shoes. They are killing my feet."

Storm smiled and was glad that because of the darkness, Jayla couldn't see the heated gleam in his eyes. He couldn't wait to get her back to the hotel to get her out of something else. The sight of her in that dress had nearly driven him mad all night. He couldn't wait to see just what she had or didn't have underneath it.

"Lift your feet into my lap and I'll be glad to give you some temporary relief," he murmured, wanting to touch her any way he could. She didn't waste time taking him up on his offer and she shifted her body to slide her legs across his lap. He knew there was no way she could not feel the hardness of his groin with her legs resting across his thighs.

He went about removing the silver stiletto heels and began massaging her feet. Her panty hose felt smooth and silky to his touch, and the thought that he'd never pampered another woman this way suddenly hit him. He tossed the thought from his mind as he continued to gently and methodically stroke her feet, thinking there was nothing like a great pair of legs and she had a pretty nice pair.

"Umm, I could get used to this. You have gifted hands, Storm."

He smiled. "Anything to make you happy." He thought about what he'd said and shook his head. He wondered what it would take to make a woman like her completely happy.

"We got back too soon," Jayla said, and he glanced out of the cab's window to see they had arrived back at the hotel. He strapped her shoes back on her feet and felt an immediate sense of loss when she pulled her legs out of his lap.

He glanced over at her, determined to remove that disappointment from her voice. He leaned over, pulled her against him and captured her lips. The taste of her was arousing…as if he needed to be aroused more than he already was. In minutes, he had her groaning and liked the sound of it.

"My room or yours?" he whispered softly against her lips.

She stared at his mouth a moment before answering in a voice that increased his heart rate another notch. "I've never been inside a man's hotel room before and since this trip to New Orleans has been a first for me in a lot of ways, let's go to your room tonight."

He kissed her again, devouring her soft lips and thinking he could definitely get used to this.

Jayla awoke when she heard the ringing of the telephone. A quick glance at the clock on the nightstand indicated it was the wake-up call she had ordered. She watched as Storm reached over, picked up the receiver and, without answering, hung it back up. He then met her gaze and for a moment she thought she saw a quick instant of regret in his eyes when he said, "I guess it's time."

"Yeah, it seems that way," she said softly, not wanting to get out of bed and get dressed, although she knew that she should. She needed to go to her room and pack. Her flight was scheduled to leave in a few hours and she had to make sure that she arrived at the airport on time.

Heat spread low in her belly when Storm continued to look at her. Whenever he looked at her, it did things to her. She would remember every moment of last night. She had entered his hotel room and he had closed the door behind them. She had walked into his embrace and the kiss they'd shared had been blazing and within seconds he had removed her dress and panty hose, leaving her wearing only a thong.

She would never forget the way he had looked at her, how he had swept her up into his arms and carried her over to the bed and made love to her as if pleasing her were the most important thing in his life. The lovemaking that they had shared had been simply amazing.

"Do you need help packing?" he asked, looking breathtakingly handsome, sleep-rumpled and delicious. He smiled as he braced himself up on one elbow and looked down at her. He reached out and gently touched the nipples of her breasts. They hardened with his touch and she felt a warmth begin to build between her legs.

She returned his smile, knowing if she were to take him up on his offer she would never finish packing. "Thanks for the offer, but I believe I can manage."

She felt her smile slowly fade away as reality set in. Although she did not regret any of the time she had spent with him, she knew it was about to end. There was no other way, and it would be for the best. She had to shift her focus away from Storm and back to the baby she wanted more than anything. As soon as she got home, she would schedule an appointment with the fertility clinic to get things started. A continuation of Storm in her life would only complicate things and she didn't do well with complications. Besides, she knew there was no Mr. Right for her, especially one by the name of Storm Westmoreland.

So why was it so hard for her to get out of his bed? And why did she want to make love to him again, one last time before she finally walked out the door?

"I enjoyed our time together, Jayla."

His words interrupted her thoughts and she met his gaze, studied his eyes. "I did, too, and still no regrets, right?"

He reached out and threaded his fingers through her hair. "No regrets. We're adults and we did what we wanted to do."

A smile curved her mouth. "Thank you Storm for showing me how great lovemaking can be."

He looked at her, countered her smile. "You're welcome."

"But life goes on," she decided to say when more than anything she wanted to kiss him.

He nodded. "Yes, life goes on, but it won't be easy. If I were to run into you anytime soon," he said, gently smoothing his fingertips across her cheek, "there's no way I'll see you and not think about that red dress and those killer high heels, not to mention the only thing you were wearing under that dress."

She chuckled. "Shocked you, huh?"

A huge smiled tipped one corner of his mouth. "Yeah, you shocked me. You also pleased me."

Storm decided that what he couldn't tell her was that she was unlike any woman he had ever known. She was some-one who could laugh with him, tease him and talk to him just about anything. And the sex had been amazing and there was no way he could let her go without making love to her again. He needed this one last time to seal the mem-ory of their time together into his mind forever.

Forever.

That was a word he had never included in his vocabu-lary, one he had never associated with a woman. He didn't do forever, and never thought about it. But he had to admit that with Jayla Cole, he thought of things he had never thought of before. And he was glad for the time they had spent together. He had learned things about her that he oth-erwise might not have known, such as her passion for strawberry cheesecake and how she volunteered her spare time at Emory University Hospital's Cancer Center.

"Storm, I need to get up, get dressed and leave."

He stared at her, feeling a sense of finality and a part of him felt a sense of loss he'd never experienced before and one he couldn't explain. And then, suddenly, he wanted her with an urgency he had never wanted her or any woman before. Blood rushed through his veins and he breathed in deeply.

"Storm…"

He looked at her and his breath stopped. He had to have her again, this one last time. He eased her beneath him the same moment that he lowered his head and captured her lips, tasting her, mating his tongue over and over with hers. She had stamped her mark on him and now he was going to make sure he stamped his on her.

For just a little while, he would make her *his*, and if he

lived a hundred years, there would be no regrets. What he would have were memories to last a lifetime.

And from the way she was returning his kiss he could tell she wanted those memories, too.

Six

"So, how was your trip to New Orleans?" Lisa Palmer asked as she sat back in her chair at Jayla's kitchen table.

Jayla looked up and met her best friend's curious stare. "It was fine. Why do you ask?"

"Because I've noticed that since you've been back, you haven't said much about it."

Jayla drew in a deep breath and wished she could ignore Lisa's curious scrutiny. It was just like Lisa to pick up on her reference about the trip. She knew that sooner or later she would have to come clean and tell her friend everything, including her planned trip to the fertility clinic.

"Umm, why do I get the feeling that you're not telling me something?"

Cupping her chin in her palm, Jayla forced a smile. "You're imagining things."

Lisa shook her head. "No, I don't think so." She gazed

at her thoughtfully, then said, "There's something different about you. You look more relaxed and well-rested which can only mean one thing."

Jayla swallowed, wondering if she really had a different look about her. "What?" she asked softly.

Lisa's lips tilted into a deep smile. "That you got plenty of rest this trip, which is a good thing that I didn't go with you. Had I gone I would have worn you out with endless shopping and—"

"I ran into someone."

Lisa lifted a brow. When seconds ticked off and Jayla didn't say anything else, Lisa scooted closer in her chair. "Okay, are you going to keep me in suspense or are you going to tell me?"

Jayla took a sip of her lemonade before responding. "I ran into Storm Westmoreland."

Lisa placed her glass of lemonade down on the table. "Storm Westmoreland? The Perfect Storm?"

Jayla chuckled. "Yes, that Storm."

Lisa stared at her for a moment as she recalled Jayla once telling her about the crush she'd had on Storm Westmoreland at sixteen. And, like most women in the Atlanta area, she also knew about his reputation as a womanizer, and that's what bothered her the most. "What was Storm Westmoreland doing in New Orleans?" she asked, having a feeling there was a lot more to the story.

Jayla chuckled again. "He was attending a conference."

"And…?"

Jayla was quiet for a moment. She knew Lisa had a thousand questions and decided she might as well tell her everything or else she would get grilled to death. "And we ran into each other and one thing led to another and we ended up having an affair."

She almost grinned when she saw Lisa's jaw drop. She then watched as Lisa picked up her glass and drained it as if it contained something stronger than lemonade.

Lisa then turned her full attention to her. "You're no longer a virgin?" she asked as if her mind were in shock.

Jayla did grin this time. "Nope."

Lisa then slumped back in her chair and pinned her with a look. Jayla was well aware of *that* look. It was a look that said you'd better tell me everything and start from the beginning.

"Like I said," Jayla said, before she was hammered with relentless questions, "Storm and I ran into each other, decided to spend time together and one thing led to another."

"Evidently."

Now it was Jayla who pinned Lisa with a look. "And don't expect me to tell you *everything* because there are some details you're better off not knowing." Her mind was suddenly filled with thoughts of everything she and Storm had done. They had made love so many times she had lost count, and each time had been better than the last.

What she held special was the first time and how, afterward, he had drawn her bath water, gently picked her up into his arms and carried her into the bathroom. But it was the last time they'd made love on the morning she'd left, that stood out in her mind more than the others.

With a loving tenderness that had almost brought tears to her eyes, he had used his hands and mouth to drive her over the edge, making her body burn out of control for him. And it was only when she was about to come apart in his arms did he fill her and begin moving back and forth inside her, combining tenderness with compelling need, and sending her escalating into a sharp, shattering orgasm that had taken her breath away and had left her sated, exhausted and spent. And as much as she'd tried to stay awake, she had drifted off to sleep. They both had. When they had awakened, she'd dressed quickly and returned to her room to pack.

He had gone to her room with her to help her pack and the last kiss he had given her before she had walked out of the hotel room door for the airport had been off-the-charts fantastic. She knew that if she never made love to another man, she would always remember having that time with Storm. It had been more than just good, mind-blowing sex. For three days, he had made her feel special, as if knowing he'd been her first had been extraordinary and he was still in awe of the gift she had given him.

"Jayla?"

She jumped when Lisa snapped a finger in front of her face. "What?"

"You haven't answered my question."

Jayla frowned. "What question?"

"Do you have any regrets?"

Jayla immediately shook her head. "No. Twenty-six years was long enough to be a virgin, but I'd never met a man I felt worthy of giving myself to until Storm."

Lisa raised a dark brow. "With Storm's reputation, you thought he was worthy?"

"Yes, because he didn't try to snowball me into doing it with him. In fact, at first he actually tried resisting my advances. I'm the one who came on to him. And he always behaved like a perfect gentleman, giving me choices and not assuming anything."

Lisa nodded, and then a curious glint shone in her dark eyes. "Is everything we've heard about him true?"

Jayla tried to ignore the heat that was settling between her legs when she thought about just how true it was. When it came to lovemaking, Storm Westmoreland was a practiced and skillful lover. She couldn't help but smile. "Yes, everything we've heard is true."

A silly smirk appeared on Lisa's face and she sat back in her chair. "Damn. Some women have all the luck," she said with envy. She then smiled. "So when will the two of you see each other again?"

Jayla tried to ignore the ache that suddenly settled around her heart, convincing herself it was only indigestion. "We won't be seeing each other again. What we shared was nothing more than a no-strings-attached affair, and since neither of us is into relationships, we decided that when we returned to Atlanta, he would continue to do his thing and I would continue to do mine."

Lisa lifted a brow. "You don't have a 'thing' to do. You basically live a boring life. All you do is go to work and come home, except for those days when you're volunteering at the cancer center."

Jayla knew what Lisa said was true, but in a few weeks all of that would change. She smiled. "Well, I want you to know that my life will no longer be boring. I've decided to take the first step in doing something I've wanted to do for a long time."

"Oh, and what's that?"

"Have a baby."

Jayla watched Lisa's expression. She looked as if someone had just pulled a chair out from under her. Lisa looked at her long and hard before finally saying something. "What do you mean, have a baby?"

"Just what I've said. You of all people know how much I love children."

Lisa shrugged. "Hey, I love them, too, but I'm not planning to have any until Mr. Right comes alone and I'm ready to settle down and get married."

Jayla raised her eyes to the ceiling. "Well, yeah, but for some of us there is no Mr. Right, so I've decided not to wait any longer."

Lisa was quiet for a moment as she pinned Jayla with that look again. "Tell me you didn't deliberately try and get pregnant by Storm Westmoreland."

Jayla couldn't help but laugh. Lisa's question was so ridiculous. Storm Westmoreland would be the last man she would want to father her child. He was too controlling. "Trust me, that thought never crossed my mind. Besides, I would never trick any man that way. I made all the necessary arrangements before I left for New Orleans, and I'm going to go to a fertility clinic and have the procedure done."

Lisa quickly held up her hand. "Time out. Back up. What are you talking about?"

Jayla smiled. The expression on Lisa's face was both endearing and maddening. They were as close as sisters and she knew her best friend well enough to know that she would not agree with her decision regarding the fertility clinic. But then, Lisa didn't have any problems finding a Mr. Right since she was already involved in a serious relationship with a wonderful guy. Added to that was the fact that Lisa came from a big family, so she didn't know the meaning of loneliness.

"I'm talking about my decision to have a baby. I've already done the preliminary paperwork and they'd located a potential donor who fits the profile I've requested. All that's left is for me to take another physical, which is scheduled for next Friday. Once it's determined when I'm most fertile during my cycle, I'll be going in to have the procedure done. If I'm not successfully inseminated on the first try, then there will be another try and if necessary, a third or however many times it takes. I'm sure my eggs will eventually be ripe for some donor's sperm," she said smiling.

Lisa, Jayla noticed, wasn't smiling back. In fact, she looked mortified. "Tell me you're joking about this, Jayla."

Jayla sighed deeply. She then worked her bottom lip between her teeth several times, which was something she tended to do when she was bothered by something. Over the years, Lisa may not have agreed with everything she did but had always supported her. Jayla knew because of her friend's traditional beliefs, this would be a hard sell, which was why she had put off telling Lisa about her plans.

She lifted her chin. "No, I'm not joking, Lisa. I've made up my mind about this. You may not agree with what I'm doing, but I really do need you to support me on this. I want a baby more than anything."

"But there are other options, Jayla."

"Yes, and I considered those other options and none will work for me. I want a baby not an involvement with a man who may not be Mr. Right, and I don't have time to wait until I finally get lucky. Times have changed. A woman no longer needs a man to get pregnant or to raise a child, and that's the way I want to do things."

Lisa didn't say anything for a long moment, then she reached across the table and captured Jayla's hand in hers. "Although I can understand some women having the procedure done in certain situations, your case is different, Jayla, and what you plan to do goes against everything I believe in. When it's possible, I think a child should benefit with the presence of both the mother and father in the home. But if you're hell-bent on going through with it, then I'll be there to do whatever you need me to do."

Jayla blinked back the tears in her eyes. "Thanks."

"Hey, Storm, get your mind back on the game, stop daydreaming and throw out a card."

Thorn Westmoreland's words recaptured Storm's attention and he threw out a card then leaned back in his chair and frowned. "I was not daydreaming and my mind *is* on the game," he said throwing out a card.

After another round of bid whist, Stone Westmoreland shook his head. "If your mind is on the game then you're a lousy card player since you just threw out a diamond instead of a heart which means you've reneged." A huge smile tilted the corners of Stone's lips. "But I'm not complaining since that puts me closer to winning."

Storm pushed back his chair and stood, glaring at his four brothers. Apparently they'd found his lack of concentration amusing but he didn't find a damn thing funny about it. "I'm sitting out for a while. I need some fresh air."

While he was walking away he heard his brother Thorn ask the others, "What's wrong with him?"

"Don't know," his brother Dare replied. "He's been acting strange ever since he got back from that conference in New Orleans."

"Maybe the pressures of being a fire captain is getting

to him," he heard his brother Chase add. "There's nothing worse than letting a job stress you out."

"Yeah," his other brothers agreed.

Storm shook his head when he opened the door and stepped out on the lanai. His brothers didn't know how wrong they were. His new promotion or work-related stress had nothing to do with the way he'd been acting since returning from New Orleans.

He glanced up and noticed a full moon and the stars in the sky. It was a beautiful night and he was glad he had come outside to appreciate the evening for a little while.

After Thorn and Tara had gotten married, they had moved into Tara's place since it was larger than Thorn's, but only temporarily. They were building their dream home on a parcel of the Westmoreland family homestead, which was located on the outskirts of town. It was a pretty nice area if you liked being out in the boon-docks and cherished your privacy.

Storm shook his head as an image of a woman forced its way into his head. It was the same image he'd been trying like hell to forget the past week. Jayla Cole.

He balled his hands into fists at his side as he wondered what was wrong with him. He'd had affairs before but none had affected him the way this one had. No woman had ever remained in his thoughts after the affair had ended. He'd known there would be memories, hell he had counted on savoring them. But he had wanted them safely tucked away until he was ready to revisit them. He hadn't counted on having no control of his own memories.

Visions of Jayla in the red dress were taking him to the cleaners and wringing him out. And then there were those images of the sway of her hips whenever she walked, whether she was in heels or flats. It didn't matter. The woman was sensuality on legs. She was a mouthwatering piece flat on her back as well. All he had to do was close his eyes and he was reliving the evenings filled with their mind-boggling, earth-shattering lovemaking.

She had fired up and completely satisfied a need within him that he hadn't known existed. Each and every time he had taken her to bed they had made incredible love. He could get her so wet, so hot, so ready, and likewise she could get him so hard, so needy, so out-of-his-mind greedy, to the point where getting inside her body was all he could think about; all he wanted.

And then there was the look on her face whenever she came. It was priceless. It was as if the force of what she felt stole her breath and the intensity of it exploded her world into tiny fragments as she tumbled into mindless completion. Seeing that experience on her face would then push him over the edge into the most potent climax he'd ever experienced; usually more than one—back to back.

"Damn," he let out a low growl and wiped a sheen of perspiration from his forehead with his hand. He was used to sexual experiences, but getting seduced by memories was something that he was not used to or comfortable with. Hell, he had even thought about dropping by her house to make sure she was all right. If that didn't beat all. He had never checked up on a woman after the affair ended.

"Storm, are you okay?"

He inhaled deeply when he heard his sister-in-law's voice and quickly decided that although it was dark, it wouldn't be a good idea for him to turn around just yet. There was a glow of light filtering out from the living room and he had gotten hard just thinking about Jayla.

"Storm?"

"Yeah, Tara, I'm fine." Seconds later when he was sure he had gotten his body back under control he turned around and smiled.

Tara Matthews was beautiful and had nearly blown Storm and his brothers away the first time they had seen her at their sister Delaney's apartment in Kentucky. And he might have even considered having a relationship with her, but he'd soon discovered that Tara was a handful. He and his brothers had quickly concluded that the only man who could possibly handle her was their brother Thorn, so they had deemed her Thorn's challenge. Now, a little more than two years later, she was Thorn's wife. But she still held a special place in his heart as well as the hearts of his brothers because in the end though Thorn may have handled her, Tara had proved that she was capable of handling Thorn, which wasn't an easy task.

He met her gaze and saw concern in her eyes. "I was worried about you," she said softly. "When I passed through the dining room and saw you missing, your brothers said you had needed fresh air. I didn't know if you were coming down with something, especially when they'd said you'd been playing badly tonight."

Storm laughed, then gave her a playful grin. "Hell, they claim I play lousy even when I'm winning."

Tara nodded smiling. "So, how was your trip to New Orleans?"

Funny you should ask, he thought as he slumped back against a column post. He sucked in a deep breath when another vision of Jayla floated through his mind. He envisioned his mouth finding her most sensitive areas, especially her ultra-hot spot and tilting her up to his mouth and making her scream.

"Storm?"

"Huh?"

"I asked how was your trip." She took a step closer to him and looked deeply into his eyes. "Are you sure you're okay, your eyes seemed somewhat dazed."

And my body is hard again but we won't go there, he thought, thinking the best thing to do was go back inside and play cards and hope that this time he could keep his mind on the game. "I'm fine and I had a great time in New Orleans. I even saw Ian while I was there and he mentioned that he would be in town for that charity benefit that you're working on."

A smile touched the corners of Tara's lips. "Really," she said excitedly. "That's the night we'll unveil the charity calendar for Kids' World and everyone will get to see Thorn as Mr. July."

Storm laughed. "I don't think that's the only reason Ian is coming, Tara," he said, thinking that maybe if he kept talking he wouldn't have to worry about visions of Jayla intruding. "The main reason Ian's coming is because you asked him to, but there's another reason."

Tara lifted her brow. "And what reason is that?"

A grin appeared on Storm's face. "He figures there will be a lot of pretty, single women in attendance."

Tara shook her head smiling, finally getting the picture. "Well, I'm sure there will be plenty of single women there since eleven of the men who posed for the calendar are still single. Thorn is the only one who has gotten married since those photos were taken."

Something suddenly pulled at Storm's memory. He remembered Jayla mentioning that she would be meeting Tara for lunch the Tuesday after returning to work. Unless those plans had changed, that meant the two of them would be meeting tomorrow. There was no way he could ask Tara about it without her wondering how he'd known. But if they were to meet tomorrow for lunch and if he knew where, he could unexpectedly drop by and pretend that he'd been in the area. For some reason he wanted to see Jayla again and if they *accidentally* ran into each other, she wouldn't think he had intentionally sought her out…although in essence, he would be doing just that.

"So, Tara, how about if I took you, Madison and Shelly to lunch tomorrow?" he suggested. He knew Dare's wife Shelly hadn't returned from visiting her parents in Florida, Stone's wife Madison would be leaving with Stone tomorrow on a book-signing trip to Kansas City, and if Tara had made other plans for lunch then he would find out soon enough.

"Thanks, Storm, that's really sweet of you, but Shelly and Madison will be out of town and besides I already have a lunch date. I'm meeting with a woman who's working with me on the charity benefit. Her company has agreed to pick up the tab for all the food and drinks that night."

Bingo. He was suddenly beginning to feel pretty good now. Confident. Cocky. Smug. He straightened from leaning against the post. "Oh, that's too bad. Where are you going?"

Tara lifted a brow. "Excuse me?"

He inhaled slowly, knowing he couldn't appear too inquisitive. The last thing he needed was for Tara to get suspicious of anything. "I asked where are you going for lunch? It might be a place where I've eaten before. Perhaps I can tell you whether the food and service are good."

Tara smiled. "Trust me, I know you've eaten at this

place plenty of times and can definitely vouch for the food and service being the best. My lunch date left it up to me to select a place and although I haven't told her yet, I'm going to suggest that we have lunch at Chase's Place."

His heart suddenly did a back flip and his mouth curved into a huge smile. Things couldn't have worked out better if he was planning things himself. Tara was taking Jayla to his brother's restaurant, a place where he ate lunch on a regular basis, so it wouldn't seem out of the ordinary if he showed up there tomorrow. "I think that's a wonderful choice."

She shook her head smiling and before she could say anything, Thorn's loud voice roared through the air. "Storm, get back in here if you're in this game, and you better not be out there kissing my wife."

Storm laughed. "He's a jealous kind of fellow, isn't he?" he asked, taking Tara's hand as they walked back inside

She grinned and he could see her entire face light up with absolute love for his brother. "Yes, but I wouldn't have him any other way."

"Chase's Place?" Jayla asked, making sure she had heard correctly.

"Yes," Tara said brightly on the other end of the phone. "It's a soul-food restaurant that's owned by my brother-in-law Chase Westmoreland, and the food there is wonderful."

Jayla rose from behind her desk, no longer able to sit. She knew the food there was wonderful but at the moment that wasn't what was bothering her. She recalled Storm saying that he routinely ate at his brother's restaurant. She was tempted to suggest they go someplace else but quickly remembered that she had been the one to suggest that Tara select the place for lunch. She sighed deeply. "I've eaten there before and you're right the food is wonderful."

"And he's promised to take good care of us."

Jayla raised a dark brow. "Who?" She heard Tara chuckle on the other end before answering.

"Chase. He's good at taking care of people. "

"Oh." It was on the tip of Jayla's tongue to say it must run in the family because Chase wasn't the only Westmoreland who was good at taking care of people. She vividly remembered the way Storm had taken care of her, fulfilling and satisfying her every need.

She tried forcing the memories to the back of her mind. "What time do you want us to meet?"

"What about around one-thirty? That way the noonday lunch crowd won't bombard us. But if you think you'll be hungry before then we can—"

"No, one-thirty is fine and I'll meet you there." After ending the call, Jayla sat back at her desk. If she saw Storm again, what was the correct protocol to handle the situation? Women and men had affairs all the time and she was sure that at some point they ran into each other again. Did they act casually as if nothing had ever happened between them and they were meeting for the first time? Or were they savvy enough to accept that they had shared something intimate with no regrets, moved on and didn't make a big deal about it? She decided the latter would work. It wasn't as if they had been total strangers.

She glanced at her watch. One-thirty was less than five hours away. Although Atlanta was a big town, she and Storm were bound to run into each other soon or later, but part of her had been hoping it was later. She had expected to see him at the charity benefit, but had figured she would be prepared to see him by then. It was more than a week since they had been together, nine days, if you were counting, and unfortunately, she was.

She closed her eyes and exhaled a deep breath. If she saw him, she would play it cool, take the savvy approach and hope and pray that it worked.

"Is there a reason why you're hanging around here?"

Storm shrugged and shot his twin a beguiling smile. "I like this place."

The expression he read on Chase's face said he knew better, since he only dropped by to eat and rarely hung around to socialize. He usually was too busy pursuing women to visit with his brother for very long. His answering machine had maxed out while he'd been out of town and his phone hadn't stopped ringing since he'd been back. But for some reason, he wasn't interested in returning any of those women's calls.

"Well, if you don't have anything better to do with your time, how about waiting tables?" Chase said, interrupting his thoughts. "One of my waitresses called in sick and we're shorthanded."

Storm glanced at his watch while shaking his head. "Sorry. I like you, Chase, but not that much." He turned and glanced at the entrance to his brother's restaurant and wondered if perhaps Tara and Jayla had changed their minds and decided to go someplace else since it was past lunchtime. No sooner had that possibility crossed his mind, than the door swung open and the two women entered.

His breath caught at the sight of Jayla. Because he was sitting at the far end of the counter, he knew she wouldn't be able to see him but he could definitely see her. She was dressed differently than she'd been in New Orleans. Today, Jayla was Miss Professional in her chic navy blue power suit. She still looked stunning and as sexy as sin. Storm could feel his libido going bonkers. He swung around to Chase. "Hey, I've changed my mind. I will help you out after all."

Chase raised a suspicious brow. "Why the change of heart?"

"Because if a man can't depend on his twin brother in a time of need, then who can he depend on?" Storm asked, giving Chase a boyish grin.

Chase cast a speculative glance over Storm's shoulder and said dryly, "I hope the person you're all fired up at seeing is the woman with Tara and *not* Tara. I would hate for Thorn to kill you."

Storm chuckled. "Relax. I got over Tara a long time ago. I just like getting a rise out of Thorn."

He leaned over the counter and snagged a pencil from Chase's shirt pocket and tucked it behind his ear. He then picked up a pad off the counter. "Who's working the table where they're sitting?"

"Pam."

Storm smiled. "Then tell Pam to take a break or, better yet, tell her to find another table to work. I got that one covered." Before Chase could say anything, Storm stood and headed over to where Tara and Jayla were sitting.

"We made perfect timing," Tara said smiling. "Had we arrived any earlier this place would have been packed." The menus were in a rack on the table and she passed one to Jayla.

Jayla nodded as she opened the menu. She was tempted to glance around but decided not to. Chances were if Storm had been there earlier as a part of the lunch crowd he would have already left.

After they had looked over the menus for a few moments, Tara glanced up, smiled and asked, "So what are you going to get?"

Tara's question recaptured her attention and she couldn't help but return the other woman's smile. Already she'd decided that she liked Tara Westmoreland. They had spoken several times on the phone, but this was the first time they had actually met in person. Jayla thought the woman was simply gorgeous and could quickly see how she had captured the heart of motorcycle tycoon, Thorn Westmoreland.

"Umm," Jayla said smiling as if in deep thought as she glanced back down at the menu and licked her lips. "Everything looks delicious, but I think I'll get—"

"Good afternoon, ladies, what can I get you?"

Jayla's head snapped up and she blinked upon seeing Storm standing beside their table. "Storm!" Without thinking, she said his name as intense heat settled deep in her stomach.

Storm's mouth curved into a devilish grin, and that grin reminded her of sensations he could easily elicit, tempting her into partaking in any number of passionate indulgences. "I'm not on the menu, Jayla, but if I'm what you want, I can definitely make an exception."

Seven

"**I** take it the two of you know each other," Tara said curiously as a smile touched her lips. She glanced from Storm to Jayla.

Jayla cleared her throat, wondering how much she should say. Before she could decide on how to respond, Storm spoke up.

"Jayla's father was my first fire captain and was like a second father to me," he said, giving them his killer-watt smile. "So, yes, we know each other."

Jayla swallowed deeply, grateful for Storm's timely and acceptable explanation.

"It's good seeing you again, Jayla."

She smiled. "It's good seeing you, too," she said, meaning every word, although she wished that she didn't.

"And you look good, by the way."

Her smile widened. "Thanks." He looked rather good, too, she thought. He was dressed in a pair of khaki trousers and a polo shirt. And he smelled good. His cologne could always jump-start her senses. It was a good thing she was already sitting down because she could actually feel her knees weaken. Everything about Storm was a total turn-on—the rippling muscles beneath his shirt, his extraordinary butt, long legs, his too-hot grin and eyes so dark they reminded you of chocolate chips.... Had she forgotten that she had a weakness for chocolate chips just as bad as her weakness for strawberry cheesecake?

She glanced over at Tara and saw that she was still watching them and Jayla decided it wouldn't be a bad idea to go ahead and place her order. She cleared her throat. "I'll have today's special with a glass of iced tea."

"All right." Storm scribbled down Jayla's order, not knowing and not really caring what today's special was. The only thing on his mind was that he was getting the chance to see her again.

He then turned his attention to Tara and smiled. "And what will you have Mrs. Westmoreland?"

Tara lifted a brow. "An explanation as to why you're waiting on tables."

Storm chuckled. He was busted. Leave it to Tara to ask questions. She'd been hanging around his brother Thorn too long. "Chase was shorthanded so I thought I'd pitch in and help him out."

Tara nodded, but the look she gave let him indicated that she knew there was more to the story than that. He wondered if parts of their conversation last night were coming back to her. "That was kind of you, Storm, and I'll have today's special, as well, with a glass of lemonade."

Storm wrote down her order, then said, "I'll go ahead and bring your drinks." He winked at them and then walked off.

Jayla watched him walk away. When she returned her attention back to Tara she knew the woman had been watching her watch Storm. "Small world, isn't it?" she asked trying to pull herself together before she actually started drooling.

Tara smiled. "Yes, it is a small world," she agreed as she studied Jayla. Storm had been blatantly flirting with the woman, which was nothing surprising. Tara had seen Storm in action many times before. But something was different with the way he had flirted with Jayla; however, at the moment she couldn't put a finger on just what that difference was.

"I'm looking forward to the charity benefit," Jayla was saying, rousing Tara from her musings and reminding her of the reason for their meeting.

"So am I, and the committee appreciates Sala Industries agreeing to be our food and beverage sponsor. Kids' World will benefit greatly from their contribution. The money raised from the calendar will be more than enough to make the children's dreams come true."

Jayla smiled in agreement. "Doesn't it bother you that your husband is Mr. July on that calendar?"

Tara laughed as she remembered how she'd maneuvered Thorn into posing for the calendar. Actually, they had come to an agreement only after Thorn had made her an offer she couldn't refuse. "No, I'm not bothered at all. It will be nice knowing other women will find my husband as sexy as I do."

Jayla nodded. She had seen Thorn Westmoreland before in person and the man was definitely sexy. But she didn't think anyone was sexier than Storm. She couldn't help but glance to where he had gone. He was behind the counter preparing their drinks and, as if he knew she was looking at him, he lifted his head, met her gaze and smiled.

It was a smile that sent shivers all the way through her body. It was also a smile that seemed to say, *I remember everything about those days in New Orleans.* She couldn't help returning his smile as she also remembered everything about their time together.

When she turned her attention back to Tara, Jayla realized that Tara had noticed the silent exchange between her and Storm. "Umm…I, well—" she started to say, feeling somewhat embarrassed that Tara had caught her ogling Storm.

Tara reached across the table and touched her hand. "No need to explain, Jayla. I'm married to a Westmoreland so I understand."

Jayla pulled in a deep breath, wondering how could Tara possibly understand when she didn't understand her feelings for Storm. "It's nothing but simple chemistry," she decided to say to explain.

Tara smiled, thinking of her reaction to Thorn Westmoreland the first time she had seen him. "Happens to the best of us, trust me."

Jayla laughed, suddenly feeling relaxed and thinking that, yes, she really did like Tara Westmoreland.

Chase shook his head as he stared at his brother. "Are you going to stand there all day and stare at that woman with Tara?"

Storm met Chase's gaze and grinned. "I like watching her eat. I love the way her mouth moves."

Chase's gaze followed Storm and he didn't see anything fascinating about the way she was eating, although he would be the first to admit that she was good-looking. He turned his attention back to Storm. "Who is she?"

"Adam's daughter."

Chase snapped his gaze back to the table where Tara and the woman were sitting. "Are you saying that's Adam Cole's girl, all grown up?"

"Yes."

"Wow. I haven't seen her since she was in high school. He would bring her in here every once and a while for dinner." He let out a low whistle. "Boy, has she changed. She was a cute kid, but now she is definitely a looker. I'd say she is a woman who looks ripe for loving."

Storm turned and glared at his brother as he leaned against the counter and shoved his hands deep into his pants pockets. "I'm going to ignore the fact that you said that."

Chase smiled. "Hey, man, I didn't know things were *that* way with her," he offered by way of apology.

Storm's glare deepened. "And what do you perceive as *that* way?"

Chase's smile widened. Storm was so used to getting a rise out of people that he couldn't recognize when someone was trying to get a rise out of him. "You're interested in her. *That's* obvious."

Storm shrugged. "Of course I'm interested in her. Adam was someone I cared a lot about. He was like a second father to me. He was—"

"We're not talking about Adam, Storm. We're talking about his daughter. Come on and admit it. You're interested in her as a woman and not as Adam's daughter."

Storm frowned. "I'm not going to admit anything."

Chase chuckled. "Then why did you get jealous a few minutes ago?"

Storm blinked, then looked at his twin as if he were stone crazy, definitely had gone off the deep end. "Jealous?" he repeated, wondering how Chase could think such a thing. "The word *jealous* is not in my vocabulary."

Chase studied his brother's face and knew he had pushed him enough for one day, but couldn't resist taking one final dig. "Then it must have been added rather recently. Not only is it now in your vocabulary, you should spell the word with a capital *J*. And I thought the reason you were acting strange had to do with work. The way I see it, that woman sitting over there definitely has her hook in and is reeling you in."

Storm drew in a deep breath, squared his shoulders. The eyes that stared at his twin were hard, ice cold. "You're going to regret the day you said that."

Chase laughed. "And I have a feeling that you're going to regret the day you didn't figure it out for yourself."

Jayla slipped off her pumps as soon as she walked into the house and closed the door behind her. She let out a deep breath. Lunch with Tara Westmoreland had gone well and they had finalized a lot of items for the charity benefit. But what stood out in her mind more than anything was seeing Storm again.

More than once she had glanced his way. The heat in his eyes had ignited a slow, sensual burn within her. Across the distance of the room, he had silently yet expertly aroused her, almost making concentration on her discussion with Tara impossible.

And when he had placed their meals on the table, her

eyes had been drawn to his hands and it didn't take much to remember how skilled his fingers were, and how those fingers had known just the right places on her body to touch to drive her crazy. It was only when he had left the restaurant, shortly after serving their lunch, that her mind had become functional. Only then had she been able to zero in on the business that she and Tara had needed to accomplish.

On her drive back to the office, she had to remind herself several times that there was nothing between her and Storm and that any future involvement with him was out of the question. They each had a different agenda. To consider a possible relationship between them would only complicate things. What they had shared in New Orleans, just great sex, was over.

Placing her purse on the counter that separated the kitchen from her dining room, she started sorting through the mail she had retrieved from her mailbox and smiled when she saw a letter from the fertility clinic.

Tearing it open, she quickly scanned the contents and her smile widened. It was a letter reminding her of the physical that was scheduled for the next week and information about the insemination procedure.

Placing the letter in the drawer, she laughed, feeling elated, happy beyond words. She anxiously awaited that day—after the procedure was done—when a doctor would confirm she was pregnant. Although Lisa didn't totally agreed with what she planned to do, at least her friend would be there to support her. And, of course, Lisa had agreed to be her child's godmother.

In her heart, Jayla believed things would work out. She had a good friend who would stand by her and she had a good job. And as she had told Lisa, if the artificial insemination didn't work the first time around, she would try a second and, if need be, a third time. She would repeat the procedure as many times as it took to get pregnant whatever the cost. Thanks to the trust fund her father had left for her, as well as the insurance funds that had been left after all the burial expenses had been taken care of, she could afford making her dream of having a baby come true.

She decided to take a shower and relax before fixing dinner. Later, she would find a comfortable spot on her sofa to sit and prop her feet up on her coffee table and enjoy a good book. She tried shaking off the lonely feeling that she suddenly felt. Lisa had a date with her boyfriend Andrew tonight, which meant she wasn't available for a chat.

She tried not to recall that this time nearly a week and a half ago, she had been in New Orleans with Storm. Nor did she want to think about how much she had enjoyed his company. Of course, the time they had spent in bed had been great, but there had been more than that. She had discovered a fun side to Storm. Before New Orleans, she'd always assumed that he was a really serious sort of guy.

She had enjoyed laughing with him, talking to him, dancing with him, sharing food with him and going sightseeing with him. He had been full of surprises in more ways than one. She couldn't help but compare him to the last guy she had dated, Erik Turner. Erik had turned out to be an A-number-one bore and had expected they'd go straight to her bedroom when he'd brought her home from their first date. He had actually gotten pissed off when she'd turned him down.

Frowning, she headed for her bedroom as she remembered how angry she had gotten, too, that night. Angry for having such high expectations that most men would treat a woman like a lady, decently respectable and not assume anything—especially on the first date. Erik had been included in a long line of disappointments for her, but he had definitely been the last straw and had been an eye-opener. That night Jayla realized that she didn't want to be one of those women who were in such a frenzy to be involved in a relationship that they failed to look at the signs that said, "This may not be the best person for me."

Another pitfall she had avoided, which was the main reason she had remained a virgin for so long, was the mistake some women made of equating sex with love. She'd learned from listening to the women she worked with, that some women still believed that if a man slept with her, it meant he loved her. She definitely hadn't assumed such a thing with her and Storm. It had been her hormones and not her heart that had been raging out of control. Storm didn't love her and she didn't love him. She hadn't expected anything from him and he hadn't expected anything from her. They had communicated well both in and out of bed, and the one thing they understood and agreed upon was that their affair would be one that led nowhere.

Sighing, she began removing her clothes for her shower. But as much as she didn't want to think about it, she couldn't get the memory of Storm and the way he had looked at her today out of her mind.

Drawing in a deep breath, Storm raised his hand to knock, then pulled back as he asked himself, for the umpteenth time, why he was standing in front of Jayla's front door. And no matter how many times he asked the question, the answer always came up the same.

He still wanted her.

Seeing her today had done more harm than good and what Chase had said hadn't helped matters. The notion that Jayla had hooked him was preposterous. Okay, he would admit she was still in his system. He had discovered that a man didn't have sex with a woman at the magnitude that he'd had with Jayla and not have some lingering effects. Lingering effects he could handle; the notion of some woman reeling him in, he could not.

Tonight, and only tonight, he would break his rule of not performing repeats after an affair ended. But he had to make sure that the only thing that was pulling him back to her was the incredible sex they'd shared. Physical he could handle, but anything that bordered on emotional he could not.

Taking another deep breath, he finally raised his hand and knocked on the door. As he waited for her to answer it, he hoped to God that he wasn't making a huge mistake.

He was about to knock again when he heard the sound of her voice on the other side. "Who is it?"

"It's me, Jayla. Storm."

She slowly opened the door and the anticipation of the removal of the solid piece of wood that stood between them sent a shiver of desire up his spine and down to his midsection. When she opened the door enough for him to see her, the sight of her nearly knocked him to his knees like a gale-force wind. It was obvious that she had just gotten out of the shower. Her hair was loose, flowing around her shoulders, and there were certain parts of her, not covered by her short bathrobe, that were still wet. He itched to take the robe off her to see what, if anything, she was wearing underneath it.

"Storm, what are you doing here?"

Her voice, low in pitch yet high in sensuality, rapidly

joined forces with desire that had already taken over his body. He was almost afraid to stand there and look at her. Too much longer and he might be driven to topple her to the floor and make love to her then and there.

"Storm?"

Claiming that he just happened to be in the neighborhood would sound pretty lame when she lived in North Atlanta and he resided in the southern part of town. Believing that honesty was the best policy, he decided to tell her the truth as his gaze locked on hers. "Seeing you today made me realize something," he murmured softly as he leaned in her doorway.

He watched her throat move when she swallowed. "What?"

"That I didn't get enough of you in New Orleans. I want you again."

He heard her inhale sharply and the sound triggered the memory of how her voice would catch just seconds before she came. His mind was remembering and his body was, too. He was tempted to pull her close and let her feel just how hard she was making him. "May I come in?" he decided to ask when she didn't say anything.

"Storm…"

"I know I shouldn't have come and I'm just as confused about showing up here as you are," he quickly said. "But seeing you today *really* did do something to me, Jayla, and it's something that's never happened to me before. It was as if my body went on overload and you're the only person who can shut it down. Since returning from New Orleans, I've been constantly reminded of the best sex I've ever had, and tonight I couldn't handle things any longer."

He sighed deeply. There. He'd said it. He'd been honest and upfront with her, although it had nearly killed him to admit such a thing. Even to his ears his predicament sounded almost like an addiction. His blood was pumped up a notch. Every muscle in his body ached at the thought of making love to her again and a part of him knew the look in his eyes was just shy of pleading. He might even go so far as to follow the Temptations' lead and sing out loud, "Ain't Too Proud To Beg."

It was all rather pathetic, but at the moment there wasn't a damn thing he could do about it. Jayla Cole was under his skin…at least temporarily. Just one more time with her should obliterate this madness. At least, that's what he hoped.

He watched her as she tried to make up her mind about him, but patience had never been one of his strong points and he couldn't help asking, "So are you going to let me in?"

Silence filled the air.

Moments later, Jayla sighed deeply. Her mind was in battle over what she *should* do versus what she *wanted* to do. She knew what she should do was send Storm packing after reminding him of their agreement. But what she really wanted to do was give him what she knew they both desired.

Just one more time, she decided. What could possibly be wrong in giving in to an indulgence just one more time? However, more than just once would be a complication she didn't need. Her heart hammered hard in her chest. She knew once he stepped inside and closed the door behind him, that would be the end of it…or the beginning. But as her body began to slowly tremble, her control began slipping. She knew that tonight she needed him just as much as he seemed to need her. He was right. This *was* madness.

"Yes," she finally said, taking a step back. "You can come in."

He entered and closed the door behind him. Locked it. The click sounded rather loud in the now awkward silence between them. That small sound was enough to push her heart into overdrive, making it beat that much faster.

"Thirsty?" she asked, deciding she should at least offer him a drink.

"Yes, very."

She turned toward the kitchen and was surprised when he reached out, gently grabbed her, pulled her close to him and wrapped his arms around her. "This is what I'm thirsty for, Jayla. The taste of you."

When her lips opened on a breathless sigh, his tongue swept into her mouth as if he needed to taste her as much as he needed to breathe. His lips were hot and demanding, and his tongue was making love to her mouth with an intensity that overwhelmed her. Helpless to do anything else, she looped her arms around his neck and held on while the heat of him consumed her, breaching any barrier and snatching away any resistance she might have had.

Too late. He was inside and intended to fill her to capacity in more ways than one.

She pushed good judgment, initial misgivings and any lingering doubts aside. She would deal with them later. Right now, being in Storm's arms this way was most important and demanded her full concentration. And everything about him—his scent, his strength, his very sensuality—permeated her skin, seeped into her blood and sent her senses spinning.

When he tore his mouth away from hers, she drew in a long audible sigh. She looked up at him and the air surrounding them seemed to crackle with ardent awareness. He reached out and traced a slow path down the center of her neck, then slowly pushed aside her robe to reveal what was underneath.

Nothing.

She heard his sharp intake of breath and he pushed the robe off her shoulders to the floor. "A few moments ago, I was thirsty for your mouth, but now I'm starving for this," he said reaching out and stroking her between the legs. "Once I get you in bed, I plan to make love to you all night."

His voice was low, uneven and so sexy that it sent shock waves all through her body. She met his gaze, saw the deep darkening of his eyes and any grip she had on reality slipped, joining her robe on the floor.

"That's a promise I intend to hold you to, Storm Westmoreland," she said on a breathless sigh, just seconds before he swept her into his arms.

Eight

"**W**hich way to your bedroom?"

"Straight ahead and to your right."

Storm didn't waste any time taking her there and immediately placed her naked body in the middle of the bed. He took a step back to look at her. For a moment, he couldn't move, too overwhelmed by her beauty to do anything but to take it all in…and breathe. He ached to make love to her, and sink his body into the wet warmth of hers.

Love her.

Air suddenly left his lungs in a whoosh and he summoned all the strength he could not to fall flat on his face. The thought that he wanted to love her had been unintentional, absolutely ridiculous, outlandish and totally absurd. He only did non-demanding relationships and short-term affairs. He wasn't into strings, especially the attached kind.

He suddenly felt a tightening in his chest at the same time that he felt a bizarre quickening around his heart.

Hell! Something was wrong with him. Then, on second thought, maybe nothing was wrong with him. He was merely imagining things. He was aching so badly to be with Jayla again that he wasn't thinking straight. That had to be it. When he got home later tonight, on familiar turf, his mind would be clear. And spending a day at the station tomorrow around the guys would definitely screw his head back on straight.

"Are you going to stand there all night, Storm?"

He blinked, attempting to clear his mind and immediately became entranced with the warmness of Jayla's smile and the teasing heat of intimacy in her eyes. He swallowed deeply and tried to get a grip, but all he got was a harder arousal. "Not if I can help it," he said, suddenly needing to connect with her that instant. He needed to touch her, taste her, mate with her.

Right now.

He yanked his T-shirt over his head and then began fumbling with the fastening of his jeans, and became irritated when the zipper wouldn't slide down fast enough because of the size of his erection. Finally, he was able to tug his jeans down his legs and quickly stepped out of them. He reached down and took a condom packet out of the back pocket of the now discarded garment.

After he took the necessary steps, he looked at her and one corner of his mouth quirked up. "Now to keep that promise."

Simply looking at Storm caused Jayla's blood to pump rapidly through her veins. The look in his eyes said that he would hold nothing back. Her pulse quickened as he slid his body onto the bed. He moved, with the grace of a leopard, the prowl of a tiger and the intent of a man who wanted a woman. Overhead, the glow from the ceiling light magnified the broad expanse of his chest. He was perfectly built, his flesh a chocolate brown and every muscle well defined.

When he joined her on the bed she couldn't stop herself from reaching out to touch him. Her fingers trembled as she ran them through the dark, tight curls on his chest, and she smiled when she heard his breathing hitch. Hers did likewise when she felt the hardness of him press against her thigh. Her gaze was drawn to his nipples. They were hard, erect, and she wanted to know the texture of them under her tongue. He had tasted her breasts many times, but she'd never tasted his.

Leaning forward, her mouth opened over a stiff bud and her tongue began sliding around it, tasting it, absorbing it, sucking it. But for her, that wasn't enough. Reaching down she took hold of his hard heated flesh and her thumb and forefingers began caressing the hot tip. This was the first time she had ever tried to bring a man pleasure, to drive him insanely wild with desire with her hands. And from the sounds Storm was making, it seemed she was doing a good job.

When she heard him groan her name, the sound forced from deep within his throat, she lifted her head, but continued to let her hand clutch him, caress him, stroke him. "Umm?" she responded as she moved her mouth upward to take a tiny bite of his neck, branding him.

"You've pushed me too far, Jayla," Storm growled, as the need within him exploded. With one quick flick of his wrist, he tumbled her backward, ignoring her squeal of surprise. But she didn't resist and instead of moving from him, she moved to him, reaching up and looping her arms around his neck as he placed his body over hers, pressing his erection against the heat of her feminine core.

"Gotta get inside," he whispered brokenly as his hand clutched her waist, his thighs held hers in place. Taking her arms from around his neck, he captured her wrists and placed them above her head. He looked down at her, met her gaze at the same time he pushed himself inside of her.

He gasped. The pleasure of being inside of her was almost too much. He tipped his head back and roared an animalistic sound that mirrored the raging need within him. Then he began moving, in and out, straining his muscles, flexing his pelvis, rolling his hips while holding her in a firm grip, rocking her world, just mere seconds away from tumbling his own.

The bed started to shake and the windows seemed to rattle, but the only storm that was raging out of control was him, pelting down torrents of pleasure instead of sheets of rain. He didn't flinch when he felt her fingernails dig deeper into her flesh, but he did groan when he felt her inner muscles squeeze him, clench him, milk him. The woman was becoming a pro at knowing just what it took to splinter his mind and make him explode. No sooner had he thought the word, he felt her body do just that.

"Storm!"

And while she toppled over into oblivion, he continued to move in and out, claiming her as his.

His.

The thought of her belonging to him, and only to him, pushed him over the edge in a way he had never been pushed before. He thrust deep into her body, burying himself to the hilt, as his own release claimed him, ripped into him—not once, not twice, not even three times. The ongoing sensations that were taking over his body were more than he could stand.

"Jayla!"

And she was right there with him, lifting her hips off the bed, opening wider for him, moving with him, as they drove each other higher and higher on waves of excruciating pleasure.

The first light of dawn began slipping into the windows, fanning across the two naked bodies in bed. Jayla slowly awoke and took a long, deep breath of Storm and the lingering scent of their lovemaking.

It was there, in the air, the scent of her, of them—raw, primitive—the aftermath of her crying out in ecstasy, clutching his shoulders, pushing up her hips while he drove relentlessly into her, going as far as he could go, then tumbling them both over the edge as their releases came simultaneously.

She closed her eyes as panic seized her. What on earth had she done? All she had to do was open her eyes and glance over at Storm who was lying on his side facing her, still sleeping with a contented look on his face, to know what she had done. What she needed to really ask herself was how had it happened and why.

Storm had a reputation of not being a man who looked up a woman for a second helping. Once an affair ended, it was over. If that was the case, then why had he dropped by? What was there about her that had made him come back for more?

Jayla's features slipped into a frown. Although most

women would have been ecstatic that Storm had deemed them special enough to grace their bed a second time, to her he was a distraction. And a distraction was the last thing she needed now, especially with her upcoming appointment at the fertility clinic. If he were to find out about her plans, like Lisa he would probably try and talk her out of it. But unlike Lisa, he wouldn't understand her decision, or support her anyway, even if he disagreed with her.

She took a quick glance at him and wondered why it mattered to her that he might not support what she planned to do? Jayla was pretty sure Storm would frown upon the idea of her having a baby by artificial insemination. Like her father, Storm was a traditionalist. He believed in doing things the old-fashioned way. She had to admit that at least in the bedroom she found Storm's old-fashioned, always-remain-a-gentleman ways endearing. Being a gentleman didn't mean he wouldn't engage in some off-the-charts, blow-your-mind hot sex like they had definitely shared last night. It simply meant that he would never try anything that made her feel uncomfortable. Nor would he ever assume anything. The only reason he was still in her bed at the crack of dawn was because he had asked if it was okay for him to stay the night. He hadn't just assumed that it was. If only she could shake his belief that a woman could not manage both a career and motherhood. How primitive was it for someone to think that way in this day and time?

She shook her head as she quietly slipped out of bed thinking Storm had definitely earned his rest. The man had energy that she wished she could bottle. No sooner had they completed one climax, he was going down for another, and somehow he always managed to take her with him. It was as if his orgasms—and the man had plenty—always triggered hers. Multiple orgasms were something she'd read about and at the time, the thought of it happening to anyone seemed too far-fetched to consider. But she was living witness that it was possible. She smiled thinking Storm had spoiled her. She wouldn't know how to act if another man ever made love to her.

Her smile slowly died at the thought of making love to another man. Would she spend the rest of her life comparing every future lover to The Perfect Storm? She shook her head as she made her way into the bathroom for a shower. She was getting in deeper by the minute.

Storm woke slowly to the sound of running water and the scent of jasmine. He smiled, closing his eyes again as visions of what he and Jayla had done played through his mind like a finely tuned piano.

He reopened his eyes, thinking he was just as confused now as he'd been the night before. He wasn't sure why he was here in Jayla's bed instead of his own bed. Then he remembered. He'd had to be with her last night. He had been willing to say or do anything to get back into her bed. Even if it had meant begging.

He glanced at the clock on her nightstand. It was early, but time for him to go. He had to report to the station today to pull a twenty-four hour shift. He thoroughly enjoyed his new position of fire captain. To move from the ranks of lieutenant had meant many nights and weekends of studying for the fire department's promotional exam. During that time, he had given up a lot of things, including women. And even then, the thought of going without one hadn't bothered him. There hadn't been one single woman that he could name that he had missed making love to during all that time.

He closed his eyes again, not ready to move, not sure that he could if he wanted to. But the thought of Jayla, naked, wet and standing beneath a shower of water suddenly made him go hard, as if his body could do anything else around her.

He sighed deeply and suddenly the features of that old woman, the one who had read his palm in New Orleans, flitted across his mind at the same time the words she had spoken rang through his ears: *You are about to make unexpected changes in your life and although you yearn for peace, turbulence is in your future. Keep your sights high, be patient and let destiny take its course.*

He opened his eyes, quickly sat up and glanced around the room. It was as if the old woman's voice were right there. He shook his head, thinking he was definitely losing it.

He turned when he heard the sound of a door opening and glanced over his shoulder to see Jayla walk out of the bathroom with a towel wrapped tightly around her. She gave him a soft smile that immediately made him go hard...as if he wasn't already. And no matter how much he thought he was crazy this morning, he didn't have one single regret about last night.

"You should have woken me up and I would have joined you in the shower," he said standing, and crossing the room to her.

He watched as her gaze took in his nakedness, as it left his face to slowly roam down his chest, down past his stomach to settle...yeah, right there. He felt his erection get larger, become harder and saw her eyes grow dark with desire and her cheeks become flushed.

"You like being in your natural state, don't you?" she asked, lifting her gaze back to his.

He smiled. "Yes, and I like you being in your natural state, too."

She shook her head and chuckled. "I think we need to talk."

"I'd rather do something else." His smile widened. All she had to do was to drop her gaze back to his midsection to know what he had in mind.

She cleared her throat. "Well, unfortunately we both have jobs to go to this morning, right?"

"You would have to remind me of that, wouldn't you?" he asked, pulling her into his arms. "Have dinner with me at Anthony's tomorrow night."

She quickly pulled back. "Dinner?"

He dipped his head and captured an earlobe in his mouth. He'd heard the surprise in her voice. Hell, he was even surprised that he had suggested such a thing. "Yes, dinner. We can talk then, okay?" He knew what she wanted to talk about. She wanted to know why he was not adhering to their agreement. He hoped when he saw her again he would have some answers.

"Storm…I don't think that we—"

He lifted her chin with the tip of his finger so their eyes could meet. "Like you said, we need to talk, Jayla, and we can't do it here or at my place."

She nodded, understanding. At least at Anthony's, there wouldn't be any bedrooms around. "Okay."

Then Storm captured Jayla's mouth in a kiss that he definitely needed. The taste of her was like a drug to which he was addicted. She was a problem that needed a solution, but for now…

* * *

Wednesdays had always been referred to as over-the-hump day and it wasn't until today that Jayla actually understood what it meant…at least in terms of her and Storm.

It was almost lunchtime and Jayla was still besieged with constant memories of the night she'd spent with Storm. She glanced around to make sure no one noticed the blush that had to have appeared on her face, even with her dark skin tone.

She was in a room with, of all people, the vice president of the company, as well as the sales and advertising managers for Sala Industries. It was that time of the year when she needed to prepare the annual public relations report that the company distributed to the general public, interest groups and stockholders to make everyone aware of the company's activities and accomplishments the previous year. One of Sala's main goals for the year had been to increase their involvement in community affairs. Being a part of the charity benefit for Kids' World was one of the many projects they had undertaken to do just that.

Jayla had worked for the company since college and up until recently, the job had been the single most important thing in her life outside of her relationship with her father. After his death, she had moved her job up to the number one spot, which was why she had made a decision to have a baby. She had needed a life outside of work and someone to share that life with her. She smiled, thinking that she had only eight days to go before she went to the fertility clinic for her physical, the first step toward making her dream come true.

She glanced across the conference table and saw Lisa looking at her strangely. She lifted a brow and Lisa surreptitiously lifted one back. Jayla couldn't help but smile. Evidently, Lisa had seen her blush a few times.

As soon as the meeting was over, Lisa pulled her back the moment she was about to walk out the room and whispered, "We need to talk."

Playing dumb she smiled and asked, "What about?"

"Like the fact you sat through most of the meeting like you were zoned out. It's a good thing Mr. McCray didn't notice."

Jayla sobered quickly as she came to her senses. Having erotic flashbacks on her time was one thing, but having them on her employer's time was another. "Sorry."

Lisa laughed. "Hey, girlfriend, don't apologize. I'd trade places with you in a heartbeat. You've been with Storm Westmoreland again haven't you?"

Wondering how Lisa could know such a thing, Jayla asked innocently, "What makes you think that?"

Lisa raised a dark brow. "It's either that or you're reliving some dynamite memories. My guess is that you're reminiscing about the past twenty-four hours."

Jayla sighed as she closed the door so that she and Lisa could have total privacy. She sat back down at the table and Lisa joined her. She met her best friend's curious gaze. "Storm dropped by last night."

Lisa leaned back in her chair and grinned. "That's a first. I heard that once an affair was ended, Storm Westmoreland never looked back. Booty calls are not exactly his style."

Jayla shot her a frown and Lisa held up her hand apologetically. "Sorry. I was just making an observation."

Jayla let out a breath. That was one observation she didn't need. "He wants to take me out tomorrow night. To dinner. At Anthony's."

Lisa smiled. "Real classy place, so what's the problem?"

Jayla returned the smile. Lisa could be so good for her at times. "The problem is what you indicated earlier. Storm is not a man who looks up women from his past. I knew that in New Orleans and he knew that, and it was understood that when we returned to Atlanta we would have no reason to seek the other out."

Lisa nodded. "And he's seeking you out."

"Yes, and I can't let it happen."

Lisa sat up and leaned in closer. "Is it okay for me to ask why?"

Jayla dragged a hand through her hair, and drew in a frustrating breath. "Because it's lousy timing. My life is about to undergo some major changes, Lisa, for Pete's sake. My physical is set for next Friday and soon after that, I plan to get inseminated. The last thing I need is Storm deciding, for whatever reason, that I'm a novelty to him."

"Hey, Jayla, don't sell yourself short. There might be another reason that Storm Westmoreland finds you interesting, other than you being a novelty. The guy might actually like you. I mean really, really *like* you. There's a chance that you've blown him away."

Lisa's comments gave Jayla pause. She thought about that possibility all of two seconds and shook her head. "Impossible. Even if there was a remote chance that was true, Storm and I could never get serious about each other."

Lisa lifted a brow. "Why?"

Jayla frowned. "He's too much like my father. He would want to keep a tight rein on me. He actually believes a woman should be a stay-at-home mom. I guess he thinks the ideal woman is one he can keep barefoot and pregnant."

Lisa smiled. "Hey, I could do barefoot and pregnant with a man like him," she said, wiggling her eyebrows.

"Well, I can't. I have my life mapped out just the way I want, thank you. I'm having a baby without the complications of a man. The last thing I need is someone dictating how I should live my life and there's no doubt in my mind that Storm would be very domineering."

Lisa's smile widened. "Yeah, but also very sexy."

Jayla raised her gaze to the ceiling. "But I can't think of sexy when all I can see is domineering."

Lisa laughed. "Evidently you could last night if those blushes were any indication. But if you feel that way, you should let him know. It should be simple enough to tell him you aren't interested and to stop coming around."

Jayla nodded. Yes, that should be simple enough and she would tell him tomorrow night at dinner.

Storm walked into Coleman's Florist Shop and glanced at the older woman who was standing behind the counter. Luanne Coleman was considered one of the town's biggest gossips, but he still enjoyed doing business with her. And besides, none of the women he ever ordered flowers for lived in College Park, the suburb of Atlanta where he and the majority of his family resided and where his brother Dare was sheriff.

"Good morning, Ms. Luanne."

She glanced up from looking at the small television screen that was sitting on the counter. Her soaps were on. "Oh, hello, Storm. You want to send the usual?"

He smiled. By the usual, she meant a bouquet of fresh-cut flowers. "No, I want to send something different this time."

He knew that would grab her attention. She stared at him

for a long moment, then raised her brow over curious eyes and asked, "Something different?"

"Yes."

She nodded. "All right, what do you have in mind?"

He glanced around. "What do you have that will last a while?"

"I have plenty of live plants and they make beautiful gifts."

Storm nodded. He didn't recall seeing a live plant in Jayla's home and thought one would be perfect, especially in her bedroom for her to look at and remember. "Good. I want you to pick out the biggest and prettiest one, and this is the person I want it delivered to," he said, handing her a slip of paper.

She took it and glanced at the name. She then looked at him and smiled. "How much do you want to spend?"

A huge grin touched his lips. "The cost isn't important. Just add it to my account. And make sure it's delivered this afternoon."

She nodded and smiled as she quickly began writing up his order. "She must be very special."

Storm sighed heavily. There. He had heard someone else say what he'd been thinking all day, so the only thing he could do was smile and agree. "Yes, she is."

Jayla blinked at the man holding the huge potted plant in front of him. The plant was almost larger than he was. "Are you sure you're at the right address, sir?"

"Yes, I'm positive," the older man said, peeping from behind the bunch of healthy green leaves of a beautiful and lush looking areca palm. "It's for you."

Jayla nodded as she stepped aside to let the man bring

the plant inside, wondering who on earth could have sent it. When the man had placed it down, he turned to leave. "Wait, I need to give you a—"

"The tip's been taken care of," the man said. And then he was gone.

Jayla quickly pulled the card from the plant and read it.

> *Whenever you look at this, think of me.*
> *Storm*

Jayla's heart skipped a beat. No it skipped two, possibly three. She blinked, then sank down on her sofa. Storm had sent her a plant, a beautiful, large, lush green plant and for the first time in a long time, she was at a loss for words.

Nine

"Thanks again for the plant, Storm. It's simply beautiful."

"You're welcome and I'm glad you like it."

"And thanks for bringing me here, tonight. Everything was wonderful."

"You're welcome again."

Then she glanced around Anthony's, the stunning and elegant antebellum mansion that had a reputation of fine service and delicious food. Being here reminded her of New Orleans, and she wondered if perhaps that was the reason Storm had chosen this place.

She glanced back over at Storm and their gazes met. He'd been watching her, something she noticed he'd been doing all evening. He had arrived at her house promptly at seven and since she'd been ready, she had only invited him inside long enough for her to grab her purse and a wrap.

At least, that's what she had assumed.

The moment he had stepped inside her home, he had pulled her into his arms and kissed her, making her realize that although she wished otherwise, there was definitely something going on between them, something that had not ended in New Orleans.

She regarded him with interest and although she knew that she should broach the subject of why they were here, she wasn't ready to do that yet. Tonight was too beautiful to bring up any unpleasantries just yet. "So, how are things going at work?" she asked, after taking another sip of her wine.

In New Orleans, he had told her that he had made the transition from lieutenant to captain rather well, but hadn't gone into much detail. Because her father had been a fire captain for years, she was familiar with all the position entailed. She was well aware that today firefighters needed more training to operate increasingly sophisticated equipment and to deal safely with the greater hazards that were associated with fighting fires in larger, more elaborate structures, as well as wild fires.

In her eyes, all firefighters were heroes, but she knew being a fire captain also required strong leadership qualities. A captain had to possess the ability to establish and maintain discipline and efficiency, as well as direct the activities of the firefighters in his company.

"Work is fine, and how are things at Sala Industries?" he asked rousing her from her musings.

She smiled. "Things are great. In addition to working with Tara on the Kids' World charity benefit, I'm working on another project that involves an environmental agency."

He nodded. "And what about that project you were excited about? How is it going?"

She swallowed, knowing exactly what project he was

referring to. She worked her bottom lip between her teeth several times before responding. "I haven't started it yet."

She decided it was time to discuss the reason they were there. They had dodged the subject long enough. She met his eyes and a shiver ran through her when she saw the desire in their dark depths. Wanting to make love with him seemed natural. Too natural. It was a good thing they were in a public place.

Her body continued to stir and an unbearable heat spread through her. Trying to ignore her torment, she considered him for a long moment, then spoke, her voice barely above a whisper. "You said you would explain things tonight, Storm."

I did say that didn't I? Storm thought as his gaze continued to hold Jayla's. The only problem was that he wasn't any closer to answers today than he had been yesterday. The only thing that he was certain of was that he wanted to continue to see Jayla. He enjoyed being with her, taking her out and having fun with her and wanted to continue to do all those things they had done together in New Orleans. For some reason, she had his number and he was helpless to do anything about it.

"Storm?"

He blinked and realized while he'd been thinking that he had been staring at her like some dimwit. He cleared his throat. "Jayla, is there a possibility for us to start seeing each other?"

It was evident from the look on her face that his question surprised her. "Why?" she asked, regarding him as if the question were totally illogical.

"I like you."

She blinked, then threw him a grin that caught him off guard. "Storm, you like women. I know that much from your reputation."

He didn't like hearing her say that. They weren't talking about other women; they were talking about her. He didn't place her in the same category with those other women he'd dated before. To him, none of them could be compared to Jayla.

He watched as she leaned over the table and, with a curious arch of her brow, whispered, "It's the virginity thing, isn't it?"

Storm nearly stopped breathing. He blinked, not understanding just what she was asking him. Seconds later, it dawned on him just what she'd insinuated and he frowned. "Why would you think something like that?"

She straightened back in her chair and shrugged. "What else could it be? I was your first virgin. You said so yourself. So I'm a novelty to you." She picked up her wine glass to take another sip, smiled, then said, "Trust me, you'll get over it."

His frown deepened. "Tell me something," he said, leaning back in his chair. "When did you figure that out?"

Her smile widened. "What? That I'm a novelty to you or that you'll get over it?"

"That you're a novelty to me."

She licked her lips and Storm felt his gut catch. "The night you showed up at my place. Seeking me out was so unlike how you're known to operate, so I figured there had to be a reason, since any woman can basically please a man in bed. It slowly dawned on me why I was different."

Storm inhaled deeply. He was glad they were sitting at a table in the rear of the restaurant in an area where they were practically alone. He would hate for anyone to over-hear their conversation.

He shook his head slowly. Everything she'd said had sounded logical. With one exception. It was so far from the truth that it was pitiful.

He smiled. "First of all, contrary to what you think, Jayla, any woman cannot please a man in bed. When making love to a woman, most men…and women for that matter, experience various degrees of pleasure. On a scale from one to five, with five being the highest, most men will experience at least a three. In some situations, possibly a four, and only if they're extremely lucky, a five."

She lifted a brow. "How did I rate?"

Storm's smile widened. He'd known the curiosity in Jayla would give her the nerve to ask. In fact, he'd hoped that she would. "You rated a ten."

She blinked, then a smile touched the corners of her lips. "A ten?"

He chuckled. "Oh, yes, a ten."

He watched as she thought about it for a second, then she shook her head, perplexed and confused. "But—but how is that possible if a ten isn't on the chart?"

He reached across the table and captured her hand in his. "Because you, Jayla Cole, were off the charts." He watched her smile widen, evidently pleased with herself. Then he added, "And it had nothing to do with you being a virgin, but had everything to do with the fact that you are a very passionate woman."

He tilted his head and said, "It also had a lot to do with the fact that the two of us are good together. We click. When we make love, I feel a connection with you that I've never felt with another woman." What he didn't add was that when he made love to her, he felt as if they were made for each other.

"Wow, that's deep, Storm," she said regarding him seriously.

He sighed as he nodded. "Yeah, it is deep and that's why I'd like for us to continue to see each other."

Jayla inhaled. She would like to continue to see him, too, but she knew that wouldn't be a wise thing to do. In less than a month, she would be getting inseminated and hopefully soon after that, she would become pregnant. The last thing she needed was to get involved with anyone, especially Storm, no matter how tempting the thought was.

"Jayla?"

She met his gaze. "I don't think that would be a good idea, Storm. This new project will take up a lot of my time, and I won't have time for a relationship."

He considered her words. He was still curious as to what kind of project she would be working on. He had asked her about it in New Orleans and she had danced around an answer. The only thing he could come up with was that it involved her job, perhaps a confidential, top-secret assignment. "And there's no way we can work around this project?"

"No."

Her response had been quick. Definite. "When will you start?"

She shrugged. She would have her physical next Friday and then hopefully within three weeks after that, she would go in to have the procedure done. "Possibly within a month."

He met her gaze levelly. "Is there any reason we can't continue to see each other until then?" Slowly, he raised her hand to his lips and kissed it.

Jayla swallowed and knew what she should say. She should tell him yes, there were plenty of reasons why they couldn't continue to see each other for the next month, but for some reason she couldn't get the words out. What Storm had said earlier was true. They were good together. They clicked and they connected. And deep down, a part of her felt she needed this time with him. Afterwards, at least she would have her memories of their time together.

"No, there's no reason," she finally said. "But you will have to promise me something, Storm."

He kissed her hand again before asking. "What?"

"When I say it's over, then it's over. You won't drop by and you won't call."

He shook his head. "I can't agree to that, Jayla. I promised your father that I would periodically check on you and—"

"I'm not talking about that, Storm. I'm taking about you dropping by or calling with the intention of us becoming involved again. You have to promise me when I say it's over, that it will be over. No questions asked."

Storm stared at her for a long moment as emotions tumbled inside of him. They were feelings he didn't understand, but he knew that no matter what, things would never be over between them, project or no project. He would see to it.

"All right," he agreed. "You'll be calling the shots and I'll abide by your wishes."

"Hey, Storm, are you in this game or not?"

Storm glanced over at Thorn and frowned. "Yes, I'm in."

"Well, keep your mind on the game. You're daydreaming again."

Storm's frown deepened. "Yeah, whatever." He glanced across the table at his four brothers who had smirks on their faces. "What's so funny?"

It was the oldest brother, Dare, who answered. "Word's out on the streets that some woman has finally caught the eye of the Storm. I pulled old man Johnson over the other day for running a Stop sign, and he said that he'd heard you were so besotted with some gal that you can't pee straight."

When Storm narrowed his eyes, Dare held up his hand. "Hey, those were Mr. Johnson's words, not mine."

Chase chuckled. "And I've heard that you're sending so many flowers to this woman that the money Coleman Florist is making off you is the reason Mrs. Luanne has that new swing on her front porch."

"And I heard," Stone piped in, as a huge smile touched his lips, "that you've been seen all over Atlanta with her and that she's a beauty. Funny that we haven't met her yet."

Thorn added, "Hey, Storm, what happened to your 'love them and leave them' policy?"

Storm leaned back in his chair thinking that Thorn's question was a good one, but one he didn't intend to answer.

"I've seen her," Chase said grinning. "She came into the restaurant one day to have lunch with Tara."

"Tara?" Thorn asked, raising a curious brow. "Tara knows her?"

Chase nodded. "Evidently, since they had lunch together that day. However, I don't know if Tara knows that Storm has the hots for her."

"Excuse me, guys," Storm said interrupting his brothers' conversation. "I don't appreciate you discussing my business like I'm not here."

Stone chuckled. "All right, then we'll discuss your business like you're here." He then looked at Chase. "So, is she as good-looking as everyone claims she is?"

Chase grinned. "Yeah. She's Adam's daughter all grown up."

Thorn frowned. "Adam? Adam Cole, Storm's boss who died a few months back?"

"Yep."

Stone glanced over at Storm. A curious glint shone in his eyes. "You're actually seeing Adam Cole's girl?"

Angrily, Storm stood and threw down his cards. "That's it. I'm out of the game."

Dare stared up at his youngest brother. Being the oldest, he had to occasionally bring about peace…and in some situations, order. "Sit back down, Storm, you're getting overheated for nothing. And to be quite honest with you, for all intents and purposes, you've been out of the game since you got here. You haven't been concentrating worth a damn all night."

One of Dare's dark eyebrows lifted. "And what's wrong with us wanting to know about this woman that you're seeing? As your brothers, don't you think we have a right to at least be curious?"

Storm inhaled deeply as he glanced around the table and glared. "I don't appreciate any of you discussing her as if she's like the other women I've dated."

Dare nodded. "If she's not like the other women you've dated, then it's up to you to tell us that. There's nothing wrong with letting us know that you think she's special, instead of trying to keep her a secret," he said in a low voice.

Storm sat back down and glanced around at his brothers. They were staring at him, waiting expectantly. He sighed deeply. "Her name is Jayla Cole and yes, she's Adam's daughter all grown up and we're seeing each other. We're taking things slow, one day at a time, and yes, she's special. Very special."

Stone smiled. "When will we meet her?"

Storm leaned back in his chair. "I'll introduce her to everyone the night of the charity benefit for Kids' World. Her company is a corporate sponsor and she's working closely with Tara to pull things together for that night."

Dare nodded. "And all of us will look forward to meeting her then." He glanced around the table and grinned. "Now let's play cards."

Jayla sat curled up on her sofa and glanced around her living room, thinking the past week had been like a scene from a romance novel. Storm had sent her flowers practically every single day and had wined and dined her to her heart's content.

On Saturday night, they had gone to a laser show on Stone Mountain and then on Sunday evening, he had taken her to a movie. Because he had been at the station all day Monday, she didn't see him again until Tuesday night, when he'd dropped by with Chinese food. They had sat eating at her kitchen table while she had told him about how her day had gone and how things were coming together for this weekend's charity benefit.

They had talked about his day, as well. He had told her that he had been selected to head up the city's fire prevention program for the coming year and that he was excited about that.

She glanced down at the letter she had in her hand, the same letter that had arrived last week from the fertility

clinic reminding her of tomorrow's appointment. Seeing
it and rereading it had reaffirmed her decision to have the
procedure.

She nearly jumped when she heard the phone ring.
Thinking that perhaps it was Storm, she placed the letter
on the table, then quickly moved across the room to answer
it. He had called earlier and said he would be playing cards
tonight with his brothers rather late and that he would see
her tomorrow. "Yes?" she said, after picking up the phone.

"It's Lisa. How are things going?"

Jayla smiled. Lisa had been out of town most of the week
on business. "Everything's going fine. How was your trip?"

"Wonderful. I love Chicago. You know that."

Jayla chuckled. Yes, she did know that. Lisa enjoyed
shopping and Chicago was her favorite place to shop.

"So, are you planning to keep your appointment
tomorrow?"

Lisa's question immediately silenced Jayla's thoughts.
She frowned. "Of course, why wouldn't I?"

"Because from what you told me every time I've called
this week, you and Storm have been seeing a lot of each
other."

Jayla shrugged. "So? What Storm and I are sharing is
short-term. I know that and so does he."

"But it doesn't have to be that way, Jayla. I believe
things could last if you gave them a chance."

Jayla rolled her eyes to the ceiling. "Lisa, trust me, they
won't. What Storm and I share is physical. I'm enjoying
his company and he's enjoying mine. Why does it have to
be more than that?"

For a long moment, there was silence. Then Lisa asked
softly, "What are you afraid of, Jayla?"

Jayla flinched. "I'm not afraid of anything."

"I think that you are. Storm Westmoreland is every-thing a woman could want in a man and you are in a good position to be that woman. Why are you willing to turn your back on such a wonderful opportunity?"

Jayla closed her eyes. She could never be the kind of woman Storm wanted. Besides, he wasn't what she wanted, either. At the moment, no man was. She wanted a baby and not a complicated relationship. She'd long ago given up on finding Mr. Right. The "married with children" routine was a fairy tale that might never come true for her. Her biological clock was ticking and she had made the de-cision to start a family sooner rather than later.

She turned when she heard a knock at the door. "Look Lisa, there's someone at the door. I'll talk with you later. Bye."

After hanging up the phone, she glanced at the clock on the wall, then crossed the living room to the door. It was late, after midnight. The only reason she was still up was because she had taken the morning off for her physical at the fertility clinic. Since her appointment wasn't until nine, that meant she would get to sleep late.

She knew before she got within a foot of the door that her late-night visitor was Storm. That would explain the reason her heart was beating so fast and her senses were getting heated. She tried forcing her conversation with Lisa out of her mind. Her best friend was wrong and she wasn't afraid of anything, especially a serious relationship with Storm. She merely chose not to have one.

"Who is it?"

"Storm."

She quickly opened the door and he stood there, staring at her. His eyes were dark, intense, and she immediately recognized the look in them. Her lips curved into a smile. "Hi."

He returned her smile and the heat infiltrating her senses kicked up another notch. "Hi, yourself. The card game ended and I wasn't ready to go home."

"Oh?"

"I had to see you, Jayla."

A teasing glint shone in Jayla's eyes. "Okay, you see me. So now what?"

He slowly took a couple of steps forward, and she took a couple of steps back. When he was completely inside the house, he closed the door behind him and locked it. He walked the few feet over to her, cupped her shoulders in his hands and pulled her to him, her mouth just inches from his. "Now this," he breathed against her lips.

Then kissed her.

As soon as their mouths touched, Storm felt something hot rush through his bloodstream. The scent of Jayla, as well as the taste of her, was getting to him and the only thing he could think of doing was devouring her, making love to her. Suddenly, some emotion that he'd never felt before flared within him, almost bringing him to his knees, and he finally acknowledged it for what it was.

Love. He loved her.

Storm drew back and stared at her for a quick second before his mouth came back down on hers again. His hands were everywhere as he began removing her clothes, and broke off the kiss just long enough to remove his own. Then he swept her into his arms and carried her into the bedroom.

What should have been a no-brainer had been hard as hell for a staunch bachelor like him to figure out. The reason he had wanted a relationship with Jayla had nothing to do with them being great together in bed, but everything to do with emotions he hadn't been able to recognize until tonight.

He was in love with Jayla Cole. She had caught more than the eye of the Storm. She had captured his heart.

Ten

Anchoring himself above Jayla on his elbows, Storm looked down at her and smiled. Dang, she always looked beautiful after experiencing an orgasm. What more could a man ask for than to be right there to experience each one with her.

He sighed deeply. Now that he knew he loved her, he had to figure out a way to get her to fall in love with him as well. First, he would have to gain her complete trust, and then he had to make sure she clearly understood that he was her Mr. Right and wanted a long-term relationship with her, one that ended in marriage. A smile curved his lips. Yeah, that's what he wanted, Jayla as his wife.

"Why are you smiling?"

He met her gaze. Her eyelids were heavy and her cheeks had a sated flush. Leaning down, he brushed a kiss across her lips. "After what we've just shared, how can you ask me that?"

As usual, everything had been perfect. The way their bodies had come together while a trail of fire had blazed between them. It was a fire he hadn't wanted to put out, but instead had done everything within his power to ignite even further, to make it burn out of control.

And it had.

By the time he had entered, she had been delirious with desire, begging breathlessly for him to make love to her; she'd been a she-cat, clawing his back and nipping his shoulders. And when they had finally come together, she had cried out his name and he had continued to move inside of her, taking them to heights of profound pleasure.

He loved her, he thought in wonder, as he leaned down and murmured her name against her cheek. "Mind if I stay the night?"

He felt her smile against his lips. "Umm, I would be highly disappointed if you didn't," she said softly.

He chuckled. "In that case, I'll stay." He pressed his mouth to hers and kissed her, needing the taste of her again. Moments later, he slowly pulled back and flicked his gaze over her features. Heat immediately surged through his groin. If he didn't get out bed, he would be making love to her all over again, and she needed her rest.

"I'll turn off the lights," he whispered.

"All right, but hurry back."

He grinned as he eased out of bed and slipped into his jeans. And just think he'd assumed that she needed her rest. He glanced at the huge plant that sat in the corner. It was just where he'd wanted it, in her bedroom so she could think of him whenever she saw it.

As he walked out of the bedroom, the image of Jayla's sexy smile when she'd told him to hurry back filled his mind and made him want to do just as she'd requested. When he got to the living room, he leaned down to turn off the lamp near the sofa and his gaze caught sight of a letter lying on the coffee table. It was a letter from a fertility clinic.

Without thinking that he didn't have any right to do so, he picked up the letter and read it. A few seconds later, he sank down on her sofa, not believing what he had just read. He felt stunned. Confused. Jayla had sought out the services of a fertility clinic to get artificially inseminated with some stranger's sperm? Why?

He reread the letter, thinking there must be a mistake but again the contents were the same. She was scheduled to have a physical tomorrow—which actually was today—and then, when it was determined her body would be most fertile, she would go in to have the procedure done.

"You were supposed to hurry back."

Storm stood when Jayla walked out of the bedroom. When she saw the letter in his hand, she quickly crossed the room and snatched it from him. "You had no right to read that, Storm."

He just stared at her as every muscle in his body vibrated. Confusion gave way to anger. "Then how about you telling me what this is all about."

She glared at him. "It's private and personal and doesn't concern you."

"Doesn't concern me? Like hell, it doesn't. If it concerns you, then it concerns me. Are you actually considering having your body inseminated with some man's sperm?"

Jayla tipped her head back; her anger clashed with his. He'd made it sound as if what she planned to do was something filthy and degrading. "It's not what I'm considering doing, it's what I will be doing. I made the decision months ago."

Taken back by Jayla's statement, he wiped a hand down his face as if doing so would erase his anger. When he looked over at her, she was standing with her hands on her hips, glaring at him. A thought suddenly popped into his head. "Wait a minute. Is this the project you've been so excited about lately?"

"Yes."

He shook his head, not believing the conversation they were having. "I understand the need for that procedure in certain situations, but not with you. Why would you even consider doing such a thing, Jayla?"

Her eyes were consumed with fire. "Because I want a baby that's why! I want a baby more than anything."

Storm was shocked by that revelation. She had once mentioned she wanted to have kids, but she had never given him the idea that she'd been obsessed with having one. "And you want a child to the point where you would actually consider having a baby from someone you don't know?"

"Yes. In fact, I prefer it that way. I want a baby and not the baby's father. I don't want a man coming in my life trying to run things."

"Run things how?"

"Like telling me how to live my life, forcing the issue of whether I can have a career outside of my home, a man who'd try to control me and keep a tight rein on me."

Of all those things she'd named, Storm recognized only one that he might eventually become guilty of.

"And what's wrong with a man wanting the sole responsibility of taking care of his wife so she won't have to work outside the home?"

Her glare thickened. "For some women, nothing, but I prefer taking care of myself. I don't want to depend on anyone."

Storm frowned and crossed his arms over his chest. "So, for your own selfish reasons, you're willing to deny your child a father?"

"If it means not wasting my time looking for a Mr. Right who doesn't exist, then yes."

Storm tried to keep his anger in check. Why couldn't she see that he was her Mr. Right? He slowly shook his head again. "If you want a baby, then I'll give you *my* baby."

"What!"

"You heard me. I'll be damned if I'll let another man get the woman I love pregnant."

Jayla was shocked at the words he'd spoken. "The woman you love?"

Silence shredded the air and Storm knew he had to get her to understand the depth of how he felt. He crossed the room and with his fingertip, lifted her chin to meet his gaze. "Yes. I love you, Jayla, and if you want a baby, then we'll get married and I'll give you one."

She stared at him as if she didn't believe he'd suggested such a thing. And then she took a step back from him. "Things wouldn't work between us, Storm. You would want more from a wife than I'm willing to give."

"And what about the fact that I love you?"

She shrugged. "I believe you like sleeping with me, but I find it hard to believe that you really love me, Storm."

She sighed deeply when he didn't say anything but continued to stare at her. "We agreed that we would end things between us whenever I was ready," she finally said to break the silence. "Well, I'm ready. For us to continue seeing each other will only complicate matters."

"Complicate matters like hell!" he said, his voice rising. "I tell you that I love you and that I want to marry you and give you the baby you want, and you're telling me that you don't believe a word of it and to get out of your life? And to top things off, you plan to continue with this crazy scheme to have a baby from a man who not only doesn't love you, but a man *you* don't even know?"

"I don't owe you an explanation for anything I do, Storm. And considering everything, it would be best if you left."

Storm stared at her for a moment, then moved past her to the bedroom. Moments later, fully dressed, he came back into the living room. He stood in front of her and said softly, "I hope that one day you'll take your blinders off. Maybe then you'll recognize your Mr. Right when he comes and stands right in front of you."

He then turned and walked out the door.

When Storm left, Jayla moved around the house trying to convince herself that she was glad they would no longer be seeing each other. The last thing she needed was a man trying to control her life.

After closing things up and turning off the lights, she slipped back into bed, and tried to ignore the scent of Storm that still lingered there. She closed her eyes.

I love you, Jayla...

She opened her eyes, flipped on her back and stared up at the ceiling as she tried to convince herself that she wasn't the one with blinders on, he was. Couldn't he see that what he was feeling wasn't really love but lust? Die-hard bachelors like Storm didn't fall in love in a blink of an eye or after a few rolls between the sheets.

She turned to her side and closed her eyes, trying to

force thoughts of Storm from her mind. But she couldn't. Steeling herself, she sighed, knowing the memories of the times they'd spent together were too deep, too ingrained in her memory.

Getting over him wouldn't be easy, but dammit she would try. She would shift her focus elsewhere and appreciate the good things that were happening to her. Everything she'd wanted was falling in place. Tomorrow, she would go to the fertility clinic for her physical and then she would wait eagerly for the day when she would be inseminated.

Storm was not the most important thing to her—having a baby was.

"Hey, Captain, you got a minute?"

Storm glanced up from the stack of papers on his desk. After having a sleepless night, he had gotten up at the crack of dawn to come into the station. Most of his men hadn't arrived yet. Although it wasn't a requirement, he was one of those captains who preferred working the same hours as the firefighters he supervised.

"Sure, Cobb, come on in. What can I do for you?"

Darryl Cobb had recently become a father again. Four months ago, his wife Haley had given birth to their third child. Darryl was a few years younger than Storm and they had known each other since their high school days. He'd also known Darryl's wife, Haley, from high school, as well, and remembered Darryl and Haley dating even back then. Evidently, Haley hadn't had a problem recognizing Darryl as her Mr. Right since the two of them had been married for over ten years now and always seemed happy together.

"I was wondering if I can take a few hours off today. The

baby has a doctor's appointment and Haley just called. Her boss called an important meeting for later today."

Storm nodded. Haley was a computer programmer for a financial management company. "That shouldn't be a problem," Storm said, turning to check the activity board. "You're supposed to teach a class on fire prevention at that elementary school today. Do you have a replacement?"

Darryl smiled. "Sure do. Reed has agreed to cover for me."

Storm nodded. The one thing he liked about the men he supervised was that they got along and were quick to help each other out when something unexpected came up. "In that case, your taking a few hours off won't be a problem," he said making a notation on the activity sheet.

He glanced back over at Cobb. "So how has it been going since Haley returned to work?"

Darryl chuckled. "Crazy."

"Then why did she go back?" he asked, then quickly felt he'd been out of line for asking such a question. But from the laugh Cobb gave him, evidently he hadn't been surprised by the question. From Storm's early days as a firefighter, it had been a joke around the station that his views on women working inside the home were unrealistic and so outdated they were pitiful. He'd been told that it would be hard as hell to find a woman who'd agree to do nothing but stay at home, barefoot and pregnant.

"Well, that humongous house we just bought in Stone Mountain was one good reason for her to return to work," Darryl said, still chuckling. "But another reason is that Haley enjoys what she does and I'm not going to ask her to give it up." He looked pointedly at Storm and said, "That's where a lot of men make their mistakes."

Storm raised a brow. "Where?"

Darryl smiled. "In assuming that they are the only ones who have it together. I personally think it's women who really have it together, and we're merely bystanders looking in. Besides, with Haley and me both sharing equally in the raising of our kids, I feel I'm playing just as an important role in their lives as she is, and that's important to me. It has nothing to do with which one of us is bringing home the bacon, but mainly how the both of us are serving the bacon. Together, we're forming a deep, nurturing attachment to our children and are giving them all the love we have, which is a lot. And to me that's the most important thing."

A few moments later after Cobb had left, Storm stood at the window in his office and looked out as he thought about what Darryl had said. Was one of the reasons Jayla hadn't recognized him as her Mr. Right was because in her mind he was all wrong?

Had what Nicole done to him all those years ago driven his beliefs that a husband should be sole provider for his wife and family? He would be the first to admit that because of Nicole's rejection, he'd always wanted to prove the point that a man, highly educated or not, could take care of his household. His father had done it and had raised a family on a construction worker's salary.

He thought of his brothers and their wives. Even married to a sheikh, his sister Delaney was still working as a pediatrician and doing one hell of a job raising their son Ari, who was beginning to be a handful. But then her husband Jamal also played an equally important role in raising their son. Then there were his sisters-in-laws, Shelly, Tara and Madison. Although Shelly and Dare were the only ones who had a son, eleven-year-old AJ, Storm was fairly certain that if Tara and Madison were to get pregnant, they wouldn't consider giving up their careers.

He closed his eyes and remembered the scene that had played out in Jayla's living room last night. The woman he loved was planning to let another man get her pregnant only because she was convinced there wasn't a Mr. Right for her. She actually believed there wasn't a man who could and would understand her need to be in control of her life.

He opened his eyes and glanced down at his watch. According to that letter he'd read last night, she had a physical at nine this morning at that fertility clinic. After the physical, it would probably be two to three weeks before the actual procedure could be performed. Hopefully that would give him time to convince Jayla that he really did love her, and that he would satisfy all her needs, including her need to remain independent…to a certain degree. Changing his conventional views wouldn't be something he could do overnight, but it was something he could definitely work on, especially for Jayla.

The most important thing was to show her that he was the right man for her. The only man for her. For the second time since returning from New Orleans, the old fortune teller's words crept into his thoughts.

You should keep your sights high, be patient and let destiny take its course.

He smiled. Perhaps the old woman hadn't been a flake after all and had known exactly what she'd been talking about. Tomorrow was the night of the charity benefit and because of her involvement, he knew Jayla would be there. He would start wooing her with the intensity of a man who had one single goal in his mind.

To win the love of the woman he intended to marry.

* * *

"You can go ahead and get dressed, Ms. Cole," the nurse said smiling. "The doctor will return in a few minutes to go over the results of your tests."

"Thanks."

Jayla sighed deeply as she began putting her clothes back on. She'd had a sleepless night and hadn't been as excited about the appointment this morning as much as she'd wanted to be because of thoughts of Storm. And it hadn't helped matters that she'd been crying most of the morning.

She walked over to the mirror in the room and looked at herself. She looked pathetic. Her reflection revealed a woman who was truly drowning in her own misery. And it was a misery well deserved. Even Lisa hadn't given her any slack when she'd called this morning and she'd told her about the argument she'd had with Storm. And when she'd mentioned that Storm had told her that he loved her and wanted to marry her, her best friend had actually gone off on her. But then, what was a best friend for if she couldn't give you hell when you needed it?

The sad thing about it was that everything both Storm and Lisa had said was true. She wouldn't recognize her Mr. Right if he came to stand right in front of her.

She sighed deeply as she slipped back into her panty hose. So what if Storm was one of those men who wanted to take care of his woman? Wasn't it better to have a man who wanted to take care of you than to have a man who expected you to take care of him? And was it so awful that he was a little on the conventional side? She would be the first to admit that she found some of his old-fashioned ways sweet. Besides, if his conventional way of thinking became too much for her, couldn't she just make it her business to modernize him? And so what if he had ways like her father? Adam Cole had been a great parent and a part of her could now say she appreciated her strict upbringing. A couple of the girls she had wanted to hang around with in high school had either gotten pregnant before graduating or had gotten mixed up with drugs.

Upon waking this morning, it had taken several hours of wallowing in self-pity, as well as being forced to listen to Lisa's tirade, before she'd finally taken the blinders off. Storm loved her and he was her Mr. Right and she loved him. She couldn't fight it, nor could she deny the truth any longer. She loved him and had always loved him.

Oh, she understood now why he had kept his distance so many years ago but still, it had been a bitter pill for a young girl to swallow. A part of her had built up an immunity against ever being rejected by him again. But now she was a woman and she wanted what any other woman would want—a man to love her. And that man had offered to marry her and give her the baby she wanted. How blessed could a woman be?

Her feeling of euphoria quickly disintegrated when she remembered she had thrown his words of love back in his face. She had a feeling that Storm was a man who wouldn't take rejection well. What if he never wanted to see her again?

She quickly slipped into her skirt, thinking she had to work fast to correct the mistake she'd made or she would lose him completely. And the first thing she had to do was to cancel her plans to get inseminated. The only man she wanted to father her child was Storm.

She turned when she heard a knock at the door. "Come in." She smiled apologetically when Dr. Susan Millstone walked in. Before the doctor could say anything she quickly said, "I've changed my mind."

After closing the door behind her, Dr. Millstone tilted her head and looked at her. "You've changed your mind?"

"Yes. I've decided not to go through with the artificial insemination procedure after all."

The doctor leaned against the closed door. "May I ask the reason you've changed your mind?"

Jayla smiled. "Yes. The man that I love wants to marry me and give me his child, and I want that, too, more than anything." *And I hope and pray I haven't lost him*, she thought.

Dr. Millstone chuckled as she shook her head. "What you've just said will make what I have to tell you a little easier."

Jayla raised a brow. "Oh?"

"I just went over the results of your physical and it seems you're already pregnant."

The news was so shocking that Jayla dropped into a nearby chair. She looked back up at the doctor, not believing what she'd been told. "I'm pregnant?"

The doctor chuckled again. "Yes. You're almost a month along."

Jayla shook her head, as if trying to keep it from spinning. She was almost a month pregnant! "New Orleans," she said softly, as a smile touched her lips.

"Excuse me?"

She met Dr. Millstone's grin. "I said New Orleans. I got pregnant in New Orleans. But how is that possible when we were careful?"

A smiled played at the corner of Dr. Millstone's mouth. "I deliver a lot of babies whose parents thought they were careful, too. No birth control is one hundred percent."

Jayla chuckled. "Evidently not."

"So, can I assume that you're happy with the news?"

Jayla jumped up as the feeling of euphoria took control of her again. "Yes, I'm happy! I am ecstatic!" she said, laughing joyously. She just hoped and prayed that Storm would be happy and ecstatic, as well, when she told him that she loved him and was having his baby.

Eleven

Everyone who was somebody in Atlanta had turned out for the Kids' World charity benefit. There were politicians, CEOs of major corporations, celebrities and well-known sports figures, all of whom considered Atlanta home.

There was also a sheikh in attendance, the very handsome Prince Jamal Ari Yasir, who was dressed in his native Middle Eastern attire and causing quite a stir among the ladies, single or otherwise. Jayla smiled, knowing the stir was a waste of time and effort since it was well known that Prince Yasir was happily married to the former Delaney Westmoreland, Storm's sister.

Jayla glanced across the room at the group of men standing together laughing and talking. Although Storm hadn't arrived yet, it didn't take much to recognize the men as Westmorelands. Their kinship was clearly evident in their facial features, their height as well as their sex appeal.

She began wondering if perhaps Storm had changed his mind about coming. After leaving the clinic yesterday, she had decided to take the rest of the day off. Too excited to work, she had gone home and called Lisa and invited her to lunch.

She'd barely gotten the words out after Lisa arrived when she burst into tears of happiness. Then she told Lisa of her fears about telling Storm. What if he no longer loved her? What if her rejection had killed his feelings for her?

Lisa, in her usual optimistic way, had assured her that although Storm might be a little angry with her right now, she doubted his love could have died so quickly.

Jayla had wanted to call and ask him to come over, but then she'd remembered he was on duty at the fire station. So, instead of talking to him yesterday, she had walked around the house wondering what she would say when she saw him tonight.

"Everything looks beautiful, doesn't it?"

Jayla turned when she recognized the voice of Tara Westmoreland. Tara was accompanied by three other women whom Jayla didn't immediately recognize. At first, Jayla thought each of the women was beautiful in a unique way. Like Tara, they were smiling and each of their smiles reflected a sincere friendliness. Jayla returned their smiles as Tara made the introductions.

The women were Shelly Westmoreland, who was married to Sheriff Dare Westmoreland; Madison Westmoreland, who was married to Stone Westmoreland and Storm's sister, Delaney Westmoreland Yasir. Jayla swallowed deeply. All three women, like Tara, were part of the Westmoreland clan. Somehow, Jayla found her voice to respond to Tara's earlier comment. "Yes, everything is beautiful and your committee should be proud of what they've accomplished."

Tara chuckled. "Yes, but your company also played a huge role. The food is wonderful. Everyone is talking about the catering service that is being used. It's quite evident that Sala Industries went out of their way tonight."

"Thanks."

"And I have to say the dress you're wearing looks simply gorgeous on you," the woman who had been introduced as Madison Westmoreland said.

"Thank you," Jayla said smiling, beginning to feel more relaxed.

She and the women launched into a discussion of styles in clothing and movies they'd recently seen when they heard a sudden buzzing from a group of single women standing not far away. A quick glance at the entrance to the ballroom revealed why. Storm and his cousin Ian had walked in and were crossing the ballroom floor to join the other Westmoreland men. Both men looked dashing and handsome dressed in black tuxedos.

Part of Jayla wished Storm would look her way; then, seconds later, she decided maybe it would be best if he didn't when she overheard the conversation between two women standing not far away.

"Hey, I'm going to make it my business to go after 'The Perfect Storm' tonight," the more statuesque of the two said.

The other women giggled and said. "Storm Westmoreland has a reputation of not doing the same woman twice."

"Yeah, but I heard that just once is all it takes to blow your mind and I definitely intend to have that one time," the statuesque one countered.

A flash of jealousy raced through Jayla, and she started

to turn to the woman and tell her that when it came to Storm, hands off. But she couldn't do that. She didn't have the right.

She glanced up when she felt someone gently touch her arm. "I wouldn't worry about what the 'hottie duo' are saying if I were you," Shelly Westmoreland whispered, smiling. "I heard from a very reliable source that Storm has found a special lady and only has eyes for her."

Jayla blinked in surprise at Shelly's words and glanced at the other women standing beside her. They all nodded; evidently, they'd heard the same thing. Was it possible that they knew she and Storm had been seeing each other? And who was this reliable source Shelly Westmoreland was talking about? Had Storm mentioned her to members of his family?

Her heart stopped and she wasn't sure what to say to the four women who were staring at her with such genuine and sincere smiles on their faces. Tears pressed at the corner of her eyes.

"I may have lost him," she whispered, as her mind was suddenly filled with doubt and regret.

Delaney Yasir chuckled and placed an arm around Jayla's shoulder. "I doubt that. My brother hasn't taken his eyes off of you since he arrived."

Hope ran through Jayla. "Really?" She was standing with her back to Storm so she couldn't see him.

Madison Westmoreland grinned. "Yes, really."

"Hey, Storm, you want something to drink?" Jared Westmoreland asked his cousin as he grabbed a glass a wine off the tray of a passing waiter.

"Storm doesn't want anything to drink," Ian said, grinning. "The only thing Storm wants is that woman who's standing over there talking to the Westmoreland women."

Stone Westmoreland lifted a brow and glanced across the room. The woman's back was to them, so he couldn't get a look at her. "You've met her?" he asked in surprise.

Ian chuckled. "Yes, Storm introduced us in New Orleans."

That comment got everyone's attention. Chase stared at Storm. "You took her to New Orleans with you?"

Before Storm could respond, not that he would have anyway, Ian spoke up. "Of course he didn't take her to New Orleans with him," he said, as if the thought of Storm taking any woman out of town with him were ludicrous. "They just happened to be in the same place at the same time. Her father was Storm's old boss, Adam Cole."

Thorn Westmoreland took a slow sip of his drink and said, "Her parentage is old news, Ian, but her being in New Orleans with Storm is definitely something that we didn't know about."

"And something all of you are going to forget you heard," Storm said. The tone of his voice matched the look on his face. Highly irritated. Totally annoyed. Deadly serious. "And I thought I told you guys that I don't like you discussing my business like I'm not here."

Chase gave his twin a dismissive shrug and said, "Yeah, whatever." He then turned his attention back to Ian. "So what else can you tell us about Storm's lady?"

Ian met Storm's gaze and got the message loud and clear, although it was obvious his brothers hadn't…or they chose no to. Ian grinned and decided to play dumb. "I forget."

Storm smiled. He knew he could count on Ian to keep his secrets, just as Ian knew he could count on him to keep his. Things had always been that way between them. He then turned his attention back to Jayla and wished the crowd would thin out so his view wasn't as blocked, or that she would at least turn around so he could see her. He wanted to look into her eyes to let her know that no matter how much she might want him out of her life, he was there to stay.

Moments later, as if he had willed it to be so, the crowd thinned out and she turned and met his gaze. His heart almost stopped when he saw how radiant she looked. And what made her even more beautiful was the fact that she was wearing that red dress.

His dress.

It was the same one he had picked out for her in New Orleans. He wondered, hoped and prayed that there was a hidden meaning behind her wearing that dress. Could he dare hope she might realize that he was her Mr. Right? Knowing there was only one way to find out, he walked away from the group.

His destination was the woman he loved.

Jayla's breath caught in her throat when she saw Storm heading toward her. She couldn't tell from his expression whether he was glad to see her or not, but one thing was certain—he wasn't going to avoid her. But maybe she was jumping to conclusions. Although he was headed to where she was standing, he might be coming over to say hello to his sister and sisters-in-law since they were standing next to her.

"Here comes Storm Westmoreland," she overheard one of the women from the "hottie duo" say. "And I think he's seen my interest and is coming over to talk to me."

"Fat chance of that happening," Tara whispered. Jayla couldn't help but smile and hoped Tara was right. As Storm got closer, her hope went up a notch when she saw he was still holding her gaze. She sighed deeply when he stopped in front of her.

"Hi, Jayla."

She smiled up at him and tried to keep her heart from pounding erratically in her chest. "Hi, Storm."

It was only then that he released her gaze and glanced at his sister and sisters-in-law. "Good evening, ladies, and, as usual, all of you look beautiful and bestow much pride upon the Westmoreland name."

He glanced back at Jayla. "And you look beautiful, as well, Jayla."

"Thanks." And before she lost her nerve, she asked, "Is there a chance I might speak with you privately for a moment?" The man standing before her looked so irresistibly handsome, so utterly gorgeous that it almost took her breath away.

Her pulse quickened when he stared into her eyes with an intensity that made her shiver. He nodded, then said, "Sure." He shifted his gaze from her to the others and said, "Please excuse us for a minute." After taking her hand in his, Storm led her through the doors and outside into the lobby.

"There're a lot of people here tonight," Storm said, as they continued walking down the elegant and immaculate hallway.

"Yes, there are," Jayla replied. The benefit was being held in the ballroom of the Atlanta Civic Center and the facility was the perfect place to host such an event. She wondered where Storm was taking her. It was obvious that wherever it was, he wanted them to have privacy.

They stopped walking when they came to a beautiful

atrium. All the greenery, flowering plants and the huge waterfall added warmth and even more grace and style to their surroundings. Jayla suddenly felt nervous, not sure of herself, but then she knew she had to say her piece. No matter what, he deserved to know about their baby, but she couldn't tell him that now. If he wanted her back, it had to be because he still loved her and not because he would feel obligated because she was carrying his child.

She cleared her throat. "Storm."

"Jayla."

She smiled when they had spoken at the same time. She glanced at him and his features were expressionless and she had no idea what he was thinking.

"Ladies first," he said, meeting her gaze.

Jayla swallowed. She knew that a lot was at stake here, but she remembered the words her father would often say—*nothing ventured, nothing gained.* She cleared her throat. "I kept my appointment at the clinic this morning."

He contemplated her silently for a moment, and then asked, "Did you?"

She expelled a soft breath, still unable to read him. "Yes, but I've decided not to go through with the procedure." She thought she saw relief flash through his gaze but wasn't sure.

He held her gaze steadily, studied her for a moment. "Why did you change your mind?" he asked.

Jayla swallowed again as she lifted her chin. "Because I realized that you were right and that I did have blinders on. So I took them off and when I did, I could see things a lot clearer."

Tension hummed between them; she felt it. "And what do you see, Jayla?" he asked softly.

She breathed deeply and decided to tell him just what she saw. "I see a tall man who is so strikingly handsome I can barely think straight, who has eyes so dark they remind me of chocolate chips and a voice so sexy it sends shivers down my spine. But most importantly, since taking my blinders off, I can see my Mr. Right standing right in front of me. Now. At this very minute. And I pray that I haven't ruined things, and there's a possibility that he still wants me, because, since taking off my blinders, I've also discovered just how much I love him and just how much I want him in my life."

Jayla held her breath, not knowing what he would say, not knowing if he would accept her words. Then, she saw a slow smile come into his face and spread from corner to corner on his lips. And those lips leaned down and came mere inches from hers and whispered. "I'm glad you quickly came to that conclusion, Jayla Cole, because I love you and there was no way in hell I intended to let you go."

Before she could say anything, he captured her mouth in a kiss. It was a kiss that was so powerful and tender that it immediately brought tears to her eyes. Storm loved her and she loved him and she believed in her heart that everything would be okay. Together, they would make their marriage work because love was the main ingredient and she believed they had plenty of that.

He reluctantly broke off their kiss. "I know you can't leave until everything is over, but I have to get you alone."

Jayla grinned and glanced around. "We're alone now, Storm."

He chuckled. "Yeah, but this place is too public for what I want to do to you." His features then turned serious. "But more importantly, Jayla, we need to talk and come to an understanding about a few things, all right?"

She nodded. "All right. But no matter what, we'll work things out."

He pulled her back into his arms. "Most definitely."

It was well after midnight when Jayla entered Storm's home. The evening had been perfect and a lot of money had been raised for Kids' World, which meant that plenty of terminally ill children's dreams would be coming true. It wasn't hard to guess that the calendars would sell like hotcakes. Over one hundred thousand calendars had been sold, and an order had already been placed for that many more.

And it hadn't come as a surprise to anyone that the single women had gone wild over the twelve men who had posed for the calendar, especially Mr. July, Thorn Westmoreland. However, any women who might have given thought to the possibility that she had a chance with Mr. July, married or not, discovered just how wrong they were when, after receiving the plaque that had been presented to all twelve men, Thorn crossed the room and kissed his wife, proclaiming to all that Tara Westmoreland was all the woman he wanted and needed.

And, Jayla thought as she inwardly smiled, Storm had made a number of declarations himself tonight. That single woman who'd vowed that she would get at least one time with Storm had been brazen enough to approach him while he and Jayla had stood together talking. Storm had smoothly introduced Jayla to the woman as his fiancée. The woman had congratulated them and walked off, thoroughly disappointed.

He had also introduced her to his parents and the rest of his family. She even got to meet the newest additions to the Westmoreland clan, his cousins Clinton, Cole and

Casey. She had quickly decided that the Westmoreland family was a very special one and they all stuck together like glue.

"Would you like something to drink, Jayla?"

She turned and watched as Storm closed the door and locked it. "No, thanks." She nervously glanced around and stopped when her gaze came to rest on a framed photograph that sat on his fireplace mantle. It was a photo that the two of them had taken with her father at his last birthday party, the one the men at the fire station had given him. Her father had insisted that she and Storm stand next to each other while he stood in the background. Because of Adam Cole's six-seven height, he appeared to be towering over them. And he was smiling so brightly that she couldn't help wondering if perhaps he'd known about her feelings for Storm and, in his own special way, had given them his blessings that night, because less than five months after that picture was taken, he'd died.

Storm followed her gaze and after a few moments said, "Whenever I look at that picture and really study it, I think that your father was a lot smarter than either of us gave him credit for being."

Jayla nodded. Evidently their thoughts had been on the same page. She inhaled deeply and then met Storm's gaze. "I agree." She broke eye contact with him and continued her study of his home. With earth-toned colors and basic furnishings, it was clearly a bachelor's place. But everything was neat and in order. "Nice place."

"Thanks. A few months ago, I decided to sell it and get a bigger place," he said as his gaze roamed over her from head to toe. "Thanks for wearing that dress. It's my favorite."

Jayla smiled. "That's the reason I wore it. I was trying to give you a sign, or at least make you remember the time we spent together in New Orleans. I figured the only other person who would know I'd worn this dress before was Ian, and I counted on him not noticing."

Storm lifted a brow. He hated to tell her, but Ian had noticed. In fact, every man who'd been present tonight had noticed Jayla Cole in *that* dress. And each and every time he saw a man looking at her, even when trying not to, he was inwardly overjoyed that she belonged to him.

And now with her standing in the middle of his living room, there was nothing he was itching to do more than to take that dress off her because chances were, like before, the only thing underneath that dress was a pair of thongs. But he knew before they could get to the bedroom, there were issues that needed to be resolved between them.

Sighing, he slowly crossed the distance that separated them and took her hand in his. "Come on, let's sit down and talk."

She nodded and then he led her over to the leather sofa and they sat down. "I've done a lot of thinking, Jayla, and you're right. There's nothing wrong with a woman working outside the home if she wants to do so. The reason I was opposed to it was because years ago, while a senior in high school, I thought I was in love with a girl who threw my love back in my face when I told her of my decision not to go to college but to attend the Firefighters Academy instead. She said that a man without a college education could not properly take care of the needs of his family. When she said that, something snapped inside me and I intended to prove her wrong and, with college or not, I wanted to be a man who could sufficiently provide for all of my family's needs."

Jayla nodded. She could see the pride of a man like Storm getting bruised with a woman saying something like that. She sighed, knowing it was time to get rid of her emotional baggage as well.

"Because Dad was so strict on me while I was growing up," she started off by saying, "I had this thing against marrying a man who I thought would try and control me. But now I see that Dad had the right approach in raising me, or no telling how I might have turned out."

She inhaled in a deep breath, then added, "I believe all those times I thought I was looking for Mr. Right I failed miserably because it wasn't time to find my Mr. Right. It wasn't time until I saw you again in New Orleans."

Storm lowered his mouth to hers and the kiss he gave her was filled with so much intensity and passion, Jayla couldn't help the groan that purred from her throat. Nor could she ignore the sudden rush of heat that threatened to consume her entire body as Storm continued to claim her mouth, staking a possession all the way to the darkest recesses of her soul. She kissed him back, putting into the kiss all the love and feeling that he did, claiming his mouth as well and staking her possession.

He pulled back, stood and pulled her into his arms. "Will you marry me, Jayla Cole? Will you love me for better or worse, richer or poorer, in sickness and in health, till death do us part?"

Tears gathered in Jayla's eyes. "Yes! Oh, yes! I love you."

Storm grinned. "And I love you, too." His gazed locked with hers and smiled. "Tell me again what you see."

She smiled up at him, knowing it was time to tell him her other news. "I see my Mr. Right…and," she whispered softly, "I also see the man who is the father of my baby."

Jayla watched Storm's expression and knew the exact moment it dawned on him what she'd said. For a moment, he continued to gaze at her, his dark eyes clouded with un-certainty, hope. "Did you just say what I think you said?" he asked breathlessly.

She smiled. If there was any doubt in her mind that he wanted a baby, their baby, it evaporated when she saw the look of sheer happiness in his eyes. "Yes. After taking my physical, I told the doctor that I had changed my mind about the insemination procedure and she said it was a good thing since I was already pregnant."

Jayla chuckled. "By my calculations, I got pregnant in New Orleans but I still can't figure out how that happened when I know for certain that protection was used every time we made love."

Storm laughed. "Yeah, but a condom can only hold so much, sweetheart. When a man is driven to have multiple—"

Jayla placed a finger to Stone's lips and grinned. "Okay, I get the picture."

He swept her into his arms and chuckled. "I'm glad that you do and I guess you know what your pregnancy means," he said as he moved toward his bedroom.

"What?"

"There's no way we'll have a June wedding, even if you wanted one. We're getting married as soon as possible."

She laughed. "How soon?"

"Tomorrow isn't soon enough for me."

"What about in a month?"

"Umm, that's negotiable," he said as he placed her in the middle of his bed.

When he stood back, Jayla's gaze swept over him. When she saw the magnitude of his arousal, she inhaled deeply. "I have a feeling I might not be able to move in the morning."

He smiled as he began removing his clothes. "I have a feeling you just might be right. And I have a feeling that if you weren't pregnant now, you would very well be in the morning."

Jayla smiled and her gaze met his. "And you're sure you're okay with becoming a father, Storm? It's a lot for a devout bachelor to take on a wife and child at the same time."

His smile widened. "But I won't have a ordinary wife and child," he said coming back to her, completely naked. "They will be extraordinary because they are mine. And I promise to take very good care of them, Adam's daughter and grandchild, just as I believe he knew that I would."

He leaned over and slowly peeled the dress from Jayla's body. Then he quickly removed her shoes and panty hose. Finally, he removed her thong. "I really like that dress, but I like you naked a lot better."

He then joined her on the bed. "Do you know what is about to happen to you, Jayla?"

She laid a hand against his cheek. "No, tell me," she implored softly, seeing the dark, heated look of desire in his eyes. It was a look that sent sensuous shivers all through her body.

He smiled. "You're about to be taken by *Storm*."

Jayla smiled. She was definitely looking forward to that experience.

Epilogue

A month later

"**Y**ou may kiss your bride."

As the Westmoreland family looked on in the backyard of his parents' home, Storm smiled as he turned to Jayla and captured her mouth in the kind of a kiss that everyone thought should have been saved for later, but one he was determined to bestow upon his bride anyway.

"At least he has his own woman to kiss now," Dare whispered to Thorn.

"It's about damn time," Thorn Westmoreland replied, grinning.

Finally, Storm tore his mouth away from Jayla and smiled. He then leaned over and whispered something in her ear and whatever he said made her blush profusely.

"Umm, I wonder what he said that made her blush like that, considering the fact she's already pregnant," Stone whispered to Chase.

Chase shrugged. "You know Storm. Nothing about him surprises me."

"Well, hell, I'm still in shock," Jared Westmoreland said, shaking his head. "Storm was the last Westmoreland I thought would marry, and just think in less than nine months he'll be a daddy."

Jared then chuckled as he glanced at Dare, Thorn, Chase and Stone. "What is it with your side of the family? All of you are tying the knot."

Chase frowned. "Not all of us."

Stone smiled. "Your time is coming, Chase." He then glanced over at his cousins, Ian, Jared, Spencer, Durango, Quade, Reggie, Clint and Cole. "And all of yours."

Durango narrowed his eyes. "Don't try putting a damn curse on us like that old woman put on Storm."

Dare shook his head laughing. "She didn't put a curse on Storm, she merely read his palm. Besides, if it's going to happen, then it's going to happen. The big question is who's next."

He studied his remaining single brother and his eight male cousins. He smiled, having an idea just who the next Westmoreland groom would be, and he couldn't wait to see it happen.

He grinned. "All I have to say is that when it happens, don't fight it. You'll find out later that it will be the best thing to ever happen to you."

Quade Westmoreland frowned. "No disrespect, Sheriff, but go to hell." He turned and walked off, and the other single Westmoreland men did likewise.

Dare laughed and he kept on laughing while thinking there would definitely be another Westmoreland wedding before long. He would bet on it...if he were a betting man.

* * * * *

JARED'S COUNTERFEIT
FIANCÉE

To my husband Gerald Jackson, Sr, with all my love.
To my family and friends for their continued support.
To Dr Angela Martin, GYN. Thanks for all your
invaluable information.

An intelligent man is always open to new ideas.
In fact he looks for them.
—Proverbs 18:15

Prologue

Jared Westmoreland glanced up from the legal document he'd been reading when he heard a commotion outside of his office door.

He heard his secretary say, "Wait a minute, miss. You just can't barge into Mr. Westmoreland's office unannounced," moments before his door flew open and a gorgeous but angry woman stormed in.

Jared's heart rate quickened and his pulse accelerated. He forced back the blatant desire that rushed through him as he walked from behind his desk. The woman was absolutely stunning. Even her apparent anger didn't detract from her beauty. In one smooth glance, he took in a mass of dark brown curls that framed her face and the smooth, creamy texture of her skin—the color of rich mahogany. Then there were her beautiful dark brown eyes with perfectly arched brows, a delectable pair of lips and rounded cheeks with dimples that not even her anger could hide. A sleek, curvy body in a pair of slacks and a tailored blouse completed the vision of beauty.

"Mr. Westmoreland, I tried to stop her but she—"

"That's all right, Jeannie," Jared said to his secretary, who had raced in behind the woman.

"Do you want me to call security?"

"No, I don't think that will be necessary."

Jeannie Tillman, who'd worked for him for over five years, didn't look too convinced. "Are you sure?"

He stared at the seething woman who was standing with both hands on her hips, glaring at him. "Yes, I'm sure." Jeannie gave him a hesitant nod and turned to leave, closing the door behind her.

Jared turned his full attention to his beautiful intruder. He was fairly certain that she was not a client since he didn't forget a beautiful face. In fact, he was sure he'd never met her before.

Dana Rollins met Jared's stare and tried to keep her intense reaction to him from showing. She had heard about Jared Westmoreland, Atlanta's hotshot, millionaire attorney. Now she was seeing him for herself and it seemed that all she'd heard was true. He was definitely the stuff dreams were made of. A sharp dresser, all the way down to his expensive-looking leather shoes, he was tall, with a body that was well built. Solid as a rock. He had coffee-colored skin, dark brown eyes, a solid jaw, straight nose and close-cut black hair. They were handsome features on a sensual face; the kind that would definitely make her do a double take. But she couldn't dwell on how sexy he looked. She was here for business and nothing more.

"I'm sure there's a reason why you barged into my office, Miss…"

"Rollins," she supplied sharply. His words reminded her of what that business was. "And yes, there is a reason. This!" she said, pulling an envelope out of her purse. "I received this certified letter from you less than an hour ago demanding that I return my engagement ring to Luther. I tried calling him but was told he's out of town so I immediately came here to get an explanation."

Jared took the letter from her and looked at it. The assessment didn't take long. He glanced back at her. "I gather you have a problem with returning the ring, Miss Rollins?" he asked.

"Of course I do. Luther decided he wasn't ready to give up his single status and called off our wedding a week before it was to take place. Besides the embarrassment and humiliation of everything—explaining things to my friends and returning shower gifts—I was left with all the wedding expenses. And to pour salt on the wound, I received that letter from your firm."

Jared inhaled deeply. Evidently she hadn't yet realized that Luther Cord had done her a favor. "Miss Rollins, I suggest you consult your own attorney to verify what I'm telling you, but my client has every right to ask for the engagement ring back. An engagement ring represents a conditional gift. The proposition is that the condition is marriage and not a willingness to marry. Thus if the engagement is broken, for whatever reason, the expectation is that the ring is returned, just as you returned the wedding presents and shower gifts," he said.

He watched as she crossed her arms over her chest and the angry frown on her lips deepened and turned rebellious. "I refuse to give it back. It's the principle of the thing."

Jared shook his head thinking that principle had nothing to do with it. The law was the law. "Unfortunately, Miss Rollins, you're faced with a losing battle and a very costly one. Do you want to add a bunch of legal fees to everything else right now?"

He knew the mention of finances would help make her think straight. And knowing he had her thinking in the right direction, he pressed forward. "I know what you're going through must be painful, but my advice to you is to try and put this episode behind you and move on. You're a beautiful woman, and I believe there's a man out there who's truly worthy of you. Evidently Luther Cord isn't. Perhaps you should count your blessings."

Jared knew his words weren't what she wanted to hear but he wanted to be as honest with her as he could. There was only so much he could say, considering the fact that Luther Cord was his client. In fact, he had said too much already. But for some reason he wanted to help end her heartache as soon as possible.

Moments passed and Dana didn't say anything, but he could tell she was thinking about what he'd said. Then he watched as she pulled a small white box from her purse and handed it to him.

He met her gaze when she said softly, "I appreciate your advice and although it's a bitter pill to swallow, I'll return the ring."

He flipped it open and saw the dazzling diamond solitaire before placing the small box on his desk. "You're doing the right thing, Miss Rollins."

She nodded and extended her hand to him. "The last thing I need is to get into more debt. Luther isn't worth it."

He accepted her hand, liking the way it fit neatly into his. "I hope things work out for you," he said with complete sincerity.

Dana gazed intently into his eyes and smiled appreciatively. Although she hadn't wanted to hear what he'd said, she couldn't help but be grateful for his honesty. In her experience, compassion and kindness were two emotions attorneys seldom possessed. "Somehow they will. I know I interrupted your work by barging in here the way I did and I apologize," she said.

"You didn't interrupt anything," Jared said smoothly. "And as for my advice, consider it a favor."

The smile that touched her lips widened. "Thanks. Maybe I'll be able to return the favor some day. I owe you one."

As he released her hand and watched her turn and walk out of his office, Jared thought to himself that Dana Rollins was as sensual as a woman could get.

One

A month later

Jared Westmoreland was having one hell of a morning.

It began with the message his mother had left on his answering machine last night, reminding him that his father's and his uncle's birthdays fell on Easter Sunday this year and requesting that he set an example for his five brothers by bringing a date to the huge dinner party she and his aunt Evelyn had planned.

His cousin Storm's recent wedding had made his mother, Sarah, take stock and realize that her six sons had yet to show serious interest in any woman. And of course, since he was the eldest, she felt he should be the first and had every intention of prodding him in the right direction. It didn't matter that he and his brothers were successful and enjoyed being single. She felt that the only way any of them could truly be happy was to find that special woman and tie the knot. The only one who wasn't experiencing the heat was his brother Spencer, whose fiancée Lynette, had died in a drowning accident three years ago.

Jared rose from his chair and walked over to the window. To add to the annoyance of his mother's call, he had arrived at work an hour later than usual because of traffic. And as if things couldn't get any worse, he had just received a phone call from entertainer Sylvester Brewster, who wanted to file for a divorce—from wife number three. Sylvester was good for business, but it was hard to watch him involve himself in relationships that didn't last.

When Jared heard the buzzer sounding on his desk, he turned around and sighed heavily, wondering if the morning could get any worse. Crossing the room he picked up the phone. "Yes, Jeannie?"

"Mr. Westmoreland, your mother is on the line."

Jared shook his head. Yes, his morning could get worse. It just did. "Go ahead and put her through."

A few moments later after hearing the connection, he said. "Hi, Mom."

"Did you get my message, Jared?"

Jared raised his gaze to the ceiling before saying. "Yes, I got it."

"Good. Then I'll be setting an extra plate out for dinner next Sunday."

Jared wanted to tell her in a nice, respectable way that if she set out the plate there was a strong chance it would sit there empty. But before he could get the words out, his mother quickly added, "Remember, you're the oldest and I expect you to set an example. Besides, you're not getting any younger."

She made it seem as if he was fifty-seven instead of thirty-seven. Besides, his mother knew how he felt about the institution of marriage. He was a divorce attorney for heaven's sake. He ended marriages, not put them together. He'd handled enough divorce cases to know that marriage wasn't all it was cracked up to be. People got married and then a lot of them eventually got divorced. It was a vicious cycle; one that made him money, but sickened him at the same time. Although there were long-lasting marriages in the Westmoreland family, he considered them exceptions and not the norm. It would be just his luck to have the first failed marriage in the family and he had no intention of becoming a statistic.

"Jared, are you listening?"

He sighed. When she used that tone, he had no other choice but to listen. "Yes, but has it occurred to you that Durango, Ian, Spencer, Quade, Reggie and I like being single?" he asked respectfully.

"And has it ever occurred to any of you that your father and I aren't getting any younger and we'd love to have grandchildren while we're still of sound mind to enjoy them?"

Jared shook his head. First, she was trying to shove marriage down their throats and now she was hinting at grandchildren. But he was smart enough to know that the last thing he needed was to butt heads with caring, stubborn Sarah Westmoreland. He would rather face an uncompromising judge in the courtroom than oppose his mother. It was an uphill battle that he just didn't have the energy for right now.

"I'll see what I can do," he finally said.

"Thanks, Son. That's all I ask."

"Really, Dana, I wish you would think about going with us."

Dana Rollins glanced up at Cybil Franklin, who stood in the middle of her office with a determined frown on her face. Cybil was Dana's best friend from high school and the primary reason she had relocated from Tennessee to Atlanta three years ago to take a position at Kessler Industries as a landscape architect.

"Thanks, Cybil, but I'm sure you've heard the saying that three's a crowd. I don't think going with you and Ben to North Carolina this weekend is a good idea."

Cybil rolled her eyes. "It's just a camping trip to the mountains. I feel awful knowing you'll be spending Easter alone."

Leaning back in the chair behind her desk, Dana smiled easily. "Hey, I'm a twenty-seven-year-old woman who can take care of herself. I'll be fine and I have no problem spending Easter alone." *It will be just like every other year since Mom and Dad died.*

None of the holidays were the same anymore since her parents had been killed in a car accident on their way to her college graduation five years earlier. Since she had no other family, their deaths had left her truly alone. She'd thought all that had changed when she met Luther. They began dating in early spring and after six months, he had asked her to marry him.

"It's times like these when I'm tempted to find

Luther Cord and kill him," Cybil said angrily. "When I think of what he did to you, I get so mad."

Dana smiled softly, no longer able to muster up anger when she thought about Luther. He had paid her an unexpected visit last week to tell her that he was moving to California. He told her that his decision not to marry had nothing to do with her, that he'd come to terms with his sexual preference, and that in his own way he loved her, but not in the way a husband is supposed to love his wife. At first she had been shocked, but then she'd acknowledged that the signs had all been there. She couldn't, or hadn't wanted to see them. Dana hadn't told anyone about Luther's confession, not even Cybil.

Dana turned her attention back to her friend. "I told you that I'd be fine. It won't be the first or the last holiday that I spend alone."

"I know but I wish that—"

"Cybil, let it go. You need to get out of here if you're meeting Ben for lunch," she said, trying to propel her out the door.

"Okay, but call me soon?"

As soon as Cybil left, Dana released a huge sigh.

Since her breakup with Luther, Dana put all of her time and energy into her job. Work wasn't a substitute for having a family and a personal life, but it did take her mind off her loneliness.

She glanced at the calendar on her desk. It was hard to believe next week was Easter already. Her parents would make every holiday special and even while in college she enjoyed going home during spring break to spend Easter with them. She remembered their last

Easter together. They had gone to sunrise church service and later they had feasted on the delicious dinner her mother had prepared, not knowing it would be the last holiday meal they would share together.

She sighed deeply, not wanting to relinquish the memories just yet but knowing that she had to. Somehow she would get through another holiday without her parents. She had no other choice.

"What would you like to order, sir?"

Jared studied the huge menu posted on the wall behind the counter and made his decision. "Umm, give me a ham and cheese all the way on whole wheat, an order of French fries and a glass of sweetened tea."

"All right. Your order will be ready in a minute."

Jared nodded then glanced around. Usually he met clients for lunch at restaurants that served the finest cuisine; and at other times he would order in and eat lunch at his office. But he had decided to take advantage of how beautiful a day it was and walk the block from his office to the deli.

The place was crowded and he hoped that he would be able to find a seat by the time his lunch was ready. He was even willing to share a table or booth with someone if the person didn't have a problem with it.

As his eyes scanned the crowded restaurant, he tried to find someone sitting alone. Abruptly his gaze stopped on a familiar-looking woman at a booth, who was reading a book while leisurely munching on a French fry. A memory suddenly flared in his mind, jump-started his senses and instantly stirred heat within him.

Dana Rollins.

It had been a month since she had stormed into his office, but he vividly recalled the impact she'd made on his male senses when she'd barged in that day. He felt blood race through his veins, reminding him that he'd been so busy at work, he hadn't been with a woman in over eight months.

He was accustomed to beautiful, gorgeous women, but there was something intrinsically special about Dana Rollins. He hadn't been this attracted to a woman since heaven knows when. Now it seemed he was making up for lost time.

"Sir, your order is ready."

Jared turned and took the tray loaded with his food from the man behind the counter. "Thanks." He then glanced back over at Dana Rollins and after making a quick decision, he crossed the room to where she sat.

She was so absorbed in her book that she didn't notice him standing next to her. She was leaning forward with both her elbows on the table while holding the book in front of her, so that the neckline of her blouse gapped open enough for him to get a generous glimpse of her cleavage. He liked what he saw—firm, full breasts.

Knowing he couldn't stand there and continue to ogle her, he cleared his throat. "Miss Rollins?"

She quickly glanced up and recognized him. He watched her shimmering bronze lips tilt into a smile guaranteed to turn him on. "Mr. Westmoreland, it's good to see you again."

Her dimpled smile made him acutely aware of just how beautiful she was. "It's good seeing you again, too. It's rather crowded in here and I saw you sitting alone and wondered if perhaps I could join you?"

Her smile widened into a grin. "Yes, of course," she said, placing her book down on the table, making sure not to lose her spot.

"Thanks," he said, sliding into the seat across from her in the booth. "How have you been?"

Her lashes fluttered downward before sweeping up with her gaze to meet his. "I've been fine and have done what you suggested and moved on."

Jared nodded. "I'm glad to hear it, Miss Rollins."

Her smile widened. "Please call me Dana."

He chuckled. "Only if you call me Jared."

After saying grace, he took a sip of his drink then proceeded to put ketchup on his fries. He glanced her way and smiled. "So what are you reading?"

She took a sip of her drink then picked up the book and held it up. "A book of poems by Maya Angelou. She's a wonderful poet and I love reading her work. It can be so uplifting."

He nodded. He had read several of her poems himself. Dana met his gaze. "Do you read a lot, Jared?"

He shrugged broad shoulders under an expensive suit. "The only pleasure reading I have time for these days is my cousin's novels. He writes under the pen name Rock Mason."

Her eyes lit up and showed her surprise. "You're related to Rock Mason?"

Jared laughed. "Yes. His real name is Stone Westmoreland."

Dana smiled. "Wow. I've read all of his books. He's a gifted writer."

Jared chuckled. "I'll make sure I tell him you said that when I see him again. He and his wife, Madison, are in Texas visiting cousins we have there, but they'll be back for our fathers' birthdays next weekend."

"Your fathers' birthdays?"

He smiled. "Our fathers are fraternal twins and they turn sixty this year. Since their birthdays fall on Easter Sunday, our mothers are hosting one huge celebration."

"Sounds like all of you will have a wonderful time."

He chuckled. "We usually do when we all get together. The Westmoreland family is big. What about you? Are you from a large family?"

He watched sadness appear in her eyes. "I don't have any family. I was an only child and my parents were killed five years ago in an auto accident en route to my college graduation."

"I'm sorry."

She met his gaze and saw the sincerity of his words. "Thank you. It was hard for me, but I got through it. Since my parents didn't have any siblings, and their parents are deceased, I don't have a family."

He watched as she caught her lower lip between her teeth as if to keep it from trembling with the remembered pain. "What are your plans for Easter Sunday?" he couldn't help but ask.

"I don't have any. I'll go to a sunrise service at church and will probably spend the rest of the day at home relaxing and reading."

He lifted an eyebrow. "What about dinner?"

She shrugged. "I'll pull out a microwave dinner and enjoy the day that way."

Jared tried shifting his attention back to his food but couldn't fully concentrate on what he was eating. Because of his large family, he had grown up loving the holidays and even looked forward to them, although lately his mother's interfering had tempered his anticipation.

An idea suddenly popped into Jared's head. His mother was expecting him to bring someone to dinner so why not Dana? When his mother and his aunt Evelyn got together, the two women cooked up a storm. That had to be better than a microwave dinner. "How would you like to join me for Easter dinner at my parents' home?" He could tell that his invitation surprised her.

"You're inviting me to dinner at your parents' place?"

"Yes."

She shook her head, as if still not understanding. "But, why? We barely know each other."

Jared knew he had to level with her. "It just so happens that you can help me out of a jam."

Dana lifted a brow. "What kind of jam?"

"My mother is obsessed. Lately, a number of my cousins have gotten married and since none of her six sons are rushing to follow suit, she's taken it upon herself to prod us along. I'm the oldest so I'm feeling the heat more than the others. She expects me to set an example by bringing someone to dinner. And since I recall you owe me a favor, I figured now's the time to collect."

Dana blinked and then she released a deep sigh. Jared could tell she had forgotten about her promise. "But I'm sure there're plenty of women you've dated who would love going to dinner with you at your parents' home," she implored.

Jared nodded as he continued to smile. "Yes, but if I take any of them they might get the wrong impression and think that I'm actually interested in a serious relationship. Besides, my mother and aunt are good cooks. All you'll have to do is show up with me, endure the likes of my family and join in with the birthday festivities. I understand it's a lot to ask, but I'd really appreciate it if you'd come. It will definitely get Mom off my back."

Jared watched as she nervously gnawed her bottom lip. He had presented the situation just as it was.

Dana met his gaze. She had felt that pull between them, that physical attraction, so to consider being in Jared's company for any reason wasn't a good idea. But, she did owe him a favor and she'd always been taught to keep her word. "And it's just this one time?"

"Yes, just this one time," he assured her. "But to pull this off, we'll need a convincing story. I think it would be a good idea if I called you one day this week to discuss answers to the questions I have a feeling my family will ask."

Dana frowned. "What kind of questions?"

Jared grinned. "Oh, the usual, like how long have we known each other? When and how we met? How serious are things between us? And there's a strong chance my mother might get downright personal and want to know if you've moved in with me yet, whether you're capable of producing babies and if so, how many you're willing to have."

Dana blinked, then laughed out loud. Jared thought it was a beautiful sound; and in all honesty, the deep rumble in her throat was a blatant turn-on.

"You aren't serious, are you?" she asked, bringing her laughter under control.

He chuckled. "Unfortunately, I am. Just wait until you meet my mother for yourself. Marrying off one of her sons seems to be her number-one priority."

Dana raised an arched brow. "And marriage is something you have an aversion to?"

"Yes. I handle enough divorce cases to know that most marriages don't last."

He watched as she sat back in her chair with a thoughtful expression on her face. "So will you be my date that day?"

Dana considered Jared's invitation. After a few moments she nodded her agreement.

Jared smiled, pleased with the turn of events. "Thanks, Dana. I appreciate you helping me out of this jam. You don't know how much it means to be able to get my mother off my back."

TWO

Dana glanced down at her watch. Jared was coming to pick her up at any moment and she was a nervous wreck.

They had talked on the phone earlier in the week to get prepared for his family's inquisition. Just hearing his voice had sent sensuous chills all through her body and reminded her that she was definitely a woman, something she had forgotten since her breakup with Luther.

That reminder came with a mixture of empowerment and restraint. The last thing she needed was to test emotional waters that were best left uncharted. All she had to do was remember what had happened with Luther to know that, woman or not, the last thing she wanted was to become vulnerable to any man again.

Dana almost jumped when she heard the sound of her doorbell. She inhaled deeply and reminded herself that she probably wouldn't see Jared again after today so there was no reason for her to come unglued. She released a sigh of relief and opened the door.

Jared gazed at Dana and quickly pulled in a deep breath. If he thought that she was gorgeous before, today she had surpassed his memories. He'd always had a healthy sex drive, but seeing her standing in the doorway with all that glorious hair spread over her shoulders and wearing a pair of jeans that hugged her curvy figure and a pretty knit top, had him wondering how he would get through the day.

"Hi, Jared, please come in."

"Thanks. You look nice."

She smiled and stepped back as he entered and closed the door behind him. "Thank you. I just need to grab my purse," she said, walking off toward a room he assumed was her bedroom.

He was glad for the extra time to pull himself together. The woman was sexy and feminine all rolled into one.

Trying to distract himself, he glanced around her living room. It was nicely decorated in bright colors and with upscale furnishings. He felt something rubbing against his leg and looked down and smiled. "Hey, where did you come from?" he asked, leaning down and picking up a beautiful black cat.

"I'm ready now," Dana said, reentering the room. She smiled when she saw him holding her cat. "I see you've met Tom."

Jared chuckled. "Oh, that's his name?"

"Yes. I've had him for a couple of years, since he was a kitten. Now he's spoiled rotten but great company."

"He's a handsome fellow," Jared said as he continued to pet the animal.

"Shh, don't say that too loud. He's conceited enough
already," Dana whispered.

Jared smiled as he placed Tom back on the floor.
When he straightened back to his full height he met
Dana's gaze. Desire shot all the way through him and
with an effort he swallowed. "Ready?" he asked.

"Yes, I'm ready."

"Welcome to our home, Dana. I'm so glad that Jared
brought you."

Dana suddenly found herself swept into strong arms
as a woman who she figured to be Jared's mother gave
her a gigantic hug. She had expected a nice welcome
but certainly not this outpouring of affection.

"Thanks for having me," Dana said once the woman released her. She glanced up at Jared. Their gazes
met and held. His expression was unreadable and she
couldn't help wondering what he was thinking.

Dana noticed a sudden thickness in her throat when
she remembered how she'd felt when Jared had arrived
at her place, exactly at noon. The only thing she could
think was that even dressed in jeans and a pullover shirt
he looked polished, suave, debonair and sensual.

"You two can give each other that dreamy-eyed look
later," Sarah Westmoreland said, beaming. "Come on
in, everyone is anxious to meet Dana."

Jared shook his head, catching himself and regain-
ing his concentration. The last thing he wanted was for
his mother to get any ideas that Dana was more than just
a dinner date. "I take it that we're the last to arrive," he

said, placing his hand at the small of Dana's back while his mother led them through the foyer.

"Quade isn't here but he called to say that he's on his way."

Jared nodded. His brother Quade was involved in security activities for the Secret Service and often missed family gatherings because of it. But it wasn't from lack of trying to be present. Like all Westmorelands, Quade enjoyed family get-togethers.

Jared could hear voices coming from the living room and took another look at Dana. He had intended it to be a quick look but even in the daylight, the soft glow from the crystal chandelier overhead seemed to enhance her beauty. There was something about the shape of her mouth—he wondered how it would feel under his when he…

"My goodness, Jared, will you stop staring at Dana like that!" his mother scolded in a chuckling voice.

Damn. He hadn't realized he'd been staring again. He kept forgetting just how observant his mother was; her eyes missed nothing. His mother was smiling and for the first time he wondered if perhaps he had made a mistake in inviting Dana. If his mother noticed his attention to her, he could just imagine what the other family members would think. That meant he had to keep his cool and not appear so taken with her.

"It's about time you got here."

Jared's head jerked around and he frowned. His brother Durango, the man who thought all women were made for his pleasure unless they had another man's stamp on them, was talking to Jared, but looking at Dana.

"Durango," Jared acknowledged when his brother came to join them.

Durango nodded but his gaze went straight back to Dana. "And who is this beautiful creature?" he asked smoothly, as a smile touched both corners of his mouth.

"This is Jared's girl. And she's off-limits to you, so behave," Sarah Westmoreland spoke up.

Jared's girl. Jared rubbed the back of his neck, feeling the heat already.

"Are you sure that you don't want any more birthday cake, Dana?"

Dana smiled at Sarah. "Thanks for asking but I don't think I can eat a single thing more. All the food was wonderful, Mrs. Westmoreland."

Dana was completely overwhelmed when Jared had escorted her into the living room and introduced her to his family. The house had been decorated with birthday streamers and balloons from corner to corner. It didn't take long to see that the Westmorelands weren't just a clan but a whole whopping village. The love and warmth between them was easy to see and feel.

There were Jared's male cousins, Dare, Thorn, Stone, Chase, Storm, Clint and Cole. They all favored each other and it was easy to tell they were kin. There were few women in the Westmoreland family: Jared's cousin Delaney who was married to a Middle East sheikh, a tall, dark, handsome man; his cousin Casey who lived in Texas and was sister to Clint and Cole, as well as Shelly, Tara, Madison and Jayla, the wives of Dare, Thorn, Stone and Storm. She also met Jared's uncle Corey and his wife, Abby.

She had never seen so many relatives gathered in one place before, and for a moment a part of her had felt a tinge of jealousy that some people had such a huge family while others had none. But that bout of jealousy soon dissolved when she saw just how friendly and down-to-earth everyone was. At first they had been curious because Jared had never brought a woman to any family function before, but eventually they began to treat her like one of the family, without hesitation, but with a few questions that she felt she effectively answered to satisfy their curiosity. When Jared's brother Quade arrived, all of the attention had momentarily shifted off her, but now it was back on her again.

Jayla was pregnant with twins and the women invited Dana to join them on a shopping trip they had planned for next weekend to help select items for the babies' nursery. Since Dana knew Jared intended for this to be the last time she socialized with his family, she declined, coming up with an excuse about all the errands she had to do Saturday morning, but had thanked them for the invitation.

She glanced over to where Jared stood talking to his brothers and cousins and her heart thumped an unsteady beat just watching him. As if he felt her looking at him, he cocked his head in her direction and their gazes connected. Goose bumps skittered along her arms and she expelled a long, silent breath before breaking eye contact with him.

Needing to distract herself, she glanced out of the window. Jared's parents' home sat on three acres of land and the huge, two-story, Southern style structure was simply stunning. A huge window provided a view of a lake. It was late afternoon and getting dark, which was a stark indication that Easter was almost over.

"I need to talk to you privately for a moment," Jared whispered softly in her ear.

She sucked in a sharp breath. She hadn't heard him approach and the warmth of his breath touched her neck and the faint spicy aroma of his aftershave made her skin tingle.

She wondered what he had to talk to her about and knew his family wondered, as well, when he took her hand and guided her into the kitchen, closing the door behind them.

He leaned against the kitchen counter and for a moment they stared at each other, not saying anything. Then he cleared his throat. "I should have given you this earlier at your apartment when I picked you up but I forgot." Jared knew he could have waited until he returned her home, but for some reason he wanted to get her alone, even if only for a few minutes. "Luther Cord sent a special delivery to me on Friday with instructions that I give you this. After arriving in California he evidently had a change of heart and decided he wanted you to keep it."

Dana raised a curious brow as she watched Jared reach into his pocket to pull out a small white box. She immediately knew what it was. "My engagement ring?" she asked startled.

Jared saw the surprised, but pleased look on her face and couldn't help but smile. "Yes, it's for you," he said handing the small box to her.

"I knew it! I just knew she was the one!"

Jared jerked his head around when his mother burst through the kitchen door. Her face was all aglow.

"I happened to be passing by the door and heard the words engagement ring. Oh, Jared, you have made me so proud and happy," his mother exclaimed between bouts of laughter and tears of joy. She then hugged Dana. "Welcome to the family."

Jared's head began spinning when it became crystal clear what his mother had assumed. He was just about to open his mouth to set her straight when the kitchen door flew open again and his entire family poured in.

"What's going on?" Jared's father asked when he saw his wife in tears.

Again Jared opened his mouth to speak but his mother's voice drowned out any words he was about to say. "Jared and Dana. They just got engaged! He gave her a ring! Oh, I am so happy. I can't believe that one of my sons is finally settling down and getting married."

Jared and Dana suddenly became swamped with words of congratulation and well wishing. He glanced over at Dana and saw she was as shocked with the way things were escalating as he was. He reached over and gently squeezed her hand, hoping that he was assuring her that he would straighten things out. He knew that he should do so now but couldn't recall the last time he'd seen his mother this happy.

Sarah Westmoreland began crying again. "You have really made me happy today, Jared. Who would have thought that of all my sons you would have a change of heart about marriage? But I could feel the love flowing between the two of you when I opened the door and saw you standing there together."

Dana glanced over at Jared. She read the message in his eyes that clearly said: *Trust me, I'll get us out of this mess, but for now, please let my mother have her moment of happiness.* She gave him a silent nod to let him know she understood what he was asking. She inhaled deeply. Of all the misunderstandings she'd heard of, this one was definitely a doozy.

"Dana and I are leaving," Jared said, taking Dana's hand and leading her out of the kitchen.

"But—but we haven't celebrated your good news," his mother called out when he headed for the door.

He turned to look at his relatives, wanting to tell them that they wouldn't be celebrating it, either. They had followed the couple to the door and were crowded around them. He frowned at the "glad it's you and not me" look on the faces of the other single Westmoreland men. "I'll see everyone tomorrow," he told his family.

Then without saying another word and holding Dana's hand firmly in his, he walked out of his parents' house, closing the door behind him.

"I'm sorry about what happened back there," Jared said. Talk about the wrong information getting blown out of proportion. "I just couldn't tell my mother the truth. She was so happy."

Dana nodded. "I understand."

Jared lifted his head and gazed over at Dana, met her gaze and something about the way she was looking back at him told him that she really did understand. "Thank you."

She smiled. "You don't have to thank me. This was a special day for your family. I saw how happy your mother was when she'd thought we'd gotten engaged."

Jared nodded, grateful for her understanding. "I'll

talk to her tomorrow and straighten things out," he said quietly.

"All right."

Satisfied, Jared put his car in gear and backed out of his parents' driveway. At the first traffic light they came to, he glanced over and noticed the engagement ring was on Dana's finger. He frowned, remembering his mother's insistence that she put it on. For some reason he didn't like seeing her wearing Luther Cord's ring. "Now that you have the ring back what are you going to do with it?" he asked, trying to keep his voice neutral.

Dana glanced over at him before looking down at the ring. "What I had planned to do all along. Hock it and use the money to pay off the remaining wedding expenses. I'm surprised Luther returned it to me."

Jared wasn't surprised. During the last conversation he'd had with Cord, he had suggested that he do the decent thing and relieve some of the financial burden breaking the engagement had placed on Dana. He had strongly recommended that although he wasn't legally obligated to do so, he should consider letting her keep the ring. Evidently the man had taken his advice.

When the traffic light changed, Jared glanced over at Dana. Her eyes were closed and her head was back against the headrest. He couldn't stop the smile that touched his lips. No doubt this had been a tiring day for her. He was used to his huge family, but a stranger might be overwhelmed.

"Considering everything, do you regret going to my parents' home for dinner?" he couldn't help but ask.

Although she didn't open her eyes, a smile touched

her lips. "No, I had a wonderful time, Jared. Being around your family and seeing your closeness, brought back so many memories of how close I was to my parents and how they used to make every holiday so special for me." She opened her eyes, tilted her head to him and smiled. "I really appreciate you sharing your friendly, loving pack with me today."

The warm look Dana gave him sent heated sensations down Jared's spine. She might have enjoyed spending time with his family, but he could admit that he had actually enjoyed spending the day with her, as well. She was a charming person to be around and, unlike a lot of his other dates, Dana had not demanded his complete attention, by clinging to him or refusing to let him out of her sight.

He had watched how easily she had blended in with his family and how quickly she had won them over. He could see why his mother thought he had fallen for her.

Jared's hand tightened on the steering wheel. Thinking he was falling for her was one thing, but actually believing that he was engaged to her was another. How could his mother assume such a thing? She knew how he felt about marriage. Did she actually believe one woman could make him change his whole thought process on something he felt so strongly about?

Moments later he pulled into Dana's driveway and brought the car to a stop. He glanced over at her and saw that she had fallen asleep. He hated waking her but knew that he had to. So as not to startle her, he leaned over and softly whispered, "Dana, you're home."

He watched as her eyes slowly opened, then of its

own accord his gaze latched on to her lips, full, luscious, tempting. He would give anything to know how they tasted.

"I think I'd better walk you to the door," he said, fighting the urge to pull her into his arms and kiss her.

He watched as she took a deep breath and nodded. "All right."

Opening the door he got out of the car and walked around to open the door for her; then together they walked to her door. She turned to face him. "Thanks again, Jared, for such a beautiful day. It was special."

He nodded. He wanted to say that she was special, too, but knew that he couldn't. This was their only time together and he had to accept that. "Thanks for being my date. I'll talk to my mother tomorrow."

"Okay."

He watched as she put her key in the door and moments later she turned to him. She hesitated for a moment, then asked, "Would you like to come in for a drink?"

He suddenly decided that he wanted to go in, but not for the drink she was offering. He wanted to do something he'd been thinking of all day. "Yes, I'd like that."

He followed her inside, but when she headed toward the kitchen he placed his hand on her arm. "I can't think of a better way for this day to end than this," he said softly, before leaning down and gently capturing her mouth with his, needing to taste her as much as he needed to breathe.

Shivers of profound pleasure shot through every part of Dana's body the moment their lips touched and her eyelids automatically fluttered shut. When Jared's tongue slipped into her mouth, tasting of the sweet tea he had sipped earlier, she shuddered as a delicious shiver ran up her spine.

Sensations she had never felt before consumed her and when she felt his hands wrap around her middle, pulling her close to the fit of his hard body, she could have melted right where she stood. His assault of her mouth was deliberate, sensuous, unhurried. It was meant to tantalize and awaken every part of her and it did.

Then he deepened the kiss, taking it to another level as he continued to take her mouth slowly, thoroughly, passionately. A part of her wanted to pull back, but he was right. This was the perfect way to end the day. They had been attracted to each other from the first and to pretend otherwise would be a complete waste of time. And since this was the last time they'd spend together, they could at least have this moment.

So she hung in and continued to let him kiss her, finding exquisite pleasure in every moment that he did so. Then he changed the rhythm of their kiss as his tongue played seek and retreat with hers, making a whimper rumble from deep within her throat.

Heat throbbed within Jared as he continued to kiss Dana. Initially, he had meant for the kiss to be nothing more than a way of saying goodbye, to satisfy his curiosity and hunger, but the moment he tasted her sweetness he was helpless to do anything but sink in and savor.

He made sure his kiss was gentle but thorough as he relentlessly explored her mouth. His tongue dueled with hers in a slow sensuous motion and when she wound her arms around his neck and arched her body to the hard length of his, he was consumed with hot waves of desire. There was something about her that had his senses pulsating. Never before had he been this driven to devour anyone.

Moments later with a fevered moan, he lifted his mouth away from hers although he continued to track her lips with his tongue. "You're beautiful in every way that a woman can be, Dana," he whispered roughly against her ear, burying his face in her neck and placing a kiss there.

His compliment touched Dana's very core. No one had ever said such a thing to her. "Thank you."

"Don't thank me. It's the truth," he said, releasing her slowly and taking a step back. "And I want to thank you again for helping me out today."

"I want to thank you, as well. Like I said, your family is wonderful."

He nodded. There would be no reason to see her after today. He tried racking his brain for some excuse to drop by, but couldn't find one. He ran a frustrated hand across the back of his neck. No woman had ever had him this reluctant to say goodbye. He glanced around the room, stalling for time. "Where's Tom?" he asked, trying to prolong the time by even an additional second if he could.

"He's probably in my bed."

Damn lucky cat. Jared met her gaze and knew he should leave before he did something really crazy such as grabbing her and starting to kiss her again. "Goodbye, Dana."

"Goodbye, Jared."

"Take care of yourself." And with those final words he turned, opened the door and walked out of the house.

Three

Around ten the next morning, Jared walked into his parents' home. His nine o'clock court appointment had gotten canceled, which afforded him the opportunity to visit his mother and straighten out yesterday's misunderstanding.

"Mom! Dad!" he called out while walking through the living room to the kitchen.

"I'm out back," was his father's reply.

Jared opened the kitchen door and stepped onto the sun deck his father had built last year. He saw him busy at work putting a coat of polish on his classic Ford Mustang. "Good morning, Dad."

"Morning, son. What a nice surprise to see you on a Monday morning."

"I had a canceled court hearing this morning. Where is everyone?"

"Durango stayed over at Stone's place last night and Ian and Spencer are having breakfast with their cousins at Chase's Place. Quade had to fly out first thing this morning to return to D.C. and Reggie, I imagine went to work."

Jared nodded and glanced around. "I need to talk to Mom. Is she upstairs?"

His father sighed deeply. "No, she had a doctor's appointment this morning."

Jared frowned. "A doctor's appointment? Is anything wrong?"

His father shrugged. "I hope not, but you know your mother. If something is wrong then I'll be the last to know. She thinks if she tells me anything I'd worry myself to death. I wouldn't know about her appointment today if I hadn't heard the message the doctor's office left on the answering machine reminding her of it. Appears they found another lump during her checkup last week."

Jared's frown deepened. Three years ago his mother had been diagnosed with breast cancer and had undergone a series of chemo and radiation treatments before being given a clean bill of health.

"Mom's car is in the driveway so how did she get to the doctor's?"

"I offered to drive her but she had already made arrangements for your aunt Evelyn to take her. You know those two. They have been best friends for years."

Jared nodded. Everyone in the Westmoreland family knew how the two women who had been best friends since high school had ended up marrying the Westmoreland twins, becoming sisters-in-law. "Do you think it's anything serious?" he asked.

He couldn't help but remember how things were the last time. The cancer treatments had made his mother sicker than he'd ever remembered her being. He, his brothers and his dad had made the mistake of hovering over her as if she was an invalid. That hadn't helped matters, which was probably the reason she hadn't mentioned this doctor's appointment to any of them. They would have all shown up at the doctor's office with her today.

"To be honest, Jared, I was beginning to get concerned. I could tell she was worried, although she tried pretending that she wasn't. But then all that changed yesterday."

Jared raised a brow. "Yesterday? What happened yesterday?"

"You made her one extremely happy woman when you and Dana announced your engagement."

Jared opened his mouth to say that he and Dana hadn't exactly announced anything. His mother had assumed the wrong thing and jumped to conclusions.

"I think your engagement actually gave her a new lease on life, a determination to handle whatever it is the doctor is going to tell her today and for that I'm grateful. You know how depressed she got the last time she had to undergo all those treatments. If that's the verdict again, and God knows I hope it's not, she'll be more of a fighter because she knows she has an important day to look forward to."

"What day?"

"The day you and Dana will marry," James Westmoreland said smiling. "That's all she talked about last night and this morning. She likes Dana and thinks she'll make you a fine wife. So do I. You selected well, Jared, and your timing could not have been better. If there's a chance your mother's cancer has returned and she has to undergo more treatments, she'll do whatever she has to do to retain her health to help plan your wedding."

"My wedding?"

"Yes, your wedding. Thanks, Son, for giving your mother a reason to fight whatever we might be up against. She'll be able to handle anything now since she knows one of her sons is finally getting married and will eventually give her a grandchild."

Jared stood in stunned silence. One thing was clear—he couldn't tell his mother the truth about Dana now.

Dana glanced through her peephole and raised an arched brow. She and Jared had said their goodbyes yesterday, so why was he standing on her front porch at six o'clock in the afternoon?

She swallowed the knot in her throat and tried to stop the rapid beating of her heart. It didn't take much for her to remember the kiss they'd shared, a kiss she had thought about most of the day. Instead of concentrating on her work, her mind had been filled with memories of Jared Westmoreland and how well he could kiss, not wanting to think about what else he was probably an expert at doing.

She continued to study him through the peephole. He was dressed in his business suit, which meant he had probably come straight from the office. He looked coolly reserved, in control and professional. Yet at the same time he also looked devastatingly male, incredibly sexy and he was affecting her in that man-woman kind of way. Swallowing hard, she blew out a slow breath and told herself to get a grip as she opened the door.

"Jared?" She sounded breathless, even to her own ears and could only imagine how she might have sounded to his. And the way he was looking at her with those dark, intense eyes wasn't helping.

"Dana, I hate to bother you but I need to talk with you about something important."

Her eyes widened. Whatever he had to say sounded serious. "All right."

She stepped aside to let him in and closed the door behind him. "Can I get you something to drink?" she asked, leading him to her living room.

"No, I'm fine," Jared said, but feeling anything but fine. His conversation with his father had thrown a monkey wrench into what he'd planned to tell his mother. Out of the corner of his eye Jared saw Tom race from where he had been near the sofa to the vicinity of the kitchen.

Jared took the seat Dana offered him on the sofa and watched as she sat in the chair across from him. With everything on his mind, the last thing he needed was to notice the skirt and blouse she was wearing. But he hadn't been able to look away when she sat down and he caught a glimpse of thigh that her short skirt revealed. Nor could he dismiss the way her blouse hugged her breasts.

"Jared? You said you had something important you needed to discuss with me."

Her words reminded him of the reason he was there and he met her curious gaze. "I went to see my mother this morning to clear up the misunderstanding, but things didn't go the way I had intended. She wasn't home so I talked to my dad instead."

Dana nodded. "And you told him the truth."

"No."

"Oh?" Dana said, confused.

"There seems to be a problem," Jared said, knowing that he needed to tell her everything. He decided to start at the beginning.

"Three years ago my mother was diagnosed with breast cancer. The lump was removed and she went through eight weeks of both chemo and radiation. She had good days and bad days and my father, brothers and I saw just what a remarkable woman she was."

The sincerity in Jared's words touched Dana. She could imagine what Jared, his brothers and father had gone through. After spending time with his family yesterday, it was easy to see just how much Sarah Westmoreland was adored by everyone.

"Anyway," Jared said, reclaiming Dana's attention, "I talked to Dad this morning and before I could tell him the truth about us, that there really wasn't an 'us,' he told me that the doctors found another lump in my mother's breast and if it's malignant, we might be talking about cancer treatments again."

"Oh, no," Dana whispered and immediately moved from her chair to sit next to Jared on the sofa. She reached out and touched his arm. "I'm sorry to hear that, Jared," she said in all sincerity.

He slowly stood and shoved his hands into his pockets. Her touch had elicited sensations throughout his body, sensations he didn't want to deal with right now. He had to stay focused.

"So am I," he said slowly. "However, knowing my mother, she will handle this like the fighter that she is.

But there's something I can do to make the fight a little easier for her."

"What?"

Jared met her gaze. "It's a crazy idea but at the moment I'd do anything for my mother, including lie."

Dana frowned, wondering what he would lie about. "Jared, what do you need to lie about?" she asked, rising from her seat to come stand in front of him.

His jaw muscles tightened and he briefly glanced away. When he met her gaze again, his eyes were intense and her breath caught at the tormented look she saw lodged there.

"Jared, what do you need to lie about?" she asked again.

He hesitated for a moment then said, "Us. My father made me realize just how happy my mother is, believing that I've finally decided to settle down and get married. Considering everything right now, I don't want to take that happiness away from her."

Reeling in confusion, Dana felt the need to take a step back. "What are you saying?" she asked, not sure she was following him.

"I have a proposal for you," he said, holding her gaze.

Dana swallowed. "What kind of a proposal?"

He gave her a not-so-easy smile. "That we continue to pretend we're engaged for a little while longer…for my mother's sake."

It would have been easier, Dana thought, if she had been sitting down instead of standing up. Nevertheless, the impact of Jared's words slammed into her.

She stared at him, looked for some sort of teasing glint in his gaze that indicated he was joking. But all she saw was an expression that said he was dead serious. Her mouth went dry and her heart began hammering in her chest. "Pretend we're engaged?" she finally found her voice to ask.

"Yes."

She inhaled slowly, deeply. "B-but we can't do that."

For several seconds he just looked at her. His shoulders straight, his gaze intent, clear. "Yes, we can. I never realized how much seeing at least one of her sons settling down meant to Mom. Now I do and I will do whatever I can to make her happy."

"Even get married?"

He frowned. "I hope I don't have to go that far, Dana. I think her believing I'm engaged will help at least until the worst part is over."

"And then?"

"Then I tell her things didn't work out between us and that we broke our engagement. It happens."

Deciding that standing wouldn't work, Dana sank back onto the sofa. "Trust me, I know all about broken engagements, Jared."

He sighed deeply. "I'm sorry. I know it's a lot to ask of you, considering your broken engagement with Luther, but I don't know what else to do."

The warmth in his gaze touched her. She wet her lips and leaned back in her seat, trying to absorb everything he'd told her. She couldn't help but admire him for his willingness to be a sacrificial lamb. He had no intention of ever getting married and had made that fact very clear. Knowing that, she was sure he didn't want to get involved in any of the trappings that led to marriage, either pretended or otherwise. Yet, for the love he had for his mother he would do what he felt he had to.

She lifted her chin and rubbed nervous hands against her skirt. "If I went along with you on this, Jared, just what would you expect of me?"

Jared moved to sit in the chair across from her. He was glad she was at least considering his proposal. "I've never been engaged before but you have. How were things with you and Cord?"

Dana sighed. "In the beginning I could actually see us spending the rest of our lives together. But now I have to admit that I wanted to marry him for all the wrong reasons. Love had nothing to do with it. He was handsome, successful—"

"And gay."

Dana raised a surprised eyebrow. "You knew?"

Jared shrugged. "I wasn't absolutely certain until I met you. The first thing that crossed my mind when you walked into my office was that no straight man in his right mind would let you slip through his fingers."

Dana couldn't help but smile at the compliment. "Thanks. I had no idea about Luther's sexual preference until recently. He came to see me and told me the truth. I can only appreciate that he broke our engagement when he did."

Jared nodded. "The two of you dated for over a year and you had no idea?"

Dana shook her head. "Not even a clue, although I realized afterward that the signs were all there but I ignored them."

Jared's brow furrowed. "What signs?"

Dana met his gaze. "Sex for instance."

A knot formed in Jared's throat. Silence grew between them—rather awkwardly, then he asked in a strained voice, "Sex?"

"Yes, sex. We decided that we wouldn't sleep together until after we were married."

Jared nodded. "Soo." He drew the word out, as if his mind was befuddled. "Whose idea was that?"

Dana bit her lip before answering. "It was Luther's idea and of course I went along with it since sex is overrated."

Jared's gaze was puzzled. It wasn't overrated in his book and he wondered how she could think such a thing. "Is it?"

"Yes."

She had him curious and he couldn't resist asking for clarification. "Why would you think that?"

She shrugged. "I'm not a virgin, Jared. I've had sex before and frankly I've never experienced anything worth losing sleep over."

He wondered who the men were who had disappointed her? He met her gaze, locked on it. "Maybe you haven't done it with the right person."

His softly decreed words spurred a hot little quiver that moved down the length of Dana's spine before blossoming out to every part of her body. She couldn't help wondering if a tumble between the sheets with him would make her think differently, then decided it was something she would never know. But still the thought caused a warm pool of heat to form in her belly.

She cleared her throat, needing to regain control of her senses. "Trust me, twice was enough. I can possibly understand the blunder in college, but I was involved with someone a few years ago and my opinion hasn't changed."

He leaned back in his chair, surprised that she was able to dismiss such a profound intimate act from her life just like that. "A few years ago? How far back was that?"

"Three years, closer to four."

Jared raised a dark eyebrow. "Are you saying that you haven't slept with a man in almost four years?" he asked, not sure if he had heard her correctly.

Dana lifted her chin, wondering how they had gotten on such a personal subject, but decided to answer anyway. "Yes, that's just what I'm saying."

Deciding she had given him enough information about herself, she said, "So tell me what things you expect us to do during this pretended engagement?"

He watched as she licked her lips again and wished it were his tongue at work instead of her own. And if that wasn't bad enough she crossed her legs and his gaze moved down the length of them, catching sight of the thigh he'd gotten a glimpse of earlier. His gut clenched when he thought of licking those legs and thighs.

Damn! He couldn't help but curse his bad luck. He was still way too attracted to her and the last thing he needed was a reason to spend more time in her company. In this situation, his mother's needs came before his own. But boy did he have needs and the enormity of those needs was hitting home—in this case right below his belt. He shifted in his seat to relieve the strain he felt behind his zipper. He could definitely use some sexual playtime and would've loved to suggest a purely physical relationship, with no emotions involved. But after her broken engagement, the last thing he wanted to do was take advantage of the situation by suggesting such a thing.

He cleared his throat. "What kinds of things did you and Cord do together?" He gave her a lopsided grin. "You've already told me about one particular activity the two of you didn't do."

Dana smoothed down her skirt. He watched as she then rolled one shoulder, which made his gaze move from her legs to her breasts. Suddenly he felt tension in his fingers. He would give just about anything to cross the room, lift her top, unhook her bra—if she was wearing one—and take his fingertips and graze her flesh before taking his mouth and latching on to a nipple and sucking—

"Luther and I went out a lot," she finally said, snatching back his focus. "We attended concerts, plays and parties. He was a sales representative with his company and often had to do a lot of socializing."

For several seconds Jared looked at her, thinking because of his clientele he often did a lot of socializing, as well. However, recently he'd cut back because of his workload. "We can do those same things. However, my mother is big on family gatherings and would expect us to also attend any. Can you handle that?"

Dana thought about how much she had enjoyed herself yesterday, almost too much. "Yes, I can handle that. Like I told you yesterday I think you have a wonderful family. But I'd hate deceiving them."

"It's for a good reason." A grin turned up the corners of his lips. "And I'd like to think that a pretended engagement with me wouldn't be so bad. I'm a pretty decent fellow."

Decency was the last thing on Dana's mind at the moment although she knew it shouldn't be. Heat was curling in her stomach just from staring at him. "How long do you think this pretended engagement will have to last?"

"That will depend on my mother's condition. If this is a false alarm, then we're only looking at a couple of weeks. But if we're looking at treatments, the last time they lasted for eight weeks. Will that be too long for you?"

Dana sighed. Any length of time would be too long as far as she was concerned. "No, umm, that would be fine."

Jared hated the uncertainty, the wariness he saw in her eyes but knew those emotions mirrored his own. He swallowed hard as he stood, shoving his hands in his pockets. "So, you're willing to keep on pretending to be my fiancée?"

Several tense minutes passed before Dana answered. She knew she might be asking for trouble, considering how attracted she was to him. But under the circumstances, there was no way she could turn him down. "Yes."

A relieved smile touched Jared's lips. He crossed the room and taking her hand he pulled her from her seat. "Thanks, Dana. Now I'm the one who's in your debt."

Having Jared in her debt stirred strange sensations in Dana's belly. She licked her dry lips, tried to smile and said teasingly, "That's okay. I won't demand anything that I don't think you'll be able to deliver." As far as she was concerned that left the options pretty wide-open.

Jared's gaze was drawn to Dana's lips; lips that were still moist from the recent sweep of her tongue. They stood so close that all he had to do was lean down and capture what he wanted most in his mouth and feast on it.

"So what's first?"

Her question made him lift a dark brow. He was about to say that a tongue-sucking kiss wouldn't be so bad, but changed his mind. "What's first?"

She smiled and he wondered if she knew what he'd been thinking, since his gaze was still glued to her lips. "Will your family need to see us together again any-time soon?"

He inhaled slowly. It's a good thing she'd asked. He had almost forgotten. "Yes. My brothers are remaining in town until Sunday, except for Quade. He had to get back to D.C. and flew out this morning. The folks are planning a cookout on Saturday evening."

Dana nodded. After spending time with Jared's fam-ily she knew his brother Quade worked for the Secret Service; Durango was a park ranger who lived in Mon-tana; Ian was a ship's captain whose luxurious riverboat cruised the Mississippi River and whose home was in Memphis, and Spencer was a financial advisor, who lived in the quaint and quiet community of Sausalito, California. Jared and his youngest brother, Reggie, were the only ones living in the Atlanta area.

"Do they know what's going on with your mother's health?" she asked.

Jared shook his head. "No, and knowing Mom she'll tell us as little as possible and only what she thinks we need to know. It's her way of protecting us. But I'm go-ing to tell them what I do know. We're meeting for din-ner at Chase's Place in an hour, and I'll call Quade with details later tonight."

"Will you tell them the truth about us?"

Jared shook his head. "No. The less people who know the better. I won't take a chance on one of them letting something slip. I don't want to give my mother any reason not to think our engagement isn't the real thing."

Dana nodded. Suddenly, she remembered something. "The ring!"

Jared frowned. "What about it?" His gaze went to her left hand. He had noticed earlier that she wasn't wearing it.

"I don't have it anymore. I took it to a jeweler during my lunch hour. I needed the money to pay off some bills."

Jared rubbed the back of his neck. Although he hadn't much cared for seeing Cord's ring back on her finger, that ring symbolized their engagement. "Where did you take it?"

"Garbella Jewelers. Do you think they still have it?"

Jared inhaled as he checked his watch. Garbella was a well-known jeweler that was frequented by a lot of high-profile individuals. "Even if they do, chances are the shop is closed now. I'll check with them first thing tomorrow. If they still have it, I'll get it back."

"And if they don't?"

Jared inhaled again. "Then I'll get you another one."

"B-but your family saw *that* ring. They will think it's odd for me to start wearing a different one."

Jared nodded, knowing that was true. "Then I'll have to think of a good reason to tell them why I changed it."

Dana nodded. Whatever reason he came up with would have to be good. "All right."

He checked his watch again. "I need to leave if I'm going to be on time to meet my brothers for dinner."

Dana focused on putting one foot in front of the other as she walked him to the door. Concentrating on him was too mind-boggling.

They stopped when they reached her door. She lifted her gaze to his. His eyes appeared darker, the same color they had become right before he'd kissed her yesterday.

"I'll call you tomorrow," he said huskily. "Will there be a problem with me calling you at work?"

"No, there won't be a problem. Wait, I'll give you my business card."

Jared watched as she quickly crossed the room to a table, tempted to let out a low whistle. Heat flared through him as his gaze wandered down her hips, thighs and legs. He took a deep breath and released it. Dana looked particularly sexy in her short skirt. She definitely had all the right body parts for it.

"This has all of my contact information," she said, returning to where he was standing.

He took the card from her and felt her shiver when their hands touched. "Thanks."

She cleared her throat when he didn't make a move to leave. "Is there anything else, Jared?"

Her question made him realize that, yes, there definitely was something else on his mind. "It would be a good idea to seal our agreement and I think this way is more appropriate than a handshake."

Before she could gather her next breath, he leaned down, slanted his mouth across hers and captured her lips in his, tasting her the way he had wanted to since entering her home. He heard her purr, felt her nipples tighten against his chest, all the way through his jacket, which only made him intensify his hold on her mouth as his tongue continued to devour her.

His heart missed a beat with every stroke of his tongue and the multitude of sensations he encountered while kissing her washed over him, short-circuiting whatever functioning brain cells he needed in order to think straight. As if they had a mind of their own, his fingers inched downward to touch her thigh and to trace his fingertips along the hem of the short shirt that had been driving him mad for the past half hour. A warning flared in his mind that this woman was pure, unadulterated temptation.

He released her slowly and fought to control his breathing, his desire and his lust. The only word he could think of was—wow! Seducing Dana Rollins was not part of his proposal but...

"Do you think that was wise?" she asked in a low whisper.

His gaze went to her lips, lips that were still moist from his kiss. He liked the sight of them and a smile touched the corners of his mouth. "Yes, in all honesty, I think that was the smartest thing I've done all day."

Jared glanced around Chase's Place as he sipped his drink. The meeting with his brothers had gone rather well and everyone was in agreement that they wouldn't hover over their mother as they had the last time. They'd also agreed that Jared's engagement had been perfect timing, although they were glad it was him and not them.

"You okay?"

He glanced up and stared into the dark eyes of his cousin Dare. He and Dare were only months apart in age and had always shared a rather close relationship. "Yes, I'm fine, considering everything."

Dare took the chair across from him. "Durango told me and Chase what's going on with Aunt Sarah. You know the family is here if you need us for anything, but I know things are going to be fine."

Jared nodded as he rubbed a hand down his face. "God, I hope so. I don't even know how Mom's appointment went today. I stopped by earlier but it was like getting blood out of a turnip. The only thing she wanted to talk about was my engagement."

Dare chuckled. "Well, you have to admit that has given the family something to talk about. Who would have thought that you of all people would decide to finally tie the knot?"

Jared frowned. "It's just an engagement, Dare."

Dare nodded. "Yes, but unless you know something that I don't, most engagements are the prelude to a wedding. You'll be marrying Dana eventually."

Jared took another sip of his drink as he met Dare's gaze over the rim of his glass. One thing he'd learned as a successful attorney was knowing whom he could trust to keep their mouths closed and whom he couldn't.

"The engagement isn't real."

Dare straightened in his chair. "Excuse me?"

Jared spent the next ten minutes telling Dare the entire story, including how he and Dana had originally met.

"Damn, a pretended engagement. You know what

happened when Shelly and I tried pretending a court-ship. It became the real thing," Dare said, remember-ing that time.

Jared stared at Dare. "That won't happen to me. You know how I feel about marriage."

Dare chuckled. "Yeah, and you know how I felt about it, too. But I can't imagine not having Shelly in my life now."

"The two of you had a history. And then there was AJ."

Dare nodded when he thought of the son he hadn't known about until Shelly had returned to town after having been gone ten years. "But even with all that, Shelly and I had to get reacquainted, find ourselves all over again. It was only then that we discovered that we still loved each other."

Jared snorted. "At work I see marriage at its ugliest—when two people who'd vowed to love each other till death do them part, face each other in a judge's cham-ber with hatred in their eyes, wanting to strip the other bare of anything and everything."

He chuckled before continuing. "The man I'm rep-resenting in court tomorrow is fighting his soon-to-be ex-wife for custody of the dog."

Dare shook his head sadly. "Don't let what you see in your profession discolor your opinion of marriage, Jared."

Jared sighed deeply. "It already has, Dare. This thing with Dana is for Mom's sake and there's no way I'm going to forget it."

Four

Dana glanced up from her desk and smiled when Cybil walked in. "Good morning."

"Umm, I don't know how good it is when you find out your best friend has been keeping secrets."

Dana raised an arched brow. "Excuse me?"

Cybil frowned as she crossed the room to stand in front of Dana's desk. "I don't know whether you're excused or not. News of your engagement made the society column today," she said, waving a section of the *Atlanta Constitution* in front of Dana's eyes.

"What!" Dana snatched the paper from Cybil to read the article. "I didn't know."

Cybil lifted a confused brow as she crossed her arms over her chest. "What didn't you know? That you're engaged to one of Atlanta's most eligible bachelors or that news of it would appear in today's paper?"

Hearing the hurt in her best friend's voice, Dana lifted her gaze from the article to meet Cybil's gaze. "I can explain."

"Do tell."

Sighing deeply, Dana stood and crossed the room to close her door. She turned to Cybil. "You better sit for this."

It took a full twenty minutes to explain everything. It would have taken less time had her best friend not interrupted every five minutes to ask so many questions.

"Boy, this is unreal. The entire office is buzzing. I hope Jared gets you a different engagement ring. People will have a lot to say if they see you wearing the same ring Luther gave you."

Dana blinked. Jeez. She hadn't thought of that since she hadn't expected news of their engagement going public.

"Who do you think tipped off the papers?" Cybil asked.

"I'm not sure but it really doesn't matter at this point." Dana knew it had to have been someone in Jared's family, probably his mother. The article had been nicely written, letting all Atlanta know that one of the city's most sought-after bachelors had gotten engaged to Dana Rollins over the Easter weekend. "I wonder if Jared has seen it."

Cybil smiled that little knowing smile that meant her mind was churning and usually in the wrong direction. "My guess is that he has." She chuckled. "I can assure you that everyone in this office has."

Dana looked at her with a concerned expression on her face. "What are they saying?" She knew if anyone knew about the office gossip it was Cybil. Not that she participated in it but everyone knew that her two staff members, Mary Bonner and Helen Fisher, were Kessler Industries' biggest gossips.

"They're perplexed since no one noticed a ring on your finger. But I think most of them are happy for you considering your breakup with Luther. They've gone from pitying you to envying you, especially since you've snagged the handsome and wealthy Jared Westmoreland."

Cybil's smile suddenly faded before she continued. "But, once you and Jared break this engagement everyone will go back to feeling sorry for you again and wondering how you could let two good men get away." She met Dana's gaze. "I have a feeling I'm not going to like the way this will turn out, Dana."

Dana wasn't all that crazy about how things were going to turn out, either, but it was too late now. She had given Jared her word. She opened her mouth to tell Cybil not to worry, that in the end things would work out okay when the phone on her desk rang.

Grateful for a moment's reprieve she reached over and picked it up. "Hello?"

"Good morning, Dana."

Dana couldn't help the flutter that suddenly went through her midsection upon hearing the husky, sexy sound of Jared's voice. It would not have been so bad if she didn't also remember their kiss yesterday, not to mention the feel of his hand on her thigh. His kisses were getting bolder, hotter and more earth-shattering.

"Good morning, Jared." She glanced over at Cybil then quickly looked away when she saw how intently her friend was watching her.

"Have you seen this morning's paper?" he asked.

She considered his question and glanced over at Cybil again. This time she gave her a pointed look, one that requested privacy. However, Cybil just sat there, ignoring her request.

Dana sighed after giving Cybil a mean look and answered Jared's question. "Yes, I've seen it."

"I apologize for not letting you know about it, but I didn't know myself until I read it this morning. It seems my mother's happiness is getting the best of her."

"Yes, it appears that way, doesn't it," she responded, not knowing what else she could say. From his tone he didn't seem upset. In fact there appeared to be an underlying tenderness and warmth in his voice. Or was she just imagining things?

"Will you have lunch with me?" he asked.

"Lunch?"

"Yes, at Jenzen's."

Dana's eyes widened. Jenzen's was an exclusive restaurant in North Atlanta. She'd heard that reservations had to be made well in advance, oftentimes weeks. It was certainly not someplace that she frequented.

"Lunch is fine. Do you want me to meet you there?" she asked. She hated admitting it but she was looking forward to having lunch with him and a part of her chafed at the thought of that.

"No, I'll come pick you up. Is eleven-thirty okay?"

She checked her watch. She had a meeting that would be ending a few minutes before then. "Yes, that will be fine. I'll be standing in front of the building."

"Okay. I'm looking forward to seeing you again, Dana."

Dana hung up the phone, closed her eyes and bowed

her head wondering how Jared could set off so many emotions within her. Emotions she'd never felt before.

"You okay?"

Dana snatched her head up. She had forgotten Cybil was still in her office. "Yes, I'm fine. That was Jared."

Cybil smiled. "So I heard." She then stood. "Enjoy lunch but promise me one thing."

"What?"

"That you won't get yourself in too deep. I saw the expression on your face when you heard Jared's voice."

"And?"

"And I don't want to see you get hurt again."

Dana waved her hand in the air, dismissing Cybil's concerns. "Hey, I know the score between me and Jared. I'm merely doing him a favor."

"Some favor. I've seen him before and he's a hottie, every woman's fantasy. How far do you plan to take this pretended engagement? Will the two of you get intimate?"

Dana swallowed. "Intimate?"

Cybil grinned. "Yeah, you know, sleep together. Share the same pillow. Bump and grind. Have orgasms."

The scenario that suddenly played out in Dana's mind had her heart beating so fast she thought she would pass out. "Of course not!"

"Are you sure about that?"

Before Dana could respond Cybil opened the door and walked out.

Jared gazed across his desk at Sylvester Brewster, hating to admit that he hadn't looked forward to their meeting.

At twenty-eight, Sylvester was a well-known recording artist who toured the country performing songs that consistently hit the number-one spot on any billboard charts.

Unfortunately, in addition to his blockbuster hit records, Sylvester had this serious problem of wife-boredom. The man changed wives like he changed shirts, but one thing was always certain, when he cast one off to take on another he was extremely generous with the alimony.

Jared sighed deeply. It seemed Brewster was ready to dump the third Mrs. Brewster for wife number four. The only glitch in his plans was that his current wife wanted more alimony than Sylvester was willing to give her, which had his client fuming.

"I don't want to give her one penny more, Jared. Baby or no baby."

Jared lifted a brow. This was the first he'd heard of a baby. "Your wife is pregnant?"

"She says she is and could well be, but it makes no difference since it's not mine."

Jared's brow inched even higher. "Do you know that for certain?"

"Yes," Sylvester said with a frustrated sigh. Then lowering his voice as if the office might possibly be bugged, he whispered. "I'm sterile, man. As sterile as a new hospital on opening day. It's the result of a childhood illness. So if Jackie's claiming she's pregnant with my child then it's not mine."

Jared sighed deeply. "If what you're saying is true, that won't be hard to prove with a paternity test."

"It is true and nobody is going to try to lay a claim that I'm their baby's daddy."

Jared watched Sylvester pace around the room. "Should I be surprised if you remarry within hours of your divorce being final?" he asked, knowing that was usually the norm.

Sylvester stopped his pacing and met Jared's gaze and he actually saw deep hurt in the man's eyes. "No. I loved Jackie and wasn't involved with anyone else. With her there was never a dull moment, man, always excitement. She was something else. For the first time in my life I fell in love and look what happens. And that's what makes it so bad. Jackie refuses to level with me even after I told her I was sterile and there was no way that baby was mine. Now she's claiming that I'm the one who's lying." In anger, he hit his fist on the desk. "Women can't be trusted, man. I'll never marry again."

Jared was silent for several moments before he nodded, although not for one minute did he believe Brewster would keep that promise. Marriage was an addiction to Brewster, one Jared was glad he didn't have.

"I'll contact Jackie's attorney next week. I'm sorry things have come to this because I thought the two of you made a nice couple. But if you're certain she's been unfaithful then—"

"I'm certain. I don't have the name of the man she was involved with but there was an affair. Her pregnancy is proof enough."

Half an hour later, Jared had completed dictating information into his recorder for his secretary to transcribe. Standing, he walked over to the window and looked out. This was another morning that wasn't going well. First off the bat, while drinking his coffee and reading his newspaper, he had come across the article announcing his engagement to Dana.

Then he had arrived at Garbella Jewelers as soon as their doors had opened only to find that they had already sold Cord's ring. He had ended up purchasing another ring and was racking his brain for an excuse to give his family as to why Dana would no longer be wearing the original one. In his opinion, the only saving grace was that the one he'd purchased had a diamond that was twice as large and was closer to what he imagined Dana might like.

He sighed as he checked his watch. It was time to leave if he wanted to pick Dana up for lunch on time.

Dana.

She was becoming a major problem. He didn't consider his proposal a business arrangement. Otherwise he would have drawn up formal documents between them. She was merely doing him a favor. They had exchanged favors before so he knew she wouldn't go back on her word. But there were factors thrown in the equation that he hadn't counted on.

Like his strong attraction to her. And the dreams he'd been having.

Last night he had actually dreamed about her legs and thighs, in addition to other parts of her that he hadn't seen. In his dream, he had gotten all the way under that skirt she'd been wearing yesterday, first caressing the soft skin of her inner thigh before letting his fingers slide inside her damp heat. And then there were the kisses they had shared. His mouth tingled just remembering the taste of her on his tongue. Just thinking about her body parts and their kiss made his arousal thicken against his zipper.

For the life of him he couldn't understand this unusual brand of sexual chemistry. It wasn't as if he didn't come into contact with beautiful women. He'd once dated a former Miss Georgia for heaven's sakes. So what was there about Dana Rollins that had him counting the minutes, the seconds before he would see her again?

He hated admitting it, but the women he'd dated in the past were usually self-centered, aggressive and accustomed to getting their own way. But not Dana. She was strong-willed, but although he had witnessed her explosive temper the first day they'd met, he knew she was a kind person. She had cared enough about his mother's welfare to go along with his outrageous proposal of a fake engagement.

And speaking of his mother, Sarah Westmoreland definitely liked Dana. Yesterday she had gone so far as to suggest they have a short engagement and a June wedding. He had immediately burst a hole in her bubble by letting her know that was out of the question. But still, seeing the look of happiness on his mother's face made him realize that no matter what, this pretense of an engagement with Dana was worth it.

Jared rubbed the top of his head as he remembered his conversation with Dare last night. He'd meant what he told his cousin. Nothing, and he meant nothing, would develop between him and Dana, no matter how attracted he was to her. It wouldn't be the first time he was attracted to a woman and it wouldn't be the last.

His meeting with Sylvester had reaffirmed his conviction that marriage wasn't all that it was cracked up to be and he intended to enjoy his remaining days on this earth as a single man.

* * *

Whatever pep talk he'd given himself an hour earlier stood on shaky ground when lust took control of his body. A jolt of sexual awareness raced up his spine when he pulled up and saw Dana standing in front of her office building.

She was the model of professionalism with her upswept hairdo and two-piece navy-blue powerhouse suit. Her knee-length skirt was longer than the one she'd been wearing yesterday, thank goodness. He wasn't sure he'd been able to resist putting his hands on her bare thighs again.

She opened the car door and slipped inside. "Hi, Jared."

He swallowed. The air was suddenly charged with sexual energy. "Dana."

He watched as she snapped her seat belt in place and tried not to notice how her skirt inched up a little, exposing those thighs and long, shapely legs he had dreamed about. He breathed in the scent of her, a womanly fragrance that was just another sexy detail for his fantasies.

"Were you waiting long?" he asked, adjusting his sunglasses and trying to control the rapid beat of his pulse.

She smiled as she pressed back against the car's leather interior, unintentionally showing more leg and thigh. His heartbeat raced right along with his pulse. "No, I walked out a few minutes ago. Your timing was excellent."

His grip tightened on the steering wheel as he eased into traffic. There were cars everywhere, and he needed to focus on his driving and not on how firm Dana's breasts looked against her blouse. And heaven forbid he thought about her mouth and how it had parted under his yesterday, inviting him to deepen their kiss.

"Were you able to get the ring?"

He allowed his gaze to travel over to her when he came to a traffic light. "No. They had already sold it so I had to buy another one." He watched as that sexy mouth twisted into a frown.

"What will we tell your family?"

"That I liked this one better." Jared sighed deeply. That was the truth. He still didn't understand why it bothered him to see Cord's ring on her finger. Probably because he knew the whole story and felt she'd deserved better.

He glanced over at her again and watched as she pursed those same sexy lips and saw the frown lines appear between her prettily arched eyebrows. "It's going to have to sound convincing when you tell them that," she said.

He chuckled as he shifted his gaze from her to stare straight ahead. "I'm an attorney, remember. My job is to be able to convince people."

A grin spread over her face. "Yes, you're right. Sorry, I forgot." She was quiet for a few moments then said, "It was for the best anyway."

He lifted a brow. "What was?"

"Getting a different ring. That article in the newspaper this morning has my office buzzing and of course everyone wanted to see my ring. It didn't occur to me that had I kept Luther's ring they would have remembered it."

Jared blew out a breath. That hadn't occurred to him, either. "What did you tell them?"

"That it was being sized."

He nodded. "Sorry you were put in a sticky situation like that."

She shrugged. "No problem. I just hadn't expected that announcement to appear in the papers. I thought I only had to pretend this engagement for your family, not all Atlanta."

"Will that cause you problems?" he asked, seeing how deep the extent of their deceit was going.

"No, not as long as it doesn't cause you any problems."

Jared's forehead furrowed in confusion. "What kind of problems?" The car came to a stop at another traffic light and he glanced over at her.

"Your livelihood. You're one of Atlanta's most eligible bachelors. Being engaged takes you off the market for a while."

One corner of his mouth curved slightly. Being engaged would definitely change his life, but only temporarily. "Umm, I guess it does, but only for a short while." He held her gaze, studied it, looking for something, anything that would indicate she wished otherwise.

He let out a slow breath when he didn't see anything. He was glad that she understood that nothing could and would develop between them. Those hot and heavy kisses hadn't meant a thing and he didn't want her to get lust confused with love. Not that he thought that she would. But still, he had to be certain they were on the same page.

Their engagement was a game and nothing more.

* * *

Dana was very much aware of the man who sat across from her in the exclusive restaurant, and had been since he had picked her up for lunch. The twenty-minute ride had been taxing when all she could do was remember what Cybil had asked about their physical relationship.

The thought that Jared might expect them to become intimate was confusing and something she knew they should discuss. But she hadn't been able to bring it up. During the drive they had talked about several things but had played it safe and avoided mentioning their engagement. Instead they had discussed the weather, the new movies that had come out over the Easter weekend and Georgia's recent elections.

She wasn't surprised to learn that he lived in Country Club of the South, an affluent subdivision in North Atlanta, in the suburbs of Alpharetta. The houses were priced in the millions and a number of celebrities and sport entertainers lived there.

"You're quiet."

Dana glanced up and met Jared's dark gaze. He had been watching her. Something flickered in the depths of those eyes that made her catch her breath, made something unbearably hot flow through her veins. She picked up her coffee cup to break eye contact. Cybil had warned her not to get in too deep and she had assured her friend that she wouldn't. When she said it she had been sure, confident, but now all that assuredness was skating on thin ice. Jared Westmoreland was not a man to take lightly. He had made it clear in the car that their arrangement was temporary. She was smart enough to read between the lines. He'd been letting her know that he was not a man to whom any woman should give her heart. "Umm, I was just thinking about things," she finally said.

"Are you thinking of changing your mind about this?" he asked quietly.

She looked up and met his gaze again. Although she couldn't read his expression she really didn't have to. She knew how much keeping his mother happy meant to him and she couldn't help but admire the lengths he would go to for her. "No, I'm not, but there's something I think we do need to discuss," she said softly.

He nodded. "All right. What would you like to talk about?"

Dana sighed deeply. Even now she felt it, the hot, sultry passion that radiated between them, that was always there whenever they were together. It was that passion, the sexual chemistry, the strong attraction that let her know she was walking on dangerous ground with him.

"Our kisses," she said, almost in a whisper. But the sudden intensity of his expression let her know he had heard her.

"Our kisses?"

She looked down at her coffee cup again when she saw the desire that darkened his eyes. After pulling in a deep breath she met his eyes again. "Yes."

He tilted his head at an angle that seemed to make his gaze focus in on her. Only on her. "What about our kisses, Dana?"

Her palms were beginning to feel sweaty and her insides felt like molten liquid with his question. She wished she could respond by stating that she wanted more of them, but knew that would definitely be a wrong answer. She could barely handle the ones she had gotten so far.

She cleared her throat. "I—I don't want them to lead to other things."

He stared at her a moment then asked, "Does your definition of *other things* include what you and Cord never got around to doing?"

She bit her lip and tried not to look at him. "Yes."

After a brief pause he said, "Dana?"

The way he said her name only forced her to look at him. "Yes?"

"Why does the thought of making love to me bother you?" he asked softly.

She felt a tiny pull in the pit of her stomach at the silky timbre in his voice. The thought of making love to him didn't bother her but it did keep her constantly off balance and made her imagine some wild and purely wicked things. It also had her conscious of her sexual state more so than ever.

She hadn't slept with a man in almost four years. That fact hadn't bothered her before. It had seldom crossed her mind. Now it did. She was experiencing wants and desires for the first time and had a feeling that a sexual experience with Jared would obliterate her long-standing belief that sex was highly overrated. She knew to ask for a purely platonic relationship would not be realistic. After all, she was a woman and he was a man unlike any other she'd ever known. He had a way of making her feel attractive, wanted and desired.

The silence between them had stretched long enough

and she knew that he deserved an answer. "It doesn't bother me, Jared. It confuses me."

He didn't say anything for a long moment, and then he said, "Although I want to share a physical relationship with you, would it help to give you my word that I won't push you into doing anything you aren't ready for?"

She frowned. "That's just it, Jared. How will I know when I'm ready for anything? All of this is rather new to me."

"You'll know, Dana. You'll know better than anyone," he said softly. "I'd be telling a lie if I said I didn't want you. Even now, I want you so bad I ache with the thought of having you. I'm not Luther Cord. But since our engagement is not the real thing, I won't expect or assume anything. How far we take things will always be up to you."

"Thank you."

A warm shudder of awareness passed through them as well as an understanding and acceptance of their predicament. Jared recognized the depth of desire in her eyes although he knew she did not.

A part of him wanted to curse the two fools that had made her think that lovemaking wasn't worth losing sleep over. There was no doubt in his mind that if he ever made love to her, sleep wouldn't be involved. just constant pleasure, gratification and enjoyment all night long.

"And as far as the kisses," he said. "They can be dangerous but necessary. Engaged couples do kiss, so a certain degree of open affection will be expected. And although we don't have to kiss when we're alone, I enjoy kissing you and hope you enjoy kissing me, as well. But if you prefer that—"

"Kissing is fine," she interrupted. "Now that we have an understanding. Like you said earlier in the car, our pretended engagement is only temporary."

The drive back to her job was done mostly in silence. There really wasn't a whole lot left to be said. They understood each other and the situation they were in.

"Here's the new ring," he said, when he parked the car in front of her office building and she'd unsnapped her seat belt.

She accepted the gray velvet box and opened it up. He heard the gasp that escaped her lips and watched as she blinked then blew out a long whistle. "Wow!" She quickly looked over at him. "Don't you think this is a bit too much?" She took it out of the box and slipped it on her finger. It was a perfect fit.

Jared's mouth tilted into a smile. For some reason he liked seeing that ring on her finger instead of the one Luther had given her. "No. If I'm going to convince my family there was a good reason for me to change rings then seeing is believing. I'll just tell them that I saw this one and thought it would look better on your hand. They'll buy that story."

Dana nodded. Anyone would. Jared hadn't just given her a ring, he had given her a rock. It had to be the most beautiful ring she had ever seen and the design was unique. She knew it most have cost him a fortune. Of course she'd return it when their fake engagement was over. She held her hand out in front of her. "It's simply beautiful, Jared."

Smiling at her, Jared reached out and captured her

hand in his and brought it up to his lips. "I'm glad you like it."

Dana swallowed when he released her hand. Jared kissing her hand had been totally unexpected and she felt a sizzle all the way to her toes.

"Now I have a question for you," he said quietly before she could gather her wits.

"What?"

"Are those two people friends of yours? They have been standing there and staring at us ever since I pulled up."

Dana followed his gaze and saw Mary Bonner and Helen Fisher standing at the entrance of the building, pretending to be engaged in deep conversation. "They're co-workers, not friends, and two of the biggest gossips in the building."

A mischievous glint appeared in Jared's eyes. "Then how about if we gave them something to gossip about."

Dana smiled. She knew where he was coming from although she also knew his plan included another kiss. But they had said at lunch that engaged couples were expected to publicly display a certain degree of affection. And if she was totally honest, she wanted to feel his lips against hers again. "Okay."

Dana's breath hitched when Jared reached over and nearly pulled her out of the seat into his lap and captured her mouth with his. Her body respond instinctively. The kiss was soft, gentle, slow and hot. It was also thorough—so methodically complete that she felt blood race all the way down to her toes. Kiss number three was everything the last two had been and more. He was making her concentrate on his taste and the slow build-up of desire that was flowing through her. His tongue tangled with hers and she felt desire and urgency consuming him and overtaking her, as well. His hard shaft was pressed against her stomach and she knew for him to have gotten that aroused meant they were definitely putting on a show.

He slowly pulled back and she placed her hands against his muscled chest as she tried to restore her breathing to a normal pattern. Her insides felt like mush and heat, and an intensity she had never felt before settled smack between her legs.

"So…do you think that worked?" he asked, lowering his head to lightly taste the sides of her mouth while placing her back in her seat.

His breath was warm, his tongue moist and her control was steadily slipping. "Yes," she said, barely able to get the single word out. "I'm sure they won't be able to stop talking about us."

Five

Lanterns furnished a translucent glow to the Westmorelands' backyard. Chairs and tables were assembled in front of the lake and an area had been cleared for dancing. There was the mouthwatering smell of ribs and chicken cooking over charcoal, and a huge tent covered a number of tables that were loaded with all kinds of delectable foods.

In addition to Jared's brothers and cousins, former classmates and friends had been invited to the cookout. Dana sighed as she glanced around. She had been introduced to everyone as Jared's fiancée and when asked when the wedding would take place she would smile and say they hadn't set a date, but doubted it would be anytime that year.

"I can certainly see why Jared preferred this ring," Madison was saying, pulling Dana's attention back to the conversation around her. Jared had been right. His family had accepted the reason he'd given about the change in rings without question.

"It certainly makes a statement, doesn't it?" Tara inserted. "It's such a beautiful ring. The other one was really nice but this one is more like Jared."

Dana was about to ask Tara what she meant when Jared's mother appeared by her side smiling. "Are you enjoying yourself, Dana?"

Dana returned the older woman's smile. "Yes, and thanks for inviting me."

"No thanks needed. You're family now."

Dana nodded. She hated deceiving the older woman.

"You've been Jared's best-kept secret. Not once did he let on that he was seeing anyone seriously, in fact I assumed the opposite. For the longest time he claimed that he would never marry. That just goes to show what can happen when a person falls in love. And it's plain to see that he's fallen hard," Sarah added chuckling. "He hasn't taken his eyes off you all evening. I've never seen him this attentive to anyone before, and I'm supremely happy about it."

The thought crossed Dana's mind that continuing that "supreme happiness" was the only reason Jared had propositioned her to take part in this sham of an engagement. She wondered why that had her feeling oddly let down.

"What do you think of Jared's theater room?" Jayla asked a few minutes later when the topic had switched from Dana and Jared to the movies that were now playing at the theaters.

Dana looked puzzled, not knowing what Jayla was

talking about but knowing it was something that she should. "His theater room?"

Shelly grinned. "You mean he hasn't told you about all the remodeling he's done? When was the last time you were over at his place?"

Dana didn't know what to say. To say that she had never been to Jared's house would definitely seem odd. She opened her mouth to make something up when suddenly Jared materialized by her side. He leaned over and kissed whatever lie she was about to fabricate off her lips.

"Come dance with me, sweetheart." He glanced over at his mother and his female cousins. "Excuse us for a moment," he said before leading Dana off to the make-shift dance floor.

Taking her into his arms he looked down at her. Holding her close, he liked the feel of her breasts against his chest and the perfect fit of her body against his. "Was my rescue quick enough?" he asked, smiling and searching her face. He wished they were alone so he could end the torture and kiss her the way he'd thought of doing all evening. "I was on my way over to get you when I heard Jayla's question about my theater room."

Dana tilted her face up, and chuckled quietly. "Yes, you were quick enough. It would have seemed awfully odd for me not to know about your house. Is there something I should know about this room so when the next person asks I can be prepared?"

Jared lightly skimmed his fingers down her bare arm. He felt her shiver and liked the fact that he had caused it. But then, she was causing things to happen to him as well—like the unbearable ache that was building in his groin. He wanted her, and with their bodies so close, there was no way she wasn't aware of his aroused state. "I like watching old movies and I've installed a state-of-the-art home theater system, the latest in plasma technology. The sound system is three times clearer than in a movie theater." In truth, he didn't want to talk about his theater room. What he really wanted to do was nudge Dana's body even closer to his, latch on to her mouth, ignore everyone around them as he kissed her crazy.

Dana smiled up at him. "Umm, I'm impressed."

It was on the tip of his tongue to tell her that besides being impressed she was also hot. Her heat was burning him, further arousing him and making him want her even more. He had to give her a lot of credit. She knew how to make a statement in anything and everything she put on her body. Tonight she was wearing a V-neck green dress that stopped just above her knees. The way the dress hugged her curves showed just what a small waist and well-toned bottom she had. Her outfit had been murdering his senses ever since he had picked her up and was still killing them. He stifled a groan. Dana Rollins was subtle, but provocatively sexy.

"I think it's time you visited my home so you won't be left in the lurch again. I'd love to fix dinner for you at my place," he said, leaning down and caressing her lips with his. He looked for any reason to kiss her and didn't mind performing for an audience. At least that's what he tried to convince himself. But he knew he wasn't performing, liking the feel of her mouth against his. He couldn't wait to get her alone.

She gave a soft laugh as she gazed up at him. "Can you cook?"

He grinned. He was on a low simmer even now. "Yes. So what about this weekend?"

Her smile faltered. "I'll be going away this weekend, to Brunswick. Saturday is my mother's birthday and I want to put flowers on her grave."

His gaze focused on her eyes and he saw that the sparkle had gone. He had also heard the sadness in her voice and knew going back to where her parents were buried would be hard on her. "My thoughts will be with you this weekend," he said softly. He pulled her close against him. Moments later he asked, "What about dinner at my place the week after you return?"

She looked up at him and smiled. Knowing he would be thinking of her this weekend touched her. "I'd love to," she said just as the music ended.

It was close to one in the morning when Jared returned Dana to her home. Although it was late she invited him in for coffee and, not surprisingly, he accepted. They had shared several slow dances, and each time she had been fully aware of his aroused state, and just as certain he had been aware of hers. At one point, he had guided her to a darkened area of the yard and had been seconds away from kissing her when Durango had cut in. She had seen the murderous look in Jared's eyes, but his brother had merely laughed it off. But now she was home, he was here with her and they were alone.

As soon as the door closed behind him, he pulled her into his arms and she went willingly, wanting his kiss as much as he wanted to give it. The mating of their mouths seemed endless, his tongue was torture of the most brazen kind.

Lust ignited within Jared with the way Dana's body seemed to dissolve into his, and at that moment he had to touch her, taste her, further stroke the heat building between them. He stroked his palms over her shoulders and upper arms, hearing the sound of her whimpering and moaning in his mouth. He continued to kiss her hungrily, greedily, needing her taste as much as he needed his next breath. And she clung to him, kissing him in return, sending him more over the edge than he already was.

Moments later he pulled back before he was tempted to sweep Dana into his arms, take her into the bedroom and make love to her all night long.

He met her gaze. Saw the heated look in her eyes and his entire body immediately reacted. Leaning forward he kissed the bare skin of her neck, liking the way it tasted, tempted to taste her all over. Beneath his tongue he felt her shiver, felt himself get harder and knew if he didn't stop what he was doing, temptation would get the best of him.

But he didn't want to stop. He wanted her with an intensity that almost took his breath away and had him working on minimum control and very little else.

With much effort he leaned away to look at her. He would give anything to take that dress off her body and get her naked. Then he would take his hands and cup her breasts and after driving her wild with his tongue on her nipples he would get on his knees and kiss a path all the way down her body until he reached—

"Jared?"

Her soft whisper interrupted his thoughts. "Yes?" he responded, his voice husky, thick with sexual need.

"I think you should leave now."

He took a deep breath, losing his calm as he'd lost his control. He knew that asking him to leave was her way of letting him know that she wasn't ready for the bedroom yet, and if they continued at this pace he would definitely take her there. He heard her words but still a part of him—that part that wanted her, needed her—felt inclined to push.

"You want me, Dana. I can see it in your eyes. I can hear it in your breathing. I can taste it in your kiss. Why deny what you want?"

She placed her fingers to his lips. "Yes, I want you, but I can't become involved in a meaningless affair, Jared. As soon as your mother is given a clean bill of health you'll be ready to break this fake engagement and walk away. Do you deny that?"

She stared at him, waiting for an answer, and he gave her the only one that he could give. "No, I don't deny it."

"Then Counselor, not giving in to my desires is the right thing," she said, taking a step back away from him.

He frowned. "I can't give you more, Dana," he said, annoyed with the circumstances surrounding them.

"And I haven't asked you to give me more, Jared. But then you shouldn't expect me to give you more than I can, either."

Exasperated, he rubbed a hand down his face. "Why make things complicated?" he asked, clearly frustrated.

"That's the last thing I want. In fact I'm trying not to complicate things. If I thought for one minute that I could handle an affair with you then we would be in my bedroom right now, getting it on. But I can't," she said feeling just as frustrated as she knew he was.

Jared sighed and reached out and pulled her tensed body into his arms. "Look, I'm sorry. I didn't mean to push, especially when I said that I wouldn't. But I want you in a way that I shouldn't. I don't think I've ever wanted a woman as much as I want you."

Jared was consumed by a need to do nothing but hold her. He didn't know how long he could hang on with their pretense but knew he had to see it through. Somehow he needed to build an immunity against the wants and desires that overtook him whenever he was within ten feet of her.

Moments later, he pulled back and looked at her. "I'll be out of town this week and won't be returning until late Friday night. When are you leaving town?"

"Early Saturday morning. It's about a seven-hour drive because I like to take the scenic route and spend the night on one of the Sea Islands."

He draped an arm casually around her shoulders. "Which one?"

"Jekyll Island. It's beautiful and close to Brunswick. My parents used to take me camping there each year."

"When will you be back?"

"Probably late Sunday evening."

Jared nodded. If she was leaving early Saturday morning that meant he wouldn't see her again until she returned. He leaned down and gently kissed her once more. And now since they were alone, he nudged her

body closer, liking the feel of his palms on her backside. He felt the tips of her breasts harden against his
chest and reacted by pressing his erection low against
her belly. The sensations spreading through him were
relentless and fierce, and he plunged his tongue even
deeper into her mouth, tasting her, devouring her, driving them both crazy with desire. "Miss me while I'm
gone," he whispered, when he finally released her
mouth. He knew he had to leave. If he stayed one
minute longer, he wouldn't be able to control his actions. "Goodnight, Dana."

He then opened the door, stepped out and closed it
quietly behind him.

Dana sighed deeply and leaned back against the
door, missing Jared already. She had to be realistic
about her pretended engagement or else she would fall
head over heels in love with him. And that was something she could not and would not let happen.

Two hours later Jared was in his bed wide awake, flat
on his back and staring up at the ceiling. Maybe he was
moving too fast with Dana and should slow down. He
had a reputation for being an in-control kind of guy, but
lately he'd been losing control whenever it came to her.

He wished there was some way he could close his
mind and thoughts to wanting and desiring her so much
but was finding it impossible. He never intended for their
pretended engagement to lead to a brief affair. It was hard
getting his mind back in focus, and nearly impossible to
remember that their relationship wasn't real.

Even his brothers and cousins had teased him relentlessly tonight about how hard he had fallen for her. And

on top of that, his father had taken him aside and asked if he was sure he could wait another year for a wedding.

Jeez. Was it blatantly obvious to everyone just how much he wanted her? And for a while tonight, while introducing her to neighbors and friends, he had actually considered Dana his.

His.

His heart slammed against his ribs at the thought of anything so foolish. He'd never considered a woman his because he didn't want any woman to consider him hers. He was only interested in the physical side of a relationship and not the emotional. He had enough of emotional entanglements with the cases he handled.

Crossing the room to his dresser, he opened a drawer and pulled out a pair of swimming trunks. Removing his pajamas bottoms he eased the trunks over his still aroused body thinking that a swim in the pool might cool him off and help calm his mind.

It was almost dawn when Jared returned to his bedroom. His body was exhausted but his mind still swam with thoughts of Dana.

The next few days were busy for Dana. The buzz around the office about her engagement had settled down, however, word had quickly spread about the rock she was wearing on her finger. More than once, a curious co-worker had stopped by her office to get a look at it. Tara had been right. Jared certainly knew how to make a statement. It was just too bad the statement he was making was not true.

On Tuesday morning, she got an unexpected call from Jared's mother.

"Mrs. Westmoreland, this is a pleasant surprise," she said smiling, and meaning every word. The more she was around the older woman, the more she liked her, mainly because she reminded her a lot of her own mother—friendly, outgoing and devoted to her family.

"Dana, how are you dear? I was wondering if you could join me for lunch at Chase's Place?"

Dana lifted an eyebrow as she checked her watch. "Sure. Would noon be fine?"

"It would be perfect. Do you know how to get there or do you need directions?"

Dana chuckled. "Yes, I know how to get there. It's a favorite for a lot of my co-workers. I've even eaten there a couple of times myself. The food is fantastic."

"Yes it is. Chase still uses some of the Westmoreland family's secret recipes."

A few hours later as Dana drove to Chase's Place, she couldn't help but think about Jared. He had left a message on her answering machine last night to let her know where he'd gone, which was definitely information a fiancée should know should anyone ask. He'd even left the number where he could be reached should she need him.

But she didn't need him.

Unfortunately, she had to remind herself of that very thing pretty often these days. She shouldn't make more of what was going on between them than there really was. Even he had admitted that when this sham was no longer needed he would walk away without a backwards glance.

So why don't you just enjoy whatever moments you have with him? an inner voice screamed. *Why does*

*there have to be regrets after goodbyes? You may not
want to fall in love with him but you're halfway there
already. Admit it.*

A lump formed in Dana's throat. She refused to admit anything. Hadn't she learned a cruel lesson about
depending on others for her happiness? First there was
the loss of her parents and then Matt and Luther, two
men who had walked into her life and then walked
out…just like Jared intended to do.

She'd known the score going in so, unlike the others, when he did his disappearing act she would be
ready.

Dana saw Jared's mother sitting at a table the moment she entered the restaurant. She thought Sarah
Westmoreland was a beautiful woman at fifty-seven
with short black hair she wore in an Afro. She had dark
brown eyes, dimples in both cheeks and a medium-size
figure. Her smile was always gracious and sincere and
Dana knew she wouldn't just be a mother-in-law to her
sons' wives, she'd be like a second mother.

"Mrs. Westmoreland," Dana said as she approached
the table.

"Dana, it's good seeing you again," the older woman said, standing and giving her a huge hug. From the
first, Dana had decided that Jared's mother was a warm,
loving person. And there was so much excitement in the
older woman's voice on seeing her that no one would
think they had just seen each other on Saturday, which
was only three days ago.

"And it's good seeing you, as well," Dana responded, thinking she could get used to all the love and affection the woman generated.

Once they took their seats Mrs. Westmoreland smiled and said, "How are things going at work? Jared mentioned you're a landscape architect. That sounds like a real interesting profession."

Dana smiled. "It is. My parents owned a nursery so I got interested in trees, plants and shrubs fairly early in life." She paused while the waitress gave them glasses of water and their menus. Then she continued. "A lot of people don't understand the involvement of a landscape architect whenever a building is constructed. My job is to make sure the outside area is not only functional but also beautiful and compatible with the natural environment. "

Sarah Westmoreland nodded. A sad look then appeared in her eyes. "Jared told me about your parents' passing. That must have been devastating for you."

Dana nodded. "Yes, it was. I was the only child and was very close to my parents. Their deaths left me without any family."

Sarah smiled warmly as she reached out and covered Dana's hand. "Well, all that's changed. Like I told you the other night, the Westmorelands are your family now and I want you to feel like a part of us."

"Thanks." Dana felt a deep lump in her throat. She hated deceiving Jared's family, although she knew it was being done for a good reason. Dana looked down to study her menu. There was no way she could look at Mrs. Westmoreland right now.

"So, dear, have your heard from Jared since he's been gone?"

Dana glanced up. At least her answer wouldn't be a total lie. There was no reason Mrs. Westmoreland needed to know that, although Jared had called, she hadn't actually spoken with him. "Yes, he called last night."

"I'm sure that he's missing you."

Dana smiled. She doubted Jared was missing her but she definitely was missing him, although she didn't want to. She spent her days trying not to think about him, but found herself doing it anyway.

Dana took another sip of her water and decided to shift the topic off her and Jared. "So, how have you been?" she asked the older woman.

Sarah smiled. "I'm fine. I'm sure Jared told you that I had breast cancer a few years ago and that recently the doctor found another lump. But there's a chance it's nothing more than fatty tissue. I'm having it removed in two weeks and then we'll know the results. Whatever it is, I'll deal with it. I'd be the first to admit chemo and radiation were hard on me, but if I have to go through them again, then I will. I'm a fighter, Dana. My family gives me a lot to fight for. And I'm looking forward to the day when I become a grandmother," she said excitedly. "Jared told me that the two of you wanted children."

Dana inwardly thought that that was a lot for Jared to have said, considering they had never discussed children, not that they really planned on having any together.

At that moment the waitress walked up to take their orders and Dana was grateful for her timely arrival. A pretended engagement was bad enough. The last thing she needed to think about was having Jared's baby.

Six

On Wednesday evening after feeding Tom, Dana curled up in her favorite chair to read and relax. It had been a hectic day. One of her clients had been difficult, upset that the city's ordinances would keep him from constructing a huge man-made waterfall on the property where he planned to erect his company's building.

Not wanting to think about the problems that had plagued her that day any longer, she switched her thoughts to the lunch she'd shared with Jared's mother yesterday. Afterward she felt a special bond toward the woman that she shouldn't feel and didn't deserve. She wondered what his family would think when they ended their engagement, which just might be two weeks from now if his mother's test indicated her lump was benign.

She glanced up from her book when she heard the

sound of the doorbell. It was barely six o'clock and she wasn't expecting anyone. Cybil and Ben had decided to take the week off to visit his brother in Tennessee.

The moment she glanced out of the peephole, her heart stopped. It was Jared. She hadn't expected him back until late Friday. Taking a deep breath she slowly opened the door. "Jared, you're back."

He leaned in the doorway, and they stared at each other for a moment before he said, "Yes, I finished up earlier than expected but I haven't made it home yet. I thought I would drop by here first."

Dana was curious why he would come by her place before going home. The only thing she could think of was that maybe he'd heard about her having lunch with his mother and wanted an update. But then he could have called her to get that information. She cocked her head and looked at him. He stood in front of her door with such a strong, manly presence, she barely found her voice to say, "Come on in."

Jared sighed deeply as soon as he walked into Dana's home and the door closed behind him. Her expression had indicated that she was surprised that he had come straight from the airport. Hell, he was surprised himself. He had missed her like crazy and the only thing he could think of was that when the plane landed he had to see her.

He looked at her, thinking that the late-afternoon sun that shone through the living-room window seemed to make Dana all aglow. He could only stand there and stare at her, thinking just how beautiful she looked while wearing a pair of shorts and a T-shirt that said I'm Yours. Boy did he wish. Every fiber in his body stirred at the thought.

Being alone with her was causing his brain to short-circuit and he felt heat slowly move around in his belly. He breathed in her womanly scent and watched all the questions that were forming in the depths of her dark eyes.

"Did you miss me?" he finally asked. Needing to know. Wanting to know. Hoping like hell that she did and at the same time not understanding why he cared if she had or hadn't.

Dana tried shoving aside the shiver that raced up her body. Yes, she had missed him. Damn him for asking. It didn't take much to recall what happened the last time they were together, in this very same room—the heated kiss that had had her tasting him for days afterward. She could lie to him and say that she hadn't missed him or she could tell the truth.

But first, before she would admit to anything, she had a question of her own. "Did *you* miss me?"

Slow amusement lit the depths of Jared's dark eyes at the way Dana had turned the tables so he would be answering her question instead of her answering his. He smiled. She was about to get an answer he doubted she was ready for. But she *had* asked.

"Oh, yeah, I missed you. I thought about you every day, although I didn't want to. I also dreamed about you every night, and in those dreams I did all those things that you aren't ready for me to do. I made you realize how wonderful it can be when two people—the right two people—make love."

He crossed his arms over his chest and after a short moment of silence he said, "Okay, I've answered your question so how about answering mine. Did you miss me?"

They stood facing each other, both intently aware that something had shifted between them. They were doing more than wavering on the edge; they were hanging on for dear life. The chemistry between them was more powerful than ever, explosive, and deliriously potent. At that very moment, Dana wondered what could be the worst thing to happen if she told him she *had* missed him, *and* with the same intensity he'd claimed and so vividly stated.

She had also dreamed about him each night and each time he had invaded her sleep he had made love to her. In the deep unconsciousness of her mind she had easily and willingly given everything to him and he had pleasured her in ways she could only imagine. She had felt safe in knowing that when she awoke, she could face reality. But a secret part of her yearned to see how close her dreams were to the real thing. Could he actually make her reach an orgasm that many times? Even reaching one would be a first for her.

"Dana?"

He reclaimed her attention. "Yes?"

"I asked if you missed me," he said softly.

Yes, he had. And she would try to answer him, although not in the same depth that he'd done. "Yes, I missed you. And I dreamed about you, too." She watched as his nostrils flared and she heard his quick intake of breath.

He slowly uncrossed his arms. "And in these dreams…"

Dana tilted her head and looked at him. "That's for me to know."

A smile touched the corners of his lips as he took a couple of steps toward her. "And for me to find out?"

She held his gaze. "I doubt that you can."

Jared lifted a dark eyebrow and Dana immediately knew her mistake. She had given him a challenge.

She couldn't help but let her gaze lower to his fly and felt herself stirred by what she saw. He was an unashamed, very aroused man. She swallowed deeply and snatched her gaze back to his face. She tried desperately to remember the last conversation they'd had here in this house. Hadn't it been a mere five days ago? But for the life of her, her mind was getting fuzzy, heated and filled with more desire than she could handle.

"I thought we decided not to complicate things," she said, trying to hold on to her sanity as much as she could.

Another smile curved his lips. "Finding out just what kind of dreams you had is the most uncomplicated thing I'll ever do. Uncomplicated and very satisfying for the both of us."

Dana saw the look of intent in his eyes and took a step back. She folded her arms beneath her breasts. "I won't sleep with you, Jared."

She saw him lift another eyebrow as he regarded her. She realized too late that she had made another mistake because she had intentionally given him another challenge.

"And I told you, Dana, that I won't push you into doing anything you aren't ready for."

She frowned slightly. "And what do you think you're doing now if not pushing."

He lifted a shoulder in a shrug. "Making an attempt

to destroy your theory that sex is overrated. But, I don't have to sleep with you to do that."

"You don't?"

"No."

Dana swallowed, saw the intensity in his gaze. She believed him. Now she understood why he was one of the most successful attorneys in Atlanta. "You're smooth," she decided to say, meaning every word. He was using every weapon at his disposal to break down her defenses. There was the huskiness of his voice, the look of heated desire in his eyes and his very obviously aroused body. Even his stance was provocatively sexy.

"I'm also thorough, Dana."

She swallowed again and wondered why on earth was he making this difficult? But then another part of her couldn't help but be curious. Could he really prove that sex wasn't overrated without sleeping with her? What would he do to prove it? Just thinking about what approach he might use stirred her up. Boy, was she tempted to find out. And his penetrating stare wasn't helping matters. He was definitely rattling her resolve and kicking good common sense straight out the window.

"You once asked me how you would know when you were ready for me, Dana," he said softly, reclaiming her attention—not that he'd fully lost it. "You might not be ready to sleep with me but I think you're ready for this. What do you think?"

Dana sighed. How could she know if she was ready for *this*, when she didn't have a clue what *this* entailed. But she did know that whatever it was, it would be something she would regret not experiencing if she sent him away.

Her gaze swept over him thoroughly one more time before she made her decision. "I think you might be right."

He nodded slowly. "It's your call."

There was considerable silence. Then finally, Dana retraced the distance between them and stood before him, met his gaze, held it. Everything inside of her stirred with heated lust. "Then I'm making it."

Jared smiled. He liked everything about her—her smile, her body, her mind. He shook his head. Forget about what he liked. It was time to focus on what he wanted. Dana Rollins was one hell of a seductive woman.

And he wanted her.

He had told her they wouldn't sleep together, but he intended to drive her as far over the edge as she could go. "Do you trust me, Dana?"

She nodded, realizing what he was asking and why he was asking it. She stared deeply into his eyes when she answered. "Yes, I trust you."

"Good." And then without wasting any more time, he swept her into his arms and quickly moved in the direction of her bedroom.

"But—but you said we wouldn't sleep together."

He gazed down at her. "We're not. We're going to play a game."

She clutched the front of his jacket to hold on to since he was walking so fast. "A game?"

"Yeah. My version of Red Light, Green Light."

"Oh."

Jared smiled thinking of the possibilities as he placed her on her bed. He was glad Tom was nowhere around, and just to make sure the cat didn't show up later, Jared walked over to the bedroom door and closed it.

He sighed when he turned back to Dana and saw the look of uncertainty in her eyes. He had to remain composed for both their sakes. "Do you want to change your mind about this?" he asked softly, respecting her doubts and fears. It wasn't about taking care of his body's needs but rather, introducing her to how wonderful things could be between a man and a woman.

She met his gaze as she settled back in the bed. He tried not to concentrate on her legs and thighs and was finding it near impossible not to. "No, I don't want to change my mind, Jared."

"Are you sure?"

She nodded. "Yes."

He moved away from the door and came to stand by the foot of the bed. "Then let me tell you about this game," he said, removing his jacket and tossing it on a chair in her room. "The light will always be green, letting me know it's okay to move forward. But at any time you feel rushed, overwhelmed or want me to stop, all you have to say is red light. Understand?"

She slowly nodded, although at the moment the only thing she fully understood was that he looked good standing at the foot of her bed, especially in his extremely aroused state. She wondered what he would be getting out of this since they wouldn't be sleeping together.

He must have read the questions in her eyes. "This isn't about me, Dana. It's about you. I can handle things and how I do so is only for me to know."

"And for me to find out?"

Jared laughed. The first real good laugh he'd had in a long time. "Yes, maybe one day."

He moved slowly toward the bed and braced one knee on the mattress. He pulled her into his arms and whispered, "Green light." Bending his head he captured her lips. The moment his tongue slid inside her mouth, heat consumed him in a way it never had before. It was hard to believe that he could want a woman this badly, with this much intensity and desire. He kissed her the same way he had dreamed about and was thrilled that she was returning his kiss with equal fire, with an urgency that only made him want her even more.

Suddenly, she broke off their kiss. "Red light," she said breathlessly, barely able to get the words out.

He stopped kissing her and met her gaze. "I needed to breathe," she explained. He didn't say anything but continued to look at her. He watched as she took slow uneven breaths and licked her lips. Moments later she said softly, "Green light."

He was ready. He captured her mouth again in his and pulled her up against his erection, wanting her to not only see but to feel what she did to him. He palmed her bottom, and then moved his hand to stroke her thighs. He slowly shifted his hand to the area between her legs, wanting to touch her and not intending for a pair of shorts to stand in his way.

He pulled back. "Red light," he said and smiled when he heard Dana whimper in protest. He met her gaze. "May I remove your shorts and T-shirt?"

Dana stared at him for a moment, melted under his seductive gaze and whispered, "Green light."

Jared's breathing almost stopped. She had given him

the go-ahead and he intended to take it to the max. Leaning toward her, he whipped the T-shirt over her head and tossed it across the room, leaving her in a black lace bra. His mouth itched, his tongue thickened at the thought of how her breasts might look. Whether he got to find out or not would be her decision. But he was a man who was used to compromising. If she wanted to keep her scrap-of-nothing bra on, he could taste her breasts without taking anything off.

He shifted his attention to her shorts, reached out and when she lifted her hips he slowly eased them down her legs to reveal black lace panties. He'd never appreciated black lace so much until now. He tossed her shorts aside to join her T-shirt. Then on his knees he leaned over her and gently lifted her bra to uncover her breasts. Dana whimpered, but didn't protest. At that moment he couldn't have looked away even if someone yelled "Fire." He had to actually fight to control his breathing. She had the most beautiful, luscious pair of breasts he had ever seen on a woman. They were full and firm.

He met her gaze. She was looking at him just as hard as he was looking at her. "The light still green?" he asked softly, in a shuddering breath.

"Yes."

One day he would show her his undying gratitude. But for now…he reached out and cupped her breasts, tracing a fingertip around the dark tip of her nipple, first one and then the other. He heard her sharp intake of breath and it heated him more. Leaning over he captured a nipple gently between his teeth and holding it captive he used his tongue to make her as hot as he was.

Dana curled her hand into a fist as feelings she had

never encountered before slammed through her. She could barely stay on the bed, with the sensations Jared was evoking heightening her gratification to a level of pleasure she hadn't thought existed. He was taking one breast, and then the other, tugging at a nipple drawing them into his mouth, torturing them with his tongue.

She closed her eyes, feeling herself being pulled under the most sensual haze ever. A moan escaped her throat. She heard it and knew he heard it, as well. But he didn't stop doing what he was doing. She had dreamed about him doing this to her but her dreams weren't anything like the real thing.

When she felt him release her nipples she opened her eyes and met his heated gaze. "Light's still green?" he asked huskily.

She nodded. She couldn't speak. "Then lie back for me," he requested softly.

She did what he asked and her stomach clenched when he began tracing a trail of kisses from her breasts all the way to her navel. And if that wasn't bad enough, she felt his fingers easing inside her panties, setting off a deep throb between her legs. Any thoughts of resisting were forgotten. She had given him the green light to do as he pleased; and it seemed his most fervent desire was pleasing her.

Jared felt her heat. He smelled her scent and his erection got harder, increased in length. He ignored the tremendous ache in his groin as he forced his mind to concentrate on Dana. He eased his finger inside her panties and found her wet heat.

He let his fingertips have their way and Dana automatically parted her legs for him. Then he went to work, stroking her back and forth, over and over again, glorying in the sounds of her moans, the sensuous catch in her breath, her purrs, the way she groaned his name.

Without missing a beat with his fingers, he eased his mouth away from her navel and back to her lips, nipping at them, tracing his tongue from corner to corner. And then he went into her mouth with an urgency that was earth-shattering, increasing the stroking of his fingers, feeling her getting wetter, hotter, slicker. She couldn't stay still and wiggled her bottom and pushed up against his fingers.

"Jared!"

And then it happened. He felt it and continued what he was doing but lifted his head to look at her. He thought that she was beautiful while having an orgasm and knew at that moment he would want to see her in the throes of passion for the rest of his days.

For the rest of his days. He blinked, quickly pushed that thought away and wondered what craziness would make him even think such a thing. Dana had no place in his future. No woman did. But knowing that couldn't keep him from reaching out and pulling her into his arms and kissing the sweet taste of sweat from her forehead as her spasms slowly subsided.

He felt his erection throbbing and he fought back his own need for release. This was her time and as far as he was concerned, it was only the beginning. One day his time would come. Meanwhile…

He brought his head down and captured her mouth. Needing the taste of her with an urgency that he didn't quite understand. The kiss was quick, hard and deeply satisfying. She sighed into his mouth and his groin tightened at the feelings it stirred.

"How about going out with me tomorrow night," he whispered close to her ear moments later when she lay curled in his arms while he held her. In the back of his mind he could still hear her cry out her response to what he'd done to her.

Dana gazed up at him. How on earth could he think of tomorrow when she was still sensually stirred up from what had happened today? She hadn't known such pure hot pleasure existed and all with the use of his fingers. She didn't want to think about what would happen if they were to actually make love. In her mind she would die a slow death, several times over.

"Tomorrow?" she said, barely getting the word out.

"Yes, tomorrow. We can go out to eat, take in a movie and then afterward walk around Stone Mountain. Anywhere that doesn't have a bed. You, lady, are too much temptation. I can only take so much."

She shifted in his arms and gazed up at him. Maybe it was her hormones talking, but when it came to Jared, she wanted to take all he had to give and not think of the consequences. "Okay, wherever you want to go is fine. I'll let you decide."

He nodded and she watched as he eased from the bed to stand. He still had his shirt and pants on and looked as rumpled as she felt. She then remembered something very important. "That was my first you know."

He glanced over at her and raised an eyebrow. "Your first what?"

She hesitated, not knowing exactly what to say or how she should say it. But as he waited for her response she knew she had to tell him of his gift to her. "My first orgasm."

He gazed at her. Shocked. When it wore off, he dropped back down on the bed and pulled her into his arms, made her look at him. "I'm glad you shared your first with me," he said huskily, meaning every word.

She smiled. "Me, too."

Jared leaned over and kissed her again, and she felt his desire but also a tenderness that overwhelmed her. He slowly pulled back, stood and crossed the room to get her shorts and T-shirt. Coming back over to the bed he took the time to redress her. He didn't say anything and neither did she.

When her clothes were back in place she looked up at him. He reached out and slid a slow finger across her cheek. "I'll call you tomorrow."

"Okay." She then remembered she needed to tell him something else. She sat up straight and pushed the hair out of her face. "I had lunch with your mom yesterday."

He startled. "You did?"

"Yes. She called and invited me to have lunch with her at Chase's Place. She's so nice, Jared, and I really hate lying to her even though I know why we're doing it."

He nodded and fixed dark eyes on her. "Don't worry about it. Things will work out."

She gave him a shaky smile. "I hope you're right." But a part of Dana wondered how things could possibly work out when the one thing that she hadn't wanted to happen was happening anyway.

She was falling in love with Jared Westmoreland.

Seven

"**W**hat do you mean there's a possibility the child is mine?" Sylvester Brewster shot to his feet.

Jared slid the documents out of the envelope and across the table as he met the man's shocked gaze. "What I'm saying is that according to this medical report, based on the physical that you took last week, you're not sterile. In fact you have a very high sperm count."

Sylvester sank back into his chair. "B-but what about that childhood disease?"

"According to Dr. Frye, you may have had a low sperm count at one time but there's no indication you were ever sterile and nothing is documented in your medical history."

Sylvester shook his head, squeezed his eyes shut. "This doesn't make sense, Jared."

"You were misinformed. Whatever doctor told your parents you were sterile evidently misdiagnosed your condition. And since you are capable of producing children, there's a strong possibility that your wife's child is yours…just like she claimed."

Sylvester dropped his head on Jared's desk with a solid thump. "Damn, Jared, you don't know what all I said to her, all the things I accused her of."

Jared nodded. He could just imagine. "All that medical report does is indicate you aren't sterile. It doesn't prove the child is definitely yours. The next step is to order an amniocentesis."

Sylvester lifted his head. "A what?"

"An amniocentesis. It's a test that's done to the mother, generally during the fourteenth to twenty-fourth week of pregnancy to determine the paternity of an unborn child. We can have the results back in two weeks."

"No."

Jared lifted a brow. "No?"

"No. I've humiliated her enough. Did you see the tabloids this morning, man? Someone leaked my accusations to the papers and it's all in the news. Jackie is never going to forgive me for not trusting her."

Jared knew that was a very strong possibility. That very morning, he had spoken to Jackie Brewster's attorney, who had informed him that his client was hurt and upset, but would be more than happy to undergo a paternity testing. Once it's proven that Sylvester *was* her baby's father, she planned to sue him for every cent he had for publicly humiliating her.

Jared met the man's stare. "I suggest you don't make decisions about anything today. Take the report home and read it and then let's meet one day next week to discuss how we're going to proceed."

"I don't want a divorce, Jared. I want my wife back. I was wrong. I should have trusted her. I love her and I owe her a huge apology."

It was on the tip of Jared's tongue to remind Sylvester that two weeks ago, when he was certain he was sterile, he'd been singing a totally different tune. "Yes, that might be the case but I doubt a reconciliation is what Mrs. Brewster has on her mind right now. According to her attorney, she doesn't want to see or talk to you. As your attorney, I suggest you don't try to contact her until we've determined our next course of action."

Thirty minutes later, Jared was standing at the window in his office looking out. Sylvester had gotten himself in a real mess this time. The love he had for his wife had gotten overshadowed with mistrust. Was there any hope of the marriage surviving? For Sylvester's sake, he hoped so.

Jared sighed deeply as he switched his thoughts from Sylvester's problems to his own. He could sum up his troubles with one name.

Dana.

There were very few times in his life when he'd been faced with a situation that he couldn't figure out or adequately handle. And this was one of those times. Frustrated and annoyed, he drew in a deep breath. What had happened between them yesterday had touched him in a way that it shouldn't have. And what was so extraordinary about it was that they hadn't made love. Yet he had shared something with her that he hadn't ever shared with another woman.

While in that bed kissing her, touching her, he had felt as if she was the only woman he could ever want. The only woman that he wanted in his lifetime. Damn, but this pretended engagement was going to his head, zapping him of common sense and confusing the hell out of him.

It hadn't been easy to leave her last night and before he'd left he had sat on the bed and pulled her into his arms. For the longest time she had sat curled up in his lap with neither of them saying anything. The only sound that had intruded on their moment had been the soft meowing of Tom at the bedroom door. Even now, just thinking about her made his chest tighten with a need he wasn't used to.

He glanced down at his watch. He would be picking her up at six for dinner. And the only thing he could think about was seeing her again and kissing her with the desperation he felt. Dana Rollins was definitely getting under his skin.

"Would you like some more wine?"

"No, thank you, Jared." Dana bit down softly on her lip and tried not to stare at him. Every time their gazes met she felt a tiny pull at her heart.

"Are you ready for your trip this weekend?"

She met his gaze and forced a smile. "Yes, I'm ready. Since it's not a long trip, a lot of packing isn't necessary."

"I'd like to go with you."

Dana's eyes widened in surprise. "Why?"

Jared shrugged as he sank back in his chair. That was a good question since he had just made the decision. "I don't like the idea of you driving so many hours alone."

Dana couldn't help but appreciate his concerns. "It's something I do every year, Jared. And when my father's birthday comes around in September I'll be doing it again. No big deal."

Jared frowned. To him it was a big deal. "You shared my father's birthday with me and I want to be there to share your mother's birthday with you."

Dana glanced down at her wineglass. How could she not fall in love with him when he said something like that? She slowly lifted her head and met his gaze. "Thanks, Jared, but that's not necessary."

He smiled. "It is to me." He leaned closer over the table. "Besides, it's been years since I've been to Jekyll Island and I'd like to go there again."

Dana inhaled deeply. The part of her that was fighting what she was feeling for Jared wanted to tell him to find another time to go, that she needed time alone, time away from him, but she couldn't say that. She decided to use another approach. "I don't think it's a good idea for us to go out of town together, Jared."

"Why? Because of last night?"

Dana felt a jolt to her body at the memories, something she'd tried to downplay all day. She had played Red Light, Green Light, many times as a child but never like that and never with a playmate like Jared. He gave the game a whole new meaning. "That, among other things," she finally said softly. *And please don't ask me what those other things are,* she silently screamed. *I don't want you to know that I'm falling in love with you.*

"I know your thoughts on us sleeping together, Dana. You've been pretty clear on that and I think I've been straightforward in saying that I won't push you into doing anything you're not ready for. But this isn't about us sharing a bed."

Dana met his gaze. "Then what's it about, Jared?"

His eyes held hers. "It's about me being with you and enjoying your company. I like talking to you."

Dana knew he was holding something back. She had been around him enough to know when something was bothering him. She could feel it. "Is there something else? Is everything all right with your mother, Jared?"

He stared at her for a moment and after taking a deep breath he said, "I spoke with Dad earlier today and he said that Mom got a call from the hospital. There was a cancellation and they were able to schedule her outpatient surgery for next week instead of waiting two weeks."

Dana nodded. "That's good news, isn't it?"

Jared heaved a long sigh. "Yes, but…"

She waited for him to finish. When he hesitated she asked, "But what?"

He dragged a hand over the back of his neck, seemingly frustrated. "But nothing. I guess I'm just remembering how it was the last time."

Dana understood and reached out, took his hand in hers and held it tight. A part of her was glad she was here with him and that he was sharing his innermost fears with her. "All we can do is hope and pray for the best, Jared. And I know you, your father and your brothers appreciate and love your mother. Your willingness to pretend to be engaged just to make her happy proves how much you care."

Dana let go of his hand and sat back, hoping she'd

said something to make him feel better. She could tell he was worried but a part of her believed Sarah Westmoreland would come through this just fine.

"How did your parents meet?" she decided to ask, wanting him to dwell on happier memories.

She watched the corners of his lips turn up into a smile. "My mother and Aunt Evelyn were best friends growing up in Birmingham, Alabama. When they graduated from high school, Aunt Evelyn came to Atlanta to visit her aunt. During her first week here she went on a church outing and met Uncle John. She wrote back to my mom telling her she had fallen in love and asking her to come to Atlanta to be her maid of honor. She'd only known her new groom a little more than a week!"

Jared gave her a lopsided grin. "My mother, being the levelheaded person that she is, caught a bus that same day and arrived in town to talk some sense into Aunt Evelyn. She didn't think love at first sight was possible."

Dana chuckled. She could just imagine his mother doing that. "What happened next?"

Jared smiled. "She got to town, met John's twin brother, James, and fell for him just as hard as Aunt Evelyn had fallen for my uncle. My parents got married within a couple of weeks of my aunt and uncle's wedding."

A smile softened Dana's lips. "That's a beautiful love story."

Jared shrugged as he took a sip of his drink. "Yes, it is, isn't it?" It had been a long time since he had thought about how his parents had gotten together. They had met and fallen in love immediately. They hadn't thought about any of the ups and downs they would face. They

had simply loved each other and had wanted to be together. To them that was all that had mattered.

Sighing deeply, Jared glanced down at his watch.
"Are you ready to leave? Tonight is a nice night to walk
around the park. Would you like to do that?"

"I'd love to." Dana met his gaze, suddenly understanding his need to get away for a few days and making a quick decision. "I'd love your company this
weekend if you're serious about going with me to
Brunswick."

He smiled warmly. "I am."

She returned his smile. "Good."

Over an hour later Jared returned to Dana's home and
walked her to the door. She turned and looked at him.

"I enjoyed being with you tonight, Dana," he said,
taking her hands in his.

Jared's words, spoken in a soft husky voice, immediately reclaimed Dana's attention. And his touch sent all
kinds of sensations escalating through her body. "I enjoyed being with you tonight, as well," she said honestly. "Would you like to come in for something to drink?"

He shook his head. "No, it's late and I'd better go."

Dana let out the breath she'd been holding. A part of
her was glad he had turned down her invitation but then
another part was disappointed. She wanted to be alone
with him. She wanted him to kiss her again. And more.

She gazed up at him. "Then I guess we need to say
good night."

He gently tugged on her hand, pulling her from the
shaft of light shining down on them from the porch
light to a darkened area of the porch. She saw the kiss
coming, wanted it and moaned with pleasure the mo-

ment their mouths touched. Intense heat, overwhelming pleasure shot through her as his tongue masterfully mated with hers. She could only stand there and grip his solid shoulders for support as he took her to another world, feasting on her lips as if they were a meal he had to savor.

When he finally released her mouth she had to rest her head on his chest while she caught her breath. Jared Westmoreland could incite passion with a mere touch, a kiss, a look. And she had felt his solid hard erection pressing against her, through the material of her skirt. He was as aroused and as she was.

"Go into the house, Dana," he whispered against her lips after slowly releasing her. He took a step back.

She swallowed. His voice sounded hoarse, husky, and sexy. "Good night, Jared," she said and turned to unlock the door.

"Good night. I'm playing pool with my cousins and Reggie tomorrow night, but I'll be by early Saturday to pick you up. Is seven o'clock a good time?"

She turned to him and wished she hadn't. He had stepped back into the light and stood tall and looked handsome. His coat jacket was slung over his shoulder and held in place by his fingertips. The pose was unforgettably sexy.

She cleared her throat. "Yes, seven will be fine. I'll be packed and ready to go."

"All right."

Giving him one last look, Dana opened the door and slipped inside. She leaned against the closed door when she heard him walk away, and then moments later the sound of his car leaving.

It was only then that she was able to slow down the beating of her heart and breathe easy again. How would she ever survive a weekend alone with Jared Westmoreland?

Jared stood next to Dana and watched as she placed the bouquet of fresh flowers on her mother's grave.

When he had picked her up bright and early she had been friendly and perky, the complete opposite of him first thing in the morning. He could be a bear until he downed at least two cups of coffee. But she had opened the door all smiles, packed and ready to go.

During the drive they had talked about a number of things including early memories of the time she'd spent in Brunswick, backyard cookouts with her parents, going to church together as a family on Sundays and how she would greet her father at the door whenever he'd come home from work.

They stopped once for lunch, but otherwise they had driven straight to town. Once there they had found a florist shop to purchase the flowers and had then driven to the cemetery.

He had considered remaining in the car, letting her have her private moments, but a part of him wanted to be with her, to stand beside her and let her know that he was there and that he cared. After a few moments of silence she straightened and automatically, as if it was the most natural thing to do, she leaned up against him and he offered her the support she needed.

He wrapped his arms around her shoulders and held her close to him. "You okay?" he asked softly.

She tried to smile and the effort made Jared's throat tighten when he saw the tears in her eyes. "Yes, I'm fine. It's just harder this year more than ever because today would have been their thirtieth wedding anniversary. They got married on my mother's birthday."

Dana gazed up at him through misty eyes. "Mom always reminded Dad that she should get two gifts that day instead of one, and of course he always came through. They loved each other very much, Jared. In a way I think if they had to die it was better for them to go together. I can't imagine my father living a normal life without my mother or vice versa. They had dated since high school and were so close, so connected. But the beauty of it all was that they never made me feel like I was an outsider. Dad used to say that I was the greatest gift of their love."

Jared nodded, knowing she needed to talk, get her feelings and emotions out. He was jarred into the realization that some marriages endured. Her parents' had. So had his parents' and his aunt and uncle's marriage. For a long moment they didn't say anything, they just stood there, needing the silence. He admired her ability to do this, to come here twice a year and face the pain of her loss with the poise and grace he had come to associate with her. He couldn't imagine getting a call, saying that both his parents were gone—unexpectedly, just like that. And if that were to happen, at least he had his brothers, the entire Westmoreland family. Dana had no one.

But today she had him and he wanted her to know that. He reached for her hand, linking their fingers. He was glad he had come, pleased that he was with her in this place, sharing such a personal and private moment. It meant a lot to him that it was his shoulder she was leaning on, his hand she was holding. And for the very first time in his life he felt he was in danger.

Danger of losing his heart.

"Thanks, Jared."

He tipped his head and looked at her. "You don't have to thank me, Dana. At the moment, I can't think of any place I'd rather be than here with you." And he meant it. "Ready to go?"

"Yes, I'm ready."

Back in the car, Jared headed toward Jekyll Island. His secretary had made hotel reservations for them. If Jeannie had thought it odd that he'd told her to get two separate rooms she hadn't said anything.

He glanced over at Dana. "Are you hungry?"

She shook her head. "No, in fact I think I'm beat and going to take a nap when we get to the hotel and check in."

He smiled. She might feel tired, but she didn't look it. She looked great dressed in a pair of slacks and top. He spared her another quick glance. There hadn't been one time he'd seen her that he hadn't gotten turned on by what she was wearing.

Jared could see them in one bed, in each other's arms doing a number of things, and taking a nap wasn't one of them.

Dana woke up from her dream with a start, her breathing uneven, a wave of heat slowly building and touching her in her most intimate places. She closed her eyes to recapture the moments when she had imagined

Jared in bed with her, naked with his arms around her, holding her, and his aroused body pressed intimately against her pelvis, sending her over the edge as he tried to connect with her.

She had felt the dampness of his skin, the perfection of his muscles as they clenched beneath her palms and the texture of his chest hair rubbing against her breasts, hardening the tips.

She had experienced all those things. But only in her dream.

Dana pulled herself up in bed and inhaled deeply as she pushed her hair from her face. She'd known she was a goner when he had walked her to her hotel-room door. After saying that he hoped she enjoyed her nap, he had lifted her palm to his lips and placed a kiss at her wrist. And it hadn't been your typical wrist kissing. His hot, wet tongue had slid over her wrist and then he had gently sucked the area, leaving a mark. His mark.

She glanced down at her wrist. She still felt the heat. She then looked across the room at the closed door that separated his room from hers—a shield, a barrier, a connecting door. But if it were to open…

She wondered if he was there. Had he taken a nap, as well? Had he dreamed of her as she had dreamed of him?

Slipping out of bed she stood and decided it was time to take part in some sort of physical pleasure. The other night Jared had shown her just what her body had been missing. He had given her a taste of what pleasures were out there if she decided to indulge.

Visiting her parents' graves had made her realize just how unpredictable life could be. You could be here today and gone tomorrow. Life held no guarantees, there were no promises. There were no forevers.

There was only the moment. And you had to seize it to get what you wanted, capture it, slow it down and take advantage of it, make every second count.

Jared had always been honest with her, totally up-front. She knew how he felt about serious involvements. And she knew that no matter what, he had no intentions of changing his mind about that. Next week, if things worked out with his mother, he would walk away, just as surely as there was a sun shining in the sky. But dammit, she refused to let go without at least having something to look back on and remember from their time together.

She turned when she heard the gentle knock on the connecting door. Tightening the belt of her silk robe, she crossed the room and slowly opened it. Jared was there. She inhaled gently, breathing in the manly scent of him. He stood tall, handsome, hot and sexy. His features were sharp; the eyes that were holding hers were keen. She felt her heart beat violently at such profound sexiness.

Regardless of whether Jared was dressed as a million-dollar businessman or wearing faded jeans and a chambray shirt, as he was now, he looked like a man any woman would want both in and out of her bed. The man any woman would want to strip her naked, kiss her sense-less and make love to her with an all-consuming passion.

And the man a woman would want to give her heart to on a silver platter.

Suddenly, she knew she was no longer falling in love with him. She *had* fallen in love with him. She loved him with every sense of her being, with every ounce of blood flowing fast and furious through her veins, with the breaths she was now taking—slow and uneven. Over the past couple of weeks she had seen more than a glimpse of him. She had gotten to know him as a man of high intelligence and intense integrity. He had proven it that day when she had shown up at his office, spitting fire and mad as hell. Luther had been his client, yet he had gone beyond what some would consider ethically proper and had given her off-the-record advice to save herself from further embarrassment, humiliation and financial ruin. And for that she truly appreciated him.

She also appreciated the way he showed her that sex wasn't overrated, and that with the right person it could be a definitely satisfying and gratifying experience. And even now, here, today, he had come to Brunswick with her. He had stood beside her and had given her his shoulder to lean on when the pain of losing her parents had resurfaced.

"I hope I didn't wake you from your nap, Dana."

She swallowed deeply as she stared up at him. "No, I'm awake." *In more ways than one,* she thought. "Did you sleep?"

He smiled, and his smile sent sensations oozing through the pit of her stomach. "No, I found that I couldn't sleep after all and decided to catch a tennis match on television."

He glanced beyond her and she knew his eyes lit on her rumpled bed. He returned his gaze to her. "Do you find the accommodations acceptable?" he asked softly.

Dana couldn't stop the smile that touched her lips. The accommodations were more than acceptable. He

had made reservations at one of the most expensive hotels on the beach, right on the ocean, connecting suites
with balconies facing the water. She had offered to share
the cost but he refused to talk about it. "Everything is
wonderful, Jared. Thank you. I hadn't expected such ex-
travagance."

Jared nodded. He knew she hadn't and that was one
of the things that made her so special and unique. Because of his success other women had expected certain
luxuries. Dana expected nothing but in his opinion she
deserved everything.

He considered how sexy she looked now, wearing a
leopard-print robe that was destined to bring out the
beast in any man. It hadn't helped matters when he had
glanced over and saw her bed with the messed-up cov-
ers and tangled sheets.

"Would you like to take a walk on the beach before
dinner?" he decided to ask. "We can either eat in the restaurant downstairs or, if you prefer, we can dine in our
rooms."

Dana lowered her gaze and quickly made her decision—about a number of things. She tipped her chin up
and met his gaze. "I'd love to take a walk on the beach
and if you don't mind I'd prefer if we ate here."

"All right."

She continued to hold his gaze and in the dark depths
of his eyes she knew that he recognized that something
had changed. Something elemental and deep. She also
knew he would keep his word. He would take things
slow, be patient and let her take the lead. He wouldn't
push, he wouldn't pressure, but he would be ready
whenever she was. And when he pounced, there would

be no stopping him. God, she hoped not. She wanted it all. Everything he had to give. And she knew when it happened there was no going back. Their time together was limited. The moments would be short. But she intended to make the most of them, and when he walked away, she would have special memories to last a lifetime.

"I guess I'd better let you get dressed then," he said, breaking into her thoughts.

She smiled at him. "Yes, I think you'd better if we want to take that walk while there's still a lot of daylight."

He nodded. Then slowly he leaned down and captured her lips. It was a slow, drugging kiss, gentle, tender. Whether he was kissing her this way or devouring her mouth, it didn't matter. He still knew how to rob her of her senses and want to make her scream out for more.

He slowly released her lips but kept his attention glued to them as she took her tongue and licked her mouth. She heard his sharp intake of breath, saw his guts clench and knew he was walking the same tightrope that she was.

"I'll knock on the door when I'm ready," she whispered, and when he nodded and took a step back, she gently closed the door and leaned against it. Throwing an arm over her eyes she inhaled deeply. What a kiss! Her already hot body had gone up another degree. The man was a master at seduction but she wouldn't have him any other way.

A smile touched her just-kissed lips. Jared was an excellent teacher. And although she knew there were more lessons to be learned, he had given her enough tutoring for what she needed to do.

At that moment the only thing she could think of was her plans to take on Jared Westmoreland.

Eight

If Jared didn't know any better he would swear Dana was trying to drive him mad. Mad with desire.

He doubted very seriously if he could hold on to his sanity, as well as his control, much longer. At any moment he would snap and Dana would drive him to reach across the table, snatch her into his arms and have her for dessert. *Dana Delight* would definitely be a mouth-watering temptation, a delectable treat.

The seduction started when she had knocked on the connecting door to let him know she was ready to go walking on the beach. He had been literally blown away by her outfit, a pair of denim shorts and a white halter top. He had seen halter tops before but never this enticing. He'd been tempted to untie the damn thing and set her breasts free. And he didn't want to think about how sensual her flat stomach looked totally bare, showing off the navel he'd grown so fond of a few days ago.

They had held hands while walking along the beach, enjoying the sunset and the ocean. They had talked about a lot of things. The weather, the economy, books they had read and exotic foods they had eaten. The conversation then shifted to the Westmoreland family and how they looked forward to the birth of Storm and Jayla's twins in a few months. Dana listened, hearing the excitement in Jared's voice. She felt a tinge of sadness that she wouldn't be around to share in the excitement since she would be out of the picture by then, out of Jared's life. At some point, he must have realized it, too. She glanced up, saw him staring at her and the intensity in his gaze gave her pause. The twins were a stark reminder that the two of them didn't have a future together. During the remainder of their walk, conversation ceased. They were caught up in their own private thoughts— thoughts they preferred not to share with each other.

When they returned to the hotel, they reluctantly went their separate ways to dress for dinner and within an hour's time, the food had been wheeled into Jared's suite. Even he would admit it was a night of romance with the candles burning on the table and the soft music playing in the background, compliments of the hotel's management. Evidently Jeannie had mentioned when she'd made reservations that they were a recently engaged couple and the hotel staff wanted to be remembered, in case they were undecided as to where they would spend their honeymoon.

A honeymoon that would never take place.

For the second time that day, Jared felt numb, his

feelings paralyzed. All he could think about was that he and Dana didn't have a future together. He forced himself to get a grip and refused to dwell on that now. All he wanted to think about was the woman sitting across from him, who was slowly sipping her champagne—another compliment of the hotel—as she watched him through beautiful dark eyes.

His body's temperature rose a few degrees. All during dinner he had been turned on by everything she did. Even watching as she opened her mouth to eat her food had stirred a flame of arousal within him. She had a pair of sensuous lips and every time she used them he felt his loins burning.

He couldn't help but wonder what she was thinking. She hadn't been talkative and the attorney in him, the one whose senses were sharp and mind alert, was waiting patiently for her to say something. Anything that would give him an indication of what was going on inside her head.

Since the suspense was killing him, he decided to just ask. "A penny for your thoughts."

Dana placed her glass down on the table. An intimate smile played at the edges of her mouth. "I was just thinking about you and how grateful I am that you came and how much I enjoy your company."

"I enjoy yours, as well."

And he really meant it. He had dined with other women but this was the first time he had felt so totally comfortable. So at ease with a beautiful woman that he both liked and desired.

"You mentioned earlier that you wanted to talk to me about a party that Thorn and Tara are giving," Dana said, recapturing his attention.

He fixed his gaze on her, looking fully into her eyes. "The weekend after Mother's Day is Thorn and Tara's first wedding anniversary. They're planning a huge celebration and I wanted to make sure you're free to attend with me that Friday night."

Dana's smile faltered. "But that's two weeks after your mother's surgery."

Jared nodded. "Yes. Is there a problem with that?"

She thought there was. "I assumed that if things were fine with your mother's surgery that we wouldn't…"

When it became apparent that she was having difficulty completing her statement, Jared reached across the table and took her hand in his. "That we wouldn't what?" he asked softly.

"Be seeing each other again, that you'd end things, break our engagement."

Jared stared into dark brown questioning eyes as he thought for a moment. Although he understood what she was saying and agreed that at one time he had thought breaking up with her as soon as possible was best for all concerned, there were a few things he felt they should take into account.

"My family, especially my mother, will find it rather odd that we broke our engagement so soon after her surgery. I think we should at least wait a couple of weeks before dropping the bomb on them." *And I don't know how I'll let you go.*

Dana couldn't see putting off the inevitable. "We're going to have to end things sooner or later, Jared. We can't continue to deceive everyone."

Jared stared at the hand he was holding then slowly released it. "I guess you're right. If things work out and my mother won't need any further treatments, then maybe the night of Thorn and Tara's party should be the last time we see each other. Agreed?"

Dana tipped up her chin and held his gaze. "Yes. Agreed." She knew that meant they had only three weeks left to spend together. Already she felt a deep pain in her heart but refused to let it ruin her evening.

"Dinner was wonderful," she said dabbing at her mouth with a napkin.

Heat flared within Jared. He would have been more than willing to wipe away any lingering crumbs from around her lips with his tongue.

He reached up and loosened the top button of his shirt. For dinner he had dressed casually, wearing a pair of khaki slacks and a black collared shirt. Dana was wearing a beautiful printed dress that had an endless slit up the side. That dress had nearly driven him crazy before she had finally taken a seat for dinner.

Moments later, his gut clenched. It seemed she was about to drive him crazy all over again. "I like the view from the balcony," she said, taking her glass and walking over to the double French doors.

"Yes. Gorgeous." He liked the view, as well, but he wasn't talking about what was on the other side of those French doors. The view he was feasting his eyes on was right in this very room.

"I bet it's simply beautiful at night," she said softly, turning around and meeting his gaze, looking at him with something akin to desire in her eyes. He shook his head wondering if that's what he actually saw or what he wanted to see.

"I bet it is, too," he managed to say as his gaze did a

long, slow slide down the length of her body. "If you stick around for a while, I'm sure we'll see just how beautiful it is. It won't be long before it's completely dark."

A smile creased the corners of her eyes. "Can you imagine standing out there under those stars?"

It was on the tip of his tongue to say he would rather be lying down under those stars and making love to her. He picked up his own glass and slowly walked over to her. When he came to a stop in front of her, a thick silence hung over them as he held her gaze, watched her uneven breathing and smelled her scent.

Aroused.

He was an experienced man. A man who knew women. And he would recognize that scent anywhere, especially with Dana. It was the same scent he'd drowned in that night they played Red Light, Green Light. The same one that had almost driven him over the edge while watching her first orgasm. If there was any way he could bottle that scent he would. Tonight it mingled with the fragrance of the seductive perfume she was wearing and the combination was a very passion-stirring force.

"Let's make a toast."

Her words broke the silence and his deep concentration. "And what would you like us to toast, Dana?" he asked huskily. Intense desire was mounting within him. It wouldn't take much for him to drop to his knees, lift her dress and go straight to the source of that scent. Both his fingers and his tongue itched to—

"I propose that we toast life."

He met her gaze as his mind was jerked back to attention. "Life?"

"Yes. It can be taken from you in a second, a minute, at any place, anytime. That's why you should live life to the fullest. Enjoy it. Appreciate it. Because when it's gone, it's over. And there's nothing you can do about it."

Jared considered her words. *Life.* He couldn't help but think of how different his had been since she had walked into it. Stormed into it was a better word. In a span of less than eight weeks, he had met her, introduced her to his family and given them the definite impression they were engaged, had purchased a very costly ring for her—one he intended for her to keep—and had spent the last couple of weeks pretending to be a man very much in love. To say that Dana Rollins hadn't affected his life would be an understatement.

"Okay, we'll toast to life," he said, lifting his glass to connect with hers. They took a sip of their champagne.

"Umm, want to have some fun?" she asked, holding his gaze over the rim of her glass.

Jared lifted a brow. "What kind of fun?"

A smile turned up her lips. "I'd like to play a game," she said softly.

"A game?"

"Yes. A game of hide-and-seek. I hide, you find me."

Jared smiled. He liked the thought of doing that. "And what happens when I find you?"

She returned his smile. "That depends."

"On what?"

"Where I'm found."

Jared downplayed the possibilities as he glanced around the room. "There aren't many places you can hide."

She grinned. "Oh, between my room and yours I'm sure there's a few."

Jared was tempted to tell her that hiding from him wouldn't do any good since her scent would give her away. When it came to her, his nose was like radar.

"All right. So what do you want me to do?" he asked, more than willing to play this game she'd suggested.

"Leave the room for about ten minutes. When you come back, the suite will be totally dark, and remember I'll be either hiding in my suite or yours."

Jared nodded. This was the second game they had played together, and for someone who usually lived a structured life, he was enjoying letting go and being adventurous with Dana.

He began walking toward the door. "Ten minutes. That's all I'm giving you. Then I'll be back, whether you're ready or not."

Dana watched as he gave her one last stomach-churning smile before opening the door, walking out of it and closing it behind him. She slowly crossed the room and dropped down on the floral-printed sofa and kicked off her sandals. She inhaled deeply and smiled seductively.

She would definitely be ready when he returned.

Jared returned ten minutes later. Ten minutes on the nose and not one second more.

He opened his door and stepped into the darkened room. He couldn't help but be amused as he switched on a light. Dana must have figured her scent would give her away so she had liberally sprayed his suite with the perfume she'd been wearing.

He glanced around the room and noticed her sandals

were by his sofa. Evidently she had kicked them off there. He walked over and picked one up. They were pretty and boy did she have small feet, sexy feet. He placed the shoe back down and glanced at the sofa. It seemed her shoes weren't the only thing she had left behind. He picked up the scarf she'd worn around her waist.

He glanced around, his ears on alert. The door connecting their suites was open. He crossed the room to go into hers. It was dark and he turned on a lamp. His gaze looked around, nothing looked amiss, and there wasn't a sound to be heard. And the scent of her perfume was in this room, as well. He walked out of the bedroom to the sitting area. He looked down in front of the sofa and blinked. There in a pool on the floor was her dress.

His breath caught exactly the same moment his arousal thickened. This was definitely one hell of a game she was playing. He hadn't expected it to take this turn so quickly, but he wasn't complaining. He had told her that he would leave it up to her to let him know if and when she was ready to take their relationship to another level. This was her way of letting him know she was ready.

Now it was his job to find her.

He was the hunter and would find his prey. With a determined purpose he walked across the room to the small kitchen that had a breakfast bar and table. He opened a closet door and found it empty.

He then retraced his steps back to her bedroom and went to check out her bathroom. He found it almost empty. A red lace bra was hanging from a light in the ceiling. He reached up and pulled it down.

He was getting hot.

Walking back to her room he got on his knees and looked under the huge king-size bed and found nothing. He looked in the closet and came up empty. He opened the French doors and walked out on the balcony. It was bare.

Frustration, added to intense arousal, wasn't a good thing. The pressure of his erection against his pants was almost killing him. When he found Dana she would pay dearly for this torture. He walked back through the connecting door into his suite and glanced around. The bedroom door was closed and he distinctly remembered it being open when he'd left.

An enticing possibility flooded his mind, made his body harden even more as he slowly crossed the room. He glanced down the moment he reached for the doorknob and saw red lace. Leaning down he picked it up. It wasn't much, barely a scrap, but he definitely knew what it was and where it came from.

Bringing the item to his nose he inhaled Dana's scent, a different one than the perfume. It was a womanly scent that was all hers. Privately. Exclusively. Deciding that she definitely wouldn't need it anymore tonight, he slipped her thong into his back pocket. Slowly opening the bedroom door, he walked into darkness and closed the door behind him.

Dana held her breath. Jared had finally found her. Not that she had done a good job at hiding. She thought she had made it easy for him but evidently she hadn't.

She had known the exact moment he had returned and had heard every step he'd taken around the room.

She'd known when he had searched her suite and when he had returned to his own. And now he was here, in his bedroom, and she was in his bed, totally naked and waiting for him.

Her mind was made up, her decision final, with no regrets. When he walked away she would have reminders of this night. They would be memories that would last her a lifetime because she knew whatever he did, Jared never did anything halfway. He was meticulously thorough and methodically efficient.

"I know you're in here, Dana," he whispered huskily in the darkened room. "And ready or not, here I come."

She heard his footsteps, slow, yet determined. She heard the sound of his breathing, quick and uneven. She almost held her breath when he came closer and closer to the bed. She felt his presence and smelled his masculine scent.

And when he switched on the lamp, bathing the room with a soft translucent glow, their gazes connected. Held. Then slowly, his gaze drifted from her face and moved downward to the sheet that covered her nude body. Then it moved back up to her face. It was a while before he spoke.

"I found you," he said in a raspy voice that was so husky it stirred heat all over her skin. "So what do I get?"

She paused a moment before saying, "Anything you want."

A hint of a smile touched his lips. Intense desire darkened his eyes. "Anything?"

"Yes, *anything*."

He continued to hold her gaze. "Are you sure?" he asked moments later.

"Positive."

His sensuous smile deepened. "And you're ready?" he asked, wanting to be doubly sure that she was. Once he began making love to her, he would be hard-pressed to stop. Unable to help himself he reached out and pushed away a strand of hair that had fallen in her face. He needed to touch her, connect with her on any level.

"Yes, I'm ready."

"With no regrets?"

She inhaled slowly. Knowing what he was asking and why. Nothing had changed. Sooner or later, possibly even sooner, depending on the results of his mother's surgery, he would be walking out of her life. She knew it. Had accepted it. And would be prepared when it happened.

But she wanted to seize the moment. Celebrate life. With him. "There won't be any regrets, Jared. I knew the score going into this game."

She then slowly eased up, letting the sheet fall away, hearing his sharp intake of breath when it did so. Getting on her knees she brushed her hand against his chest and moved slowly downward to feel the hard planes of his stomach. "Are we going to talk all night or are we going to get on with what we've wanted for quite a while?"

He reached out and traced a path around her nipple with his finger, teasing the darkened tip. "And what is it that you think we've wanted?"

"Some of each other."

"Some?"

Her lips smiled with warm confidence. "Okay, I stand corrected. *All* of each other."

Without giving her the chance to draw her next

breath, Jared pulled her into his arms and covered her mouth with his, igniting an explosion of passion between them. He kissed her with hungry intensity. It seemed as if a dam had burst, emotions were flooding and there was no one around to fix it.

Dana's arms came around him and held on, taking everything he had to give and wondering how she had denied herself for so long. Jared was a special man who had always treated her like a lady. And for that she would always be eternally grateful.

He slowly released her and stepped back. Her legs trembled from the impact of his kiss. He continued to hold her gaze, looking at her with virile intensity, as he unbuckled his belt. She felt heat pouring into her stomach and drifting downward between her legs as she began catching fire from his flame.

"Tonight I'm going to do all those things I've been dreaming of doing to you," Jared said, his voice a thin whisper and full of sexual need. "I want to see you reach a climax again, several of them, over and over. But this time, you won't be alone. I'll be there with you, joining in and sharing the pleasure." His words were seduction all wrapped in silk.

Dana watched as he pulled his shirt over his head. With the top of him bare, he exuded strength, power and muscular endurance. He had a beautiful chest and his dark coloring made him look even more beautiful to her. He tossed the shirt aside, then sat down in a wing chair to remove his shoes and socks. After that was done, he stood and went back to his pants, tugging the belt from the loops.

He smiled over at her. "When I told you that I

wouldn't push until you were ready, I knew that meant my patience would be tested. I've been wanting you forever and tonight I plan to show you just how much."

Dana continued to watch as he slid down his pants and underwear. She blinked when she saw the size of him. She had felt his hardened erection plenty of times against her but now seeing it in the flesh was putting a whole new spin on things. Jared was loaded. He had been very fortunate when certain body parts had been distributed.

"Umm, interesting," she whispered softly, meeting his gaze and smiling.

He chuckled. "Interesting? Is that all you can say?"

"I'll wait to make sure it can work before making any more comments."

He laughed, loving every moment of sharing this camaraderie with her, while at the same time fire bolts of desire raced through him. "Trust me. It will work. In fact I plan for it to go into overtime."

The room got quiet as the reality of what they were about to do set in. For the longest time, their gazes connected and their minds were of one accord. Naked, Jared slowly walked over to the bed and took Dana's hands in his. He brought them to his lips and kissed her palms.

"You do things to me that no other woman ever has, Dana. You make me feel things. Make me want things. I don't want you to think what we're about to do is just another roll between the sheets for me. It's something I consider exceptional and extraordinary."

The love Dana felt for Jared increased tenfold. She loved him with all her heart. Tonight she wanted to physically connect with the man she loved. Deciding he had talked enough, she tugged on his hands and they tumbled down into the bed.

Jared's body ended up on top of hers and he glanced down at her, feeling the heat of flesh touching flesh, and framed her face with his palms. He studied her features as if implanting them in his memory.

And then he kissed her. Hungrily. Devouringly. And he couldn't stop. He wanted her with a vengeance, a deep-rooted passion that he couldn't understand. He heard the gentle moan of passion that escaped her lips, and felt the warmth of her fingers caress his naked skin as his tongue continued to ravage the sweetness of her mouth. Finally, the need to breathe and to shield her from pregnancy made him pull away. "I have to protect you," he said with hot desire running rampant in his voice.

He slowly stood, crossed back over the room for his pants. He fished through his pocket, pulling out her underwear instead of his wallet. He glanced over at her and smiled. "Nice color."

She gave him a short laugh brushed with embarrassment. "Glad you like it."

Tossing them aside he then checked his other pocket for his wallet, pulled it out and retrieved a condom packet. Several. He knew she was watching as he put it on, and was overwhelmed by the sensations that rammed through him as he prepared to bury himself in her softness.

After he finished the task he glanced up and met her gaze. "What do you think?"

He saw the heated desire in her eyes, saw the slight

shivering of her body. "I think," she said softly, "that more than anything, I want you inside of me, Jared."

Jared inhaled sharply as he felt a tightening coil in his lower region. He should have known she would say or do something to endear her to him that much more. He wanted to fight it but couldn't. And he knew what he was feeling had nothing to do with the length of time it had been since he'd had a woman. It had everything to do with this particular woman.

He slowly walked over to the bed, slid in and pulled her into his arms. Emotions he'd never felt before took their toll and he kissed her while giving in to his over-heated senses. He then moved from her lips to her breasts, determined to top what he'd done to them the other day. The lips and tongue torturing her now were those of a man who wanted to make his woman as wet as she could get. Torture was too mild a word to use for what he was doing. He took his time reacquainting himself with the taste of her skin, the feel of her flesh, liking the way her nipples hardened in his mouth as he feasted on them greedily.

When her scent became intoxicating and way too potent, his hand moved in slow precision and reached downward to touch the most intimate part of her, finding her not just wet but completely drenched. He vividly remembered a scene from one of his dreams that he longed to act out. He shifted his body and moved away from her breasts, began tracing a path down her chest to her navel with his mouth, glorying in the sensual taste of her naked skin.

He continued to trail kisses all over her. Rolling her on her stomach, placed kisses all over her spine, the center of her back and all over her shoulders. He then gently rolled her back over and met her gaze. By the look in her eyes he knew she was trying to contemplate his next move. He leaned back and without saying a word, his hand traveled between her legs, parting them just seconds before he lowered his mouth to her with hungry intensity.

Of their own accord, her hips lifted to him and to make sure they stayed there, he grabbed hold of them, held them as he greedily devoured her in this very intimate way. He heard her moan with every insistent stroke of his tongue. He tasted her heat, her fire and her passion. Passion he was both creating and satisfying.

"Jared!"

He quickly pulled back and covered her body with his, interlocking their limbs. He took her mouth at the same time he entered her, sliding inside of her in one smooth thrust as she welcomed him into her body. The same heat consuming her was eating him alive. He began moving as sensations, too overpowering to be real, clamored through him, making his strokes harder, stronger and deeper, robbing him of any logical thought but one. *Don't hold back. Share everything with her and deal with the consequences later.*

And when her body exploded into what seemed like a billion pieces beneath him and carried her to a spiraling climax, he broke their kiss and buried his face in her neck. Kissed her there. Marked her. He continued to take her over the edge with steady thrusts of possession.

That same explosion, the finality of every physical sensation he could think of, overtook him. He hollered out her name as his body shook with the magnitude of an earthquake, the force of a hurricane and the electrifying power of a thunderstorm. What he had found in her arms, inside her body was intense pleasure, too magnificent to measure and too rapturous to describe.

And he knew as the earth slowly ceased spinning and his body relaxed, utterly consumed and feeling like a lifeless weight floating on shafts of air, that this was an experience he'd never shared with any woman before. He was bombarded with the need to hold her and make love to her all through the night.

At that very moment, Jared had to concede that when the time came, walking away from her would be the hardest thing he'd ever had to do.

Shortly after midnight, Jared stood barefoot on the balcony and leaned against the railing. The incessant pounding of the waves beating against the shore matched the raggedness of his breathing and the distinctive hammering of his heart.

Emotions that he had never dealt with before were coming at him from all directions, different angles, crowding in on him. He released a long deep breath as he tried to fight them. But it was useless. Dana had touched him tonight in a way no other woman had, and it hadn't been all physical.

It seemed that after making love to her that first time, an undeniable urge to do so again and again had taken over, and so they had all through the night. He had shared more than just his body with her. He had also shared his soul. It seemed as if she had somehow eased inside his heart and was still snuggled there.

After making love to her the last time he had lain

awake while she drifted off to sleep beside him. Sighs of satisfaction had continued to flow through his body long afterward. When he'd glanced over at her, he had been touched by how peaceful she looked. Struggling with feelings that were foreign to him, he had slid out of bed and slipped into his pants. Before he had left the room he had glanced back, lingering in the doorway. The moonlight shining in through the window focused on Dana curled in his bed, her naked body barely covered while she slept. Her bare breasts, firm and full, had tempted him to taste them again.

Bringing his thoughts back to the present, Jared pulled in a broken breath, knowing that no matter how many women he'd slept with before Dana and no matter how many he would sleep with after, he would only find total, complete and satisfying release in her arms. Only hers.

Jared turned slowly, sensing Dana's presence immediately. A lump thickened in his throat when he saw she was wearing his shirt, a shirt that barely covered her.

Their eyes met. Held. And then she said softly, "I woke up and decided that it was lonely in bed without you."

Jared didn't want to tell her the reason he'd left was that he had needed distance from her; he'd been driven to have a few moments alone to get his head back on straight. Making love to her had literally blown him away. Instead he told her part of the truth. "I wanted to hear the sound of the ocean and see the moon and all the stars."

He drew in a deep breath of air, not able to think beyond the need she aroused in him, and then added slowly. "But do you know what I want now more than anything?"

Dana shook her head. "No. What?"

"To make love to you again." A part of him wished he could have mustered enough strength to have said that for the remainder of the night they needed to sleep in separate beds; they were getting into something neither had counted on, something he definitely didn't want. But as she slowly began taking steps, crossing the balcony to him, the only thing he could do was open his arms.

The moment she came close, he gathered her to him, needing to hold her. He felt the willpower he had tried to regain slip away. She pressed against him, needing to be held. She wrapped her arms around his neck and they stood that way for a long moment, body to body, soul to soul. Slow warmth spread from her to him and it seemed that her every curve was molded against his firm muscled length.

And then he swooped her up into his arms and with hurried steps carried her back into the bedroom and placed her on the bed. He leaned down and caught her lips in a kiss that was deep, sensual and demanded full surrender. The sounds of pleasure emitting from her made him want her that much more and his stomach clenched with profound need.

He released her to pull the shirt from over her head, and then proceeded to remove his pants. After taking the time to put on protection, he joined her in bed. She whispered his name and the only thing Jared could think about was demonstrating with his body just what she did to him and how much he wanted her.

The knowledge that she wanted him as much as he wanted her sent his desire skyrocketing in all directions. He intended to spend the rest of the night sharing intense passion with the one woman whose name was more than a whisper on his lips. It was a name that was finding a way to his very soul.

Jared's last thought as he captured her mouth with his was that having her seep into his heart was something he could not let happen. No matter what.

Nine

"**T**hanks for being here, Dana."

Dana gave Jared an assuring smile when he reached out and took her hand in his and tightened his fingers around it as they sat side by side in the hospital's waiting room. His features were solemn and she knew he was worried about the outcome of his mother's surgery. "You don't have to thank me, Jared. I wanted to be here."

She glanced at the clock on the wall. The doctors had indicated it wouldn't be a long procedure and that someone would be out to talk to the family when it was over. Jared's youngest brother, Reggie, had accompanied Mr. Westmoreland downstairs to the coffee shop, and every so often Jared's cell phone would ring when one of his other brothers called for an update on their mother's condition. His aunt and uncle were here and so were several of his cousins and their wives. One thing she had learned about the Westmorelands was that they were a close-knit family who bonded in a crisis. She admired that about them.

Dana glanced up at Jared. "Can I get you anything?"

He gave her a reassuring smile. "No, thanks, I'm fine." He then leaned closer and whispered softly, privately, "What I really want is something I can't have right now, but there's always later."

Dana felt heat flare into her cheeks and hoped no one noticed the blush that came into her features. After returning from Jekyll Island they had begun spending more and more time together. They had dined at his place and gone out to eat a couple of times this week, had taken in several movies and had also joined his cousins last night at Chase's Place to celebrate Thorn's birthday.

And each time they made love it was better than the last. On the nights that he stayed over, she enjoyed waking up in his arms. There were never any regrets, only complete fulfillment. She could not resist Jared any more than she could stop breathing. The intimacy they shared was tangible, special and so profound, that more than once it brought tears to her eyes.

Tonight she was having dinner again at his place and was looking forward to it. She hoped they had reason to celebrate, and remained positive about his mother's condition.

For the next few minutes she tried engaging Jared in small talk since she knew that he, like everyone else, was watching the clock. His father had returned and was now nervously pacing the room.

Everyone looked up when the doctor walked into the

waiting room with an unreadable expression on his face. Mr. Westmoreland, with Jared and Reggie on his heels, quickly walked over to meet the doctor.

"How is she?" James Westmoreland asked in a somewhat shaky voice.

Dr. Miller smiled and he reached out and touched the older man's shoulder. "She's doing fine and test results confirm the lump was nothing but fatty tissue. Sarah is fine and once the anesthesia wears off, she'll be able to leave. Of course I want to see her for a follow-up visit next week."

James sighed deeply and Dana could see relief and happiness in everyone's eyes. "Thanks, Dr. Miller."

"You're welcome." Dr. Miller glanced over at Jared and Reggie. "Which one of you is engaged to be married?"

Jared lifted a brow. "I am. Why?"

The doctor chuckled. "Because that's all your mother talked about from the time they wheeled her into the operating room to right before the anesthetic kicked in. She's really happy about it and is anxious to start planning a wedding. Congratulations." He then turned and walked out of the waiting room.

Jared turned his head and met Dana's gaze. Her fingers tightened on the straps on her purse. It was an unconscious gesture that only he noticed. She had agreed to play out this charade for an additional two weeks, but he understood how everything was placing a toll on her. It was placing a hell of a toll on him as well.

He studied her face, knowing that even after their "engagement" ended, memories would remain that wouldn't leave him alone, that were bound to creep into his thoughts at any place and at any time.

He sighed deeply as he crossed the room to where Dana was standing, needing the contact, the closeness. "Mom's fine," he said.

Her smile was soft. "I heard and I'm glad," she said so quietly that he barely heard her.

Elated with the news that his mother was okay, and because he was dying to taste Dana's lips, Jared bent his head and brushed his lips across hers.

"If you two keep this up, your Mom's prediction is bound to be true," James said, grinning, coming to stand beside his oldest son.

Another deep sigh escaped Jared's lips. He had an idea but knew he was expected to ask, so he did. "And what prediction is that?"

Mr. Westmoreland looked at Dana then back at his son and chuckled. "That there will be another Westmoreland wedding before the end of summer."

Dana had fallen in love with Jared's home the first time she had walked through the double doors a week ago. The two-story structure, located in one of North Atlanta's most exclusive and affluent communities, was huge and spacious.

When Jared had given her a tour she'd seen that each and every room was breathtaking and expensively decorated, and that included the state-of-the-art theater room she had heard so much about, and a beautifully designed swimming pool. He had five bedrooms, six bathrooms, a huge country kitchen, a living room and dining room as well as a breakfast room, a library and game room. He even had a four-car garage and she had been surprised to discover that he owned a motorcycle.

He had explained that because of Thorn, all the male Westmorelands owned a Thorn-Byrd, the brand of bikes that his cousin built.

The house, Dana thought, was very much like the man who owned it, fascinating, interesting and compelling. With all the vaulted ceilings, rich thick carpeting, costly paintings that lined the walls and the expensive antique furnishings, it signified wealth but wasn't overdone. There was nothing ostentatious about the house or the man. It was obvious that Jared liked nice things, but she definitely wouldn't consider his likes eccentric or outlandish.

"Make yourself comfortable," Jared said as he glanced over at her. It was early evening. They had spent the majority of the day at his parents' home after his mother had gotten released from the hospital. He had made all the necessary calls to his brothers, assuring them that things were fine and their mother was okay.

"Do you need my help?" Dana asked as she sat at the breakfast bar and watched how efficiently he moved around in the kitchen.

"No. We're having something light and simple."

Dana chuckled. "Umm, let me guess, hot dogs and lemonade?"

Jared smiled. "No, it's something a lot more filling than that. In fact it's one of the few Westmoreland family secret recipes that Chase will share—a chicken-and-rice casserole. I prepared it this morning before leaving for the hospital, so all I have to do is warm it up. I'm also making a salad to go along with it and thought a glass of wine would be nice, as well."

She watched as he pulled a casserole dish from the refrigerator and proceeded to place it in the microwave. He then pulled out all the items he needed for the salad.

"And you're sure there's nothing I can do to help?" The last time she had shared a dinner with him here, he'd had everything catered.

He glanced up at her and smiled. "I'm positive. You've done enough already. I meant what I said about me appreciating you taking off work to be at the hospital today. It meant a lot to me and I know it meant a lot to my family, especially Mom. I'm so thankful that the test results were good. In a way I had prepared myself for the worse."

Dana heard the catch in his voice and immediately got out of her seat and came around to stand in front of him. She reached out and placed a hand on his arm. "But like you said, Jared, the results were good and that's what's important. She's okay."

Jared nodded and thought that Dana's touch felt hot on his arm. A seductive silence hung over the room as he held her gaze. Desire swirled around in his belly and he hung tenuously on to his control. He wanted her. Always wanted her. Constantly wanted her. And was always amazed at the depth of that wanting.

He recalled vividly and in living color every aspect of making love to her last night. They had returned to her place from the movies, and as soon as the door closed shut behind them, desire, the likes of which he'd never encountered before, had taken hold of him, racked his mind, rammed through his body. He had hauled her to him, picked her up into his arms and had taken her into the bedroom where he had stripped her of her clothes, and then quickly removed his own, barely taking time to protect them both before covering her body with his and making love to her.

The same way he wanted to make love to her now.

He made a move to reach out for her the exact moment the alarm on the microwave sounded. Inhaling deeply, a faint smile formed on his lips. "I guess it's time to eat."

She smiled in return. "Yes, I guess it is."

"Will you go swimming with me?" Jared asked later when they had finished dinner, cleared the table and loaded the dishes in the dishwasher. The last time she'd been over, the lining of the pool was being redone.

She slanted him a teasing grin. "What makes you think I can swim?"

He regarded her with an interest that had her toes curling and the most intimate part of her aching. "I just figured you could, and if you can't then I'll teach you."

Her eyes squinted with amusement. "You're an expert swimmer?"

"I don't do so bad."

Dana thought that if he could swim with the same degree of expertise that he made love then he was definitely an ace. "I can swim," she said, deciding to come clean. "My parents made sure I knew how before my fourth birthday. Living on the East Coast and so close to the ocean meant that I had to learn."

She tipped her head back and looked at him. "But there is one slight problem."

"What?"

"I didn't bring a bathing suit."

"That's no problem. I'm sure there's an extra one around here that should fit you."

He watched her face and saw the exact moment her eyes darkened with disappointment. "Don't bother."

He quickly realized what had bothered her. Reaching out he gently squeezed her shoulders and said, "It's a bathing suit that Delaney left behind, Dana. She used to keep several of them here in case she ever wanted to visit and go swimming." He pulled her to him, needing to hold her. "I've never gone swimming with a woman in this house before," he whispered. He never felt the need to explain his personal life to any woman, but for some reason he wanted to explain things to her.

Dana pulled back, ticked at herself for caring. Besides, he didn't owe her an explanation about anything. It wasn't as if they were really engaged. "Sorry, I don't have a right to come across like that, Jared. What you do is none of my business."

He studied her face for a long time then said, "There's no need to apologize." His breath was warm against her face when he leaned toward her and placed a gentle kiss on her lips. He deepened it then pulled back slowly, not ready to languish her lips yet as he placed tiny kisses around it. "I can say the hell with a bathing suit and let's go skinny-dipping."

Breathless, she smiled against his lips. "Yes, you can say that but then that poses another problem."

He watched as she moistened her lips with a stroke of her tongue, and was tempted to lean down and take that tongue into his mouth and feast on it some more. "What other problem?" he asked, barely able to get the words out.

"I've never swum in the nude."

The thought of her swimming naked ran fluidly through his mind, forming images that made him want to strip her bare, then and there. "You know what they say, Miss Rollins. There's a first time for everything." He leaned down and whispered in her ear, "Come on, let's go for a swim."

When they began walking, Jared slung an arm around her shoulders as he led her to the area where the pool was located. Dana tried not to let the seductive sensations that Jared generated within her, take possession of her mind.

The potent smell of chlorine teased Dana's nostrils as they entered a passageway. He reached out and flipped a switch, bringing light into a huge area filled with lush greenery. To say the pool was impressive would be an understatement. Secured in the privacy of brick walls and a vaulted ceiling made of solid glass, this private place was definitely a swimmer's haven. Dana smiled when they stopped walking and she looked up and saw how the moonlight and the stars reflected through, slanting light against the pool's blue-tinted waters.

"So, do you want a bathing suit or do you prefer going without?" Jared asked as he placed his hands on her hips.

She grinned. "I think I'd feel more comfortable with a bathing suit."

He watched her thoughtfully, wondering if this was the same woman who had played a very enticing game of hide-and-seek with him that weekend. It had been one passionate pursuit and now it seemed that she was trying to go all shy on him. However he was sure a few sizzling kisses would rid her of any degree of bashfulness.

"I may as well warn you that I plan to take the suit off of you the first chance I get," he whispered, leaning down and capturing her earlobe in his mouth and sucking gently.

A breathless sigh escaped Dana's lips and she closed her eyes. It was a good thing he was still holding her by the waist or she would have melted and slid right into the pool. "I kind of figured you'd be trying something like that."

He took her hand in his and drew her away from the pool to an area surrounded by a bevy of palm trees. "At least I gave you fair warning."

He led her to a room off from the pool area that appeared to be a large dressing room. "You can change in here," Jared said, giving her an easy smile. "Towels are in that closet and there's a bathing suit that should fit you in that drawer over there."

She looked up at him. "What about you?"

He gave her that same grin that had endeared him to her the first time she'd seen it. "I don't have a problem swimming in the nude, Dana."

And with that he turned and left her alone in the room.

Dana nervously fumbled with the buttons on her blouse as she removed it while glancing around the huge room. She saw that all the walls and the ceiling were mirrored and she felt slightly funny as she watched herself undress. She studied the daybed that sat on one side of the room and didn't want to imagine Jared and some woman in it as they watched themselves make love. He had said no woman had ever gone swimming with him in this house but who was to say that no woman had ever made out with him in this room?

Letting out a long breath, she tugged her skirt down over her hips, not wanting the picture of Jared and any other woman to form in her mind. As she'd told him, what he did was his business. But still, the part of her that loved him so much that it hurt, felt pain at the thought of him with someone else.

She tried turning her thoughts and attention elsewhere. Dinner had been delicious and the wine he'd selected had been perfect.

She could tell a huge load had been lifted off his shoulders now that he knew his mother was okay. He seemed more relaxed. Being around him made her feel things, want things and each and every time he had smiled at her, touched her—innocently or otherwise—she found herself hard pressed to keep her emotions under control.

Whenever she looked into his eyes his keen sense of intelligence startled her. He was his parents' firstborn, but had not been the heir apparent. Anything and everything Jared possessed was the result of hard work. He deserved all he had achieved and was a man like no other she'd ever known. There was a fierceness about him, yet at the same time an innate gentleness that she found sweet and endearing.

Jared Westmoreland was the man she would love until the day she died.

Dana sighed, as she tied her hair back, trying to remain clearheaded. She couldn't and wouldn't have regrets, no matter what. And she wouldn't dwell on the impossibilities of a future with Jared.

Moments later she glanced at herself in the mirror. Jared had said nothing about the bathing suit being a bikini. It appeared to be brand-new and was a perfect fit, although it showed more skin than she was used to exposing. Jared had seen her naked several times since their weekend together, but for some reason she felt shy around him tonight.

Maybe it was because every time she held his gaze for any period of time she saw desire in his eyes that was so thick it could be cut with a knife. And what he'd said earlier about her not keeping the bathing suit on for long sent passionate chills down her body. He'd said it and she had no reason to doubt it. Grabbing a towel she wrapped it securely around her waist and took a deep breath before walking out of the room.

The first thing she noticed was that Jared had dimmed the lights. The second thing was that he was already in the water, standing in the shallow end, leaning back against the pool's wall. All the way across the room she could feel the strength of him. Knowing he was completely naked only filled her with heated passion and desire. He was built and had the kind of muscles women drooled about. Each and every time she came into contact with his body, she burned.

"Get rid of the towel, Dana."

His words as well as the look in his eyes pulled her to him. She slowly walked to the edge of the pool and met his heated gaze. "And if I don't?"

A smile touched the corners of his lips. "Then I'll be

tempted to get out of the pool and remove it for you, and while I'm removing the towel I'll also remove everything else."

Dana tilted her head, picturing both things in her mind. "Mmm, that sounds like quite a seductive threat, Counselor."

She watched as he moved swiftly and agilely through the water and ended up at the side of the pool, within less than a few feet from where she stood. "No threat, Dana. It's a promise."

She took a step back when he eased his naked body out of the pool. She noticed he had on a condom, making it blatantly clear what he had in mind. Dripping wet he stood in front of her. He leaned over and kissed her tenderly while at the same time used his fingertip to loosen the knot of the towel. She felt it fall to the floor, but his mouth kept her too occupied to care. At the moment she was content to let him carry out any threats he'd made.

"You look nice," he said huskily, releasing her lips and letting his gaze roam over her body. "You're definitely wearing this bathing suit—but not for long."

With a flick of his wrist he released her top and then bending, he caressed her bare shoulders with the tip of his tongue. That was followed by slow nibbling kisses that he placed on her neck before moving to her breasts, taking the hard tips of her nipples into his mouth one at a time.

When she began to shudder he slowly lowered himself down in front of her and began easing the bikini bottom down her legs.

"Your body leaves me breathless, Dana," he whispered as his lips trailed kisses all over her stomach. "And your scent drives me crazy."

His mouth moved downward and he reached out and gently grabbed hold of her hips. Glancing up at her and seeing how she watched everything he was doing while taking measured breaths and gripping his shoulders for balance, he said, "I love kissing you all over."

He felt a shiver flow through her body and whispered huskily, "But I especially love kissing you here."

He heard her moan when his mouth closed over her most intimate part, finding her hot and wet. His tongue flicked out and began stroking her slowly and tasting her completely. When she arched against his mouth, he became greedy, insistent and possessive.

"Jared!"

She screamed his name. He felt her buckle against his mouth as every sensitive nerve in her body exploded. He wanted it all and he didn't let up until her last shudder ended and she became soft and limp. Standing, he swept her into his arms and carried her over to a huge padded bench and held her. Placing her in his lap he tightened his hold on her and drew her closer, needing the contact and not wanting to question the why of it.

"You're too much, Jared," Dana whispered on a half sigh, barely opening her eyes.

His smile was intriguing. "Is that a bad thing or a good thing?"

"Umm, I imagine it's a good thing," she said softly.

His chuckle was soft and the sound of it sent more sensual chills up Dana's body. "You imagine? You're not certain?"

She hooked her arms around his neck. "Give me a few moments to recoup and I'll let you know for sure."

"You don't have a few moments to spare, sweetheart. I want you too much," he said throatily. And then he was kissing her again, his lips hungry, his tongue hot, intense. Her body immediately responded and began to heat up all over again.

He slowly pulled back. "Come on, let's swim for a while."

He stood with her in his arms and walked over to the pool. "The water is temperature controlled, so it's warm."

They eased their bodies into the pool. After treading water for a few moments, they swam to the other side of the pool then back again. Going to the edge of the pool he gathered her close. Before she could gasp her next breath, he kissed her, touched her all over and completely shattered her sanity.

Mindlessly, she moaned his name when his finger slipped inside of her, stroking her to heated bliss. "Wrap your legs around my waist."

Meeting his gaze she placed her arms around his neck, and when he positioned her body just where he wanted it he slowly eased inside of her, finding she was still moist and hot.

And when he had gone as deep as he could go, Jared's head came down and moments before he covered her lips he whispered the words, "This is as perfect as anything can possibly get."

And then he began moving inside of her, making love to her, taking, giving and sharing. Water lapped against their skin, absorbing the heat of their naked flesh, stroking their passion to a fevered pitch.

It seemed as if it had been months, years since they had shared passion this way and all the longings Dana could possibly endure broke through, encasing her in a storm of emotions and pleasures that ripped through to her very soul. And when he increased the rhythm, she pressed closer to him, urged him to take more as passion swirled around her, driving her through turbulence that could only have one end. Each stroke he made pushed her closer and closer to release. She dug her fingers into his shoulders as liquid warmth gathered, anticipation hovered and pleasure crested.

Jared let out a deep guttural groan when he felt a shudder race through Dana's body and she ground her hips against him, pushing him deeper inside of her, to the hilt. And then he lost it, that final, fragile hold on his sanity. His next powerful thrust connected them in a way that made sensations shoot through both of them simultaneously. Blood pounded in his ears and her name trembled from his lips at the same time that his body shook in a release so strong that he was whirled into a massive impact that stole his next breath.

He felt Dana tremble in his arms, her response shameless, total and complete. The effects tore through him, ripped him in two and demanded that he give up everything, all that he had, whatever he possessed, to the fury of passion that consumed them both.

And as he crushed her to him, he surrendered to the multitude of feelings that drew them together. *She was his.*

Ten

"**I** want my wife back, Jared. She refuses to see me or talk to me so what do you suggest that I do?"

Jared sighed deeply wondering how Sylvester expected him to answer a question like that when he had his own personal issues to deal with. It had been almost two weeks since his mother's surgery and tonight was the night of Thorn and Tara's anniversary party—and the final act of the play in which he and Dana had been participants. They were supposed to officially end things tonight by breaking their engagement.

"Jared? Are you listening to me?"

Jared turned his attention back to his client who'd been pacing his office for the past half hour. Evidently, Sylvester thought that as his attorney Jared had all the answers, which was a completely false assumption. He was in the business of ending marriages and not trying to find ways to save them.

"Have you tried begging?" Jared decided to ask. The last time he had spoken with Jackie Brewster's attorney, he'd been informed that she was adamant about giving her husband the divorce he'd asked for. She refused to remain married to a man who had wrongly accused her of being unfaithful.

Sylvester frowned. "I'm serious, Jared."

"So am I. According to your wife's attorney, she wants us to proceed. She says there's no chance of reconciliation."

Sylvester, with a defeated expression on his face, dropped down in a nearby chair. "I can't lose her. I love her, Jared, and I will do whatever I have to do to save my marriage. I was wrong. I knew what a good woman she was, yet I was quick to think the worst. It was so hard to accept that someone could actually love me and give me their complete devotion."

Behind his desk, Jared leaned back in his chair. It was odd to watch Sylvester this torn up over a woman. In the past, he'd been quick to end things and move on, usually because he had some other woman waiting in the wings. But that wasn't the case this time. It was obvious Sylvester was in love with his wife.

Love.

With that one word, Dana quickly came into his thoughts. He blinked, refusing to go there. What he felt for her was desire, gut-wrenching desire, lust of the strongest kind. He'd been in relationships before and was an ace at getting out of them whenever things got sticky. And he would be the first to admit that things between him and Dana were definitely getting sticky. It was time to split—with no regrets.

"Isn't there something you can do, Jared? I'm desperate."

Sylvester's words recaptured his attention. He stared up at the ceiling in deep thought for a moment. "Maybe there is," he said, making a quick decision. "I'll do my best to arrange for you and Jackie to have a private meeting, without me or her attorney present. I can't make any promises, but I'll try. Once the two of you are alone, it's going to be up to you to convince her that you're worthy of forgiveness."

He saw the hopeful gleam that appeared in Sylvester's eyes and the optimism that lined the man's features. It was evident he was struggling to hold on to his composure. If there had been any doubt in Jared's mind of just how deeply Sylvester felt about his wife, it vanished at that very moment.

"Are you okay, Dana?" Cybil asked, studying her best friend's face.

Dana looked up from the papers on her desk and forced a smile. "Yes, I'm fine." She quickly glanced away, knowing she couldn't hide her emotions from Cybil.

"If you're fine then why have you been crying?"

Dana began studying the papers on her desk again. "Who says I've been crying?"

"I do," Cybil said quietly, crossing the room to stand in front of Dana's desk. When seconds ticked by and Dana didn't say anything, Cybil spoke again, her voice low and imploring. "I didn't want you to get hurt."

Dana slowly stood from her desk and walked over to the window. She stared out until she was certain that her voice wouldn't tremble with each word she was about to say. "I didn't get hurt. I enjoyed each and every moment I spent with Jared."

"And you fell head over heels in love with him," Cybil said, stating the obvious.

Dana met Cybil's concerned gaze. "Yes, I fell in love with him. I didn't mean for it to happen, but it did. I love Jared with all my heart and I don't have any regrets about it."

Cybil crossed the room to stand in front of Dana. "All right. Now what?"

Dana looked away, to glance back out the window. "Now we've come to the end of our road. Tonight we end things and tomorrow I go back to being an unengaged woman."

Pain settled deep in Dana's heart. How could she go back to the solitary life she'd known after being with Jared for the past six weeks? Not only with Jared, but with all the Westmorelands. For a little while, they had filled a need in her she hadn't realized existed—a need to belong to a family. It was going to be hard going back to being alone again.

"Ben and I are going to the Amelia Islands in the morning to attend the tennis tournament. Come with us."

Dana gave Cybil a reassuring smile. "I'll be fine. I will survive." She chuckled. "It won't be my first broken engagement," she said teasingly.

"But it will be the one that really mattered—pretense or not."

Dana nodded. "Yes, it will be the one that mattered."

"And will you be ready for the questions on Monday? The speculations? The gossip?"

On a long sigh Dana ran her hand through her hair. No, she wouldn't be ready for any of that but she would deal with it. She gave a wry smile. "I'm ready for whatever comes my way, Cybil."

But she knew the moment she'd said the words that they were a lie.

"Why do I get the feeling that you're not in a good mood tonight?"

Jared gave his cousin Storm a crooked smile and lifted the glass of punch to his lips, took a sip and then asked. "I don't know. Why do you?"

A chuckle escaped Storm's lips. "I've often heard if you want a straight answer, then don't ask an attorney a question."

"Yes, I've heard that one, too," Jared said, giving his cousin a wink and taking another sip of his punch. He glanced around, seeing all the people who had shown up to celebrate Thorn and Tara's first wedding anniversary. Even after a year, the thought of Thorn being married was still hard to get used to. Jared never thought there was a woman alive who was brave enough to put up with the surly Thorn Westmoreland. Evidently he'd been wrong. Tara seemed to be handling his prickly cousin very well and it didn't take much to see how in love they were.

Storm's marriage six months ago had been another surprise, and Jared couldn't help but dwell on all the changes that had taken place in Storm's life since then. The man who had once been Atlanta's most sought-after bachelor, who had been known as *The Perfect Storm* to multitudes of women, the man who swore he would never, ever marry was now a happily married man with a wife and twins on the way.

"What happened?" Jared asked. He suddenly needed answers and he'd force them out of Storm if necessary.

Storm raised a dark brow. "What do you mean what happened?"

"With you and this marriage thing. You swore you would never fall in love but you did and I want to know what happened."

A huge smile stretched Storm's lips. "Since you're engaged to be married yourself, I don't understand the need for this cross-examination. But just in case for some reason the verdict's still out, or you're attempting to find logic in all of this, the answer is simple. Love happened. I met a woman who I couldn't live without. At first I thought it was strictly physical since there was such a strong attraction between us, but then I discovered there was more to it than just being intimate. I enjoyed being with her, going places with her, seeing her smile and sharing my thoughts with her. And she was different from any woman I'd ever known."

Storm chuckled before continuing. "It took me a while to rationalize the depth of my feelings but when I did, I knew just what I wanted and who I wanted. And I also knew what I could lose if I didn't accept the truth and act on those feelings. I needed Jayla in my life, as part of my life, just as much as I needed to breathe."

Jared's troubled gaze met Storm's. "You were vulnerable."

Storm shook his head. "That's a subjective viewpoint, Jared, but also a wrong one. I was in love. I was so deeply entrenched in the throes of it that there was no way I could walk away. Jayla has added meaning to my life in ways I didn't think possible. But then from what I can tell, Dana has done the same for you. It shows every time the two of you are together. I've never seen you this attentive to any woman. For the past ten minutes you've been standing here getting agitated as you wait for her to return from touring the house with Tara. You love her, man. I thought I had it bad, but you have it worse. Hell, you're in worse shape than Thorn was and he hadn't known he was in love with Tara until it was almost too late."

Jared took another sip of his drink. He wondered what his cousin would say if he were to tell him he was wrong, that he wasn't in love with Dana, and that the entire engagement had been nothing but a sham.

Whatever he was about to say died on his lips the moment Dana walked through the patio doors with Tara. Tara and Thorn had had the house built and had moved into it a few months ago. It was a beautiful structure located in the outskirts of town on land that had been in the Westmoreland family for generations.

"Well, there's your lady, Jared. And if you're as smart as I know you are, whatever doubt that's beginning to form in your mind will soon vanish. Dana is a treasure worth having and if I were you I'd go a step further than just putting a ring on her finger. I'd make her officially mine as soon as I could."

"And what about the risk?"

Storm's eyes came swiftly to his. "What risk?"

"Divorce."

Storm shook his head. "You've been handling way too many divorce cases, Jared. When you're in love, you don't think of failure, you only think of success and prosperity. Life is full of risks. Each time I leave the station and head out to fight a fire there's a risk. You don't dwell on the what-ifs, and you have to believe that some risks are definitely worth taking. You have to believe in forever. And with that," Storm said, setting down his glass on the table beside him, "I think I'll go find my wife and give her a huge kiss."

Jared lifted his forehead. "Why?

Storm gave him a smart-ass grin. "No particular reason. Just because."

Jared watched as Storm walked away before switching his attention back to Dana. She met his gaze and smiled. He smiled back then sighed deeply as he thought of how right things seemed at that moment. From the first, Dana had blended well with his family. And when she stood in a group with his female cousins, as she was doing now, she seemed so much a part of the Westmorelands. It seemed perfectly right for her to be here with them and with him.

As he continued to hold her gaze he suddenly knew that everything Storm had said was true. As much as he wanted to deny it and *had* denied it, the truth was now crystal clear. He *was* in love. He wanted and needed Dana in his life.

He wanted forever.

How many times in the last six weeks had he reminded himself that their engagement was nothing but pretense? That no matter how much he enjoyed being with her, the time would come for it to end, and for him to go back to playing the field with flashy women who weren't looking for commitment? All the while knowing that his life would become empty without Dana in it.

How many times had he longed to keep things the way they were, but convinced himself that he didn't want or need a woman in his life? That he had seen the ugly side of marriage too much to take the risks for himself? But Storm was right. Some risks were worth taking.

The thought of Dana with someone else, sharing what they had shared was unacceptable. When they had entered into this pretense, he'd had no intention of letting his guard down around her. But he had. And she had eased her way into his heart as easily as anything he'd ever seen. He'd tried to put up resistance, had told himself countless times what he'd felt for her was nothing but lust. However, he knew just as sure as he was standing here that what he felt for her was love of the richest kind and if he was completely honest, he could even admit he had probably fallen in love with her the moment she'd stormed into his office. From that day on, he had wanted her with a passion unlike anything he'd ever felt before.

He wondered what Dana wanted. Was there a chance that she had feelings for him? Could she love him? There was only one way to find out. If she loved him, too, it would definitely make things a lot easier, and if she didn't, then he would just have to take the same advice he'd given Sylvester earlier that day. He would beg if he had to, because he had no intention of letting

Dana go. Whether it was using reason or resorting to seduction, he would do what he had to do to win Dana's heart forever.

Dana didn't have to ask Jared if he wanted to come in when he took her home that night. She wanted him to and hoped that he would. Tonight was their last night together and she wanted one more lasting memory. Besides, she needed to give him back his ring.

When she had returned from touring Tara and Thorn's house she had noticed something different about Jared. It wasn't anything that she could put her finger on, but she sensed something was up. He'd always been attentive when they were together, but tonight it seemed that he was doubly so. And for someone who was supposed to announce to his family that they had broken their engagement tomorrow, he seemed too much the adoring, doting fiancé tonight for such a thing to be believable. There had been the hand holding and the loving kisses that all painted a picture of a couple who were very much in love.

And then there were the times she had caught him looking at her, sometimes in the oddest way. Once, when their gazes had locked, without warning and right in the middle of Dare's conversation, Jared had cupped her face in his hand and kissed her in front of his family, slowly and firmly, before whispering the words, "Let's leave," seductively in her ear.

So here they were, back at her place and as he closed the door behind them she wondered what he had in mind. But whatever it was, she was determined not to lose her composure. She would get through this night as they said their goodbyes.

"It was a nice party, wasn't it?" she asked, trying to generate conversation.

Jared leaned against the door, saying nothing as he watched her with intense dark eyes. "Yes, it was nice."

"And that motorcycle that Thorn presented to Tara was beautiful, simply awesome. To think he made it with his own hands. I can't imagine all the hours it took for him to do it. That was such a special gift to her."

"Yes, it was."

"It's obvious they are so happy together," she added, knowing she had started to ramble. "It's plain to see how much in love they are."

Jared smiled. "Yes, it is. In fact all my cousins who've gotten married appear to be happily in love."

She met his gaze. "What about Chase? Do you think he'll follow his brothers into matrimony eventually?"

Jared eased away from the door to stand in front of her. "Yes, I think he will, once he finds the right woman."

Dana nodded. She wondered if Jared would ever change his mind about love and marriage or if he would always let what he saw in his profession dictate how his future would be.

Knowing there was something she couldn't put off doing any longer, she let out a long, shaky breath as she lifted her hand and eased the engagement ring from her finger. She handed it to him. "It's time to give this back."

He shook his head as his gaze continued to hold hers. He took the ring from her and placed it back on her finger. "No, I want you to keep it."

She blinked. "I can't do that," she said incredulously, shocked he would suggest such a thing.

"Why not? You wanted to keep Cord's ring."

"But only because I was stuck with all those wedding expenses. Pretending to be engaged to you hasn't cost me anything," she said softly, not wanting to admit that it *had* cost her something. Her heart.

He didn't say anything for a few moments and then he gently took her into his arms and gathered her close. He pulled back briefly, met her gaze and in Dana's mind he was looking at her the same way he had done earlier that night.

She held his gaze and every emotion Dana could think of took hold of her. Every time she thought about the fact that this would be the last time they shared together, that chances were when he walked out the door he wouldn't be coming back, despair took hold of her. But she refused to let their last night together end in gloom and doom. It hadn't started out that way and she wouldn't let it end that way.

Jared leaned down and their mouths joined. Immediately, Dana could tell there was something different about this kiss. It still packed a lot of passion that sent toe-curling sensations through her, but there was a degree of tenderness that touched her deeply, almost brought tears to her eyes. It was as if he was methodically placing his stamp on her.

Moments later when he drew away, she had to hold on to his hand to keep her balance. She could actually hear her heart pounding.

"Let's play one final game," Jared whispered softly.

"A final game?" she asked, thinking of the two others they had played together. Her heart began pounding even harder just thinking about them. And the purely seductive male look in his eyes wasn't helping matters.

He looked at her for several long, quiet moments, then said, "Yes. Let's play Truth or Dare?"

With a sigh, Dana looked down at her hands, her gaze focused on the ring he had placed back there. She looked up at him. "I haven't played that in years, since high school at a sleepover."

"Then you know how it's played?"

"Yes." But something told her that Jared would have his own version of the game. What would his dare be like? And did she really want to bare her heart and soul by telling him the truth about anything he asked?

Jared kept his gaze leveled on her. "Okay then let's get started. You go first," he murmured softly.

Dana heaved a deep breath. "Truth or dare?" she challenged.

A smile spread from Jared's lips to his entire face. "Truth."

"Okay." She paused for a moment, wondering what she could ask him and decided to go easy. "What did you enjoy the most about Thorn and Tara's party to-night?"

"Being there with you."

Dana's breath caught and goose bumps formed on her arms with his response. She hadn't expected him to say that. Before she could recover he said, "Truth or dare?"

She decided she would stick with the truth. "Truth."

"What did *you* enjoy the most about the party to-night?" he asked.

Dana sighed. She had hoped he wouldn't ask her that. She had enjoyed a lot about the party tonight, but she knew what she'd enjoyed the most. She met his gaze and told him the truth. "The moment you kissed me in front of everyone."

She saw the darkening of Jared's eyes. She heard the deepening of his breathing. Both sparked desires within her. He reached out and touched her chin, and then his finger moved slowly down the center of her neck to where her pulse was pounding. "Truth or dare," she challenged again, barely able to get the words out.

Although it was impossible, it seemed his eyes darkened more. "Dare," he said huskily.

Dana swallowed past the lump, especially with Jared's hand still there on her neck, drawing lazy circles with his fingers, stimulating both her mind and her body. She could only think of one dare at the moment. "I dare you to kiss me like I'm the only woman you could ever want." A part of Dana knew how badly that must have sounded, but it was her dare and she wondered what he would do about it.

Jared felt his groin tighten in response to Dana's dare. He doubted that she knew how beautiful and sexy she looked, waiting to see what he would do. Fulfilling her dare wasn't a problem since in his mind she was the only woman he could ever want anyway. But she didn't know it and maybe it was about time she did.

He reached out and gently pulled her to him. There was no waiting, and his mouth took hers with all the urgency and need that he felt. He heard her whimper the moment his tongue entered her mouth, and as he began mating his mouth with hers, he felt the shiver that ran down her body. He had kissed her a number of times, but now he was kissing her as the woman he had singled out to spend the rest of his life with, and he was determined to let it show in his kiss. All evening he had longed to kiss her this way. That kiss in front of his family was merely meant to tide him over until now. Until this. His heart was filled with love and his body was wired with sensuous need. Together, both were causing him to overload.

When she grabbed the back of his head, locking their mouths, his hand eased under her blouse, unhooked the front catch to her bra to touch her breasts. Her felt the tips hardened beneath his fingers, felt her body's response to it in her kiss. She moaned in his mouth and the sound sent fire through every nerve in his body. Then when breathing became a necessity, he slowly pulled back, reluctantly breaking off the kiss.

Dana swallowed a frustrated groan. She hadn't wanted him to stop kissing her. Thanks to him she knew how it felt to come apart in a man's arms. She'd discovered all the pleasure a person could experience in making love.

"Truth or dare?"

A heated flutter floated around in her chest, a tingling sensation took root in her stomach. She nervously bit her bottom lip, looked up at him and met his gaze and said, "Dare."

He smiled, seemingly pleased. Then said, "Give me your underwear."

Dana blinked, wondered if she'd heard him right, although she knew that she had. The room felt charged when she lifted her skirt. The heat in his gaze intensified and her breathing pattern became irregular.

Holding his gaze, she slowly eased her bikini panties down her legs. When they were completely off, she balled them up in her hand and handed them to him.

He took them. "Thanks."

Now it was her turn. "Truth or Dare?"

His deep penetrating gaze met hers. "Dare."

A wicked gleam appeared in her eyes when she said, "Give me yours."

Jared chuckled quietly as his hands went to his belt and he pulled it out of the loop. Next he eased down his zipper. Dana watched as he removed his jeans, then the pair of black briefs he was wearing. She inhaled deeply when he stood before her naked from the waist down. Completely naked and totally aroused.

He held her gaze. "Truth or Dare."

She gave him an intimate smile. "Dare."

"I dare you to take off the rest of your clothes."

Dana's heart began beating faster as she began unbuttoning her blouse to take if off. She then removed her bra that was half off anyway. Next was the skirt that she eased down her legs along with her half slip. Her body shivered at the intense desire she saw in Jared's gaze as he looked at her. His eyes seemed fixated with the area below her navel.

"Truth or Dare?" she asked softly, feeling totally exposed, yet at the same time, utterly sexy while standing nude before him.

"Dare," he said throatily, as if that one word had been torn from deep inside his throat.

She nodded, wondering if they would ever get back to truths when it was much more fun being daring. Just looking at him standing in her living room more naked than dressed, made her feel warm, wet and wanton. "Take off the rest of yours, as well."

All he had to do was pull his shirt over his head and

he was done. "Truth or Dare?" he challenged in a husky voice as his gaze moved down the length of her. She felt her body burn everywhere his eyes touched. She also felt her blood simmer slowly through each of her veins.

"Truth," she responded, letting out a slow breath.

"Now that we're naked, what do you want us to do?" he asked. The magnitude of desire in his eyes had her body burning.

She held his gaze. They were back to the truth again. Everything feminine within her yearned for him, actually ached. The area between her legs was throbbing unmercifully. And she could think of only one way to end the torment. "I want you to make love to me. Here. Now. And don't hold back on anything."

Her words were both a truth and a dare, Jared thought, as he filled with need and desire, and an overpowering love slammed into him. Something within him snapped and he wanted to give her exactly what she'd asked for.

He reached out, pulled her to him and kissed her, drowning in the sweet moistness of her mouth. He wanted to touch her, taste her, mark her as his. And although he knew such a thing wasn't possible, he wanted to seduce her into loving him as much as he loved her.

He tugged her down on the carpeted floor and let out a low growl of need when he left her mouth to devour the rest of her. His tongue was hot and the skin it tasted increased the fever and the hunger inside him. And Dana wasn't helping matters. Her hands were touching him everywhere, letting him know that she was driven by the same fierce urgency. When she took him into her hand, running her fingers down his hot, slick shaft, he sucked in his breath. She was burning for him the same way he was on fire for her and he knew of only one way to put out the flames.

"No more," he said, pushing aside her hands, his arousal beyond the point of control. He quickly covered her body and entered her, sheathing himself deep. Breathing raggedly, he began thrusting inside of her, holding her gaze as he moved in and out, mating with her like a man who was about to take his last breath and this was the only thing that could sustain him.

Dana followed Jared's frantic rhythm, kept up with his nonstop pace and sucked in a breath at the impact of each and every thrust. Pleasure tore through her relentlessly, urged her to wrap her legs around his hips and pull him deeper inside of her. She wanted this, had asked for it. And he was giving it to her.

"Jared!"

She gave herself to him in torrid abandonment. Shudders, unyielding and unrelenting, rammed through every part of her body, from the top of her head to the tip of her toes. A mass of sensations bombarded the area between her legs where their bodies were joined. And when he picked up the pace, increased the already frantic rhythm, and deepened his steady thrusts, she lifted her body off the floor, needing and wanting everything he had to give.

"Dana!"

Jared's body shook with the force of an orgasm that shot him into ecstasy, filled him with wondrous sensations. A deep guttural growl of satisfaction ripped from deep within his throat and he felt his body explode inside of her. He never knew, never even thought that making love to a woman could be so climactic and earth-shattering, until he'd made love with her. He had never before mated this wildly with a woman, never before wished the rapture would never end.

A short while later, he collapsed on the floor beside her and pulled her into his arms. He wrapped his arms around her as she lay sprawled lifelessly across his chest, the hunger they had for each other satisfied.

"Truth or dare?" she whispered, pressing her lips against the hollow of his throat and gently sucking there.

His breath caught and he felt himself getting hard all over again. "Truth," he said when he was able to breathe normally again.

"What are you thinking?" she asked, somehow finding strength to lean up and stare down at him.

His heart reacted immediately to her question. "I'm thinking that what we just shared is amazing, and that every time we've made love was incredible. I also think that you're beautiful, sexy and a woman any man would want to claim as his. And that I want you in all the ways a man could possibly want a woman. In bed and out of bed. I'm also thinking about the fact that we didn't use protection, but I'm not bothered by it because I don't want things to end between us tonight."

Dana lightly traced her fingers through the hair on his chest. Was he trying to say he wanted her as a lover? That things didn't have to be over after tonight? But how would he explain to his family as to why she had gone from being his fiancée to nothing more than his lover. But then another part of her knew she wanted more from Jared, a lot more than he was willing to give. She refused to sell herself short and it was best to walk away now to save herself heartbreak later.

"Truth or dare, Dana?"

His challenge interrupted her thoughts. She looked at him. "Truth."

He reached out and captured her hand. "What are you thinking?"

She inhaled deeply, then released a slow, shaky breath. "I'm thinking that I can't settle for an affair with you, Jared."

"That's good because I don't want an affair."

At the confused look that appeared on her face, he sat up and pulled her to him and placed a slow, lingering kiss on her lips. When he released her he said, "I want something more than an affair, Dana. I want you to be the woman I come home to every night."

She frowned, not sure she understood what he was saying. "I don't understand."

With a shuddering sigh he said, "Then maybe it's time to put all game playing aside and speak only the truth."

He couldn't help but think about how much he loved her and needed her in his life. "These past six weeks, pretending to be your fiancé, the man you are going to marry, have been the best weeks of my life. And tonight when I realized it was about to end, I had to face a number of truths. One of which was the fact that I have fallen in love with you."

Dana blinked, seeming thunderstruck. "You have?"

His smile showed a perfect set of white teeth. "Yes, and more than anything I want to make our engagement real." He lifted his hand to her face to caress her cheek.

"But getting what I want really depends on how you feel about me, Dana."

He saw the moment tears began forming in her eyes. "Oh, Jared, I love you, too, and more than anything I want our engagement to be real."

He chuckled with both joy and relief and pulled her into his lap. "I'm damn glad to hear that. So, Dana Rollins will you marry me? Be my wife, the mother of my children and the love of my life for always?"

He framed her face in his hands and continued. "Will you let that ring you're already wearing be a symbol of my love and promise? And will you believe that I will honor you, protect you and make you happy?"

He watched as more tears came into her eyes at the same time a soft chuckle escaped from her throat. "Yes, I'll marry you, Jared, and be all of those things."

An overpowering gush of happiness erupted from Jared's throat. "You do know this means you'll have all the Westmorelands as family?"

Tears made her choke back her laughter. "Thank God. I'd become attached to them and didn't want to give them up even though I thought this would be our last night together."

When his arms tightened around her she leaned down and rubbed her cheek against his chest. "You're a pro at making seductive proposals, Jared Westmoreland."

He grinned as his heart raced with unmeasured joy. "Am I?"

"Yes."

"Umm," he said as heat began stroking his body all over again. "I'm also pretty good at other things."

She met his dark penetrating gaze as she stared at him. "Are you?"

"Yes."

She leaned down, her lips mere inches from his. "Show me these other things. I dare you."

In one smooth move he quickly had her on her back. Their gazes locked and he knew he would love her for the rest of his life.

And that was the naked truth.

Epilogue

Two months later

Just as Sarah Westmoreland had predicted, there was another Westmoreland wedding before the end of the summer.

As Jared carried his wife down the church steps, she laid her head against his solid chest as rice rained down on them. Out of the corner of his eyes he saw his parents. He noticed his mother dab tears of joy from her eyes. To say she was happy was an understatement. But then, he knew she was already checking out her remaining five single sons to see who she should set her mark on next. He chuckled. She even had his cousin Chase within her intense scope. No one would be safe from matrimony if Sarah Westmoreland had her way.

When he and Dana were seated inside the limo, he

pulled her into his arms and kissed her with all the love he felt in his heart. His tongue swept inside to caress the walls of her mouth thinking that he would never get tired of the taste of her.

Their next stop was the grand ballroom of the Atlanta Civic Center. It amazed him how his mother and Aunt Evelyn, along with the long-distance assistance of his aunt Abby in Montana, were able to put together such an elegant wedding once he and Dana had set a date.

Jared released Dana's mouth and looked down into her smiling face. "How much ruckus do you think we'll cause if I tell the driver that we want to skip the wedding reception and go straight to the airport to catch our plane for St. Maarten?"

A smile touched the corners of Dana's mouth. "Oh, I think more than we're prepared to deal with. Your mother and aunts might never forgive us."

Jared grinned. "You're right. I guess the least we can do is show up."

"I agree."

He reached out and pulled her into his lap. It wasn't an easy thing to do considering her wedding dress. It was beautiful and she had looked gorgeous in it when she had walked down the aisle to him. Her best friend's husband, Ben, had given her away and Cybil had been her matron of honor. Delaney, Shelly, Tara, Madison, Casey and some of Dana's girlfriends from college had been her bridesmaids. Jayla had had to sit this one out since she was about to deliver at any moment. Dare had been Jared's best man and his brothers and the rest of his cousins stood in as his groomsmen.

Sylvester Brewster had asked to sing a song at the

wedding as a way to show his thanks for all Jared had done in getting him and his wife back together. After Jared had set up the meeting between them, the two had agreed to marriage counseling to make their marriage work. They were in love and wanted to put this episode behind them and move on.

Dana lifted her hand to admire her rings. She then looked at Jared's hand to see his matching gold band. She glanced up at him. She loved him totally and completely. An idea suddenly popped into her head. "Later tonight, when we're all alone I think we should play another game."

Jared lifted his forehead. "I thought Truth or Dare would be our final one."

She shook her head, grinning. "Why stop when you're having fun? And I have the perfect game for us."

She had peaked his curiosity. "And what game is that?"

"Spin the Bottle."

Jared smiled as he thought of all the possibilities and decided he could definitely put an interesting twist on that game. "Okay, I'm up for it."

Dana chuckled. "I thought that you would be."

And then with a shuddering sigh she pulled his face down to hers, her lips parting as she let him take possession of her mouth in a kiss that was full of all the passion she had come to expect from him. And as she returned his kiss with provocative urgency and overpowering passion, she knew that the best day of her life had been when she had agreed to become Jared's counterfeit fiancée.

* * * * *

THE CHASE IS ON

To Gerald Jackson, Sr, my husband and hero.

To Joyce Perry, who taught me everything I need to know about making chocolate...even some things I really didn't need to know. Thanks, JP!

An unreliable messenger can cause a lot of trouble. Reliable communication permits progress.
—Proverbs 13:17

Prologue

Eighteen years ago

"**N**ever trust a Graham."

Sixteen-year old Chase Westmoreland slid onto the stool at the counter in his grandfather's restaurant. The old man turned and spoke while placing a huge glass of milk and a plate filled with cookies in front of him.

"Why? What's wrong, Gramps?" Chase asked as he immediately attacked the stack of cookies.

"What's wrong? I'll tell you what's wrong. Carlton Graham stole some of our secret recipes and passed them on to Donald Schuster."

Chase stopped eating as his eyes grew large. He knew how his grandfather felt about the Westmoreland family recipes. They had been in the family for generations. "But Mr. Graham is your friend."

Scott Westmoreland frowned at his grandson. "Not anymore he isn't. Our friendship ended along with our partnership two weeks ago. I never thought I'd live to see the day he would betray me this way."

Chase downed a huge gulp of milk and then asked, "Are you sure he did it?"

Scott Westmoreland nodded, his features tired and full of pain and disappointment. "Yes, I'm sure. I'd heard that Schuster had added a couple of new dishes to his menu that taste just like mine, so I went to investigate for myself."

Chase nodded. "And?"

"They're mine all right. Schuster won't say where he got the recipes, but I knew they are mine."

Chase sadly shook his head. He'd always liked Mr. Graham and his chocolate chip cookies were the best. His grandfather's were all right, but Mr. Graham's had a special ingredient that made them mouth-wateringly delicious. "Did you ask Mr. Graham about it?"

"Of course I did and he denies everything, but I know he's lying. He's the only person who knows exactly what ingredients I use. He must feel guilty. That's probably the reason he's not wasting any time moving his family out of town."

Chase's eyes widened. "The Grahams are moving away?"

"Yes and good riddance. It wouldn't bother me any if I never saw another Graham again. Like I said, they can't be trusted. Always remember that."

One

The present

He needed an attitude adjustment.

That thought flashed through Chase Westmoreland's mind as he turned the corner to pull into his restaurant's parking lot. Six months of abstinence, he concluded, had to be the reason he'd been in such a bad mood lately.

It had nothing to do with the fact that in the last three years, all of his four brothers and his baby sister had gotten married. Even his cousin Jared, the die-hard bachelor and divorce lawyer, had recently fallen victim. Chase was sick and tired of varied family members looking at him with a knowing smile on their lips. If they

were waiting for him to be next, then they had a long
wait ahead of them.

And it didn't help matters that his brothers were cocky
enough to say he would change his mind when the right
woman came along. His comeback to them had been
quick and confident. The "right woman" didn't exist.

"What the hell!" He brought his car to a sudden stop in
the middle of the parking lot outside his restaurant, which
was buzzing with activity. He had forgotten that someone
had purchased the building a few doors from Chase's
Place. From the way things looked, they were moving in.

He had received notice a few weeks ago that he
would have a new neighbor.

He wasn't surprised. Atlanta was a city of international renown that had managed to hold on to its
southern charm. And the downtown section where his
restaurant was located with its charming neighborhoods,
tree-shaded streets and friendly communities, made it
a prime area for doing business. If he remembered correctly, someone would be opening a confectionery.

When he'd first heard about it, the news had brought
out his cravings for chocolate, but now seeing the mass
of confusion surrounding him all thoughts of sweets
suddenly turned sour.

Moving trucks were everywhere and taking up parking spaces his customers would need. It was barely six
in the morning and he had a huge breakfast crowd. The
last thing he needed was someone messing with the
availability of parking. It was a good thing he had a reserved spot in front of his restaurant, or there wouldn't
be any space left even for him.

He sat in his car, forcing himself to breath calmly as a truck blocked him in. This was Monday, not a good day for his patience to be tested. He was just about to hit his horn when a woman walking out of the building caught his attention. For a moment he forgot his anger. Hell, he even forgot to breathe.

As she talked to the driver of the truck blocking his path, he looked her up and down. She was a prime specimen of a woman. She was dressed in a short baker's smock, and he hoped she had on a pair of shorts since a good gust of wind would show him and anyone else what may or may not be underneath. A smile drifted over his lips. Even with the smock he could tell she had one helluva figure. And when his gaze lit on her face…

His skin suddenly felt overheated as he looked into a medium brown face too beautiful for words. She had a pair of honey-brown eyes and full, moist lips covered in what looked like juicy red strawberry lip gloss. He wanted to get out of his car, walk over to her and kiss the coloring right off her lips. Then there was her hair, a mass of dark-brown curls that tumbled over her shoulders. For the first time in quite a while Chase found himself physically affected by a beautiful woman.

That thought made him take a deep breath and he forced himself to pull back. He was a thirty-four-year-old hot-blooded male and there was nothing wrong with responding to visual stimuli. But he couldn't let a great pair of legs and a gorgeous face scatter his wits. All he had to do was remember his last year at Duke University and Iris Nelson. Thinking of Iris made warning bells go off…the sound of reason.

Sighing deeply, he let his gaze drift over her once more before backing up his car and moving around the truck. He sighed, glad he was breathing again. As soon as he got inside his restaurant he would drink a strong cup of black coffee.

Chase only wished he hadn't noticed the absence of a wedding ring on the woman's finger, making him happier than it ought to.

Jessica Claiborne smiled as she looked around her shop. After moving in she was already set for the shop's grand opening tomorrow morning. She had spent the day doing last-minute checks on inventory and confirming arrangement for deliveries. She had hired two high-school students to pass out flyers about the shop around the community. Since she intended for all of her products to be baked fresh daily, she had made a call to the children's hospital and offered to donate any treats she didn't sell tomorrow. Also, she had signed contracts with a couple of the hotels around town to supply their restaurants and coffeeshops with baked goods.

She glanced out the window. It was a beautiful day in early October. The movers had gotten everything set up on Monday and the artist she'd hired had come that morning to paint her shop's name on the display window. Delicious Cravings was the name she had decided on, and she would be forever thankful to her grandmother for making her dream come true.

Sadness settled in Jessica's heart whenever she thought about the grandmother she had simply adored and the inheritance she'd been left when her grandmother had died last year on Jessica's twenty-fifth birthday. The money had made it possible to walk away from her stressful job as a corporate attorney in Sacramento and pursue her dream of owning and operating her own confectionery.

She sniffed the air, enjoying the smell of chocolate cooking. Already today she had made a batch of assorted pastries including éclairs and tarts. But what she had enjoyed more than anything was whipping up chocolate nut clusters and an assortment of cookies for her neighbors as an apology for inconveniencing them during her move.

Mrs. Morrison who owned the seamstress shop next door had accepted her apology but declined her treats since she was allergic to chocolate but had said she would love to try her shortcake. The Criswell brothers, who owned the karate school, had accepted her gift and apology graciously, welcomed her to the strip and said they looked forward to patronizing her shop. The only person left was the owner of Chase's Place. Jessica hoped the restaurateur was just as understanding as Mrs. Morrison and the Criswell brothers had been and that he had a sweet tooth.

Grabbing the box she had filled with sweet treats, she walked out the door and locked it behind her. She had hired a part-time helper, an elderly woman who would come in during the busy lunchtime hours.

It was early afternoon but she could tell the restaurant was packed and hoped the business would eventually trickle over to her once people realized she was open. Before she got within ten feet of the restaurant she could smell the mouth-watering food and realized she hadn't eaten anything since breakfast.

She walked into Chase's Place, immediately liking what she saw. It was a very upscale restaurant that some-how maintained a homey atmosphere. Lanterns adorned each table and the tablecloths matched curtains that hung in the windows. There was a huge counter with bar stools and soft jazzy music coming from a speaker lo-cated somewhere in the back.

"Welcome to Chase's Place, where you're guaran-teed to get the finest in soul food. Are you dining in or carrying out?"

Jessica smiled at the young woman who greeted her. "I'm the owner of the new confectionery a few doors down and wanted to bring the owner a gift for any in-convenience he might have encountered while I was moving in."

The woman nodded. "That would be Chase and he's in his office. If you follow me I'll show you the way."

"Thanks."

Jessica followed the woman down a hall that led to the back of the restaurant. Everything looked tidy, even the storage room they passed. The hostess knocked when they reached the office door. "Who is it?" a deep, husky voice called out.

"It's Donna. Someone is here to see you."

"Hell, I'm surprised anyone can get through with all that chaos that's been going on in the parking lot. I have a good mind to go over there and give my inconsider-ate new neighbor a piece of my mind for all the prob-lems she's caused me the last couple of days. I couldn't get my own deliveries through for—"

Chase stopped talking when his door swung open

and the woman he had checked out Monday morning walked into his office past a speechless Donna. "I guess I've saved you a trip. I would think, considering the circumstances, you would have been just as understanding as my other neighbors and…"

Whatever the woman was saying Chase had stopped listening mere seconds after she walked into his office. Heat flared through all parts of his body and his full concentration centered on the shorts and tank top she was wearing.

Up close her legs were more of a turn-on than they had been on Monday morning. He blinked. The closer she got, the better she looked, especially those moist strawberry lips. She was angry…sexy as hell.

In addition to the honey-brown eyes and curly dark hair that tumbled around her face, she possessed perfect cheekbones and a cute perky nose. He couldn't help noticing that the mouth that was moving was beautifully shaped and ready to be kissed.

"And I hope you choke on these!"

He was jolted from his lust-filled thoughts when a box was suddenly shoved against his chest. It took only a split second for him to realize his visitor was leaving. When the door slammed shut, he looked at Donna, ignored the silly smirk on her face and asked, "What the hell did she say?"

He watched Donna's try to hide a laugh. "I think, boss, that you've been thoroughly told off. I can't believe you weren't listening."

No, he hadn't been listening. He looked down at the box.

"That was supposed to be a peace offering," Donna explained. "She came to apologize for the inconvenience over the past couple of days. I think that was downright neighborly of her. I guess she hoped you'd be more understanding of the chaos she caused while moving in."

Chase nodded, suddenly filled with regret that he hadn't been more understanding. But he'd been in a foul mood for the past week and had wrongly directed his anger at her. She was a woman after all, and a woman, or actually the lack of one, was the root of his problem.

Granted he wasn't the ladies' man his twin brother Storm had been, but usually he could pull out his little phone book and contact any number of women, who, like him, were more interested in getting down than getting married. But for some reason doing so didn't suit him. The last woman he dated had read more into the relationship and he'd had one hell of a time convincing her that bedding her didn't mean he'd be wedding her. He wasn't into serious relationships of any kind and had told her that in the beginning. Evidently somewhere along the way she'd forgotten.

He dragged a weary hand down his face. Some women saw the single Westmoreland men as challenges. His brother Storm's philosophy—before his wife Jayla had entered his life—had been that he enjoyed women too much to settle down with just one. Chase believed in learning from his mistakes, and his biggest one had been a woman by the name of Iris Nelson.

While in college at Duke, he had seemed headed for

a pro basketball career when an injury had ended his dreams. He'd found himself facing an endless future when Iris, the girl he had fallen in love with, decided that with no chance at the pros he was no longer a good prospect.

Over the years he'd become wary of opportunistic women who only entered relationships to find out what was in it for them, and when the going got tough, they got going. Making women secondary in his life was the best way to eliminate the chance of a repeat heartbreak.

"So what are you going to do?" Donna asked, interrupting his thoughts.

He didn't have a clue. One thing was certain, he owed his new neighbor an apology. "Tell Kevin to prepare a today's special to go and be generous with the servings."

Chuckling, Donna nodded. "You think you'll find her soft spot with food?"

He looked down at the box he held in his hand and inhaled the aroma of chocolate. "Wasn't that her game plan?"

Donna gave him a long look before slowly shaking her head and closing the door behind her as she left.

Chase placed the box on his desk. The top was marked Delicious Cravings. He thought of how she'd looked Monday morning when he had first seen her and just moments ago standing in the middle of his office. The name was definitely appropriate.

He opened the box and immediately fell in love— with the sweets. Yes, he definitely owed the woman an apology and before the evening ended he would make sure she got one.

* * *

That man had a bad attitude!

Jessica took a deep breath, refusing to get any more upset than she already was. How dare he say she was inconsiderate? She was one of the most considerate people she knew. It was one of the reasons she had walked away from her high-paying job as a corporate attorney.

She had gotten fed up with having to fight for things she didn't believe in, pushing policies that ruined people's lives, being forced to put corporate profits before the consumers' best interests.

And her consideration for her family's wishes was the only thing pushing her to seek out members of the Westmoreland family to right a wrong made against her family years ago. The nerve of them thinking her grandfather had been a dishonest man! He had been one of the most honest men she knew and if it was left up to her, she would give the Westmorelands a good piece of her mind and tell them just what she thought of their accusations. But before taking her final breath her grandmother had made her promise to come to Atlanta to clear the Graham name without starting World War III, and she intended to do that. After doing research on the area, she decided Atlanta would be a good place to live and not just visit. And so she had made the decision to relocate to the area.

She sighed as her thoughts drifted back to the owner of Chase's Place. He had reminded her of dark chocolate of the richest kind and she knew one of the reasons she had gone off on him the way she had was that she couldn't afford to get caught up in his sheer beauty. Even with his horrible attitude she had to admit that he was handsome as sin. Taller and well-built, his features took her breath away. He had reminded her that she was a woman, something she often tried to forget.

The last thing she needed was to get attracted to a man. She refused to get so carried away that she forgot how deceitful they were. She had learned her lesson even if her mother never had. Jeff Claiborne may have been the man who had fathered her, but he was also the man who had kept her mother dangling on a string for over fifteen years with promises of marriage. When Jessica had been born he had given her his name, but her mother's last name had remained Graham.

It had taken her grandfather's paid investigator to deliver the news that there was no way Jeff Claiborne could ever marry Janice Graham. He was already married to another woman and had a family living in Philadelphia. The news had been a terrible blow to her mother—one that she had never recovered from. She took her own life rather that live with the heartache and pain.

At the age of fifteen Jessica had watched as her mother's coffin was lowered into the ground and had vowed never to give her heart to any man. She wouldn't be fooled by a man as deceitful as her father had been, one man who could take undying love and abuse it in the worst possible way.

Her grandfather, angry and hurt over what Jeff Claiborne had done, had made sure the man didn't get away unscathed. He had paid a visit to Jeff Claiborne's wife and had presented her with documented proof of her husband's duplicity. Jennifer Claiborne, a good woman, hadn't wasted any time filing for a divorce and leaving her husband of eighteen years. And Jennifer had gone one step further by welcoming Jessica into her family, making sure she got to know her sister and brother, and making sure Jeff Claiborne contributed to her support. She knew Jennifer had been instrumental in helping to set up the college fund that had been available when she had graduated from high school.

Savannah and Rico were as close to her as any brother and sister could be. And Jennifer was like a second mother to her. She'd known she could always go visit her extended family in Philadelphia.

Jessica heard a knock at the door and frowned. Dusk was settling in but she could plainly see through her display window that her unexpected visitor was the man from the restaurant.

She had a good mind to ignore him. For the last couple of weeks since moving to Atlanta she had begun thinking she had finally found peace, but now he was convincing her otherwise.

She heard his knock again and decided that she wouldn't hide. Like everything else in life she would deal with her problems, and in this case, her problem was him. He had sought her out and she supposed she needed to make nice because she'd be seeing him a lot. This building was not only the place she would work but thanks to space above the shop, it was also her new home.

Deciding she had let him linger long enough, she made her way to the door and unlocked it. She took a deep breath before opening it. "What do you want?"

He had been standing with his back to her, looking up at the sky. The day had been beautiful but it seemed that tonight it would rain. He turned around and as soon as their gazes locked she felt the temperature go up about one hundred degrees.

He still reminded her of rich dark chocolate rum balls but now something else had been added to the mixture, she thought, as her gaze moved from the baseball cap on his head to the features in his face. A slight indention in the bridge of his nose indicated it may have been broken at one time but she didn't even consider that a flaw. Nothing, and she meant nothing, distracted from this man's good looks.

Jeeze. That wasn't a good sign.

And to make matters worse, his smile was so potent that she was forced to grip the doorknob to support her suddenly wobbly knees. Forcing her eyes away from that smile, she met his gaze once more and it angered her that he had this kind of effect on her. "I repeat, what do you want?" she all but snapped.

His grin widened. He was either oblivious to her less-than-friendly mood or else he chose to ignore it. "I came to apologize and to deliver a peace offering," he said, widening that killer smile even more and holding up a bag that smelled of delicious food.

"I was out of line earlier," he said. "And I do understand how it is moving in. The only excuse I can give for my behavior is that this has been one hell of a week. But my problems are not your fault."

His apology surprised her, but it didn't captivate her

as he had evidently assumed it would. Long ago she had learned to be cautious of smooth-talking men.

"Will you accept my apology?"

She jutted her chin. "Why should I?"

"Because it will prove that you're a much nicer person than I am and someone with a forgiving spirit."

Jessica leaned against the doorjamb, thinking that she was definitely a much nicer person than he, but she wasn't all that sure about having a forgiving spirit. She inhaled deeply, deciding she didn't want to accept his apology. She didn't like the chemistry she felt flowing between them and she also decided she didn't like him. She knew it all sounded irrational, but at the moment she didn't care. "There are a lot of things I can overlook, but rudeness isn't one of them."

Chase lifted a brow and frowned. "So you aren't going to accept my apology?"

She glared at him. "At the moment, no."

His frown deepened as he peered down at her. "Why?"

"Because I don't feel like it. Now if you'll excuse me I need to—"

He held up a hand, cutting her off. "Because you don't feel like it?"

"That's what I said."

Chase felt frustration take over his body. He had dealt with many unreasonable people, but this woman gave new meaning to the word. Yes, he had been rude. But he had apologized, hadn't he?

"Look," he said slowly, while trying to overlook the irritation plastered on her face. "I know things got off to a bad start between us, and for that I apologize. And you're right. I was rude, but now you're the one who is being unreasonable."

Jessica sighed deeply. The dark-brown eyes focused on hers were intense, sharp, and to-die-for, but still...

"But still nothing, Jessica Lynn," she could hear her grandmother saying in the recesses of her mind. *"You can't judge every man by your father. You can't continue to put up this brick wall against any man who gets too close."*

Sighing again, she smoothed a hand down her face. Her grandmother was right but the need to protect herself had always been elemental. For some reason she had an inkling that the man standing before her was someone she should avoid at all costs.

"Please accept my peace offering as I did yours, okay?" Chase asked, interrupting her thoughts. "By the way, everything was delicious, especially the chocolate chip cookies. They're my favorite and I haven't tasted chocolate chip cookies that delicious in years. They were melt-in-your-mouth delicious." He slanted her a smile. "And I didn't choke on any of them."

"Too bad," she said dryly. Their gazes held for a moment, and she knew she was a puzzle he was trying to figure out. No doubt other women didn't cause him any trouble. He probably flashed his smile and got whatever he wanted. Just like her father.

She wrapped her arms around herself knowing he didn't intend to leave until she accepted his apology. "Okay, I accept your apology. Goodbye."

He grabbed the door before she could slam it shut in

his face. He held up the bag and smiled. "And the peace offering?"

She snorted a breath. "And the peace offering," she said reaching for the bag.

Chase chuckled. "Now we're getting somewhere." Instead of giving her the bag he held his hand out to her. "We haven't been properly introduced. I'm Chase Westmoreland. And you are?" he asked taking her hand.

Jessica knew if she had a lighter skin tone he would have seen all the blood drain from her face. "Westmoreland?"

He grinned. "Yes, does the name ring a bell? There's a bunch of us living in Atlanta."

Deciding she wasn't ready to tell him just how familiar it was, she shook her head. "No, I recently moved here from California."

He nodded and after a few moments he said smiling, "You never told me your name."

She blinked, recalling that she hadn't. "I'm Jessica Claiborne."

His smile widened. "Welcome to Atlanta, Jessica. Do you have family here?"

"No," she answered truthfully, "I have no family living here." Her head was still spinning at the realization that he was a Westmoreland.

There was a bit of silence between them when Chase remembered the bag he was holding. "Oops, I almost forgot. Here you go," he said handing the bag to Jessica. "It's today's special. I hope you enjoy it."

"Thanks."

He hesitated for a moment then said, "I guess I'd better get back. The dinner crowd is arriving. Will you be living upstairs?"

"Yes," she said, gripping the bag in both hands. She needed to get away from him to think.

"Well, every once in a while if it's a late night, I sleep over my place, too. If you ever need anything, just let me know."

Don't hold your breath, Jessica thought, closing the door on temptation.

Two

Jessica leaned back in the chair and licked her lips. That had to have been the most delicious meal she'd eaten in a very long time. The smothered pork chops had been tender, just the way she liked and the mashed potatoes had made her groan out loud. No wonder Chase's Place was packed. The dessert, a slice of carrot cake, had been melt-in-your-mouth delicious. And she knew baked goods. Her grandmother had been the best baker she'd ever met.

She'd always enjoyed baking because of all the times she had spent with her grandparents in the kitchen growing up. She had even considered going to culinary school instead of law school. But her grandfather had talked her out of it, saying there were enough cooks in the Graham family.

As she cleaned up, Jessica glanced around her apartment. It was just the right size for her, with a large living room, a bath, a small kitchen and a bedroom. She loved the hardwood floors and the huge window in the living room.

She smiled at the thought that she actually owned this place, the entire building. Downstairs in the shop, there was a huge cooking area and a small office in the back. It had been just what she'd been looking for. According to the real estate agent, all the buildings were newly renovated and business in the area was always good. She moved over to the window and glanced out again at all the people gathered at Chase's Place.

Her breath suddenly caught when she noticed Chase walk out of his restaurant with another man. It was plain to see the two were related since there were distinct similarities in their features. But Chase was the one holding her attention. The sun had gone down, but the faint light illuminated him. He looked good in his jeans and black pullover shirt, and even from where she was standing she could see his perfectly chiseled features.

She sighed deeply, and as if he had heard, he glanced toward her window and their eyes met. She felt it, the moment their eyes connected, a jolt in the lower part of her body, a current of electricity that spiked up her spine. Both feelings suddenly rejuvenated that part of her that had been dormant since her first year of college. The one and only time she'd ever had sex had been an awful experience she hadn't ever wanted to repeat.

But now, looking at Chase perpetuated more than mild curiosity; for a single moment she wondered if making love with him would be different. She blinked, and stepped away from the window. How could she have forgotten just who Chase was? He was a Westmoreland, for heaven's sake! She refused to become a lust-crazed lunatic over someone from a family of liars who had accused her grandfather of being a thief. It didn't matter to her that Chase was the epitome of everything male. He was a Westmoreland and that meant he was definitely off-limits.

"Who is she?"

A smile caught the corner of Chase's mouth as his attention was drawn from the window where Jessica had been standing back to his brother Storm. "Need I remind you that you're married?" Chase replied.

Storm chuckled as he shook his head. "No. Jayla is the love of my life and all the woman I'd ever need, and the girls are the icing on the cake," he said of his three-month-old twin daughters. "But it seems to me that she has gotten your attention."

The smile faded from Chase's lips. Jessica Claiborne had definitely caught his attention and from the moment they met. "Her name is Jessica Claiborne. We didn't hit it off at first."

Storm's lips tilted in amused humor. "And now?"

Chase leaned against the building. "I think she still doesn't like me."

Storm lifted his brows. "First impressions can be changed if you work hard at it," he said as he watched his brother's gaze shift back to the window where the woman had been standing earlier. He glanced at his watch. "I have to go. I just wanted to make sure you knew about the christening on Sunday."

"Yes, Mom mentioned it. I think the restaurant is perfect for the after-christening dinner."

Storm smiled. "Are you sure? I wouldn't want you to go to any trouble."

"No trouble for my nieces. Consider it done. Tell Jayla that I'll call her sometime tomorrow to discuss the menu."

"Ok, I'll do that."

Chase watched his twin brother get into his car and pull away. He hesitated for a moment not ready to go back inside and glanced at the confectionery again, wondering whether Jessica had enjoyed the meal he'd had prepared for her. There was only one way to find out.

Shoving his hands into his pockets he walked past Mrs. Morrison's seamstress shop until he stood directly in front of Delicious Cravings. Ignoring the Closed sign on the door, he knocked a couple of times then rang the doorbell. Moments later a soft voice asked. "Who is it?"

"Chase."

She slowly opened the door and glared at him. "What do you want now?"

The bitterness that was still in her voice surprised him. He would have thought that if his apology hadn't done the trick, certainly a meal from Chase's Place had smoothed her over. Evidently not. He heaved a sigh.

She had folded her arms over her chest and he wished she hadn't done that. Although he was a leg man first, he was a breast man second and the position of her arms clearly empathized what a nice, firm, full pair she had. At that moment he actually envied her tank top.

He cleared his throat and said, "I saw you standing at the window."

Her gaze sharpened. "So?"

He smoothed a hand across his forehead. Maybe where she came from, people were unfriendly and unpleasant, but here in the South people were warm and gracious. "Is it too much to hope that you enjoyed dinner?" he asked.

She actually seemed surprised by his question. "Of course I enjoyed dinner. Why would you think that I hadn't?"

"Your attitude."

Jessica clamped down her jaw down from jutting out. Okay, so once again he hadn't seen her at her best, but there was a reason for it. He was a Westmoreland and she was a Graham.

Sighing, she dropped her hands to her side. "Look, don't take it personally, but I don't like you."

Chase leaned in the doorway and crossed his legs at the ankles. "Why?"

She waved her hand impatiently. "I'd think it would be obvious."

He lifted a brow. "You think we're opposites?"

She drew in an angry breath and met his gaze. "I don't know you that well, but I'd say we're as different as day and night."

Chase straightened and shot her a grin. "Then that explains it."

She narrowed an eye. "Explains what?"

"Why we're attracted to each other. Opposites attract."

Jessica snorted a breath. "I am not attracted to you!"

Chase's grin widened. "Yes, you are, and I'm attracted to you as well," he said, standing with his legs braced apart, his gaze intense, and shoulders squared.

"Believe whatever you want."

"Would you like to prove otherwise?"

She raised a questioning brow. "How?"

Chase shrugged. "Never mind, this isn't a good time to—"

"Wait! If there's a way I can prove that I'm not attracted to you then let's bring it on," she snapped.

Chase met her gaze. "Fine with me if you're sure that's what you want to do."

Jessica's shoulders were rigid with anger. "And just what is it we need to do to prove it?"

"Kiss."

At first Jessica was stunned. But then she figured it would be just like a man to want to prove anything by locking lips. Well, he would find out that she didn't enjoy kissing any more than she had making love. This was destined to be the shortest kiss on record.

She met his gaze and smiled. "Like I said, let's bring it on."

The way Chase returned her smile had her thinking that maybe, just maybe, she'd made a mistake. And when he walked past her into her shop, she had a sinking feeling in the pit of her stomach that that was definitely so.

Damn, Chase thought as he gazed at Jessica's mouth. He was going to enjoy every minute, every second that he devoured it. He bet it was as sinfully sweet and delicious as all those treats she whipped up. Sweeter.

As he continued to stare at her, pure, unadulterated lust rushed through his veins, pricked every pore of his skin and slashed waves of heat through his body. He could even go so far to say that he felt the cells in his groin reproducing.

Need propelled him from where he was standing across the room to her. He gently clasped the back of her head and pulled her closer, her lips mere inches from his. "I intend to kiss you witless," he whispered huskily.

She jutted her chin and narrowed her gaze. "You can try."

He smiled, liking her spunk. Chase hoped like hell that she put all that haughtiness into their kiss. "Open your mouth for me, sweetheart," he whispered in a deep, throaty voice.

Releasing a frustrated sigh, Jessica opened her mouth to tell him a thing or two, but with lightning speed he seized the opportunity and planted his mouth firmly on hers, silencing whatever she was about to say.

He groaned deep within his throat. His tongue thick and hot captured hers and savored it like spicy ginger-bread. She had never been kissed this way before; never in her wildest imagination had she envisioned some-thing like this happening to her.

Chase devoured her mouth like a dessert he had to have, doing passionate, provocative and illicit things to it. The man was skilled, trained, experienced and knew just what to do to make those purring sounds suddenly erupt from deep within her throat.

She couldn't believe it. With his kiss, sensual urges—

intense and strong—that she didn't recognize attacked her entire being, demanding that her body react and respond to him. She was grateful for the strong arms holding her close; otherwise she would have melted to the floor by now. She felt intense fire licking its way through her veins, her insides were simmering in heat. She was mesmerized to the point of no return.

But that's not all she felt.

His hardness, his strength, one hell of an erection was cradled between her thighs. She felt delirious, and when an involuntary shudder raced through her, she suddenly realized something. She was kissing him back. She never kissed men back. The thought overwhelmed her, overloaded her senses and sent intense heat rippling through her body.

If this didn't beat all. They had just met that day. He was a Westmoreland. She didn't like him. She didn't like kissing. She needed to breathe.

As if he'd read her last thought, he slowly released her mouth. As she stared up at him she couldn't believe they had shared something so powerful, provoking and intimate. A part of her wondered what one should say after such a stimulating encounter. But at the moment she couldn't say anything. The only thing she could think about was the way his mouth felt and how much she'd enjoyed kissing him.

"Let me go on record to say I only ended the kiss so we could breathe," he whispered, reaching up and sliding his fingers through her hair. "We might be opposites, but like I said earlier, Jessica, we do attract."

The huskiness of his words sent shivers all through

her and her skin was beginning to feel hot all over again. She could actually feel her blood sizzling. He took a step back and a warm smile tilted the corners of his lips.

"Best wishes on opening day tomorrow," he said softly.

She watched as he turned and walked out of the shop, closing the door behind him.

"I'm looking forward to working for you, Ms. Claiborne."

It had been a busy grand-opening day. The huge crowd had come and gone and they were now able to relax and take a breather. Jessica smiled at the woman, old enough to be her grandmother, and replied, "I'm looking forward to working with you, too, Mrs. Stewart. I'm just so grateful that you could help me out. I'd feel a lot better if you called me Jessica."

Delicious Cravings had officially opened at eight o'clock that morning. Jessica had been quite busy and was grateful when Ellen Stewart had walked in the shop at eleven to help with the lunch-hour traffic. But no matter how busy she'd gotten, she couldn't forget the kiss she had shared with Chase last night. It had been amazing.

Switching her thoughts elsewhere, she watched Mrs. Stewart as she dusted off the counter, thinking the woman was a huge asset to the shop with her knowledge of retail sales as well as her genuine friendliness. It seemed she knew everyone who had come in. She was a definite plus for business. But then so was Chase Westmoreland.

Most of the people who had dropped by to make a

purchase had mentioned that Chase claimed her treats were to die for. She hated admitting it, but she owed him a degree of gratitude as well, although the last thing she wanted was to owe a Westmoreland anything.

"I think it was very nice of Chase to send you customers. He's such a sweetheart."

Jessica stopped placing brownies in the display case and turned a curious gaze to Ms. Stewart. "You know Chase?"

The woman chuckled. "Of course I do. I know all the Westmorelands. Although most of the people living in Atlanta are transplants, there are still a few of us natives hanging around. I knew those Westmoreland boys and their cousins when they were in elementary school. In fact, I taught most of them."

Jessica nodded, remembering Mrs. Stewart had mentioned she had retired as a teacher over fifteen years ago. "They got into mischief like boys would do but I didn't know a more respectful group," Mrs. Stewart added. "Did you know that his brother Dare is the sheriff of College Park?"

Jessica lifted a brow. "No, I didn't know that."

"Well, he is and a good one at that. And then there's Thorn, who builds motorcycles and races them. Stone writes blockbuster books. There are also a bunch of Westmoreland cousins, like Jared, the well-known attorney. Oh, and I can't forget Storm, Chase's twin brother, although they aren't identical."

Jessica raised a brow, finding all Mrs. Stewart was telling her intriguing. "So I guess that means you know their parents as well."

Mrs. Stewart smiled warmly. "Yes. The Westmorelands are wonderful people. I knew the grandparents, too."

Jessica leaned against the counter. "Really? I understand that Chase's grandfather used to own a restaurant years ago."

Mrs. Stewart chuckled as she wiped off the counter. "Yes, and just like Chase's Place, it served the most delicious home-cooked meals around. Truckers made up the bulk of Scott Westmoreland's busy clientele, but people would come from miles around to eat his food made from secret family recipes handed down through generations. I understand Chase uses some of those same recipes and guards them like a hawk, especially after what happened when his granddad discovered that someone gave away the secret recipes to his chili, beef stew and broccoli casserole."

Jessica swallowed deeply. "How did that happen?" she asked innocently.

"I'm not sure but Scott claimed his partner, a man by the name of Carlton Graham, gave—"

"That is not true. He would not have done such a thing!"

At Jessica's strong defense of Carlton Graham, Mrs. Stewart eyed her curiously before saying, "I recall Carlton and Helen moved to California to be near their daughter and granddaughter." She lifted a curious brow. "Is there any chance Carlton Graham is a relative of yours?"

Jessica nodded, knowing there was no way she could lie to the woman. "Yes, he was my grandfather."

Mrs. Stewart's eyes widened. "Does Chase know that?"

Jessica shook his head. "No, and I don't intend to tell him until I can prove my grandfather's innocence."

"And how do you plan to do that?"

Jessica shrugged. "I'm going to start digging around in my spare time. Someone stole those recipes and deliberately made it look like my grandfather had done it. I promised my grandmother before she died that I would clear the Graham name of any wrongdoing."

Mrs. Stewart nodded. "You might want to ask Donald Schuster since it was his restaurant that ended up with the recipes."

Jessica lifted a brow. "Is he still around?"

"Yes. He's done well over the years. There's probably over a hundred Schuster's Restaurants nationwide, a few in every state, even out in California. And people claim they have the best chili around—chili some say was derived from a Westmoreland recipe."

Jessica nodded. She had heard of the chain of restaurants and had even eaten at one. "What can you tell me about Chase?"

Ms. Stewart sighed deeply. "He's a decent man who unfortunately had his heart broken years ago by a woman he met while at college. It's my understanding they met at Duke University where Chase had gotten a basketball scholarship. Everyone said that she clung to him like glue while he had a promising future in the pros. But when an injury ended any chance of that happening she dropped him like a hot potato. He's never dated another woman seriously."

The two were silent for a few moments then Ms. Stewart spoke again. "I'd like to give you a little advice if I can."

Jessica nodded. "Sure."

"Don't wait too long to tell Chase the truth about your connection to Carlton Graham. It will be better if he hears it from you than from someone else, and if you start asking questions that's bound to happen."

She leaned closer and paused a moment as if searching for words to explain. "Although all of this happened over eighteen years ago, Scott Westmoreland was deeply hurt by what he saw as an outright betrayal. In fact, he had a heart attack not long after that."

Jessica's eyes widened. She hadn't known that. "He did?"

"Yes, although I can't blame it all on stress involving the recipes. Scott was a heavy smoker and I'm sure that played a huge part in it, too, especially since he eventually died of lung cancer."

The older woman sighed deeply. "I'm not saying your granddaddy did or didn't do what the Westmorelands claim. All I'm saying is that they believe that he did it. Chase, the one closest to his grandfather, took the old man's pain and suffering personally and for years he'd tried to make Schuster admit they were preparing foods using Westmoreland recipes. Schuster refused to do so, and since there wasn't any proof, Chase eventually let the matter drop. But I doubt very seriously that he's forgotten about it."

A short while later, with only ten minutes left to closing time, Jessica was alone in her shop. She knew she had earned some pretty good profits for the first day. She sighed as she made her way over to the display case to pack up what was left of today's inventory. She had made prior arrangements with the children's hospital to donate any treats left from that day and knew someone was on their way to get them.

She couldn't help remembering what Mrs. Stewart had told her about Chase and the girl he'd fallen in love with at college. And although she hadn't wanted to feel sympathy for him, she had. The worst thing for someone to do is kick you when you're already down, and his ex-girlfriend had done just that. She hoped that over the years he had realized that he was better off without her. She wished at some point her mother had realized that she was better off without Jeff Claiborne.

She heard the tinkling of the bell on the front door, and turned, thinking it was the courier from the hospital.

Her breath caught in her throat when she saw it was Chase.

Three

"Hello, Jessica."

All day Chase had had her on his mind, and a part of him needed to see her, to see if what they had shared the day before had been reality or make-believe. And seeing her now let him know it had been real. She was as beautiful as he had remembered, everything about her was as much of a turn-on as he'd recalled.

When she continued to look at him without saying anything, he said, "I thought you probably didn't have time to eat lunch so I brought you dinner."

He watched her nervously nibble on her bottom lip and his guts clenched. "Thanks, but you didn't have to do that. I had planned to go to one of those hamburger places down the street."

He frowned. "The food at Chase's Place is tastier and better for you." He crossed the room and handed her a doggie bag. "You may want to get started on this while it's still warm."

Jessica took the bag from him and placed it on the counter. Chase was the last person she wanted to deal with right now. Seeing him here, in her shop, sent flashes of the kiss they'd shared through her mind. A part of her wanted to be angry at him for making her feel the way she did, but it was hard for her to continue to be mad at a man who went out of his way to be nice to her. And he was being nice....

She heard the tinkling of the bell on the door and turned around as a woman walked in. "Hello, I'm Gloria Miller," the woman said. "I'm here to pick up your donation for the children's hospital." She glanced over at Chase and smiled. "Hi, Chase."

"How are you, Gloria?"

"I can't complain."

Jessica couldn't help wondering if Chase knew practically everyone or everyone knew him. "I hope the children enjoy these," she said handling the woman the sealed box.

The woman grinned warmly. "I'm sure they will. Thanks for this delicious contribution." Moments later she was gone.

"That was thoughtful of you," Chase said as he glanced out the window and watched Gloria pull off.

Jessica shrugged. "No big deal. I operated on the cautious side today and baked more than I needed. I don't want to sell anything that isn't fresh tomorrow so I thought I'd donate what was left to the children's hospital."

"How will you handle the overstock inventory tomorrow?"

"I hope to bake only enough. I don't mind having a few items left but not as much as I had today. And speaking of today, I want to thank you."

Chase grinned. "You already have."

Jessica shook her head. "I'm not talking about dinner," she said. "I'm talking about all the referrals. A number of people who came in mentioned you had sent them and I appreciate the business."

He leaned against the counter. "I'm sure I wasn't the only one. The Criswell brothers dropped by for lunch and they were telling everyone about your fudge and how delicious it tasted. So they're responsible for increasing your business, too."

Jessica nodded. "I'll thank them as well when I see them." She walked over to the door after checking her watch. "It's closing time."

Chase checked his watch. "So it is."

When Chase didn't make any attempt to leave, Jessica put up the closed sign and locked the door. She also pulled down the shade to the display window, and the moment she did the interior of the shop got somewhat dark and way too intimate. "Will you get the lights, Chase?"

"In a moment."

She watched as he crossed the room, stopping directly in front of her. "Do you know what I thought about a lot today, Jessica?"

She didn't respond right away and she refused to meet his gaze. "No, what did you think about?"

He reached out and touched her chin, forcing her eyes to meet his. "The kiss we shared last night."

A part of her wanted to shout for him to get over it, but how could she expect him to when she hadn't? She had thought about it a lot that day as well. "We barely know each other, Chase. We just met yesterday. Things are moving too fast."

"You're right," he said gently, evenly. "So this is what I'd like to propose."

She lifted a brow. "What?"

"That we take the time to get to know each other."

"Why?" she asked, trying to understand. "Why should we do that?" The last thing she wanted was to become seriously romantically involved with anyone. She had a lot on her plate starting up her business. And all of her spare time was devoted to starting her investigation. The first person she intended to talk to was Donald Schuster. He was the one person who she hoped could help prove her grandfather's innocence.

"I think the answer is obvious," Chase said, interrupting her thoughts. "You don't like me. That bothers me because I don't understand why. Whenever I get within ten feet of you, I can feel your guard going up. I'm also bothered by the fact that I'm very attracted to you and I don't like being this drawn to a woman I don't really know. Hell, I didn't get much work done today for thinking about you."

"Then I suggest that you try shifting your attention elsewhere."

"I doubt if that will work. I want you."

Jessica went numb. She'd never met a man who expressed his interest in her so blatantly.

"I hope my directness didn't shock you."

She met his gaze. Yes, it had shocked her. Her heart was flip-flopping in her chest, not to mention the heat that had settled in the pit of her stomach. In California, men enjoyed playing games and you rarely knew what they were thinking, where you stood or what their intent was. "You're an attractive man, Chase, and I'm sure you date," she decided to say.

He smiled. "Not much and especially not a lot in the past six months." When she opened her mouth to continue, he pressed two fingers across her lips. "I'm not asking you to marry me, Jessica. I just want us to get to know each other. You're new in town and I'd like to show you around, introduce you to people, and spend time with you."

"You're a man. You'll eventually want more than that."

"Will I?"

"Yes." Panic gripped her. Never before had a man made her lose all sense of logic. Chase Westmoreland was powerful, dangerous and all male, and those three things had her worried.

Chase knew to tell her that she was wrong, that he wouldn't eventually want more, would be an outright lie. He glanced over at the bag sitting on her counter. "Go ahead and enjoy your food." Then, without missing a beat, he asked, "How about a movie tomorrow night?"

She blinked then stared into his eyes. He was smoothly changing the subject and they both knew it. "A movie tomorrow night?"

"Yes, a movie," he whispered, and the deep sensuous tone of his voice vibrated her nerve endings. "I'll pick you up around seven."

Her senses told her the last thing she needed to do was to begin dating a Westmoreland, but he might have some of the answers she needed. She couldn't overlook that fact. "A movie sounds nice. I'll be ready at seven." She then reached for the doorknob. "Now you can leave."

She pushed a wayward curl back from her face, inhaled and waited. His gaze was locked on hers, arousing her, making her nipples harden against her blouse. She wondered if he was aware of her body's response to him. His scent made her want to nuzzle her face into his neck and…

She closed her eyes, refusing to go there. When she slowly opened her eyes, he was there, his lips mere inches from hers. She inhaled sharply. The stir of sensual need suddenly overwhelmed her.

"You feel it like I do, Jessica," he whispered. "Don't ask me why it's happening because I don't know, but it's as if this place, this time, these moments between us were meant to be and we don't have any control over anything."

Jessica tipped her head back, refusing to look at things that way. But when he raised his fingertips to her lips, she instinctively parted them. He was right. It was as if neither of them had control over the moment. She didn't want to get romantically involved with him but a need to kiss him again was sending sensual charges all through her body. And from the way he was looking at her, she could tell he felt them.

She struggled to push down this passionate side she hadn't been aware she had. She was an ace at confrontation as an attorney, but Jessica was a novice when it came to the kind of deep-in-the-gut sensations that had her lips quivering.

"Please let me kiss you, Jessica."

With the sound of his voice, deep, husky and sexy, he didn't have to ask twice and she tilted her lips up to him. The moment their mouths connected, she swallowed a groan and let his tongue do all kinds of naughty things, pushing her pulse into overdrive and causing tingles to erupt inside her stomach. This kiss was based on more than mutual attraction and gratification. There were elements taking over that scared her to death. He was a fantastic kisser and knew he would be a great lover…but she didn't intend to sleep with him. Ever.

If only she really meant it.

She pulled back. He needed to leave. Now. "Goodbye, Chase."

He smiled. "Goodbye. I'll see you tomorrow night at seven."

And then he was gone.

The following evening Jessica breathed deeply as she crossed the room to open the door. It was exactly seven o'clock and, not surprisingly, Chase was punctual. She glanced down at herself. She had dressed casually in a pair of jeans and pullover sweater.

Jessica felt her pulse shudder when she unlocked the door to find Chase standing there. As expected, he was looking tall, dark and gorgeous. She wondered if he had any idea how he had disrupted her sleep the past two nights. "Chase."

"Jessica."

"Would you like anything to drink before we leave?" She felt another shudder pass through her when she noticed how his gaze was lingering on her mouth. A part of her wished more than anything she was immune to his robust masculinity but unfortunately she wasn't.

"No. Do you have any chocolate chip cookies left from today?"

Jessica couldn't help but smile. He sounded just like a little kid being set loose in the toy section of a department store. "Yes, I do and I remembered that they are your favorite. I've boxed them up already. You can have them when we get back."

"Oh, really…" he said as a smile spread over his face.

Jessica grinned. "Yes, really. Now are we ready to leave?"

"Let's go."

"Are you hungry?"

Jessica glanced up at Chase as they walked out of the theater. She couldn't help but chuckle. "Are you kidding? I'm the one who ate most of the popcorn, at least two hot dogs, not to mention a super-size drink and a box of gummy worms."

A corner of Chase's mouth tilted in a smile as he took her hand in his. "It's okay. I'm not a big fan of junk food."

"Umm, I can imagine. Who comes up with the menu for Chase's Place?"

"Usually I do, but Kevin gives his input."

"Kevin?"

"He's my cook but every once in a while if he's out, I do the cooking. Kevin and I are the only ones who know the Westmoreland family recipes and he's bound by a legal contract never to divulge our secrets. I had to take such measures after what happened to my grandfather years ago. He got burned putting too much trust in his partner."

Jessica swallowed the thick lump in her throat. She already knew the story, at least her grandmother's version. Now she wanted to hear Chase's. "What happened?"

"Years ago, a man by the name of Carlton Graham did most of the cooking while my grandfather handled the administrative duties. The two worked together for years and then had a dispute over something and parted ways. A few weeks later Granddad found out that Carlton had sold the secrets of a few of the Westmorelands' prize-winning recipes to a rival restaurant. Needless to say my grandfather never got over the betrayal. Those stolen recipes had been in the Westmoreland family for generations."

Jessica had to bite down on her lips to stop from coming to her grandfather's defense as she'd done with Mrs. Stewart. "And how did your grandfather know who stole the recipes?" she asked, trying not to give Chase a reason to question her interest.

By now they had reached Chase's car and he opened the door for her. "Because nobody else knew the ingredients. Also, my grandfather kept his recipe book under lock and key and no one else besides Carlton had access to it."

So of course he blamed my grandfather, she thought

as she slid into the leather seat of Chase's sports car. "What about other people who worked at your grandfather's restaurant?"

Chase shrugged. "As far as I can remember—I was only fifteen or sixteen at the time—the only other people who worked there were two waitresses, Miss Paula and Miss Darcy, and neither knew the recipes. Their job was to wait tables and take care of the customers."

Jessica nodded, thinking she had asked enough questions. The last thing she needed was for him to become suspicious.

She wished she could level with him and tell him that she was Carton Graham's granddaughter, but to do so would be a mistake until she could prove her grandfather's innocence.

Chase closed the door and walked around the car to get inside. He turned to her before starting the ignition. "You never said if you were hungry."

She shook her head and met his gaze. "No, I'm not hungry but if you are then we can stop and get you something."

He smiled. "I have an even better idea. How about if we go back to your place so I can dig into those cookies? And it would be wonderful if you have some milk. There's nothing like a big, cold glass of milk with chocolate chip cookies."

Just for a second Jessica wondered if taking Chase back to her place and inviting him inside was a good thing. But they had said they wanted to get to know each other better and she had found out some information from him tonight. On Monday she would ask Mrs.

Stewart about the waitresses who used to work for Chase's grandfather to see if they were still around. Maybe she could talk to them as well.

"Yes, I have milk and after such a wonderful evening the least I can do is take you back to my place and let you indulge your taste buds a little."

A corner of Chase's mouth tilted into a smile as he started the car. "Umm, indulge my taste buds? Now that's certainly one way of looking at it."

Four

"**I** don't think you really know how delicious these cookies are, Jessica."

Jessica leaned back in her chair and smiled, pleased with Chase's compliment. "I bet you say that to all the girls."

After taking a huge swallow of milk Chase licked his lips and smiled. "No, honestly, I don't. In fact most of the women I've dated couldn't cook worth a damn, which is probably the reason I was such an asset to them. If nothing else, I was able to feed them."

She grinned and wished she wasn't so affected by that smile of his. He had been at her place for over an hour, and during that time she had sipped her coffee while listening to him tell her about his family. She could actually feel the love he had for his siblings although he tried convincing her that his four brothers were nothing but pains.

However, he had spoken fondly about his baby sister Delaney, who would be flying into town tomorrow from the Middle East with her husband and son. A christening was planned on Sunday for his brother Storm's twin baby girls. And a christening dinner party would be held after the church service at Chase's Place.

"You've let me do a lot of talking, now it's your turn," Chase said, interrupting her thoughts.

She lifted a brow. "It's my turn?"

"Yes, tell me about yourself, Jessica."

For just a second she pressed her lips, together wondering what she could say that wouldn't lead him to make a connection to her and Carlton Graham. And if he remembered her grandfather then there was a strong possibility he would remember her grandmother as well.

She leaned forward, knowing she would have to be careful about what she said. She didn't want to deceive him but, for now, the less he knew the better. "I was born in Sacramento, California, but went to law school at UCLA and—"

"Law school? You're an attorney?"

She heard deep surprise in his voice and smiled. "I was and I guess legally I still am since I'm still licensed there. I worked for a huge corporation and was hired right out of law school. But over the years I saw just how much integrity the company lacked and often had to defend a lot of their practices that I knew were wrong."

She took a sip of her coffee, remembering those

times. "I probably would have still been there if it hadn't been for my grandmother. She died and left me an inheritance that I used to open Delicious Cravings."

Chase bit into another cookie. "What about your parents?"

"My mom was a single parent," she said quietly. "For fifteen years she believed my father would marry her, only to find out that he'd strung her along. He couldn't marry her because he was already married with a family living in Philadelphia."

She watched Chase go still. Saw the anger that came into his eyes and studied the frown that bunched his forehead. "How in the hell was he able to pull that off?" he asked.

Jessica sighed. "He was a salesman and traveled a lot. His home base was in Pennsylvania but he dropped in and paid us a visit whenever he was in town. He was able to pull off his duplicity for fifteen years because my mother never questioned his comings and goings."

She took another sip of her coffee then added, "I hated him the most when he would show up unexpectedly. My mother was a different person around him. She became weak, vulnerable and dependent. If he said *jump* she would purr, *How high?*"

Chase nodded. Although he had known Jessica only for a few days he knew she did not take after her mother. He couldn't picture any man dominating her that way. More than likely she had seen her mother live that kind of life and refused to live it herself. "How did your mom find out the truth?"

A part of Jessica wondered why she was telling him

any of this, but she knew the reason. She had discovered earlier that she felt comfortable with him. "She didn't find out. My granddad did. It had always bothered him that my father never married my mother and I guess he thought fifteen years was long enough. He also got suspicious of my father's drop-in visits and hired a private investigator who ferreted out the truth."

Chase wiped his mouth, then tossed his balled-up napkin into the garbage can that sat across the room. "How did your mother handle it when she found out the truth?" he asked, turning his attention back to her.

A shudder went through Jessica when she remembered that time. "She didn't handle it. In fact she was so devastated, so humiliated, that she overdosed on sleeping pills."

"I'm so sorry," Chase whispered and reached across the table, taking her hand in his. "That must have been awful for you."

Jessica's heart began beating wildly when Chase's hand enclosed hers. She studied his hands for a moment. They were large, strong and comforting. "It was," she said quietly. "I was fifteen and all alone except for my grandparents. I went to live with them after that. They were super and helped me through a very difficult time. Jennifer was also there for me."

"Jennifer?"

"Yes, Jennifer Claiborne, my father's legal wife. She divorced him after she found out what he'd done. Being the warm, loving and caring person that she is, she opened her arms and heart to me. She sent for me every summer so I could get to know my brother and sister and she became my second mom. She also demanded in the divorce decree that my father establish a college fund for me like he had for my sister and brother."

Chase smiled. "She sounds like one hell of a tough lady."

"She is and I know I can call on her if I ever need anything. She's always been supportive, and considering the circumstances, I think that's admirable. A lot of women would not have done all the things she did to help me put my life together after Mom died."

"What about your father?" he asked, leaning forward. Jessica's nostrils couldn't help but absorb his aftershave, which mingled with his masculine scent and was making her pulse rate escalate.

"After the divorce my father sort of dropped out of everyone's life. Last I heard he was living somewhere in New York."

"The bastard," Chase said, anger and disgust evident in his voice. "What made you decide to move to Atlanta?"

Jessica paused at his question. She couldn't tell him the real reason she had chosen Atlanta. "Mainly the cost of living. Compared to other progressive areas in the country, Atlanta gave me more for my buck and when the real estate agent located this building and said it included an apartment on top, I knew it was perfect."

She slowly pulled her hands out of his and leaned back in her chair. "I think you've eaten enough sweets for one night, Mr. Westmoreland." She glanced at her watch. "Besides that, I can sleep in late on Saturdays, but you can't."

Chase grinned. "True, but you'll need breakfast, too,

so how about joining me tomorrow? Kevin can throw down with grits and eggs."

She cocked her head and studied him. "Is that an invitation?"

"Yes, that's exactly what it is. Then if you aren't too busy you can go to a game with me around noon."

She lifted a brow? "A game?"

"Yes, I coach a basketball team of teens at the community center in College Park, and there's a game tomorrow. Chase's Crusaders against Willie's Warriors."

Jessica shook her head grinning. "Hey, I thought this was football season."

"To some people it is, but to parents who want their sons to become the Michael Jordan of tomorrow, every season is basketball season. So will you go with me?"

Jessica smiled. Although she knew she should turn him down, she said, "Basketball in October, how can I resist? By the way, who's Willie?"

Chase chuckled. "He's the coach for the other team and owns a video franchise a few blocks away. He played professionally for the Pistons a few years ago. We went to high school together and have remained good friends."

Jessica nodded. Of all the things they had talked about tonight, he hadn't mentioned anything about his dream to play for the pros. She watched him as he stood.

"Will you walk me to the door?"

"Of course."

He strolled across the room to check out her cooking pots as well as the molds that were sitting on the candy-making table. "One day you're going have to let me watch you make a batch of chocolate candy."

"Umm, maybe one day I will." She tried concentrating on what he was saying and not on what he was wearing, but there was something scrumptious about a man with wide shoulders and muscled arms in a black pullover sweater. Add a pair of denim jeans on a well-built body with firm thighs and what you got was one hell of a sexy man.

They walked together as she led him out of the kitchen to the door. Jessica tried to downplay the flutter in her stomach but couldn't, since she knew there was a good chance…a really good chance…that he would kiss her good-night. She hated admitting it but she was looking forward to his kiss.

"Breakfast in the morning?" he asked when they reached her door.

She shrugged. "Maybe. But the game is a definite."

"All right, I'll pick you up at eleven."

He leaned forward, his lips just inches from hers. "We're going to have to do something special next Wednesday," he said softly with his gaze totally transfixed on her mouth.

"Why?"

"We'll have known each other a week then." A corner of his mouth curved into a smile. "I can tell you're beginning to like me. For a while there I was worried."

They were standing so close that Jessica could feel the warmth of his breath across her face and the manly scent of him had settled firmly in her nostrils. "You want me to like you?" she asked, voluntarily scooting closer to him as he placed his hands at her waist.

"Yeah, I want you to like me. I'm a likable guy, but I can have my bad days just like anyone else."

"I'll try and remember that."

"Please do."

And then he lowered his mouth to hers. She had a pair of incredible lips and he would never get tired of kissing her. And her taste was so damn good. He wouldn't get much sleep tonight. He already knew that. So he figured he needed to remember every moment of this, every lick, every nibble, to get him through the night.

He liked the sound of her moaning. He liked the way her tongue was mating with his, and he liked the way she was sliding her hands up his shoulders. But more than anything, he loved her hot taste. He knew if he didn't stop now and pull back he would be tempted to sweep her into his arms and take her upstairs.

Moments later he broke off the kiss and whispered. "You are one hell of a woman." Jessica watched as he opened the door and walked out.

Closing and locking the door behind him, she inhaled deeply. Chase Westmoreland was as delicious as the chocolate treats she loved, but she couldn't allow herself to give in to the craving.

"You were missed at breakfast."

Jessica smiled as she stepped back to let Chase inside. As he walked into the middle of the shop with a cup of coffee in his hand, the morning sun that flowed through the display window highlighted his features and she immediately felt a sense of longing and desire.

"I decided to use my time doing something else besides eating," she said. "Win or lose I believe Chase's Crusaders deserve a treat so I spent the morning baking cookies."

Evidently surprised, he cocked his head and stared at her. "You did?"

She grinned. "Yes, I did. I figured it was the least I could do to contribute to such a worthy cause. I think it's wonderful that you're taking the time to spend with them."

Chase shrugged. "It's no big deal. They are a wonderful group of kids. Besides, I love basketball. It was my dream to play in the pros but an injury stopped me. So I finished college and came back here."

She nodded. "That's when you decided to open your restaurant?"

He smiled and leaned against the counter. "No, that idea didn't come until three years later. Like you, I got a job in corporate America, working as a financial adviser. It didn't take me long to get fed up with office politics and make a career change."

He laughed. "Believe it or not, the idea for opening a restaurant came from my brothers. I'm the one who spent the most time with my grandfather when he was in business. I worked at his restaurant after school and on weekends. So I was the one who he passed all the family recipe secrets to. And since I loved to cook, my brothers—who were all single at the time—usually ended up at my place for dinner, so they suggested I go into business for myself."

He took a sip of his coffee, then added, "I had some money saved, my brothers chipped in and we found the building I'm in now. At first it was a family affair where everyone pitched in and worked, even my parents. But when I started seeing a profit I figured that I could afford to hire paid help."

"And now Chase's Place is a popular hot spot known for its mouth-wateringly delicious soul food," Jessica said, remembering something Mrs. Stewart had told her earlier in the week.

His smile widened. "Yes, and I'm very proud of that."

"You should be. Have you given any thought to franchising?"

"Yes, especially lately. But I have to be certain that the warm, friendly, family atmosphere I've worked so hard to achieve won't get lost."

He glanced at his watch. "Are you ready?"

She smiled. "Yes, I just need help getting the box of cookies out to your car."

She moved across the room to go into the kitchen, and he placed his cup on the counter and intercepted her. She glanced up at him and immediately felt a flutter in her stomach. Warning flags went up—as they had last night—signaling her that they were moving too fast; it was too soon and that she shouldn't get involved with him. He was a Westmoreland—the enemy. But whenever he looked at her the way he was doing now, the last thing she wanted to dwell on was bad blood between their families.

"Let's make plans for next week," he whispered, as one corner of his mouth tilted into a smile.

"What kind of plans?" she found herself asking.

"Dinner at my place Wednesday night around eight."

She lifted a brow. "But I thought you closed early on Wednesday. At six."

His mouth curved even more. "I do. A lot of people around here go to prayer meetings at their church which usually include dinner. But I just happen to know the owner of Chase's Place and he's given me permission to bring a special guest after hours."

She chuckled. "Oh, he did, did he?"

"Yes, he did."

Again, warning flags were flapping around in her head, but at that moment she chose to ignore them and said, "I'd love to have dinner with you Wednesday night."

"Thank you."

And then he leaned down and kissed her.

"We were totally surprised when Chase mentioned he had invited someone to today's game," Tara West-moreland, the wife of Chase's brother Thorn, said smiling. "And we think it's wonderful."

Jessica was confused. "Why would you think that?" she asked. When she and Chase had arrived at the community center he had taken her to a group of four women. Three he had introduced as his sisters-in-laws—Shelly, Madison and Tara; the other was his cousin Jared's wife, Dana.

It was Shelly, Dare's wife, who answered. "Because Chase is a very private person and he's never brought a date to any of the games before."

Jessica shrugged as she leaned back on one of the bleachers. The game would be starting in less than ten minutes. "I'm not really his date. We met this week when I opened a confectionery a few doors down from his restaurant. I moved here from California, and since

I don't know anyone in town he was kind enough to invite me along today."

Madison, who was married to Stone, grinned as she patted Jessica's hand. "Trust me, he never would have brought you over to us if you weren't his date. Chase guards his privacy like a hawk." The other three women agreed and nodded knowingly.

Jessica blinked, not sure what to think. She didn't want anyone assuming that she and Chase were involved. They weren't. She glanced down at the basketball court and saw Chase talking to his brothers and cousins. Anyone who saw the group of men would know they were related. She had met the Westmoreland men earlier and found them to be nice, likeable people, although she hadn't wanted them to be.

On the car ride over, Chase had surprised her by inviting her to his nieces' christening as well as the dinner party he planned to host afterwards at his restaurant tomorrow. To include her in such an important family affair was a bit too much and she had declined. Besides, she had made plans to meet with Donald Schuster tomorrow. She had called him yesterday and he had agreed to meet with her at his home.

"Chase's looking this way again," Tara said grinning. "Smile for Chase, Jessica, so he'll know you're okay and aren't suffering from our company."

Jessica couldn't help but smile. These Westmoreland women were too much. She really liked them. She met Chase's gaze and smiled. He smiled back before directing his attention back to the group of youngsters on his team.

"Don't look now but here come the guys," Dana said, smiling, seeing her husband and his cousins climbing the bleachers toward them.

"They will be as curious about you as we were," Shelly whispered to Jessica grinning.

Jessica shot the women a nervous look. "Surely they aren't going to ask me anything about my relationship with Chase?"

Tara chuckled. "No, they're depending on us to pump you for information and later they'll corner us and expect us to come clean and divulge everything that we know."

"But don't be surprised if Dare asks you questions," Shelly added, grinning. "It's the cop in him so don't take it personally. Besides, he's the oldest of his brothers and is somewhat protective, although he'll never admit it." She leaned back in the bleachers and shook her head and chuckled. "And now that he sees how taken Chase is with you, he's bound to get downright nosy."

Jessica stared at the women, not sure if they were serious. It didn't take long for her to realize they were. She swallowed, thinking the last thing she needed was Sheriff Dare Westmoreland asking her a lot of questions.

By the time the Westmoreland men had reached them she had tried to contain her nervousness.

"So, where are you from, Jessica?" Dare asked, not missing a beat as he eased into the spot next to Shelly.

Jessica forced a smile. "Sacramento. Have you ever been there?"

"Yes, for a law enforcement convention a few years back. It's a nice area," he responded.

"Yes, it is a nice area," she agreed.

"Why did you leave?"

Jessica knew everyone was waiting for her answer. She wasn't one to get rattled easily, but Dare Westmoreland was doing a good job of shaking her composure. It wasn't that he was outright rude in his questioning, but she hated being placed in a situation where she had to explain herself to anyone. But in this case she would. It was obvious that the Westmorelands were a close-knit group and a part of her envied the care and concern that they had for each other.

"Job stress," she finally said, leaning back on the bleacher and tucking a strand of hair behind her ear. "I was an attorney in a—"

"You're an attorney?" Jared cut her off by asking.

Her gaze moved from Dare to Jared who she knew was the attorney in the Westmoreland family. She smiled when everyone fell silent. "Yes. I went to law school at UCLA and then went to work for a large corporation. Starting off I loved my job but over the years I discovered just how much the company lacked integrity and more than once I found myself defending practices that I knew were wrong."

"So you walked away?"

Her gaze moved from Jared to Tara and felt a sense of relief at the look of admiration in her the other woman's eyes. "Yes, but not before I had what I considered a workable plan. My grandmother passed and left me an inheritance, so I decided to use it to fulfill my dream of opening my own business. I've always enjoyed baking with chocolate and I decided a change in areas and careers was what I needed."

"Why Atlanta?"

Breath held, Jessica shifted her gaze from Tara back to Dare. There was something in his dark-brown eyes that made her wonder if he suspected that there was a lot more than what she was sharing with them. She forced herself to hold his gaze while saying, "I knew someone who used to live here and remembered her saying how nice it was. Besides, everyone knows this is a city on the move. There's something for everyone."

Dare opened his mouth to ask her another question but before he could get the words out, the buzzer sounded, indicating the start of the game. Everyone's attention shifted from her to the activities on the court below. Jessica let out a silent sigh and started to relax somewhat, but then she noticed Dare was still studying her curiously and knew she would have to stay on her guard around him.

"You have to be proud that your team won," Jessica said hours later as she and Chase walked out to his car. After the game the parents had served refreshments. Her delicious baked treats had been a big hit.

"Yes, I am. I think the guys did a good job. They showed good teamwork and that's what's most important, the team and not individual egos. If we can instill that mindset into them now, they'll be better athletes if and when they make it to the pros."

He glanced at his watch. "My sister Delaney and her family should have arrived by now and everyone will be over at my parents' place. Would you like to go over there with me for a while?"

Jessica inhaled deeply. She had enjoyed herself with
the Westmorelands at the game today but the last thing
she wanted was to continue to give them the impression
that she and Chase were an item. "Thanks for the invite,
but I think I'm going to turn in early tonight. This has
been one busy week for me. The grand opening was
great but tiring, and I want to spend the rest of today and
tomorrow relaxing."

"All right." He looped an arm around her shoulders
as they continued walking toward his car. Chase, Jessica was discovering, was a very nice person and she
didn't want to think about what his reaction would be
when he found out she hadn't told him everything about
herself. But for now, she couldn't. Until she could come
to him with proof of her grandfather's innocence, the
less he knew the better.

Five

As Jessica drove through the security gate that led to the Schuster estates, she was glad Donald Schuster had agreed to see her. After telling her that he had remembered her grandfather, no doubt he was curious about what she wanted.

As she approached the huge ranch-style home set on what had to be at least four acres of land, she couldn't help but think how quickly she could prove her grandfather's innocence if Mr. Schuster were to tell her who had given him the Westmoreland secret recipes. Then she could present her findings to the Westmorelands and proceed with her life as she had planned. If nothing else, this week had shown her that people wanted a pastry shop in the area and more than once she had been approached with the idea of supplying pastries for neighboring businesses.

Moments later Jessica found herself knocking on a huge wooden door and blinked when a butler dressed in a starched uniform answered. "May I help you, Miss?"

She smiled. "Yes, I'm Jessica Claiborne and I'm here to see Mr. Schuster."

The butler nodded. "He's expecting you."

The butler led the way, and Jessica followed, glancing around at the extravagant surroundings. Everything she saw said *money,* but there was something about the place that reminded her of a museum more than a home.

She stopped when the butler paused and opened a door that led out onto a glassed, enclosed patio. An older man, who would have been close to her grandfather's age had he lived, was sitting in a wheelchair looking out over a huge lake.

"Mr. Schuster, your guest has arrived," the butler announced.

The man immediately turned the wheelchair around to look at her. A smile touched his aged face. "Come in," he said in a strong voice. He offered her a chair across from him. "You said you wanted to ask me questions about your grandfather and that episode with the Westmoreland secret recipes."

Jessica nodded. "Everyone thinks my grandfather is the one who gave them to you."

The man waved a frail hand in the air. "No one gave me anything. Although some of my entrées may have tasted like Westmorelands' they weren't. I tried to tell Scott Westmoreland that, but he was too bullheaded to listen, and I guess it didn't help matters that he knew I'd been trying to convince your grandfather to become my partner. But there was this friendship thing between him and Westmoreland and nothing would shake that."

Jessica was saved from saying anything when the butler brought in a tray of iced tea. When she found herself alone with Mr. Schuster again, she said, "Evidently something did shake their friendship, since he stopped working with Scott Westmoreland."

"Yes, but he would have eventually gone back. The two got into it all the time but they would always resolve their disagreements and get back together. They made a hell of a team. Your grandfather was a great cook and Scott, bless his stubborn hide, was one hell of an entrepreneur. And I understand his grandson Chase Westmoreland is just like him. He's a fantastic chef and has a good head for business when it comes to running a restaurant."

Jessica smiled, thinking that the older man had paid Chase a nice compliment. "And you're sure there's no way you were using any of the Westmoreland recipes?"

The older man chuckled. "At my age I wouldn't bet my life on anything, but my cook at the time said they were was his own recipes, and I had no reason not to believe him."

Jessica nodded again. "Could you tell me his name?"

"Theodore Henry. But we called him Teddy for short."

"Does he still work for you?"

"Heavens no, he stopped working for me years ago. But I understand Teddy owns a catering company in town."

Jessica took a huge sip of her tea then set the glass down and smiled. "Thanks, Mr. Schuster, you've been a big help and I appreciate you taking the time to see me. I intend to find Mr. Henry and talk to him."

"Hey, Chase, will you quit looking out that window? Jessica hasn't returned yet. If I didn't know better I'd think you were really smitten with her."

Chase turned and frowned at his brother. "I just met her a few days ago, Thorn."

Thorn shrugged, smiling smugly. "So? All it took was a couple of seconds for Tara to knock me off my feet."

Better than her knocking the hell out of you. Chase shook his head, reminiscing. He could vividly recall the night Tara and Thorn had met. Tara had been so mad at Thorn he was lucky she hadn't whacked him. "No one is knocking me off my feet," he finally said.

"If you say so."

Chase inhaled deeply. Sometimes he wished he'd been born an only child.

"Dare thinks there's something suspicious about her," Thorn added.

Chase raised his eyes heavenward. "Dare's a cop. He thinks there's something suspicious about everyone."

Thorn chuckled. "That's true. I don't think he was too happy that she was so close-mouthed about herself and her family."

Chase leaned against a table, remembering what Jessica had shared with him the other night. It wasn't exactly something he'd want to share with the whole world if it had happened to him. He'd felt touched that she had told him as much as she had. "She's a private person, Thorn. Let it go."

Thorn smiled. "Hey, it doesn't bother me if your woman has secrets."

"She's not my woman."

"Who isn't your woman?" their sister Delaney came up and asked.

"The chocolate chip lady," Thorn said grinning. "She makes the best damn chocolate chip cookies."

Chase narrowed his eyes. "She made them for the guys on the team, but I couldn't help noticing that you, Stone and Dare grabbed a few."

Thorn shrugged. "They looked too tasty to pass up and they reminded me of the cookies Grampa's cook used to bake before they went their separate ways years ago. And as far as your team goes, all that sugar in a teenager's mouth isn't good. Think of all the cavities. We did their parents a favor."

Chase was about to say something when he noticed Jessica's car pulling into the parking lot.

"Looks like your woman is back," Thorn said as a smile tilted a corner of his mouth.

Chase shrugged nonchalantly. "So? What of it?"

Thorn rubbed his chin. "That's what I'm wondering myself," he said as he walked out of the room.

It was close to five o'clock by the time Chase had tidied up his restaurant and taken out the last of the trash. His brothers had hung around to help, but he was glad when they'd finally left. They had ribbed him enough for one weekend.

He locked the door to his restaurant and glanced over at Jessica's place wondering what she was doing. She'd said she would spend the weekend relaxing and he didn't want to bother her, but a part of him had to see her.

What he had told Thorn was true. He and Jessica had known each other for only a few days. But he had to admit that in such a short length of time he had learned more about her than he had about some women he'd dated for a full month. He'd learned about all the unhappiness she'd had in her life and how much she enjoyed baking. He liked talking to her and felt comfortable telling her about the injury that had kept him from going to the pros. But he hadn't mentioned anything to her about Iris and the broken heart she had dealt him during that time.

He smiled when he thought of the hit Jessica had been with the kids on his team and their parents. Everyone had appreciated her thoughtfulness in wanting to reward the team with goodies. There hadn't been a shy bone in her body while interacting with everyone, including his family. He liked the way she smiled when she found something amusing, but he also thought her frown was absolutely adorable. During the short time they had known each other, he had told her more about himself than he had shared with any woman before.

But how could he trust her, or any woman? After the episode with Iris, trust wasn't something that came easily with him, especially when it involved a woman. He was a private person, reluctant to talk about his personal business and he pretty much kept things to himself. He did share a close bond with his brothers and cousins, and once in a while he would talk to them about things that were important to him but never about women. No woman had ever gotten close enough to him again to cause that type of grief. They came into his life and they went out of his life. That's the way he wanted it and that's the way he intended to keep it.

So why was he becoming obsessed with Jessica Claiborne?

He strolled over to his car to leave, and just as he was about to unlock the door he paused. Inhaling deeply he turned and began walking toward Jessica's shop. With every step he took he tried to convince himself that he was just being neighborly by checking in on her. He didn't have to go inside. He would just say hello and leave.

But moments later, when she opened the door, all thoughts of leaving suddenly left his mind. It was obvious that she had recently showered. And that she wasn't wearing a bra under her tank top. He blinked, not wanting to stare. She had great-looking breasts. They looked full, firm and lush pressed against the soft fabric of her top. Damn, he shouldn't be looking at her breasts. He wished he could do more than just look at them. Tasting them wasn't such a bad idea right about now.

He tore his gaze away from her chest and his eyes moved downward. She was wearing shorts that showed off her gorgeous legs and he suddenly felt his attraction for her get sharper, more intense.

He should be avoiding Jessica like the plague. Their relationship was not what his brothers assumed. But still, he was man enough to admit that there was a flicker of forbidden desire that clenched his guts whenever he saw her, came this close to her. Why was he putting himself through such madness? He sucked in a deep breath and smelled her scent—like cinnamon, spice, every-thing sensual and everything nice.

"Chase?"

He heard his name and then remembered he was standing there and hadn't said anything. "May I come in?" he finally asked.

Her legs somewhat shaky, Jessica met Chase's stare. Getting rid of him would be easy enough. All she had to do was refuse his request to come in. But for some reason she didn't want to. She tried to tell herself that this intense attraction between them had gone on long enough and it was time to take drastic action. Telling him that she was Carlton Graham's granddaughter would guarantee that he would walk away for sure, but she wasn't ready for that to happen. She couldn't tell him who she was until she could also prove her grand-father's innocence.

She sighed deeply and took a step back. When he was inside with the door closed behind him, she saw the heated look of desire in his eyes. Her first instinct was to run, head up the stairs, but she had a feeling he would only come after her. So she might as well stay put and get something they both wanted. For someone who didn't like kissing, she was becoming obsessed with doing it. Her mouth had practically been branded Chase's Place.

Jessica made a move toward Chase, as if drawn by a magnet. At the same time, Chase moved closer to her. "This is crazy," she said in a breathless whisper as she walked into his arms.

"Yeah, totally insane," he said huskily, pulling her closer to him.

She tilted her face up, and he did what was becoming as natural as breathing; he captured her mouth with his, blazing the heat already sizzling between them, satisfying their need to taste each other.

Kissing him got better each time. He had that special technique of letting his tongue sweep the corners of her lips, first sipping her gently like fine wine before deepening the kiss and sucking her tongue into complete submission, mating wildly with it and driving her insane. Only with Chase could she allow herself to open fully and take part in such an intimate exchange. He had the ability to arouse feelings that she wanted to explore. She wasn't able to do anything but stand there, hold on and shudder in his arms.

Moments later, he pulled back, reached out, palmed her face in his hand and brushed a kiss over her forehead. "I wanted to check on you to make sure you were okay." Then, knowing that was really a lame excuse, he added, "And more than anything, I wanted to taste you again."

Giving in to this uncontrollable desire, he leaned closer and kissed her mouth again, wishing he could kiss her forever. He finally lifted his head and their gazes met. And he knew what they had agreed on earlier was true. This was crazy. But that didn't stop him from kissing her again before he finally left.

She never was good at counting sheep, Jessica thought a few hours later as she lay in her bed gazing up at the ceiling. Who could think of sheep when thoughts of Chase Westmoreland filled her mind?

The taste of him was still fresh in her mouth, and she didn't want to think about the feel of him. Her breath was coming out in short gasps just thinking about the size of the erection that had been cradled between her thighs as he had continued to kiss her deeper and deeper.

She'd known she could have pulled back to stop him at any time but she hadn't wanted him to stop. So he hadn't, until it became obvious that if they continued she would have found herself on the floor with her shorts off, legs spread, and Chase naked between them. After kissing her into sweet oblivion, he had told her that he hoped she slept well tonight then left.

Jessica wasn't sleeping at all. She snapped her eyes shut. Instead of a flock of sheep flooding her mind, she saw Chase as she had seen him earlier that night, just moments before he'd left. He had been standing in her shop, gazing at her with so much desire in his eyes.

She almost jumped when she heard the phone ring and quickly reached over to pick it up while glancing over at the clock. She smiled and sat upright in bed. How could she have forgotten the call she got around this time every Sunday night?

"Hello."

"Hello, Jess, how did things go?"

Jessica's smile widened upon hearing Jennifer's voice. "The grand opening was wonderful."

"Sorry I missed it."

"Trust me, I understand." And she did. Jennifer Claiborne had been appointed school superintendent in Philadelphia, and since the school year had only started a month ago, she hadn't been able to get away.

"Have you heard anything from Savannah lately?" Jessica asked about her sister who was a year older and worked mostly out of the country as a photographer.

"Yes, she called today and said she had tried contacting you, but you weren't home. And she couldn't reach you on your cell phone. Of course she didn't leave a message. You know how she hates talking into those answering machines. I also talked to Rico today and he said to let you know he'll be in your area next week and plans to stop by."

Jessica grinned. "And I'm going to look forward to his visit," she said. Rico was four years older, a private investigator and she simply adored him.

She and Jennifer talked for over an hour. She told her about the information she had gathered to prove her grandfather's innocence.

"And you're sure Chase Westmoreland doesn't have a clue who you are?" Jennifer asked for the second time.

"Yes, I'm sure. He knows me as Claiborne so there's no way he could make the connection." That was the way she wanted things until she was able to tell him everything.

"Well, I hope you're not making a mistake by not telling him the truth up front."

Jessica shook her head. "He's a Westmoreland. He wouldn't trust me. Like his grandfather didn't trust my grandfather."

"It also seems to me from what you've told me about him that he's a nice guy. Possibly someone you could become interested in."

Too easily, Jessica thought, remembering the intense attraction she and Chase shared. "You know how I feel about having a serious relationship, Jennifer."

"Yes, and like you I have reasons to feel that way, but there's a need within all of us to be loved by someone."

Jessica sighed. Until she had met Chase she would have denied that such a need existed, but now…

"I'd better let you go. I'm sure you have a big week ahead of you."

After hanging up the phone, Jessica shifted to a more comfortable position in bed. She couldn't dismiss another type of need trying to take over her mind and body. It was a need she had never experienced before, but one she always encountered whenever she and Chase kissed. It was the need to take things further and enter into a scorching affair with him, based on need, not love, something she had never done before. She wasn't sure if she could handle it. And if she couldn't stand the heat, she should probably just stay out of the kitchen altogether.

Six

"So you remember the two waitresses who used to work for Chase's grandfather?" Jessica asked Mrs. Stewart while restocking the display case with fudge.

"Paula Meyers and Darcy Evans? I sure do," Mrs. Stewart said smiling. "Paula still lives in College Park but Darcy moved to Macon a few years ago to be closer to her family."

"And what about Theodore Henry? Mr. Schuster's former cook?"

"Yes, I knew him, too. He was a single man, nice-looking, soft-spoken, pretty much kept to himself. He rarely went to church, but he didn't bother anybody. He did what he had to do at Schuster's and minded his own business."

Jessica nodded. She intended to speak to Mr. Henry and Paula Meyers by the end of the week. Getting together with Darcy Evans might take longer since she would have to drive to Macon to do so.

She preferred speaking to everyone in person. From her days as an attorney she learned that face-to-face communication was much more effective than discussing anything over the telephone.

Hours later, after Mrs. Stewart left for the day, Jessica found herself alone in her shop as she tried to decide what would be tomorrow's craving of the day. But the only craving she could think about was the one she had for Chase. She couldn't erase from her mind the enjoyment she got kissing him. It didn't take much for her to remember the gentle yet thorough sweep of his tongue inside her mouth, assailing her senses with every stroke, and how he would feast on her lips. He had the ability to dismantle each and every wall she erected around herself.

And that wasn't good.

She glanced at the clock. She had an hour left before closing time. When Donna, the waitress from Chase's restaurant, had dropped in earlier to buy some brownies, she had casually mentioned that Chase had to leave town unexpectedly for Knoxville, something about a screwup in one of his deliveries, and that he wouldn't be back until Wednesday.

Jessica had accepted Donna's statement with a small shrug, which she hoped indicated her indifference. But the truth of the matter was she wasn't indifferent. How could she be when the thought that she wouldn't be seeing Chase again until Wednesday made her miss him already?

They were supposed to have dinner at his restaurant—after hours—to celebrate a week of knowing each other. He wasn't interested in anything other than enjoying a good wholesome time with a woman, based on friendship and nothing else. Okay, so they did throw a lot of kissing into the mix, she thought. But still their relationship was based on friendship, although that might crumble when he found out her true identity.

She sighed when she heard the phone ring and reached to pick it up. "Delicious Cravings."

"Yes, I'm returning a call to Jessica Graham. This is Paula Meyers."

Jessica smiled. "Yes, Ms. Meyers. Thanks for returning my call."

"Are you sure there won't be anything else, Chase?"

Chase glanced up from looking at the invoice. He was eager to leave Knoxville and head home but it seemed that Sam Nesbitt's daughter was on the prowl again. Storm had dated Cyndi once and now, with Storm happily married, it was obvious that she had shifted her attention to his single brother. "I'm positive. Looks like everything is in order."

"I would definitely agree," she said, giving him a thorough once-over while licking her lips.

Seeing her lick her lips did absolutely nothing for him. If it had been Jessica's lips, there'd be no way he would have been able to downplay the thrill and excitement that would have rushed through him.

"I'm about to close shop, Chase. I know a place where we can go and…get it on."

Chase lifted a brow. Storm had warned him that Cyndi Nesbitt didn't mince words or waste time. She spoke her mind and told you exactly what she wanted, and most of the time she could get pretty damn graphic. As he gazed at her, he knew she could probably deliver on her offer of recreational sex. But the fact of the matter was he wasn't interested. The only woman he wanted was back in Atlanta.

Placing a polite smile on his face, he said, "Thanks for the offer but I have a few more stops to make before returning to Atlanta sometime tomorrow. Tell your father that I'm sorry I missed him."

A disappointed pout curved her lips. "Yeah, I'll be sure to tell him."

Later that evening Chase was back at his hotel. After taking a shower he lay on the bed and found his mind filled with thoughts of Jessica. Inexplicable warmth flowed through his bloodstream. He had never met anyone quite like her. He shifted his body and rubbed the back of his neck. Okay, he knew he shouldn't be thinking about her so much, but the blind truth was that he couldn't help himself. It was nothing more than a sexual attraction fueled by six months of him doing without, but still, there was something about Jessica that drew him, made it impossible for him to want any other woman but her.

He leaned forward and picked up the business card he had placed on the nightstand earlier, the card Jessica had given him on Saturday for Delicious Cravings.

Sighing deeply, he picked up the phone and began dialing. When it began to ring he glanced at his watch. It was close to eight o'clock and he hoped he wouldn't be disturbing her.

"Hello?"

At the sound of her sweet voice he released a long, deep breath. The warmth flowing through his bloodstream increased as he settled back against a huge fluffy pillow. "Hi, Jessica. It's Chase."

Jessica curled her body as she lay on the bed and a heated sensation flowed through her stomach. She took a deep breath. The sound of Chase's voice was doing things to her. "Chase, how are you?"

"A whole lot better now that I'm talking to you."

A thrill shot through Jessica at his words. He definitely knew how to break through a girl's defenses. "I had to leave this morning on an unexpected trip to Knoxville," he was saying, reclaiming her attention. "I've been having problems with my suppliers and I thought a face-to-face meeting was warranted."

Jessica nodded. "I've heard that Knoxville is a beautiful city."

"It is. I gather that you've never been here."

She smiled. "No, I haven't."

"Then I'll have to invite you to come with me the next time I make a trip this way."

Chase murmured the words low, in a deep, husky tone. His breath seemed to transcend the phone lines and warmly caress her ear, heating the flesh along her spine. His invitation wasn't helping matters. "I'd like that." She ignored the warning bells sounding in her ears. She and Chase were moving a little too fast, but she didn't see them slowing down any.

"So, how was your day?" he asked.

She didn't want to think of her meeting that afternoon with Paula Meyers. The older, sweet and seemingly gentle woman hadn't been able to tell her anything about who might have passed the Westmoreland secret recipes on to the cook at Schuster's restaurant. Jessica would be taking a drive to Macon to talk to Darcy Evans the next afternoon. When she had called, the woman hadn't seem too excited to talk with her.

"Today was wonderful," she said. "Business was good. In fact I got another contract to supply pastries for a nearby hotel."

"Sounds like you're doing well. But then, I knew that you would."

When Jessica tried uncurling her body, heat ran down her spine again. "Thanks." A few moments into the conversation she asked, "So when will you be coming home?"

"Sometime Wednesday. You haven't forgotten about our dinner plans, have you?"

She took a deep breath, not wanting to tell him that she hadn't thought of much else. Even the disappointing dead end with Paula Meyers hadn't dampened her thoughts of sharing a meal with Chase on Wednesday night. "No, I haven't forgotten. I'm looking forward to it," she said truthfully.

"So am I." After a few moments he said, "I'm sure

you've had a busy day and need your rest so I'll let you go. Good night, Jessica."

She hated that their phone conversation was coming to an end. "Good night, Chase, and thanks for calling."

After hanging up, Jessica traced the lines of her lips with her fingertips, remembering the time it had been Chase's tongue and not her finger caressing her lips. The memory sent an arousing shiver through her. As she stretched out in bed she could hear the steady tap of rain beating down on her roof.

Cuddling her pillow she shifted her body into a comfortable position knowing that the moment she closed her eyes, thoughts of Chase would consume her, even while she slept.

Darcy Evans was hiding something.

Jessica could feel it. The woman, who appeared to be in her mid-thirties, said she had only agreed to talk with Jessica because of the respect she'd had for Jessica's grandfather. Eighteen years ago she had been a seventeen-year-old unwed mother in need of a job and Carlton Graham had talked Scott Westmoreland into hiring her as a waitress. She hadn't worked there long when Scott and Carlton parted ways.

"So you have no idea how the Westmoreland recipes could have gotten into the hands of the cook at Schuster's restaurant?"

Jessica watched the expression on the woman's face. As she stood leaning her hips against the closed door, she replied, "How would I know something like that? I was just a waitress."

Yes, how indeed? Jessica wondered as she continued looking at the woman. "And you were a waitress there for a couple of months?"

"For four months actually."

"And during that time you never worked in the kitchen?"

The woman's eyes flared. "And just what are you accusing me of?"

Jessica sighed. "I'm not accusing you of anything, Ms. Evans. I'm just trying to find answers to an unsolved puzzle."

The woman lifted her chin. "Why bother? Scott Westmoreland and Carlton Graham are dead. What does it matter what happened with those recipes?"

Jessica picked up her purse and stood. "Because although they've passed away, their descendants deserve to know the truth, and until they do, my grandfather's honesty will be questioned. That's unfair to him. I want to prove he wasn't guilty of any wrongdoing."

Jessica watched the woman tense up and look around the small apartment as if not wanting to meet Jessica's eyes. "Your grandfather was a good man."

Jessica smiled. "Yes, I think so, too, but he died knowing there was a blemish on his character and that always bothered him. And I'm asking that if you remember anything that you think might help clear his name, will you please let me know."

"I won't remember anything," Darcy Evans said, much too quickly, Jessica thought as she was ushered out the door.

* * *

Chase turned and glanced around the room. His office had been transformed into a place he almost didn't recognize. While in the kitchen preparing the dinner he would share tonight with Jessica, he had given Donna instructions on how he had wanted things set up, and it appeared his ever-efficient waitress had gone overboard. The way she had changed a section of his office into an intimate dining area for two definitely met with his satisfaction, but what was up with the lit fireplace and all the flowers and candles? There was no way he could dine in here with Jessica and not think of seduction. He would want to kiss her, take her upstairs to the small apartment he used on occasion, and undress her. Then he would run his hands all over her breasts, stomach and thighs, not to mention touch that area between her legs that had definitely become his own delicious craving. He felt a tightening in his loins. He wanted to do more than touch her there. He wanted to taste her, devour her and watch her eyes fill with the pleasure he was dying to give her as she opened her legs wider and his tongue continued to—

"Everything meets with your satisfaction, boss?"

Jerked out of his racy thoughts, Chase turned and met Donna's excited features. He sighed. "You kind of went overboard, don't you think?"

Donna chuckled. "Well, considering how things went the first time Jessica Claiborne walked into your office, I figured you needed all the help you could get, and I have a feeling that she likes to be wined and dined like the rest of us."

Chase nodded as he studied the woman he had hired six months ago. Donna had become someone he could depend on. Although he didn't know a lot about her personal life since she kept that pretty private, he did know that she was twenty-three and was attending school at night to earn a degree in business management.

A few hours later when he was alone Chase's primitive instincts kicked into gear. His staff had cleaned everything up and left for the day. He hadn't seen Jessica since Sunday and although he had spoken to her on Monday night from Knoxville, he had talked himself out of calling her again on Tuesday. He had convinced himself that his desire for her was natural and he would just have to ignore the low burning need that always simmered in his gut whenever he was around her. Tonight the two of them would celebrate a week of knowing each other, although he didn't want to dwell on the fact that he'd never commemorated a week of knowing any other woman.

He sighed, almost impatient to see her again, to kiss her, talk to her, then frowned, wondering what the hell was wrong with him. He didn't have long to ponder that question when he heard a knock at the door.

Ignoring the racing of his heart, Chase opened the door and for a moment just stood there staring at the woman standing in front of him. She was dressed in a skirt and blouse that would have looked simple on any other woman. The outfit did a pretty nice job of emphasizing her full, firm breasts, tiny waist and curvy hips. And, he thought, glancing downward to take a look at her legs, which could easily be seen thanks to the shortness of her skirt, there was definitely temptation there, especially with the high-heeled sandals she wore. Her scent, hot and seductive, also triggered something within him. Like he wasn't heated up enough already.

He didn't say anything for a moment and watched as she nervously swept her bottom lip with her tongue. Pure unadulterated lust hit him with the force of Mount St. Helens erupting.

"I hope I'm not too early, Chase," she said softly, glancing up at him.

His gaze came to rest on her mouth when he said, "No, you're right on time." *And I want to taste you bad.*

He took a step back, let her in, then closed and locked the door behind her. The air surrounding them seemed to quiver and the need to take her into his arms and kiss her was slithering through every vein in his body.

"I thought I'd contribute dessert," she said, handing a covered container to him. "Chocolate cheesecake."

"Thanks." He slowly felt his control slipping and knew he had to get a grip. Grip, hell! He placed the cake container on a nearby table and reached out and pulled her into his arms. As soon as his lips captured hers he knew kissing her was becoming an addiction. It should be against the law for any woman's mouth to taste this sweet, this delicious, this able to whet his sexual appetite.

He hadn't known how much he needed this until now. He needed to bury his mouth in hers, suck her tongue, feel her breasts pressed against his chest, and hear the way she moaned when he kissed her. And then there was the way her body automatically connected to his groin, fitting his arousal dead center between her thighs—the part of her he craved most.

Damn if he didn't put a stop to this madness, he would be taking her right here, right now. Slowly, reluctantly, he lifted his head and almost drowned in the heated look in her eyes. "I thought it would be best if we dined in my office," he whispered against her moist lips. "That way no one would see the lights on in here and assume I'm open for business." In other words, he didn't want any interruptions.

"All right."

He suddenly felt warm again and he inhaled deeply, trying not to focus on her mouth. Trying to pull himself together, Chase picked up the cake container off the table and placing a hand at the center of her back, he led her down the hall. Neither said a word. When they reached his office door he pushed it open and watched as she walked into the room.

Her gaze immediately went to the table set for two, the lit fireplace and the flowers and candles. She didn't say anything for a moment, turning slowly. The eyes that met his were like a soft caress and did nothing to cool his desire, only heightened it.

A smile tilted the corner of her mouth when she said, "You didn't have to go to all this trouble, Chase."

Yes, I did, he thought, as he slowly strolled toward her, covering the distance separating them. He placed the cake container on his desk and to keep from reaching out and touching her, he tightened his hands into fists at his side.

The way her hair tumbled around her shoulders,

made her look sexier than ever, and now, within the close confines of his office, her scent, a delicious fragrance that was the very essence of her, further ignited that primal instinct already playing havoc with every part of his body. Kissing her earlier definitely hadn't helped matters.

"I hope you enjoy dinner. It's a Westmoreland secret recipe for chicken and dumplings."

Jessica swallowed. The last thing she wanted to hear anything about was a Westmoreland secret recipe. "Is it good?"

He chuckled. "I'll let you decide." He walked over and pulled out a chair at the table. "Come and let me serve you."

She nodded and sat down at the table. Jessica watched as he expertly served the food, struggling to remain calm and fighting not to stare at him. She hadn't realized until now just how much she had missed him these past couple of days. Nor had she realized how much she had needed him to kiss her. He had such a dark, handsome, sophisticated look, yet her senses told her that there was a hint of something untamed about him.

"Let's dig in," he said after they'd said grace.

During dinner they talked about a number of things. He even gave her pointers on how to promote her business on the Internet. Afterwards, they savored the cheesecake she had brought.

"Did you enjoy dinner?" he asked softly sometime later, when they stood in front of the fireplace enjoying a glass of wine.

She smiled. "Yes, I enjoyed everything. The chicken and dumplings were to die for."

She glanced around the room at the flowers and candles then turned back and looked at him. "Everything was nice, Chase, but I'm wondering…"

When she hesitated and didn't finish what she was about to say, he asked, "Wondering what?"

She nervously bit her bottom lip. "I'm wondering if perhaps it's a little too much for two people who've decided to be just friends."

Chase had crouched down in front of the fireplace to add another piece of wood to the flames. He lifted a dark brow and glanced at Jessica. "When did we decide that? We talked about things moving too fast and slowing them down a bit. We also agreed to take the time to know each other better. But I don't recall saying we wouldn't be anything more than friends. In fact I'm counting on just the opposite. I don't want to be only your friend."

He studied her as he stood, watching every nuance of her features as the words he'd spoken sank in. "What are you saying?" she whispered softly, her voice the only sound in the room other than the resonance of the fire crackling in the fireplace.

He sighed, knowing he had to give her the bare truth. No frills, no gimmicks, no lies and definitely no game-playing. He wanted to be her lover and not her friend. Usually he didn't move this fast with any woman, but with Jessica he was driven to do so. "We've already discussed the issue of us being attracted to each other. But there seems to be another problem, a deeper one."

Her brows furrowed in a frown. "What?" She tried to downplay the churning in her stomach as he looked at her. His dark eyes, shadowed by long lashes, were doing things to her.

His features were serious when he said, "I want you, Jessica, and I think you want me as well. We can do whatever we want to skirt around that fact, avoid it or ignore it, but eventually the final result will be the same."

She lifted a brow. "The final result?"

"Yes."

"Which is?"

"We *will* become lovers. If not tonight, then some other night. The chemistry between us is too strong for us not to. I would never force or trick you. But I will try my best to seduce you."

Seduce you...Chase's words flowed through her mind and as much as she didn't want them to, they stirred a sensual need in her. They did more than that, they ignited something deep and elemental. She turned to study the flames in the fireplace, but they were nothing compared to the ones inching through her bloodstream at that very moment.

For two solid days she had tried keeping her mind focused on finding out how Schuster's cook had gotten hold of the Westmoreland secret recipes, but Chase had always lurked deeply in her thoughts.

She heard him come to stand behind her. She breathed his masculine scent, and knew that what he'd said was true. Considering their families' history, an involvement with him was the last thing she needed. But he was right. Sooner or later they *would* sleep together, even though she hadn't liked sex in the past. She knew that with Chase things would be different. He'd already changed her mind about kissing.

"Jessica?"

He whispered her name just moments before he reached out and gently turned her around. Dark-brown eyes studied her intently, searching her face, heating her insides and melting her resistance. For longer than she cared to remember, she had been an independent woman, placing no aspect of her life or livelihood into a man's hands. But then those hands had never belonged to Chase Westmoreland.

The truth of the matter was that she wanted his hands to hold her, snuggle her close to him, touch her all over, give her the pleasure she had dreamed he had given her just last night. Just thinking about it made her pulse fierce, her breathing erratic, her heart beat wildly and generated an intense amount of heat between her legs. She drew in a shaky breath knowing what she was going through was more than mere lust, but at the moment she didn't want to define anything.

She struggled against the need to be sensible versus her desire to be wanton. There was a heartbeat of a pause, and then she reached out and wrapped her arms around Chase's neck and brought her body against the hard solid plane of his. She felt how aroused he was through his slacks and the intense sexual need she had been fighting since first meeting him took control.

"Chase," she murmured softly, deciding to throw

caution to the wind and take what she wanted for the first time in her life.

"Yes?"

"Seduce me."

Seven

Seduce me…

Jessica's words sent Chase's libido into overdrive. He gazed at her, thinking that not only did he plan to seduce her, he intended to drive her wild. "Will you join me in another glass of wine?" he asked quietly against her ear.

She nodded as a shiver passed through her, uncertain of his plans for her. But whatever they were she would be a willing participant. She met his gaze and held on to it. "Yes."

Emotions were churning inside her as she watched him pour them each another glass of wine. "I propose a toast," he said huskily, gazing at her with those dark penetrating eyes that had her body simmering. "To seduction."

Jessica let her gaze shift from him to stare at the hand holding his wineglass in midair. This wasn't the first time she had studied his hands and wondered how they would feel on her. Even now, just thinking about it had her senses overheating. She swallowed deeply as she clicked her glass to his then slowly drank her wine. When she had taken a couple of sips he reached out and gently eased the glass from her hand and placed it beside his on the table. He turned to a CD player that sat nearby and after he had turned a knob, soft jazz filled the air.

"Let's dance," he whispered, pulling her into his arms.

Jessica could feel her body tremble from the hardness of his pressed intimately to hers. She gave in to the seductive moment surrounding them and closed her eyes as the soft sound of the music lulled her, sharpened her feminine instincts. She nestled her face against his throat, breathing in his manly, arousing scent. The light stroke of his fingers on her back inched lower, past her waist to caress her backside. His touch was driving her insane, making her want things she'd never had. Molten heat filled her entire body.

More than once her pelvis pressed into him; she was fully aware of his erection, large and thick, and she was surprised by her ability to make him want her that much. He splayed the palm of his hand inside her buttocks, bringing her closer to him, making her breathing shallow and the area between her legs even more damp.

All too quickly, the song ended. She glanced up and met his gaze. She saw the heated look in his eyes, noted the raw primitive expression on his face mere seconds

before he leaned down to connect his lips to hers. Hands
that she had been studying earlier reached out and cradled her head, delving into her scalp, as he mated his
mouth with hers, slowly, easily, thoroughly.

Then he deepened the kiss, sucking her tongue into
his mouth, letting her know just how much he wanted
everything he could get and driving her mad in the process. He ground his aroused body against hers and she
groaned as he continued to kiss her with a passion that
had liquid heat flowing between her legs, making her
want him there. *Oh, yes, right there.*

She felt his fingers inching up her leg, moving slowly
toward her inner thigh and the feel of him touching her
made her suck in a quick breath. He pulled back, releasing her mouth and the look he gave her was so incredibly
sexy it made a deep quivering need invade her insides.

"I think you have on too many clothes," he whispered
as he reached out and began unbuttoning her blouse. "I
want you naked." He continued to hold her gaze. "Do
you have a problem with that?" he asked softly as he
eased the buttons out of the buttonholes.

She reached out and held fast to his arm. Not to stop
him but to hurry him along. His slowness was almost
killing her. "No, I don't have a problem with it," she
whispered, reveling in the warmth of his skin beneath
her fingers.

When the last of the buttons had been undone and he
saw her flesh-colored lace bra, he inhaled sharply. His
hands went first to the front fastener and, with a quick
flick of the wrist, her bra came undone and her breasts
sprang free.

Jessica heard the deep sound of male appreciation that erupted in his throat and her stomach clenched at the way he was staring at her breasts. There was hunger in his eyes. She held her breath as he eased the bra from her shoulders, letting it join her blouse on the floor.

"I've wanted you from the first day I saw you. It wasn't here in this office. It was before then. That Monday morning I saw you move into your place," he whispered. "The first thing I thought was that you had a gorgeous pair of legs," he said smiling wryly. Then his features turned serious when he added, "Gorgeous legs or not, I didn't want to get involved with you, but I soon discovered I could do nothing to stop it from happening."

He breathed in deeply. "I want you so much," he groaned just moments before leaning down and capturing one of her nipples with his mouth.

Jessica sucked in a deep breath when his mouth connected to her turgid nipple, licking at it, sucking it into his mouth and lavishing it with the warmth of his tongue. He was assaulting her emotions to the third degree, causing a purr to erupt deep within her throat, making her legs give way.

As her knees buckled, he brought her body closer to his, holding her up, not letting her go anywhere while his mouth switched breasts, tormenting the other as he had its twin.

"Chase." Jessica moaned his name on a soft sigh as her hand reached out to hold fast to his head, not wanting him to stop what he was doing to her. He was filling her with passion to a degree she'd never known could exist.

He pulled back. "I want to taste you some more," he whispered throatily, holding her gaze, making the ache within her even more profound.

She inhaled sharply and to her amazement she heard herself say, "Then do it."

The smile he gave her melted her insides and destroyed any resistance that might have suddenly popped into her mind. She watched as he undid her skirt to let it slide down her legs and pool at her feet, leaving her wearing nothing but a pair of flesh lacy thong panties.

"Sexy as hell," she heard him growl in a deep, rough tone before going on his knees and gently easing her panties down. Then he leaned back and looked up at her, letting his gaze roam all over her. His eyes came back to the area between her legs. When she saw him lick his lips she knew what was coming next. She had heard about it, read about it, but had never experienced it herself. In a few moments she would. Chase would make sure of it.

He eased closer to her and leaned over and placed a kiss on her navel, licking the area around it, making it wet then blowing warm air on it, making the heated warmth between her legs intensify. She watched him as a flush of desire surged through her.

He slowly made his way downward, past her navel, and before she could catch her next breath he was kissing her there with the same intensity that he had applied to her mouth. And to make sure she wasn't going anywhere—like she would even consider such a thing—he placed a firm grip on her buttocks, holding her still while igniting her entire body into flames.

She heard the guttural growls he was making as he kissed her and, of their own accord, her hands clutched his head. He sank farther into her warmth, deepening the kiss and tasting her in a way no man had ever done before.

With a groan, she thrust her hips closer—as if his mouth wasn't planted in place firmly already—but what she wanted was for the waves that were insistently pounding at her insides to finally drown her. It was evident that Chase would not be rushed. He intended to feast on her until he got his fill, until his hunger to taste her this way was assuaged.

But her body suddenly exploded and she screamed his name. She tried pushing him away from her, but he gripped her buttocks tighter, firmly locked his mouth to her as his tongue moved inside her wildly, uninhibitedly, stroking her, tasting her thoroughly. He didn't release his grip until the last tremble had left her body, and then he didn't stop what he was doing, but continued to taste her as his hands gently stroked her hips.

Finally, he lifted his head, eased back on his haunches and looked at her. The look in his eyes made her breath catch. He wanted more. A lot more. And as she watched him lean forward and nuzzle his face in the area between her thighs, heaven help her but she wanted more, too. "Make love to me, Chase," she whispered.

He pulled back, looked up at her, eased to his feet and then swept her into his arms.

Chase gazed down at the woman he was holding. Usually he wouldn't do what he had just done until he got to know the woman better, but Jessica was a decadent delicacy and he couldn't have resisted sampling her that way even if he had wanted to. And now that he had tasted her, his craving had intensified. She was utterly delicious.

He held her tenderly while walking up the stairs and couldn't help but notice how she cuddled in his arms, rubbed her cheek against his chest, causing his breathing to quicken, his libido to go into overdrive.

When he reached the bedroom he drew in a deep breath, crossed the room to the bed and lowered Jessica. He had felt her heat the moment she had walked into Chase's Place tonight, and now he wanted to get all into it again. But first he had to get as naked as she was. Looking at her lying there on his bed without a stitch of clothing was making him lose control of all coherent thought. Tasting her was nice, definitely a mouthwatering experience, but what he wanted to do more than anything was get inside her.

As he stood back to unbutton his shirt, he watched her watching him. The moonlight streaming in through the windows bathed her in a translucent glow, making the coloring of her body as luscious as the chocolate she used to bake with. "Say something," he whispered when the quiet stillness in the room got unbearable and it was obvious what he was doing had her complete attention. He tossed his shirt aside.

He watched as she stretched her naked body while a smile touched the corners of her lips. He liked the fact she wasn't shy or bashful. Nor was she ashamed of showing her body to him. She laughed quietly, sexily. "What do you want me to say?"

Heat flooded his brain when she took her tongue and licked her lips. He swallowed the lump in his throat as his hands went to his belt buckle. "You can say anything."

She paused, as if taking in his words, and when she licked her lips again he sucked in a quick breath. He watched as she eased to the edge of the bed, her face coming in direct contact with his midsection. She reached out and pressed her hand against the large, heavy erection clearly showing through his slacks, using her fingers to explore the firmness of it through the khaki material. "Umm, at the moment, I can think of only one word to say," she said softly and in a voice he found incredibly sexy.

"What's that?" he asked, barely able to get the words out as she continued to explore him, squeeze him, cup him.

She lifted her gaze to meet his and with a deep, throaty sound she said, "Hurry."

He smiled as he took a step back and quickly pulled the belt from his pants before easing both his underwear and slacks down his legs. He stood before her as naked as she was and got heated watching her eyes roam over him. "What are you thinking?" he asked in a strained voice.

"What I thought the first time I saw you. That you remind me of rich dark chocolate," she whispered. "And that I would definitely like to have some of it."

He chuckled and slowly moved toward the bed. "Baby, I intend for you to have all of it."

He joined her on the bed, urging her back to the middle of the mattress. Without wasting any time he pinned her body beneath his weight. "But first," he said, leaning in and bringing his face down to hers, "I need to kiss you again."

Jessica smiled. She knew all about his kisses, was well aware of how delicious and X-rated they were. Ever since meeting Chase she had become aware of the extent of the sexual desire she had stored away, denying its existence. Before she could ponder why, his mouth captured hers, making her forget everything but the way he was working his tongue inside her mouth. Memories of what he had done to her while on his knees in his office, along with what he was doing to her now, sent sensuous shudders all through her, tumbling her emotions and getting her body overheated.

When he finally released her mouth, he whispered quietly, so incredibly sexily in her ear, "Open for me, Jessica."

Instinctively she spread her legs as he continued stroking his tongue back and forth across her lips. She felt him lift his lower body and she unconsciously lifted hers. "Now take me in," he whispered hoarsely.

He leaned up and met her gaze and she knew what he was asking her to do, which was something she'd never done—lead a man into her body. But she would do it. She wanted to do it. Before, when she had made love that one time in college, things had been over before she could blink, leaving her feeling cheated, unsatisfied, disappointed. But Chase was making sure she was a part of what they were doing. He was allowing her to be more than a willing partner. He fully intended her to be an eager participant.

Reaching out she came into contact with the hairy

surface around his navel. Her fingers paused, liking the feel of the rough texture of hair there on his stomach. When her fingertips began caressing him there, she heard his sharp intake of breath.

"Jessica."

Her name was a tortured groan from his lips and she smiled as her fingers moved downward until she got hold of him. He felt hard, firm, big in her hands. She blinked. *Too big.* She wondered if they would fit.

She glanced up and met his gaze. As if knowing her thoughts he smiled and said, "Perfectly."

She breathed in deeply, deciding to take his word for it. Besides, holding him in her hand was making her lose control of all rational thought. The only thing she could think about was that the huge, thick object she was clutching would soon be inside her, mating with her and…

She blinked again. "What about protection?" she suddenly asked.

She could tell from the expression on his face that he had forgotten just as she had. He sucked in a deep breath. "Damn, I'm usually not this careless. Sorry," he said, shifting his body off her to retrieve a condom packet from the nightstand drawer. He ripped it open with his teeth and quickly sheathed himself.

She smiled, although she still wondered how they would fit. "I sort of got carried away with the moment, too." She paused, then quickly added, "I'm on the pill to regulate my periods but I haven't slept with anyone for over eight years—"

"Eight years?" A shocked look took over his features.

She nodded. "Yes, not since my first year at college.

It wasn't anything like I thought it would be and was over quickly." A part of Jessica couldn't believe she was discussing this with Chase as if they were having a conversation about the weather.

"And you haven't done it again since then?"

Jessica swallowed before answering. "No, this will be the first time since then."

Returning to her, he bent his head, took her lips, dipped his tongue into her mouth, kissing her with such gentle tenderness Jessica thought she would faint. Then he deepened the kiss, reigniting the flame between them, causing her body to ache for him once again.

"Lead me in, Jessica," he said moments later, breaking off their kiss.

His breathing was choppy and his whispered words made her entire body pulse. Holding him firmly in her hand, she guided him to her as their eyes met and held. The intensity in his gaze sent heat throbbing through her. She actually felt the muscles in her womb contract. It seemed that every part of her was ready to receive him.

When he was at her entrance she felt him take over. The tip of him eased inside, stretching her, and as he lowered his hips and she lifted hers, he went deeper. She sucked in a deep breath when he couldn't go any farther.

Chase raised up slightly and gazed down at her. "You're still... He didn't..." He broke off in amazement. He leaned down, his face mere inches from hers.

Before Jessica could fully understand what Chase meant by those words, she felt him push his body forward, and the cry of pain that tore from her lips was captured in his kiss. She'd been a virgin all this time. He continued kissing her and she couldn't recall a more precious moment.

Instinctively, she wrapped her legs around Chase's waist as he continued kissing her. Moments later, he pulled back and whispered, "Make love with me, sweetheart."

Her legs tightened around him. Her body was coiled with anticipation of what was next. And when he pushed deeper inside her, locking them legs to legs, limbs to limbs, breasts to chest, she lifted her hips to him.

He began to move. Slow at first, driving her almost insane with the way his body was moving in and out of hers. Then suddenly his strokes quickened and they mated effortlessly, smoothly, fluidly. His hips slammed into her over and over again. As if that wasn't close enough, he took his hand and lifted her and she thought she felt him touch the crest of her womb.

"Chase." She cried out his name, begging for a release that was different from the one she'd had earlier in his office. Different but just as intense. His tongue inside her had been awesome, but his sex inside her, pumping into her fast, solid, hard, was even better. Over and over he continued, nonstop. Every single thrust brought her closer to the edge. She wanted to scream, her throat ached to do so.

And she did.

She screamed his name. Her arms circled his neck and felt all the perspiration that soaked his skin. Sweat trickled down his back, slicked his forehead, and dampened her flesh. But he didn't let up and she cried out again, everything inside her exploding—including him.

She heard his guttural cry just moments before she

felt the warmth of his release. He was not holding anything back, determined to make her shatter, break free, blast off to the stars, detonate into ecstasy. And he was there with her, grinding his teeth, pushing deeper inside her as both of them continued to come apart. He relentlessly pounded into her hard and fast, and she felt his second release, just as intense and thick as the first. His head fell back and he screamed her name as explosions continued to erupt between them.

And Jessica knew at that moment that as unbelievable as it might seem, she had fallen in love with Chase Westmoreland.

Chase's body shuddered as he eased off Jessica. They had made love a second time and he'd have liked nothing better than to pin her body under his and go another round. He doubted if he would ever tire of making love to her.

His delicious craving. He'd never known a woman so damn edible.

He glanced over at her. He'd worn her out. She could barely keep her eyes open. After the first time they had made love he had gone into the bathroom. When she had seen him standing at the foot of the bed with the basin of water and wash cloth, she had drawn back and looked at him as though he'd lost his mind, not believing he would even for one minute consider performing such an intimate act on her. She had tried being stubborn about it, but in the end he had kissed her into submission. He had never slept with a virgin before. Even Iris had been experienced.

He inhaled sharply when he thought of the woman

who had wounded his pride and broken his heart. When he had been at the top of his game, at the head of the list for the NBA draft, she had been right there, on his arm and in his bed. But after his injury she hadn't wasted time moving on to bigger opportunities and even had the gall to tell him that it wasn't anything personal, but she wanted more from life than to be tied to a cripple. That had been nearly ten years ago. He no longer walked with a limp thanks to the extensive physical therapy he had endured, a very supportive family and the willpower and determination to survive as well as to succeed.

He glanced back over at Jessica and saw she had drifted off to sleep. But still he heard her murmur his name as she shifted in bed and wiggled her bottom to fit into him. His physical reaction to her cradled so snugly against him was immediate. His craving for her absolute. He splayed his palm on her stomach and gently pressed her closer to him, spooning their bodies, and he heard when she murmured his name again.

Chase frowned slightly. The last thing he needed at this point in his life was another woman getting under his skin. Once burned, it was hard not to wear a shield. He had made the decision long ago never to fall in love again. Doing so would only be asking for pain. For that reason he was troubled by his deep attraction to Jessica. Even before they had shared what they had tonight, he had been entranced by her, which wasn't a good thing. When it came to women he wasn't into attachments.

He glanced at the clock on the nightstand. It was a little past midnight. He would need to wake her before four o'clock to make sure she got dressed to return to her apartment. Some of his employees began arriving around five to handle the early-morning breakfast crowd. The last thing he wanted was for anyone to know his and Jessica's business. As far as he was concerned, what they'd shared was too precious for prying eyes at the moment. Everyone would discover sooner or later that they were having an affair, but he wished it to be later and not sooner.

Chase cursed under his breath when he thought about his brothers and cousins. They would try making a mountain out of a molehill but at that moment, Jessica shifted again in bed, bringing her bottom even closer to the fit of his front, and his brothers and cousins were the last thought on his mind.

Jessica slowly opened her eyes and felt a strong, warm arm slung across her waist. A very naked waist. It suddenly occurred to her that she was completely naked and so was the man lying so close beside her in the softly illuminated bedroom.

She peeked at the clock on the bedside table. It was three o'clock in the morning. She felt her pulse quicken at the memory of what she and Chase had shared last night, and all because of Chase's very talented mouth. She closed her eyes as heat flowed through her.

Then something else rushed through her as well. The stark memory that she had been a virgin. Chase was now the first for her in a lot of ways. The first man to give her a climax and the first man to actually make love to her in the full sense of the word. There had been nothing quick about it and the last thing she felt was cheated.

Jessica felt her face burn with embarrassment when she also remembered what he'd done after they had made love the first time, and the gentle, attentive care he had given her afterward. She had never imagined any man being that caring and concerned with a woman he'd slept with. Just thinking about what he had done to soothe her aches would endear him to her for life. And when they had made love a second time, he had been so gentle and tender it had almost brought tears to her eyes.

A sharp pain stabbed at Jessica's heart when she imagined what Chase's reaction would be when he discovered she was Carlton Graham's granddaughter. She knew Mrs. Stewart and Jennifer were right. She should tell him the truth and continue to go about proving her grandfather's innocence. From just the short time she'd gotten to know Chase, she felt that trust was an important issue to him.

Suddenly, Jessica's breath caught in her throat when she felt his arm shift from her waist as his hand moved slowly downward, toward the juncture of her legs.

"Sore?" he asked, his voice warm and soft, as he brushed his lips across an area beneath her ear.

Jessica opened her mouth to answer but she let out a soft purr instead when his fingers began caressing her feminine core, making scorching heat swirl inside her. She swallowed deeply and then tried to speak again. "Not too much, thanks to you." She felt the moistness of his tongue as he licked an area against her neck. She immediately gasped for air.

"No thanks needed."

In one smooth move he had rolled her from her side

onto her back and she found herself trapped intimately beneath his hard, solid body. The eyes staring down at her were sexy as sin. And immediately she felt the heat simmering within her ignite, flame out of control. Right now, at this very moment, she wanted him to make love to her again. She needed it. Later she would rake herself over the coals for falling in love with him, but for now…

She raised her arms to encircle his neck, bringing his mouth down closer to hers. "Make love to me again," she whispered, meeting the deep intensity in his gaze.

Although she might be the one making the request, she knew that he wanted her just as much as she wanted him. The proof was there in the thick, hard, turgid erection resting so achingly close between her thighs. But she knew that Chase was the kind of man who wouldn't make a move until she'd given him permission to give her pleasure.

And then, slowly, she began to feel him inch his way inside of her. The dark eyes she was gazing up into became even darker. Her body automatically stretched as he went deeper, and flicks of intense heat began consuming her.

"I love being inside you," he growled in her ear, and she wrapped her legs securely around him, locking their bodies as his shaft inched deeper still. When he had gone as deep as he could go, he leaned down and when her lips parted on a low, breathless moan, he claimed her mouth, at the same time as the lower part of his body began moving in deep, penetrating thrusts, over and over again.

And then it happened. Pleasure slammed into her and she was stunned by it. She had reached a climax with him before, but this one almost jerked her body clear off the bed, made her arch desperately against him, and felt as if she was coming apart, fragmenting into a million pieces. Chase lifted his mouth from hers to throw back his head and a deep howl filled the air as he experienced his own pleasure. As if she wasn't close enough, his hands cupped her bottom to bring her closer so he could go deeper, fusing their bodies as one.

Then his lips covered hers and he took her mouth with a promise of more fulfillment as exploding waves drowned them once again, sweeping them off to a place where it seemed their souls had somehow melded.

Before dawn that morning Chase opened the door of his restaurant to walk Jessica home. The air was cool and everything was quiet and still.

He automatically placed his arms around her shoulders and brought her body close to his as they strolled in the darkness passed Mrs. Morrison's shop. No words were exchanged between them and Chase wondered if Jessica felt the way he did, that what they'd shared was a dream and one uttered word would bring them awake.

When they reached her door he watched as she unlocked it. She turned back to him and Chase quickly leaned down and pressed a kiss upon her lips. He wondered how one ended what had turned out to be such a very special night. And if she were to invite him in, how would he turn down her invitation when more than anything he wanted to make love to her again—for the rest of the morning and the remainder of the day as well?

The kiss that he had meant to be short and sweet suddenly took on a life of its own, and he found himself kissing her deeply, with abandoned possession and simmering hunger. He knew he should pull away from her, but decided he couldn't imagine having his mouth in any other place at the moment.

Finally, when they heard the loud horn of a semi-truck somewhere in the distance, they moved apart. She met his gaze and he could see the same desire he felt mirrored in her eyes.

"I'd better go inside," she whispered softly. "And thanks again for dinner."

Chase smiled. "Thank you for *everything*."

Jessica's stomach clenched. She both loved him and wanted him. A deadly combination. Without thinking what she was doing she leaned up on tiptoes and brought her lips to his. He took the kiss she offered, added his own little sensual twist.

She slowly pulled back. "Good night, Chase."

A broad grin touched both corners of his lips. "And good morning to you, Jessica." He turned and then walked away.

Eight

The first thing Chase noticed when he walked into Jessica's shop at lunchtime was the slew of customers lined up at the counter that had yet to be waited on. And it appeared she was trying to work the lunchtime crowd all by herself. He wondered aloud where Mrs. Stewart was.

Jessica had glanced up when she heard the sound of his voice. She met his gaze and smiled.

"She called in. She wasn't feeling well and was determined to come in anyway, but I talked her into staying home."

Chase lifted a brow. "And you're trying to handle this crowd all by yourself?"

"Yes."

Before she could blink, he had come behind the

counter and snagged an apron off the rack. He then put on a pair of food-handler's gloves. Jessica turned and stared at him. "What are you doing?"

He smiled at her. "Helping out."

"B-but..."

He turned her back around. "You have a customer, Jessica. Don't keep Mrs. Prescott waiting. If I'm not mistaken this is her day of beauty and she can't be late at the salon."

The older woman who was standing on the other side of the counter beamed. "That's right, Chase. And Harry and I will be at your place for Friday's night's special. I'm counting on it being fried chicken, collard greens and potato salad."

Chase chuckled. "And just for you and Mr. Prescott, I'll make sure that it is."

Mrs. Prescott then turned to Jessica. "And don't put up a fuss about him helping out, young lady. I've known those Westmoreland boys since the day they were born. The last thing you have to worry about is one of them robbing you blind."

Jessica couldn't help but smile. That *was* the last thing she was concerned about. But how would she be able to do anything with Chase so close? There wasn't much space behind the counter and she didn't know how she and Chase would share it. She and Ms. Stewart were two relatively petite women, but Chase...well, Chase was well-built, muscular, had a nice set of abs, not to mention a few other qualities she considered outstanding. She'd been an eyewitness to those qualities just last night, and the memory made heat rush into her face.

"Hey, you okay?" Chase leaned over and asked her, almost too close for comfort.

She blinked and tried to control her rapid heartbeat. "Yes, I'm okay." *If you call thinking about last night okay.* "Why you ask?"

He chuckled. "Because Mrs. Prescott has been trying to give you her money for the past couple of minutes."

"Oh." Jessica turned to the older woman apologetically. "I'm sorry."

The older woman smiled. "That's okay, I understand. I used to be young once."

Jessica swallowed. Had the woman picked up on her attraction to Chase? She was more than ready for the next customer, determined to keep her concentration on her customers and not on Chase. A few moments later she discovered they worked well together. He knew just what her customers wanted and even talked them into buying something extra. For the next hour and a half they had a steady flow of customers, but by two o'clock the store was completely empty.

Jessica glanced over at Chase as he removed his gloves. "Thanks for the help. You're good for business," she said smiling.

"Umm, I hope I'm good for more than just business," he said grinning suggestively as he removed his apron and hung it back on the rack.

Jessica shook her head and chuckled. "Trust me, you are."

His grin widened. "That's good to know."

Jessica sighed. She had meant every word of what she'd said. Memories of their time together last night had kept her pretty heated much of the day. One thing the busy lunch hour had done was keep her mind occupied and off him...until he had shown up unexpectedly with his offer to help.

Chase glanced down at his watch. "I'd better go before everyone wonders where I took off to." He chuckled then said, "But then I think they'll know if Luanne Coleman has her way."

Jessica raised a brow. "Luanne Coleman?"

"Yes, the woman who was in here wearing the red dress and straw hat."

Jessica nodded, remembering. "Was she the one who held up the line for ten minutes trying to decide whether she wanted a batch of brownies or fudge and didn't make up her mind until you gave her a sample of each?"

Chase laughed. "Yes, that's the one. She and her husband own a flower shop in College Park and she is the town's biggest gossip. It's my guess that after she left here she went right over to the restaurant and spread the word that I was helping you out."

Jessica stared at Chase. "But why would that interest her?"

Chase leaned back against the counter. "The last I heard Mrs. Coleman and the other older ladies in her sewing club are betting on the next Westmoreland to get married."

"The next Westmoreland to get married?"

"Yes. Some are putting their money on me and some on my cousins Ian and Durango." At her confused look Chase chuckled again and decided to explain. "My brothers and cousins and I haven't ever wanted marriage in our future but within the past three years, all of my brothers have gotten married."

"Oh."

"Then a few months ago my cousin Jared surprised all of us by getting engaged. He and Dana got married, so quite naturally everyone turned their eyes on me since I'm the last of my brothers. Although I've told them many times I'd never marry, they don't believe me."

Jessica nodded. "And why not?"

"Because my brothers and Jared always said the same thing—that they would never marry. And although I would be the first to admit that they're all happy, it means nothing to me. The bottom line is that I'll never marry."

Jessica turned away from him, pretending to be absorbed in wiping down the glass case. She didn't want him to see how his words affected her. She may have fallen deeply in love with him, but that was her problem, not his. She had a feeling he was deliberately emphasizing something he'd said last night. She had heard him loud and clear when he'd said he was into casual relationships. A man into casual relationships didn't have marriage on his mind. She was smart enough to know that. Maybe it was time she let him know her position as well. "I never intend to get married either," she said as she wiped off the counter. She didn't look up but felt his probing eyes on her anyway.

"Why not?"

Jessica decided to look at him since he actually sounded confused. "I told you the story behind my father, Chase. What he did affected my ability to trust. Not that I think all men are the scum of the earth like he was, but I pretty much decided I have more to do with my time than worry about whether the man I'm with is trustworthy."

Chase nodded. "Yes, I know what you mean."

Jessica met his stare. "Do you?"

Chase fell silent for a moment then said, "Yes. I do. I got burned in college when the woman I thought loved me dropped me like a hot potato when my injury kept me from playing pro ball."

There was a pause and then he added, "I was quite bitter for a while but soon wised up and decided I was better off without Iris. Still, that hasn't stopped me from being cautious. I'll never trust another woman with my heart again. Trust is important to me. I can't stand deceit of any kind."

She nodded slowly, not wanting to consider the fact that at that moment she was deceiving him. "Umm, so I guess we understand each other."

Chase was quiet. Then he said, "Yes, I guess we do." He looked back at his watch again. "I'd better go." He then looked at her and asked. "What are you doing later?"

"I'm going out."

He raised his brow. "Out?"

"Yes." She decided she didn't owe him any further explanation than that. The last thing she wanted him to know was that she intended to pay a visit to Theodore Henry. The man had refused to return her calls. She had heard from Mrs. Stewart that he would be catering a fund-raising dinner in East Point, a suburb of Atlanta, tonight. She intended to show up and talk to him whether he wanted to talk to her or not.

"How about taking a two hour drive with me to Chattanooga on Saturday?"

"Chattanooga?"

Chase smiled. "Yes. I'm going there to pick up motorcycle parts as a favor to Thorn. He's busy building a bike for his next race."

Jessica thought about his invitation. She had never been to Chattanooga before and had always heard how beautiful the city was. Although she knew the best thing to do was not get more involved with Chase than she already was, the bottom line was she couldn't help it. She wanted to spend time with him. "I'd love to go to Chattanooga with you Saturday."

His smile widened. "Great. I'll pick you up Saturday morning around eight. Is that a good time for you?"

"Yes, that's a perfect time, and I'll be ready."

For a long moment neither of them said anything, but they stared long and hard at each other. And, as she gazed into his dark eyes, Jessica could feel the heat beginning to rise between them. She wondered what Chase was thinking when he tipped his head back and continued to stare at her. Was he remembering last night in his office and then later in his bedroom? She had enough memories stored for the both of them. Even now, with him standing there, she could vividly remember him kneeling between her thighs and the swirl of his tongue as he greedily devoured her.

She felt her stomach clench and her thighs actually trembled at the memory. As if he'd read her thoughts—was tuned right in to what she was thinking—he took a couple of steps toward her when the bell on the door sounded. A man walked in.

Chase inhaled deeply as he watched as Jessica turned to greet the customer. His entire body felt tight, wound-up, hot. It was as if he'd read her mind and had gotten caught up in her sensuous thoughts, her candid memories of the time they had spent together last night.

Pulling in another deep breath, he watched as a huge smile touched her lips before she raced from behind the counter to be engulfed in the man's arms.

"Rico!"

Chase frowned. Who the hell was Rico? And judging from the gigantic smile on Jessica's lips she definitely knew the guy. Was this the guy she was going out with later? Suddenly, without much glamour or fanfare, an emotion he hadn't experience in a long time attacked his insides. He didn't know who the man was, but he wanted to cross the room and snatch Jessica out of his arms.

He made a move, then caught himself, astounded that he would feel that way. Not since Iris had he felt jealousy for any woman. Fighting for control he leaned back against the counter. Okay, so he usually wasn't the jealous type, but dammit, at the moment he was seeing red.

"Maybe I should leave," he said in a somewhat angry voice.

Two pair of eyes shifted to glance over at him. Evidently the extent of his anger registered. He saw a sparkle in the man's eyes. In Jessica's he saw clear confusion. Hell, he was confused about the way he was acting as well.

"Umm, maybe you *should* leave," the man named

Rico said, smiling, although the smile didn't quite reach his eyes.

Chase's frown deepened. He straightened, suddenly filled with a desire go over and smack the man, break the pretty boy's nose.

"Rico, stop," Jessica said, chuckling. She met Chase's hard stare and the smile vanished from her lips. She wondered what had him so upset. Then it dawned on her. She had told him she was going out later today and then Rico showed up. She couldn't help but smile again at the possibility that he was jealous.

She shook her head, knowing that couldn't be possible. Men who were only into casual relationships didn't get jealous. "Chase—" she cleared her throat to say "—I'd like you to meet my brother, Rico Claiborne."

Chase lifted a brow and stared first at her and then at the man. "Your brother?" he asked, clearly astonished. The two looked nothing alike.

"Yes, her brother," the man answered smiling. He slowly crossed the room to Chase. "And you are?" he asked as though he had every right to know. Chase started to tell him off but then he remembered how he and his brothers used to behave with his baby sister Delaney's dates, and decided big brother here was due the same courtesy.

"Chase Westmoreland."

Chase watched a confused expression form on the man's face before Rico turned around to look Jessica.

Jessica inhaled deeply. She knew that Rico recognized the Westmoreland name and had questions. And she would have to give him answers.

Rico turned back around and offered Chase his hand. "Nice meeting you, Chase Westmoreland."

Chase took the hand the man offered, wondering what the hell was going on. He had picked up on something between brother and sister when he'd given the man his name and that had him confused. "Nice meeting you as well," he finally said. He then cleared his throat and said, "I'm sure you want to visit with your sister so I'll be going."

Rico smiled. "You don't have to leave on my account."

Chase inhaled deeply. Yes, he did have to leave. He had to go somewhere and think about his possessive feelings. "I was about to go anyway. I have a lot of work to do."

Rico nodded.

"Chase owns that huge restaurant two doors down," Jessica was saying. "My shop assistant got sick today and he was kind enough to help me out with the lunch-hour crowd."

Rico Claiborne nodded again, looked over his shoulder at Jessica and then back at Chase and said, "Oh, I see."

Chase frowned. He had a feeling Jessica's brother was seeing too damn much. "Nice meeting you," he said, then crossed the room to the door. Before he opened it he stopped and glanced over at Jessica. "And I'll see you Saturday morning."

She smiled. "All right."

Chase then walked out the door and closed it behind him. For a long moment Jessica didn't say anything but watched as he walked past Mrs. Morrison's shop back toward his place.

"Would you like to tell me what's going on, Jess?"

Jessica turned and met her brother's inquisitive gaze. "I'm not sure I know, myself, Rico."

Later that night Jessica walked into the ballroom of a community center and glanced around. This was a fund-raiser for a mayoral candidate and like everyone else present, she had purchased a ticket to attend. However, she was only here to get answers from the man whose company would be catering the food.

Rico had been passing through on his way to Florida and had only stayed long enough for them to share a snack and talk. She had explained as much about the situation as she could, leaving out specific details involving her and Chase but she had a feeling he had read between the lines anyway.

Jessica glanced down at her watch. She had arrived during the cocktail hour, so it wouldn't be too difficult to make her way to the kitchen and talk to the cook. All she needed was a few minutes of his time.

Moments later she walked up to one of the waiters who was carrying around a tray of hors d'oeuvres. "I'd like to see Mr. Henry. Is he around?"

The man smiled then nodded in the direction of the kitchen. "He's in there."

"Thanks."

A few moments later she walked into the kitchen and glanced across the room at the man giving orders to a couple of waiters. If this was Theodore Henry then he was a lot younger than she'd thought he would be. This man appeared to be in his middle forties.

She waited until the two young waiters left before approaching him. "Mr. Henry?"

He turned and gave her a pleasant smile. "Yes? How can I help you?" he asked, extending his hand to her.

"I'm Jessica Claiborne. I've tried calling you several times but you never return my calls." Jessica watched as the smile on his face vanished and he coolly withdrew his hand from hers.

"I am an extremely busy man. Besides, I have no idea what you were asking about."

Jessica lifted a brow. "So you knew nothing about Scott Westmoreland's allegations that my grandfather gave you Westmoreland recipes when you were Schuster's cook?"

"Oh, I heard about it but I didn't have time for such claims. I was too busy coming up with those tasty dishes to worry about two old men with nothing better to do than argue over something unimportant."

Jessica exhaled a breath. Although it was killing her, she was determined to continue questioning the man with polite professionalism. Although she definitely wanted to tell him where he could shove his arrogant attitude. "And just where *did* you get the recipes, Mr. Henry?"

His frown deepened. "Not that I have to answer that, but to clear your mind about any wrongdoing on my part, those recipes have been in my family for years. I told Westmoreland that, but he refused to believe me."

Before giving her a chance to respond or to ask him anything else, he said, "Look, Miss Claiborne, I really don't have time to stand here and discuss something that happened almost eighteen years ago. Evidently it's important to you but it's not to me. Now if you'll excuse me, I have things to do."

"Hey, boss, we're about to leave," Donna said to Chase. "You plan to stay late tonight?"

Chase pushed away from his desk. "Not too late. I just have a little bit of paperwork I need to do."

Donna nodded. "Okay. I'll see you in the morning."

Once alone, Chase leaned back in his chair and glanced around. His office looked normal, nothing like it had the night before. But still that didn't stop the memories from flooding his insides with a heated rush.

He stood for a moment, stretching his legs. As he walked around the room every step he took reminded him of Jessica being here with him last night. He remembered all the times he had kissed her, brushed his lips across her skin, touched her with his fingers, and devoured her greedily with his mouth. He was getting hard just thinking about it.

Damn. He was spending way too much time lusting after Jessica. After all, that's all it was. There was no other explanation for it. That bout of jealousy earlier today had stemmed from possessiveness, nothing more. Hell, he'd had a right to feel possessive after what the two of them had shared. She had been a virgin, for heaven's sakes. He couldn't help but smile. Even she had been surprised by that.

He stretched his shoulders and looked down at his watch. It was close to eleven o'clock. He wondered what Jessica was doing. Was her brother still there?

What if he wasn't? He sighed deeply. Damn, but he wanted to see her.

He shook his head. After last night, if he were to show up now, this late, she'd think he was making a booty call. Hmm, although the thought of that sounded nice, he knew, whether he wanted to admit it or not, that he thought of Jessica as more than a convenient body he could use. There was something about her that reached him on all levels, not just the physical one. He wished he had the strength to keep her at arm's length but knew he could not. Even when she wasn't there with him he could feel her presence. Thoughts of her were always embedded deep in his head.

Knowing he had to get out of his office he grabbed his jacket off the rack. Moments later he was locking the door behind him. He tried not to glance over at Jessica's place. But he just couldn't help it.

Fighting temptation with a vengeance, he walked to his car. He was determined not to see Jessica again today. But as he pulled out of the parking lot, intent on going home, he knew that tomorrow was only a few hours away.

Nine

"**H**ey, Chase, you got somewhere to go tonight?"

Chase glanced up from looking at his cards and met Dare's stare. He and his brothers were over at Storm's place playing a friendly game of cards. At least it always started off friendly. Hopefully tonight they wouldn't have to worry about Storm's loud complaining when he started losing. With newborn twins in the house he figured his brother's boisterous foul mouth would be kept at a minimum.

"What makes you think I have someplace to go?" he asked.

Dare smiled. "Because you seem anxious about something, and you keep looking at your watch,"

Thorn chuckled and glanced over at Chase. "And that's a sure sign a woman is involved."

Chase had no intentions of telling them if there was or if there wasn't. It had been hard going all day without seeing Jessica. Twice he had started over to her place before quickly changing his mind. They would be seeing each other tomorrow when she went with him to Chattanooga and he was satisfied that was soon enough.

Chase threw down his cards. There wasn't a damn satisfying thing about it. He glanced around the table at his brothers, who were staring at him as if he'd lost his mind. "Look, I'm out of here," he said standing on his feet.

Stone lifted a dark brow. "But for once you're winning."

Chase inhaled. No, he wasn't winning. He was losing every minute he was sitting here with them when he could be with Jessica, in her arms, in her bed.

This had turned out to be a good batch of chocolate, Jessica thought as she pulled off her cooking mitt and licked her lips. She had made more than she needed, but she figured the extra would be perfect for moulding into candy for Chase's Crusaders.

Removing the hairnet from her head, she pushed a wayward strand of hair from her face and thought about her disappointing meeting with Theodore Henry last evening. The man was arrogant. And regardless of what he'd said, she believed he had gotten those recipes from somewhere.

Today had been a very busy day and she was glad Mrs. Stewart had felt well enough to return. But the steady stream of customers hadn't stopped her from glancing over at the door every once in a while hoping to see Chase walk in. She knew Fridays were one of the busiest days at his restaurant, but still, she had missed seeing him all day. He'd had dinner delivered to her and the thought of him thinking of her made her smile. She had discovered that Chase Westmoreland—the man she had fallen in love with—was a very thoughtful man.

She glanced around when the doorbell rang. It was close to ten o'clock. Who could that be? Her pulse rate increased at the thought that it might be Chase. Leaving the shop's kitchen, she quickly made her way to the front door. The silhouette of his body through the glass gave him away. She hadn't been expecting him but she could tell by the way her heart was beating and the sizzling heat that was beginning to flow through her that she was glad to see him.

Breathing deeply she slowly unlocked the door.

Chase couldn't help but stare at the woman standing in front of him. She was barefoot and her thick black hair was pulled back into a ponytail, but a lock of hair had escaped and obscured one eye in a way he thought was sexy.

"Chase?"

He stuffed his hands in his pockets to keep them from reaching out and pulling the rubber band from her hair, totally destroying her ponytail and making her hair tumble over her shoulders.

"I was playing cards with my brothers," he said slowly, getting turned on just by looking at her standing there. "I was winning, but I couldn't keep my mind on the game for thinking about you, wondering what you were doing and wishing whatever it was, I could be here with you." He watched Jessica's mouth turn up into a smile and his guts clenched.

"Chocolate," she said softly.

He blinked then lifted a brow. "Excuse me?"

She smiled again. "I was making chocolate. At least I was just finishing up. Would you like to come in?"

Chase smiled. Would he ever. "Are you sure you don't mind?"

She met his gaze. "I'm positive." As he closed the door behind him, Chase leaned against it for support and stared at her. Her reaction to his heated gaze seemed natural, and the darkness of his eyes touched her everywhere, making a low burning need ignite through her. Seconds turned into minutes and neither said anything. If she didn't speak soon, she'd be burned to a crisp. "Would you like some?"

Too late she realized what she'd asked and watched a smile tilt the corners of his lips. It was a smile that was definitely provocative, irrevocably male. She quickly decided to clarify. "Chocolate. I made extra. Would you like to taste some?"

He nodded his head, kept his gaze directed on her. "I'd love to taste your chocolate."

She swallowed as a sharp physical reaction sliced through her and it made her wonder if they were still discussing the same thing. "There's some left on the stove."

Chase followed Jessica to the kitchen and remembered the last time he'd been inside that particular part of the shop. It had been the night he had taken her to the movies and she had invited him in for cookies and milk afterward.

"Where's your brother?" Chase decided to ask, wondering if the two of them were alone. He hadn't seen another car parked out front."

"He's gone. He was passing through and only stayed for a little while."

Chase nodded. "I would never have guessed the two of you were related."

Jessica glanced back over her shoulder at him and smiled. Most people didn't and she understood why. "Our father is African-American but Jennifer, my stepmother, is white. Rico looks like her and my sister Savannah looks like a combination of both of them."

Chase stood just inside the door of the kitchen and glanced around as the aroma of chocolate teased his nostrils. She had definitely been busy. A long table was lined with molds for chocolate lollipops. But what was really holding his attention was Jessica.

He watched as she walked over to an industrial-sized stove. "One thing about chocolate," she was saying, "is that you can never make too much, since it can be stored and reused many times over."

She turned and smiled at him. "The only problem is that tonight I've run out of storage space and I have to get rid of what's left in the pot since I won't be using it. I think it was a really good batch." Chase watched as she stuck her hand into the pot and then tasted the chocolate from her finger.

His gut clenched at the sight of her licking her finger clean, and he felt an immediate hardening of his body as his control began slipping. He met her gaze and doubted that she knew just how aroused he was getting from watching her.

"May I have a taste?" he asked, shrugging out of his leather jacket and walking toward her. He paused long enough to place the jacket on a hook near a small table.

"Sure. Is a spoonful okay or do you want—"

"Your finger."

She lifted an arched brow. "My finger?"

He came to stand in front of her. She smelled good, but he knew without a doubt that she tasted even better. "I want to lick it off your finger. Just like you did."

Jessica swallowed hard. His words made her feel tingly all over, especially in one particular spot. She turned back to the stove and stuck her finger in the huge pot. She shivered slightly as she ran her fingertip along the side and coated it with warm chocolate. She turned and held her hand up to Chase, close to his lips. "Here you go."

Without saying anything, and without his gaze leaving hers, he caught her hand in his to steady it, then stuck out his tongue and licked the chocolate off her finger. His strokes ignited the already simmering flames inside her to a torturous blaze as she watched his tongue gently but boldly caress her finger. She felt a whimper form in her throat and when he sucked her finger into his mouth, devouring it greedily, she nearly came undone. He had to reach out and catch her by the waist to stop her from melting to a heap on the floor.

When he finally released her finger, he smiled at her, licked his lips and said, "You're right. That's a good batch. I've never had chocolate that tasted that good before." Then before she could catch her next breath, he leaned in close to her lips and whispered, "And I want some more."

He kissed her, slanting his mouth greedily over hers. His seductive attack on her mouth put her on hot alert. Immediately her body responded to the feel of her breasts pressed tightly against his chest, the way her middle fit snugly against the hard length of him, and the way his mouth was mating with hers. She could feel the desire between them intensifying. They needed each other badly. He tasted like chocolate, but she figured so did she. And they both intended to indulge to their hearts' content.

Chase finally pulled back. Breathless. Something inside him snapped. The deep sexual need for her that he'd been fighting all day swiftly uncoiled. He wanted her. Desperately. Now.

He lifted up his T-shirt. Tossing it aside, he went to the snap on his jeans. The same fever consuming him was consuming her too and he watched her undo the top two buttons of her smock and pull the cotton material over her head. Within seconds he stood before her without a stitch of clothing on and she wore only a blue bra and matching lacy thong.

Driven by a need that was unlike anything he'd ever experienced before he reached out and pulled the rubber band holding her ponytail in place, letting her hair flow wildly around her shoulders. Then, with a flick of his wrist, he unfastened her bra and slipped it off her. His gaze then went to her thong, and he reached out and traced his finger along the thin scrap of material before bending to gently pull it down her legs.

He smiled and, before Jessica was aware of what he was about to do, he reached his hand into the pot of chocolate, coated his fingers and proceeded to smear the warm, creamy richness all over her chest. She made a purring sound deep in her throat at the feel of his hands coating the dark, sticky sweet substance all over her breasts. Using his fingers and gentle precision he smoothed it all over her skin, rubbing his thumb over the sensitive peaks of her breasts before moving lower.

His hand made a path down her stomach then slid lower, spreading chocolate everywhere he touched. Jessica squeezed her eyes shut as heat suffused her body, causing a burning sensation between her legs. And when he touched her there, covering her in warm chocolate, she leaned forward and pressed her lips against his neck and whispered his name.

She opened her eyes when she felt him sweep her up into his arms and walk across the room to an unused table and placed her on it. Then his mouth was everywhere as he leaned over her and began licking the chocolate from her body. With every stroke, every caress of his tongue she moaned his name, groaned a need, and her hips involuntarily came off the table as he robbed her senses blind in the most primitive way known to mankind.

The quaking of her body alerted him that she was close to coming apart. He quickly gathered her into his arms, sat down in a chair and placed her on his lap, straddling him. Purposefully, he guided himself into her. Instinctively, as if she needed this, wanted him, she pushed her body down on the hard, pulsing erection and threw her head back as her muscles drew him in deeper, clenched him, stealing his breath with every inch of him that her body absorbed.

He pulled her mouth down to his in a kiss that was downright salacious, and he began thrusting his body upward, plunging back and forth, in and out of her, setting a rhythm that was meant to drive her.

"Chase!"

He gritted his teeth, took one final plunge and gripped her hips, locking her body to his, needing the feel of his throbbing flesh exploding within the crevices of her womanly core. The thought of what was happening, the profound degree of intimacy they were sharing, made him nudge her legs wider, wanting to give her everything he had and then some.

He heard her cry out again and then he lost it. When she began convulsing in his arms he was powerless to deny himself another orgasm. A shiver of animalistic need raced up his spine and with a growl of deep satisfaction he plunged into her again. He arched his back and called her name as the most incredible climax took control of his body and mind, sending them swirling with sensations he'd never felt before. Three nights ago he'd thought this innocent whiff of a woman was almost too much for him. Now he wondered how he would survive the passion she stirred each and every time they made love.

What he had just experienced left him weak, sensuously spent and for long moments neither of them spoke. Nor did it seem were they in a hurry to separate their bodies. They needed to remain connected a while longer.

Then he lifted his head and their gazes met and at that moment he knew that what they had shared had been earth-shatteringly special, and that no matter how many times they made love, he would never get enough of her.

And he also realized something else. Jessica Claiborne was getting under his skin, and getting deeper and deeper with every passing second.

Chase awoke to the sound of horns blasting in the distance. It was morning. He glanced over at the woman cuddled beside him, remembering all that had transpired between them the night before. After making love to her in the chair he had swept her into his arms and brought her upstairs to the shower where he washed any lingering traces of chocolate from her body. He had dried her off before sweeping her into his arms to carry her over to the bed where they made love over and over again.

He closed his eyes, thinking there was no other place he'd rather be at the moment than lying beside her. But then the thought of being deeply embedded within the warmth of her body was a damn good idea, too. An even better one. He rubbed a hand over his face. If he kept at this pace he would have to start taking an extra vitamin each day.

He glanced over at the clock. It was nearly seven. His restaurant had opened without him and since his car was parked outside and he was nowhere to be found, Donna and Kevin would be able to guess where he was and what he'd been doing.

He rubbed a hand across his chin. He needed a shave. But then a slow burn began seeping up his spine making him aware of something else that he needed.

Jessica.

Oh, hell, he had to wake her up sometime. He smiled, knowing just the way he wanted to do it.

Jessica glanced over at Chase when they passed a sign that said they had reached Chattanooga. Situated along the Tennessee River and tucked away among the southern Appalachian Mountains, it was clearly a beautiful city.

She had enjoyed Chase's company during the two-hour drive from Atlanta, although she had slept the first half hour on the road. She was still filled with memories of how he had awakened her that morning. A smile curved her lips.

She sighed as she thought about the conversation they had shared during the past hour or so. He had told her more about his and his brothers' escapades growing up, and she had shared with him memories of her times with Rico and Savannah.

After taking care of the business he had come to Chattanooga for, Chase suggested that they have lunch at a restaurant on the Formal Gardens at the Chattanooga Choo Choo. After a delicious lunch of mouth-watering seafood, they had walked around holding hands, basking in the beauty of the gardens. She hadn't known so many kinds of roses existed.

As they continued walking, enjoying the beauty of so many flowering plants, he pulled her closer to him and whispered. "Last night was special, Jessica. This entire week has been. I want you to know that."

She glanced up at him and smiled. He had told her that twice already. "Spending time with you has been special to me as well, Chase."

They were silent for a moment while they continued walking, headed toward the parking lot and back to his car. He then said, "I'd like to prepare dinner for you tomorrow."

She chuckled, remembering what happened the last time she'd shared dinner with him. "At the restaurant?"

"No, my home."

They had reached his car and stopped walking. She gazed up at him. He was smiling that smile that made her feel warm and tingly on the inside. She had gotten a quick tour of his home when they had gone there that morning for him to change clothes. She thought his home in Buckhead, a very upscale and affluent section of Atlanta, was simply beautiful.

"I've love to have dinner with you tomorrow, Chase. Do you need me to bring anything?"

A sexy smile touched his lips. "Only yourself."

She laughed quietly. "Umm, I think that can be arranged."

He pulled her into his arms and just before he kissed her, he whispered, "I most certainly hope so."

Although Chase had told her to only bring herself, Jessica couldn't resist making a delicious dessert. She smiled as she glanced down at the baking dish filled with banana pudding.

But her smile faltered, the banana pudding suddenly forgotten when Chase opened the door and her gaze connected with his. He stood before her, imposing, undeniably male and irresistibly sexy. The royal blue pullover sweater he wore emphasized very broad shoulders and his jeans fit well-built hips and firm muscular thighs perfectly. She clung tightly to the little composure that she had left while drowning in everything sensual about him.

"I thought I told you that the only thing you had to bring was yourself."

She swallowed. Good grief. His voice sounded just as sexy as the rest of him. "I couldn't resist."

He smiled, moved forward and took the dish from her hand. "And neither can I, Jessica." He leaned down and kissed her, giving any neighbors who might be out and about something to talk about.

He pulled back slightly and whispered close to her lips. "Maybe we ought to finish this inside."

She licked her lips. "Umm, yes, maybe we ought to."

He stepped back, and, as soon as she was inside with the door closed, he placed the baking dish on a hall table and pulled her into his arms, kissing her more ardently than he had a few moments ago. "Kissing you has become addictive," he whispered, as he used his tongue to lick the sides of her mouth and a section of skin beneath her earlobe. "I definitely like the way you taste."

She smiled up at him. "And here I came prepared to be fed, not to become a meal."

He chuckled against her lips before licking them some more. "Oh, don't worry, baby, I'm going to feed you." He pulled in a deep breath and took a step back. "Come on to the kitchen before I have you pinned up against that door and take you right here and now. I'm just that tempted."

He picked up the banana pudding, then bent his head down to her for another quick kiss. "I hope you have plenty of energy because I intend to put you to work."

She smiled. "Work?"

"Yes, work," he said as he led her into the kitchen. "I intend for you to help me prepare one of the Westmoreland secret family recipes for dinner tonight."

Jessica suddenly went still. "But I thought you said you didn't share the secret recipes with anyone."

He turned around, looked over at her and grinned. "It's okay—I trust you. Now come on. I told you, I planned on putting you to work."

Jessica hesitated. Now was the perfect time to level with him. She should tell him the truth, especially since her investigation had hit a brick wall. There was no one else to talk to for more information. Paula Meyers and Darcy Evans said they had told her all they knew, while Schuster and Theodore Henry claimed they knew nothing. Although there was something about Darcy Evans' and Theodore Henry's version of things that she didn't believe, she had no proof to base her suspicions on. But she wasn't ready to throw in the towel. She was determined to speak to both of them again.

"Jessica?"

She glanced over at Chase. He was looking at her strangely. "Yes?"

"Are you okay?"

She inhaled deeply, wanting to tell him the truth. But she knew at this moment she couldn't. She couldn't risk what he might do. What if he kicked her out on her butt. She couldn't stand that right now. She would tell him the truth soon. But not today.

She forced a smile. "I'm okay. What do you want me to do?"

Chase placed a typed piece of paper on the counter in front of her. "I've got the recipe memorized but since you're helping I printed it off the computer."

She breathed in as she glanced down at the recipe. "You keep secret recipes stored in your computer?"

He chuckled as he pulled a can of cream out of the refrigerator. "Yes, I intend to pass my business on to one of my nieces or nephews one day."

"What about kids of your own?"

He glanced over at her. The smile he wore wavered just a tad. "I have no intentions of getting married and I don't plan on ever having any. And on the off chance that I do marry—probably a good twenty or thirty years from now—all I'd want from my wife is companionship. Our marriage will be in name only."

Jessica nodded and glanced back down at the piece of paper. Even the thought of a fifty-something Chase marrying a woman in a marriage of convenience bothered her. She loved him, dammit!

"So what do you think?"

His question almost started her. She'd been so wrapped up in her thoughts. "About what? You getting married twenty years from now to a woman you won't love?"

He shook his head and smiled wryly. "No. What do you think about the recipe? Are you up to it?"

He placed the cream on the counter and came to stand directly behind her. He reached out and drew her back against him, her tush snug against his erection. If anyone was up to anything, he most certainly was. She sucked in a quick breath when he slid his hands down past her waist to her hips.

She slowly closed her eyes. At any moment he would start inching up her skirt to slide his hand underneath. From there he would find his way into her panties. If she didn't stop him they would never get dinner done. Besides, she needed a few moments alone to pull herself together. Their conversation about the possibility of him getting married one day had messed with her mind.

She spun around quickly, almost startling him in the process. "Excuse me. I need to wash up before we get started."

Without giving him a chance to say anything, she eased by him, went into the hall bathroom, closed the door and tried to catch her breath..

After finishing off the last piece of baked chicken on her plate, Jessica leaned back in her chair and licked her lips. Every meal that Chase had prepared for her had made her want seconds. But what was so special about the baked chicken and Westmoreland rice was that they had prepared the meal together—working side by side in his kitchen as though they belonged there.

"Don't lick your lips like that," Chase murmured from across the table.

She glanced over at him and raised her eyebrows. "Why not?"

"Because it makes me want to lean over this table and lick them for you."

The air between them started to simmer, and Chase felt the need to take a step back, slow things down, savor their evening together. "Tell me about your grandparents."

She quickly glanced over at him. Panic suddenly fill her. "Why?"

"Because I think considering what you told me about your mother's situation that your grandparents must have had a positive effect on your life."

She smiled. His expression warmed her, and she could tell that he was truly interested. Memories of her grandparents flashed through her mind. "They did. Although my mom and I had our own place, my grandparents were close by." She paused before adding. "They moved to California to be near me and my mom when I was around ten or so. My greatest memories are the ones I shared with them."

Jessica knew that now would be the perfect time to tell Chase that she was Carlton Graham's granddaughter and suddenly decided to do so. "Chase."

He met her gaze and smiled. "Yes?"

She made a small sound in her throat but couldn't get the words out. At least not those words. Instead, she cleared her throat and asked. "How long have you lived here?"

"A little more than a year. Before then I had an apartment in Roswell. I visited a friend in this area and decided I liked it. What about you? Do you plan to live over your shop for a while or are you interested in buying a house someplace?"

Jessica took a sip of her coffee. "I owned a home in Sacramento. It was larger than I needed, but my boss at the corporation where I used to work believed that a big house in a posh neighborhood was a must for the attorneys he employed. And, like an obedient soldier, I did what was expected."

He nodded. "Do you miss being a lawyer?"

She shrugged. "I miss practicing law but not the corporate politics that went along with it. The straw that broke the camel's back was a case I was assigned to work on. One of the divisions of a company I represented made children's toys. We had repeatedly gotten complaints that one particular toy was dangerous and several kids had gotten injured playing with it. But it was a big moneymaker and the company refused to pull it from the shelves. When a child died, we got sued. I had to defend a product that I knew had been responsible for causing that child's death. I couldn't do it and quit."

Chase felt a rush of admiration for her. Instead of getting caught up in the woes of corporate politics and becoming just another company robot, she had taken a stand and had made what had to have been tough decisions regarding her future.

He stood, walked around the table and took her hand in his. "Come on, let's go for a walk."

She lifted a surprised brow. "A walk?"

He smiled. "Yes, the neighborhood has a nature trail. And usually around this time of the evening you can catch a fox or two roaming around. Besides, walking is a good way to work off that huge meal we just ate. And just think we haven't gotten into the banana pudding yet."

She grimaced. "Hey, don't remind me. I don't know where I'll be able to put anything else."

He grinned. "That's what you get for having a hard head. I told you not to bring anything but yourself."

A smile touched her lips. "Well, yeah, but I didn't want

you to do all the cooking. Had I known you would put me to work I would have thought twice about doing it."

He leaned over and pressed a kiss to her temple. "You enjoyed sharing the kitchen with me today. Admit it."

Jessica laughed. "Okay, I admit it. Are you happy?"

He raised his hand and cupped her face in it. He smiled down at her and held her gaze. "Yes, I am happy," he said quietly, actually meaning it. His hand tightened around hers. "Come on, let's get out of here and take that walk."

"What do you mean you haven't told him yet?"

Later that night Jessica stared down into the cup of coffee she held in her hand. She had her sister on speaker phone and Savannah hadn't wasted any time giving her the third degree.

"Jessica?"

She raised her eyes to the ceiling. This was worse than Savannah being here in person. Her tone was just that effective. "I hear you," Jessica said, taking a sip of coffee. Moments later she added. "The timing has never been right. Every time I get ready to open my mouth, he says something sweet and I can't bring myself to tell him."

"Sounds like you're making excuses."

Jessica sighed deeply. She was. "It's not easy, Savannah. I told you how I feel about him."

"Yes, but in order to give him a chance to feel that same way about you, you have to be honest with him. Put all your cards on the table."

Jessica gazed down into her cup of coffee again. Of course her sister was right. While having dinner with Chase that evening she had had at least two opportunities to come clean and tell him the truth, but had taken advantage of neither. "If I told him now, without proof of my grandfather's innocence he might think the worst."

"And what if you can't prove your granddad was innocent, Jess? What then?"

Jessica didn't want to think about that possibility. Both Darcy Evans and Theodore Henry were hiding something. She could feel it. She closed her eyes and saw the image of a very handsome Chase Westmoreland smiling at her. Then suddenly another image invaded. It was one of Chase angry at her. The sexy line of his mouth had transformed into a deep frown.

"Jess?"

Jessica opened her eyes again. "Yes?"

"You're special, and no matter what the outcome might be, if he doesn't see how special you are then you're better off without him."

"You think too highly of me, sis," Jessica laughed as she pushed her coffee cup aside. She'd had enough caffeine for one day.

"Hey, I can say the same about you."

For a long moment, neither said anything and then Jessica broke the silence. "You would like him," she said quietly.

"Yes, but as far as I'm concerned, he's already taken. You did say he has brothers didn't you?"

Jessica grinned. "They're taken as well, however he has some very good-looking single cousins."

"Umm, maybe I should come for a visit."

"You know," Jessica said smiling. "Maybe you should."

* * *

"Storm says you're pretty serious about some woman."

Chase glanced over at his cousin Quade who had made an unexpected visit to town. Quade worked behind the scenes for the Secret Service and his job protecting the president could take him anywhere. Chase took a sip of his beer before saying. "Storm talks too damn much."

Quade smiled. "Maybe he does." He thought a moment, then said, "So tell me…who is she and how did she manage to get under your skin?"

Chase shrugged one shoulder. Although he rarely saw Quade these days, that didn't diminish their friendship, best buddies since childhood, who rarely kept secrets from each other. "Her name is Jessica Claiborne and she moved here from California. She used to be a corporate attorney but got fed up with corporate politics and decided to try her hand at baking instead. She owns a confectionary two doors down from the restaurant."

Quade lifted a brow. "She gave up law to make candy?"

Chase sat back and smiled. "Yes."

Quade shook his head. "That was some career move. I wondered what her parents thought of that."

Chase spent the next ten minutes or so telling Quade about Jessica's past and her bastard of a father. "That had to have been hard on her," Quade said.

Chase nodded. "I'm sure it was, but, at least she had her grandparents."

Quade sighed. "Yes. It sounds like they were good people."

Chase thought of the woman who was beginning to mean a lot to him. "I'm glad they were there for her."

Quade sat forward. "So how did she managed to capture your attention?"

Chase stood and walked to the window. He remain silent for a moment pondering Quade's question. He turned from the window and shrugged broad shoulders. "Hell, that's a good question, but she's there, Quade, under my skin and the strange thing about it is that I sort of like her there."

Chase saw the surprised smile that touched his cousin's lips. "Next time I'm passing through I'd like to meet her."

"You will," Chase promised.

Ten

"What are you thinking about, Jessica?"

Jessica glanced up and met Chase's gaze. She had been staring down at their clasped hands as they sat at a coffee shop in Lenox Square Mall, thinking how comforting it felt for her fingers to be intertwined in his.

A week and a half had passed since she'd had dinner with him at his home and each and every day she spent with him she was falling deeper and deeper in love. But hanging over her head was the fact that she wasn't being completely honest with him.

Theodore Henry had gotten downright rude and even threatened to file harassment charges if she tried contacting him again. That meant her only hope was Darcy Evans, who hadn't returned any of her calls. She would make it her business to talk to the woman again.

She knew Chase was waiting for an answer, so she forced a smile and said, "Umm, I was just thinking about what a close-knit family you have." And she really meant that. Chase had invited her to a Monday-night football party at Jared and Dana's home to see the Falcons play the Cowboys. They had watched the game on Jared's state-of-the-art home-theater system. She had met Chase's parents and reacquainted herself with some of the family members she had met previously. And she had finally met his sister Delaney and her husband Sheikh Jamal Ari Yasir.

He smiled. "Yes, I have to admit that we are that. I can't imagine it being any other way." He leaned closer to her. "But you and your siblings are close, too, aren't you?"

She nodded. "Yes. Savannah and Rico are great. Jennifer has a sister and a brother but they're standoffish. They think she went a little too far including me in her family. After all, I'm the product of her husband's affair."

"You were also her husband's child. Besides, her husband's wrongdoing wasn't your fault. I think it was admirable of her to accept that and do what she did. But I know that many women's pride would not have let them do it."

Jessica nodded again. "Yes, I know, and that's what makes her so special to me. She made it her business to include me as part of Savannah's and Rico's life and I appreciate her for it. It really helped after Mom's died."

"I'm sure it was hard on your grandparents to lose your mother that way."

Jessica sighed deeply. "Yes, she was their only child. For a while my grandfather blamed himself for not finding out about my father sooner. Another part of him questioned whether he had done the right thing at all by hiring that investigator and telling my mother the truth. He never thought she would take her life over it."

Jessica didn't say anything for a while, then added, "For the longest time I was bitter and resented her for what she did, leaving me alone. I had to go through grief counseling to let go finally and realize that the love my mother had for my father was an obsession and a sickness. That's when I promised myself that I would never get that caught up over a man."

Chase tightened his fingers around Jessica's as he once again thought about the relationship they shared. He had to admit that the past couple of weeks had been pretty darn special. They had attended a laser show on Stone Mountain, played tennis together twice and she had watched Chase's Crusaders clinch another win one week only to lose big-time the next. Last Sunday evening, a pack of them led by Thorn had taken their Thorn-Byrd motorcycles on the road to ride all the way to Augusta for dinner. No one in the family had seemed surprised that he'd brought Jessica along, nor had anyone questioned him about the amount of time the two of them were spending together. His family had accepted that they were now an item. He wasn't sure how he felt about that.

"More coffee?"

They both glanced up at the waiter who was making his rounds. "No thanks," Chase replied, releasing Jessica's hand to glance at his watch. "In fact, I'd appreciate our bill now."

When the waiter left, Chase smiled over at Jessica. "Thanks for going shopping with me."

She chuckled. "There aren't many people I know, men specifically, who do early Christmas shopping. You still have two months left."

Chase grinned. "Yes, but like you said, I have a large family. Besides, giving out gift cards makes it easy. The kicker is trying to decide what stores they like best." His grin widened. "The saying 'beggars can't be choosers' doesn't always apply in my family."

After finishing their coffee they walked around the mall again. Although there were two months lefts before Christmas, many of the stores already had their holiday decorations up.

"This place is like a madhouse the day after Thanksgiving. You'll have to come with me that Friday to see what I mean. But the crowd puts me in the Christmas spirit."

Jessica suddenly felt breathless. Thanksgiving was a month away. That he assumed they would still be together had her walking on air. But she quickly came back down to earth when she thought of what was still lurking over her head. She decided to pay Darcy Evans another visit tomorrow. She had to give it one more try before finally telling Chase the truth.

Jessica was grateful Mrs. Stewart had agreed to work a full day so that she could make the trip to Macon to pay Darcy Evans another visit. She hated being a nuisance, but she was determined to give it another try to see if perhaps there was something the woman wasn't telling her.

Darcy wasn't at home but an older woman—Darcy's

mother—told her that Darcy owned a hair salon not far away. Thirty minutes later Jessica was parking in front of Darcy's Beauty Box.

Jessica knew the moment she walked into the shop and her gaze connected with Darcy that the woman was surprised to see her. "Ms. Evans, how are you?" she asked, extending her hand. The set-up of the shop was very chic. Jessica was glad there was only one customer sitting under the hair dryer, who wouldn't be able to overhear their conversation.

"Why are you here?" Darcy asked, reluctantly accepting the hand Jessica offered. "I thought we finished our discussion the last time we talked."

A wry smile touched Jessica's lips. "I was hoping that perhaps you might have remembered something else since then."

"No, there's nothing else. I told you everything I know."

"Are you sure?"

Darcy tore her gaze from Jessica's and glanced around the room, looking anywhere other than Jessica's eyes. "Yes, I'm sure."

Jessica still wasn't completely certain and decided to try another angle. She didn't want to push but she needed the truth. "Do you believe my grandfather passed those recipes on to someone who worked at Schuster's, Mrs. Evans?"

Darcy's eyes snapped back to hers. "No, of course not. He was one of the most honest men that I knew. I felt bad when Mr. Westmoreland accused him of doing that."

Jessica lifted a brow. "You were there the day it happened?"

"No. Your grandfather and Mr. Westmoreland had an argument and then your grandfather quit. But he and Mr. Westmoreland were such good friends we all assumed he would be coming back."

Jessica nodded. "Do you remember what the argument was about?"

She watched as the woman tore her gaze away from her again. A few moments passed then she said quietly, "It was about me."

Jessica wasn't sure she'd heard her correctly. "About you?"

The woman nodded. "I was going through a difficult time. My son Jamie who was only eighteen months old at the time was constantly sick, which kept me from work a lot. And when I was there I was so preoccupied worrying about him I was beginning to get my orders messed up."

Darcy inhaled deeply as if remember that time. "Some of the customers started complaining to Mr. Westmoreland. Your grandfather knew how much I needed my job to pay for Jamie's medical bills and asked Mr. Westmoreland to give me another chance. They argued about it. Then I heard your grandfather walked out."

The woman shook her head regretfully. "I felt bad about everything. But Paula Meyers, who had worked with your grandfather and Mr. Westmoreland a lot longer, told me not to worry about it because your grandfather had quit before after having words with Mr. Westmoreland and would be back. When two weeks went by and he didn't return, I got worried and started blaming myself."

Jessica's eyes began softening. All it took was a close look at Darcy Evans to know she was still blaming herself. "I think my grandfather and Mr. Westmoreland would have eventually patched up things, too," she decided to say. "But a couple of things happened right after that. My mother had to be hospitalized for pneumonia and my grandparents flew to California to take care of me."

Jessica smiled, remembering. "While they were there I think they decided that my mom and I needed them closer, especially when they couldn't talk her into moving to Atlanta. They returned home a week or so later and my grandfather found out about Mr. Westmoreland's accusations. His integrity had been questioned by someone he considered a good friend and he was hurt. Nothing he said to Mr. Westmoreland could prove his innocence, and I think that was one of the reasons he felt moving to California was best for everyone."

For a long moment neither she nor Darcy said anything. But Jessica could swear the older woman had an odd look on her face. And if she wasn't mistaken, it was a guilty one. "Are you sure there isn't anything else you can tell me, Ms. Evans?"

For a brief moment Darcy didn't answer, and then she said, "No, there's nothing else."

Jessica still didn't believe her. "It's important to me that if you do remember anything you contact me. I'm caught in the middle of a bad situation right now."

Darcy lifted a brow. "What kind of a bad situation?"

Jessica knew she had to be completely honest with Darcy and hoped the woman would eventually tell her whatever she was holding back. "I've fallen in love with Scott Westmoreland's grandson Chase."

Darcy nodded. "He's the one that owns that restaurant in downtown Atlanta, right?"

Jessica smiled. "Yes, that's right."

"I always knew he would be the one who would eventually follow in his grandfather's footsteps. He would hang around the restaurant and help out more than any of the others. He always seemed like a nice young man."

Jessica smile widened. "He is. We've been seeing each other for about three weeks now, but he doesn't have any idea that I'm Carlton Graham's granddaughter."

Darcy raised a surprised brow. "He doesn't?"

"No. Because of what happened all those years ago, bad blood was left between the two families. I promised my grandmother before she died that I'd prove my grandfather's innocence to the Westmorelands and end the feud." She inhaled deeply. "I hadn't planned on meeting and falling in love with Chase."

Darcy nodded. "But surely something that happened years ago wouldn't keep the two of you apart."

Jessica smiled wryly. "It might. He was pretty close to his grandfather and I can tell he's still pretty bitter about the entire thing. Besides, honesty means a lot to Chase. I should have told him who I was from the beginning. But I wanted to prove my grandfather's innocence before doing that. Now I can see I made a mistake in waiting."

"What will you do now?"

"Tell him the truth and hope he believes me. Hope he's willing to put the past behind us and move on."

Darcy didn't say anything for a few moments, then asked, "Do you think he will?"

"God, I hope so."

Chase glanced down at his watch thinking Jessica should have returned by now. He had stopped by the shop at closing time to let her know that he had to leave town unexpectedly, and found Mrs. Stewart was still there. The only thing she would tell him was that Jessica had an errand to run and she didn't expect her back before seven o'clock that night.

He couldn't help wondering what sort of errand Jessica had to do that could have kept her away from the shop practically all day. He glanced around when he heard a knock at his office door. "Who is it?"

"Donna."

"Come in."

He watched his most dependable waitress walk nervously into the room. In the months she had worked for him he'd never known Donna to be nervous about anything. But a part of him saw beyond that. For a split second he could see a hint of sadness behind those big brown eyes of hers.

When she didn't say anything he decided to urge her on. "Donna, what can I do for you?"

She looked away, hesitated, then she said, "I came to give you this."

Chase's eyesbrows shot up when she handed him a piece of paper she had in her hand. It took him a quick second to scan it. His eyes widened, and he lifted his gaze, giving her a surprised look. "You're quitting?"

She looked away again and shrugged her shoulders. "Yes. I like working here but I need to start going to school full-time if I ever want to finish. I got a letter yesterday from a college in Tennessee offering me a scholarship to finish my last two years, and I've decided to take it."

Chase smiled. Although he regretted losing Donna, he knew that was an offer that was too good to pass up. Opportunities like that didn't come often. "I'm happy for you, Donna."

At last a smile touched her lips. "Thanks. I'm pretty happy for myself. I keep rereading the letter to make sure I'm not dreaming. They want me to start in January, which means I'll have to pack up and move. With the holidays coming up I didn't want to leave you in a fix, and I wanted to let you know now, although I can probably work another month."

"And I appreciate that. You're going to be hard to replace. And if you ever need anything I'll always be a phone call away."

"Thanks, Chase."

After Donna left, Chase leaned back in his chair. He glanced down at his watch again. He had taken just about all he could stand. He needed to see Jessica. And the thought that he would be leaving town for three days didn't help matters. Hell. He'd been pretty useless all day for thinking about her. To go to her shop and not find her there had been a huge disappointment.

Chase didn't like the way his thoughts were going—he was becoming more and more obsessed with Jessica. For the first time in his life, while holding Storm's twins earlier that day when Jayla had stopped by to meet Storm for lunch, he had actually thought of having kids of his own. For Pete's sake! Just the other day he had told Jessica he didn't plan on ever having kids. Yet when he had looked down at his nieces, he'd actually envisioned Jessica as his children's mother. Panic rose thick in his throat.

He stood, suddenly not feeling at all like himself. He was encountering emotions that were best left alone. Yet for some reason he couldn't leave them alone. Not today. A sharp rush of desire flooded his insides and his main thought as he walked out of his office was that he had to see Jessica.

Chase practically launched himself at Jessica, pulling her into his arms and kissing her the moment she opened the door.

"God, I missed you today," he murmured, easing her back into the shop and closing the door shut with the heel of his shoe. He didn't care that he'd just seen her yesterday and had made love to her last night. That was then and this was now. He leaned down and kissed her.

Jessica tried not to shiver from all the love she felt flowing through every part of her body. She didn't want to think about the possibility that once she told Chase the truth tonight, he would walk away angry and not look back. But she knew what she had to do.

She pulled her mouth from his. "Chase, I have something to tell—"

Before she could finished what she was about to say, he was kissing her again, deeply, with an urgency that obliterated all her thoughts. Knowing this might very well be the last time she shared such intimacy with him, she went for sheer pleasure and attacked his mouth with the same urgency with which he was attacking hers. Moments later they were both groaning out loud.

Chase finally broke contact with her mouth, swept her into his arms and quickly carried her up the stairs. He placed her on her feet next to the bed and immediately began removing her shirt as she reached for the fly of his jeans. Both were crazed with passion, driven by need. Their level of desire had reached a boiling point.

"I want you so bad I ache," Chase whispered when he had completely removed her clothes and she had removed his. He tumbled her back on the bed, went for her breasts and greedily began licking the swollen mounds. She moaned out loud when he sucked a nipple into his mouth. His tongue began licking it, tugging on it; he was driving her crazy by holding the sensitive tip gently between his teeth and not letting go. He then gave the other breast the same torturous treatment.

"Chase!"

"Hold on, baby, I've just gotten started," he murmured, leaving her breasts to travel downward. Jessica sucked in air when his tongue began licking around her navel, circling it, branding it, kissing it.

Then he lifted his head, locked his gaze with hers and something flickered in his eyes; the heat of it made her breath catch just seconds before he lowered his mouth to her feminine core. Her legs automatically spread for him and it took all the strength that she possessed not to come off the bed under the onslaught of his skillful mouth. But nothing could stop her from shivering uncontrollably when he increased the pressure of his tongue, stroking her with a decadent lick that sent blood throbbing through her veins. She screamed his name but that only spurred him on, making him even more intent on savoring her this way. And when an orgasm hit, splintering her body into a million pieces, she screamed his name again and bucked her hips upward as he continued to ply her with quick and sure strokes of his tongue.

It was only when the last shiver had touched her body that he finally dragged his mouth away. Every inch of her felt sensitive from such a fiery response. He sat back on his haunches and the smile that played at the corners of his lips sent shivers racing through her again. He held her gaze, making her heart pound and she felt an agonizing ache rekindle between her legs.

As if he knew just what she was going through, he reached out and touched her there, began caressing her wet flesh. Then he leaned toward her and, in a voice that was deep, sexy and husky, he said, "Don't relax now, sweetheart. I'm just getting warmed up."

Chase intended to make love to his woman all night. *His woman.*

He closed his eyes when a sharpness tore through his heart, almost knocking the breath out of him.

"Chase, are you okay?"

He opened his eyes and gazed down at Jessica. He moved to position his body over her, satisfied that she was primed and ready to take him in. At that moment, he knew. She *was* his woman and he loved her. He loved her. He had never intended for such a thing to happen. But it had and there wasn't a damn thing he could do about it but accept it. And he did, without question.

"Chase?"

His heart pounded against his chest and he leaned down and kissed her lips softly. "Yeah, I'm okay, baby. At this moment I couldn't be better."

She smiled cheekily up at him and said, "Hey, I think that's for me to decide."

Chase grinned as he traced her lips with the tip of his tongue. "Then let me help you make such an important decision."

And then he was back at her lips with that skillful mouth of his, kissing her deeply as his tongue whirled around in her mouth, feasting, tasting, corner to corner, marking every single crevice.

Jessica moaned and closed her eyes when he slipped his hand between their bodies. His fingers touched the soft flesh between her legs, lightly stroking, making small erotic circles, causing sensations to flood her, making her hips buck again.

He finally released her mouth and gazed down at her as she slowly opened her eyes. He was filled with an urgency that he'd never felt before by the recognition of just how much he wanted this woman. Just how much he loved her. And suddenly he became caught up in a raging desire to be inside her.

Now.

He lifted her hips with his hands, anchored his thighs between hers and positioned his aroused member dead center where he needed it to be.

He eased inside her and she automatically adjusted her body to accommodate him, lifting her hips as he went deeper. He arched his hips and pressed forward until he reached the hilt and was buried deep inside her. He fought the urge to move, to stroke her with the rhythm that would send them both over the edge. He wanted to savor being this way, inside her, locked in tight, feeling the moist heat of her clutching him, nearly stealing his breath away.

But he refused to move just yet. He held her gaze, and because he wanted her to know just how he felt at that moment—submerged in the intensity of his love—he whispered, "I love you, Jessica."

He watched her eyes widen, her face fill with disbelief, and then he saw the tears that filled her eyes, the look of happiness on her lips when she said, "I love you, too, Chase."

Damn. He hadn't expected that. And her words were the catalyst that broke his control. His need to make love to her suddenly became as vital as his need to draw his next breath. He began moving inside her in rapid thrusts, stunned by how emotions had taken over his mind, invaded his heart, filled him with a drive to make her truly his.

Never had he known anything as beautiful as what he was sharing with her now. She was filling an emptiness inside of him that he hadn't known existed. And she was doing it in a way no other woman had. His body continued moving in and out of her as she lifted her hips, wrapped her legs around his waist to hold him tight, melding their bodies together over and over.

"Chase!"

When she cried out his name, he gritted his teeth as the same sensations that began wracking her body invaded his. An explosion erupted and mind-whirling sensations overtook them. He grasped her hips while he continued to ply her with fluid strokes and the full impact of his release. It seemed they were spiraling higher than they had ever gone before, riding wave after wave of sensation so intense he wondered if he could survive. He drove into her again and again as words of love flowed from his lips.

And when his body exploded a second time, and moments later a third, he knew that she was truly his just as he was undeniably hers.

Hours later, Chase tried not to wake Jessica as he eased out of bed. He needed to leave, go home and pack for his trip to Houston. His plane would be leaving in five hours and he would be battling morning traffic to the airport.

After putting on his clothes he walked back over to the bed, leaned down and gently kissed her lips. Moments later he slipped downstairs, deciding to leave her a note. He would also call her when he got to the airport. If this meeting wasn't so important he would change his mind about going. But lately he'd given thought to opening another Chase's Place in Texas and the group of men he was meeting with could make such a venture possible.

He opened the door to her office and glanced around. This was the first time he had been in this particular room and liked how she had things set up. It was small but furnished professionally. He walked over to the stylish oak desk to get a piece of paper and a pen. His hand went still when his gaze fell on a small framed photograph.

He picked it up, blinking, not sure he was seeing straight. It was a photo of Jessica with an older couple who he could only assume were the grandparents she loved. Chase recognized the older couple immediately. They were Carlton and Helen Graham.

Suddenly, he felt as if he'd been punched in the gut. Jessica was Carlton Graham's granddaughter? If that was true, then why hadn't she told him? His hand shook as he placed the picture frame back on the desk. He glanced around and a piece of paper caught his attention. He picked it up. He read the words written on her To Do list for today:

Talk to Donald Schuster again regarding the Westmoreland recipes.

The paper slipped from his hand as he felt a stabbing sensation in his heart. He closed his eyes in denial. There was no way another Graham was betraying a Westmoreland. It couldn't be possible. When he opened his eyes and stared at the paper and the photo once again, he saw that anything was possible. Had Schuster heard that he was thinking about franchising and made some kind of deal with Jessica to get close to him? Damn, she *had* gotten close to him, and he had even trusted her enough to share one of the recipes with her. What was in it for her? A chance to sell her sweets in all the Schuster restaurants around the country? He clenched his teeth. It hurt like hell to know she was an opportunist, just like Iris had been.

He felt angrier than he'd ever felt in his life, anger mingled with deeply entrenched pain. He left the office and raced back up the stairs. For the second time in his life he had given his heart to a woman and look what happened. Never again would he trust blindly.

He felt a tightening around his heart when he walked back into Jessica's bedroom. His body was torn with the love he felt for her and the hurt her betrayal was causing. Exhaling deeply, as if that could expel any emotions he felt for her, he walked over to the bed. "Jessica, wake up."

Fighting sleep, Jessica slowly opened her eyes when she heard the sound of Chase's voice. When he came into focus she saw that he was standing over her with features filled with anger. She pulled herself up in bed. "What's wrong, Chase?"

For a moment he didn't say anything; he just looked at her and the anger was there, clearly, in his eyes. "Chase, please tell me what's wrong."

"Why didn't you tell me you were Carlton Graham's granddaughter? Did you get a kick out of playing me for a fool?"

She sucked in a quick breath, wondering how he had found out, but then knowing it really didn't matter. He *had* found out and she hadn't been the one to tell him. "No, that's not it at all, Chase. I wanted to tell you but thought I could prove my grandfather's innocence first."

"You can't prove what isn't true."

Jessica was out of bed in a flash. She got into Chase's

face, not caring that she was completely naked. "My grandfather didn't take any recipes and I wanted to prove it. But then I fell in love with you and—"

"Hell, you didn't fall in love with me. It was nothing but an act. Do you think I'm stupid, Jessica? I saw that note about you meeting with Schuster today. Are the two of you working together to pry more recipes out of a Westmoreland? What did he offer you? A chance to peddle your sweets in his restaurants?"

Jessica shook her head. "No. How could you think something like that? Schuster has answers. Someone gave him those recipes all those years ago, and since I knew it wasn't my grandfather, I met with him once to see what he could tell me. I'm meeting with him again to get more information out of him if I can."

Chase drew in a deep breath. He wanted to believe her, but all he could think about was her betraying his love. His mouth tightened in a harsh line. "If any of what you're saying is true, why didn't you tell me who you were? We've been seeing each other for almost a month, Jessica, and during that time you've had every opportunity to tell me the truth, but you never mentioned you were related to Carlton."

Jessica swallowed, knowing he had her there. There had been opportunities when she could have shared that fact with him. "Like I told you, Chase, I wanted to prove his innocence first. I was going to tell you when you first got here last night, but I didn't get a chance to. You've got to believe me. Chase. I love you and—"

Chase laughed. It was an unforgiving sound. "Love?

Is this how you show your love? By being deceitful? Then I don't want any part of it."

He turned and walked out of the room. Jessica held her breath until she heard the door slam shut behind him. Tears flooded her eyes. She had made a complete mess of things. She hadn't cleared her grandfather's name, and worse—Chase hated her.

Eleven

Chase slipped out of bed. Whenever he traveled he made it a point to stay at the best hotels. But a nice room and a soft bed couldn't prevent his restless nights.

For the past two days he had been so thickly involved with business negotiations that he hadn't allowed anything or anyone to invade his thoughts…other than Jessica. She had managed to wiggle inside his head, although he hadn't wanted her there.

And he couldn't get her out no matter how hard he tried.

Without wanting them to, memories of that night came back to flood his mind. She had actually looked shocked by his accusation. Well, hell, how had she expected him to react? Had she thought he would embrace her with open arms? Overlook the fact that his grandfather and hers had ended up bitter enemies? For heaven's sake, she was a Graham and he was a West-moreland. He distinctively remembered his grandfather's warning never to trust a Graham. Not only had he trusted one, he had fallen in love with one.

He sighed deeply. And did she actually think he would believe her story about trying to prove her grandfather innocent? That the only reason she had met with Schuster was to find out the truth?

But then he couldn't dismiss the possibility that his reluctance to believe her was the reason she hadn't leveled with him in the beginning. She had known he wouldn't embrace her with open arms. They would have become enemies before having the chance to become friends.

On top of knowing that, there was this thought that had been nagging at him for the past two days. What if she *was* telling the truth? He couldn't let go of the fact that this was a woman who had walked away from a prestigious career for ethical reasons. A woman of strong values and beliefs. She was also a woman who had spent her free time baking goodies for the guys on his team. This was someone who definitely cared about others.

And more than anything, he couldn't forget that she had been celibate for eight years. He had a gut feeling it would have taken more than the promise of her products being sold in a Schuster restaurant for her to go as far with him as she'd gone if she didn't really care for him.

He inhaled deeply. Had he acted irrationally two

days ago? Had he been unfair by jumping to conclusions and not listening to her side of things? Had he been wrong to place her in the same category as Iris? The two women were nothing alike. Iris was an unscrupulous taker. Jessica was an extraordinary giver.

He glanced over at the clock on the nightstand. It was almost midnight. He wanted to call Jessica, talk to her. When he returned to Atlanta tomorrow he would listen to what she had to say and not be so quick to judge. No matter what, he still loved her. What happened with the Westmoreland recipes no longer mattered to him. If Jessica was hell-bent on proving her grandfather's innocence then he would help her discover how the recipes got into the wrong hands.

He took a deep breath. More than anything he wanted a future with the woman he loved.

"Listen, Jessica, if he loved you two days ago then he loves you now. Nobody can turn love on and off like a faucet, not if it's the real thing."

Jessica heard her stepmother's words but she still wasn't convinced. She had seen the look of loathing in Chase's eyes just moments before he'd left. But then she couldn't erase the memory of another look as well. It had been the look he'd given her just moments before whispering that he loved her. When he had said those words she had believed in her heart that he had meant them, just like she had meant what she'd said to him. She loved him, too.

"Even after I found out what your father had done," Jennifer was saying, "I couldn't hate him. I was hurt and

I put up a wall to protect myself from further pain, but the love was still there for a long time."

"It doesn't matter," Jessica said softly. "Chase let me know things are over between us." After a brief pause she said, "I've made some decisions."

There was a short silence, then Jennifer asked, "What sort of decisions?"

Jessica took a deep breath. "I met with a real estate agent today. I've decided to sell this place and move back to California."

"And return to law?"

"Possibly, but it won't be as a corporate attorney. I'm thinking of becoming a consumer attorney specializing in product safety."

"Do you think running away will solve anything, Jessica?"

"I'm not running away. I'm protecting my heart from further damage."

There was a brief pause again, and then Jennifer said, "Well, I think you and Chase need to sit down and talk things through."

"So do I," Jessica said quietly. "But before he left I got the distinct impression that he doesn't want to see me again. And since our businesses are separated by only one building, there's no way we can avoid seeing each other. One of us will have to leave. It might as well be me." After a brief pause she added, "Hey, I'm a survivor. You know that."

She sighed deeply. She *had* let Chase become too important to her. She had done the one thing she'd always promised herself she wouldn't do, give her heart and soul to a man. That made it harder to walk away. But walk away she would.

"What do you mean she's selling her place?" Chase asked staring hard at Donna. He had come straight to the restaurant from the airport to find Delicious Cravings closed in the middle of the day with a For Sale sign in the window.

Donna leaned back against his closed office door. "Rumor has it that she's moving back to California."

A chill of fear ripped down his spine. God, he'd been a fool to think the worst about her. He had done a lot of thinking over the past three days, and in his heart he knew Jessica loved him. He had been a complete idiot to accuse her of all those things. Unlike Iris, Jessica couldn't relate to greed.

Donna cleared her throat. "I know this might not be a good time but there's someone here who insists on seeing you."

Chase lifted an eyebrow. "Who?"

"A woman named Darcy Evans."

Chase's brow lifted higher upon remembering the name. He sighed deeply. "Please show her in."

A few minutes later, Darcy Evans walked into his office. Although she had only worked with his grandfather for a short while, no more than six months, he remembered her. She had been quiet and kept to herself, much as Donna was inclined to do.

Chase crossed the room to shake her hand. "Ms.

Evans, it's been years. It's good to see you again. Please have a seat."

When she had taken the chair across from his desk he met her gaze and asked. "What can I do for you?" Chase couldn't help noticing that she appeared nervous.

"I wanted to talk to Ms. Claiborne but her place is closed up. She came to see me a couple of times during the past month."

Chase knew he looked puzzled and confused. "Jessica came to see you?"

"Yes. She didn't believe her grandfather took those recipes from your grandfather and wanted the truth. It's my understanding that she talked to me, Donald Schuster, Paula Meyers and Theodore Henry."

Chase recognized all the names except one. "Theodore Henry?"

"Yes, he was the cook for Schuster at the time I worked for your grandfather." She sighed deeply before saying, "Theodore and I were lovers."

Chase's eyes widened and he leaned forward from his desk. "You were?"

"Yes," she admitted. "We were together for almost a year, but we kept things a secret. He felt his job as a cook with Mr. Schuster was on shaky ground and was desperate. He asked me to find a way to take those recipes. At first I wouldn't do it. I liked Mr. Graham for getting me the job and I thought your grandfather was a nice man, although he could be rather bullheaded at times."

Chase nodded. He knew his grandfather could definitely be that. "But you eventually took them, Ms. Evans?"

She nervously clutched the straps on her purse as tears filled her eyes. "Yes. I'm the one who gave them to Theodore. I got upset that Mr. Westmoreland let Mr. Graham go and wanted to do something to lash out at him. One day he left his recipe book out on his desk while he was out making deliveries. I made copies and passed them on to Theodore."

Chase was surprised; usually his grandfather had kept the family recipe book under lock and key. The old man must have had a lot on his mind that particular day. "I appreciate you coming and telling me the truth. It's finally put a lot of ill feelings to rest."

"Then it's not too late?" she asked, wiping her tears.

He reached across his desk to hand her a tissue. "Too late for what?"

"You and Ms. Claiborne. She told me that she loved you and wanted to tell you the truth, but had wanted to prove her grandfather's innocence first so that you would believe her."

Chase leaned back in his chair, feeling lower than low. Jessica had tried to tell him the truth but he hadn't listened. A bad feeling erupted in the pit of his stomach. What if she wouldn't forgive him for not believing her? What if she didn't want any part of him?

"Mr. Westmoreland?"

Chase took a deep breath and realized he hadn't answered the woman's question. "No, it's not too late. I love Jessica and together we can work out anything."

He had said the words, and he hoped to God that they were true.

* * *

Jessica noticed Chase's sports car the moment she pulled into the parking lot. Her stomach fluttered nervously as she gathered her purse and shopping bag to go inside her shop.

Moments later, barely after she'd gotten inside and closed the door behind her, there was a knock. She opened the door to find an older gentleman standing there. "Flowers for Jessica Claiborne."

Jessica smiled. It would be just like Jennifer to send her flowers to cheer her up, she thought, gazing lovingly at the huge vase of beautiful red roses. There seemed to be two dozen of them. "Thanks," she said. "If you wait a moment I'll get you a tip."

The old man grinned. "No need. It's been taken care of." His grin then widened. "He's never sent a woman flowers before. At least not from our shop."

Jessica lifted a puzzled arched eyebrow. "Who?"

The man chuckled. "I can't say, but he signed the card, and since he's aware of my wife's penchant to gab, I'm sure he knows that word of this delivery will be all over Atlanta before the sun goes down today. But evidently he doesn't care about that. Good day, ma'am." And then the man walked off and Jessica watched him get into a van from Coleman's Florist.

Closing the door behind her, a puzzled Jessica walked over to the counter, put the flowers down and pulled out the card.

Love makes you do and say foolish things.
I'm sorry,
Chase

Jessica didn't move. She barely breathed. Chase had sent the flowers to apologize! Before she could gather her thoughts there was another knock on her door. She quickly crossed the room to open it and found Donna standing there smiling.

"Hello, Jessica. I have a delivery for you, compliments of Chase's Place," she said, handing Jessica a huge bag. The aroma let Jessica know that whatever was inside would be delicious.

Jessica smiled, accepting the bag. "There's enough food here to feed two people."

Donna chuckled. "I think that's the idea."

Before Jessica could say anything, Donna was gone. Closing the door behind her, Jessica walked over to the counter and placed the bag of food next to the flowers. Before she could take a look inside, there was another knock at the door. For a moment she didn't move. Her heart knew. Her body knew. Her soul knew.

It was Chase.

Taking a deep breath she forced her body to cross the room. She exhaled deeply before gripping the handle to slowly open the door.

He stood there, leaning in the doorway holding a bottle of wine in his hand. He looked sexy, good enough to eat. Out of habit she licked her lips and watched his gaze move to her mouth. Her stomach clenched and her pulse spiked.

He didn't appear angry. That was a good thing. She inhaled deeply, knowing she needed either to ask him in or to ask him to leave. "Would you like to come in?"

"Yes." He hadn't hesitated in responding.

She swallowed hard and stepped aside to let him in. Where was extra oxygen when you needed it? she wondered, closing the door behind him. She leaned against the closed door knowing if she took one step she would fall. Her knees were too weak to support her. At this moment, she thought Chase looked more devastatingly handsome than he'd ever been before.

"Thanks for the flowers," she decided to say. "And for the food."

"You're welcome, and this is for you, too," he said, handing the bottle of wine to her.

She took his offering. "Thanks." It was only then that she forced herself away from the door to walk across the room to place the bottle of wine next to the flowers and delicious food. She slowly turned around and he was there, next to her. She hadn't heard him move. The look in his eyes was filled with regret.

"I'm sorry. I should have listened to you. I should have believed you," he whispered brokenly.

"I'm sorry, too," she said as a lump filled her throat. "I should have told you the truth as soon as I knew who you were."

He took another step to close the distance separating them. "I had three days to think about things. To think about us. And I want there to be an us, Jessica. What happened between our grandfathers is in the past. And you were right. Carlton didn't take the Westmoreland recipes. Darcy Evans came to see me earlier today. She came here first and found the shop closed. She wanted you to know the truth. She was the one who took the recipes. She and

Theodore Henry were lovers and she took them to get back at my grandfather for letting your grandfather quit."

Jessica tensed and took a step back. She met his gaze. "Is that why you're here? Because Darcy's words proved my innocence?"

Chase shook his head. "No. Even before Darcy came to see me I had made up my mind about us. I knew that I loved you. You don't have a deceitful or unethical bone in your body. You're nothing like Iris and I'm sorry I ever thought it. Please forgive me."

She met his gaze. They had both made mistakes. "I'll only forgive you if you forgive me for not being completely honest with you from the beginning. But I was so determined to prove my grandfather's innocence. I promised my grandmother on her deathbed that I would."

"And you did."

Jessica was filled with emotion at the thought that she truly had. She inhaled deeply as Chase covered the distance between them and reached out and lifted her chin with his finger.

"I love you, Jessica. I love you so much." He gathered her into his arms and whispered, "And I want forever with you. I want to put an end to the bitterness between our families. I want to form a new Westmoreland and Graham partnership. Please marry me. I want to give you my babies, love you, protect you, till death do us part and even after that."

"Oh, Chase," she said as tears burned her eyes. "I want all those things, too."

The smile Chase gave her would endear him to her forever. And then she felt herself being lifted into big strong arms. "We'll eat later," he whispered against her lips as he carried her up the stairs.

She shivered with need as he placed her on the bed. Then he was on the bed with her, kissing her, removing her clothes. She was filled with desire and love; her pulse skittered with need so overbearing it took her breath away.

When she was completely naked he stood to remove his own clothes. But she wanted to do more than watch. She wanted to help. She eased out of bed and helped him take off his sweater. Next was his belt. Then she unzipped his pants so he could strip out of them. When he stood before her wearing nothing but a sexy pair of briefs, she reached out and skimmed her hand down his chest, moving lower to his stomach, needing to touch him to make sure she wasn't dreaming.

And then she eased down on her knees to remove the last piece of clothing that shielded his body. She took her time, easing the briefs down his legs. Then she placed a kiss on his navel before leaning back and meeting his gaze.

"Come here," he whispered hoarsely, holding his hand out to her.

He gently tugged her to her feet, held her close in his arms and she felt his engorged arousal press into her quivering stomach.

She met his gaze. "I wanted to—"

"I know," he said, cutting off her words and pulling her closer. "But had I allowed you to do that, things would have been over before they'd gotten started. You're still new at all of this, and I'm going to enjoy spending the rest of my life exploring things with you."

He grinned down at her. "There will never be a dull moment at our house. You are and forever will be my most delicious craving."

Jessica's entire body swelled with love. "Make love to me, Chase," she whispered hotly against his lips.

He swept her back into his arms and placed her on the bed and joined her there. She shivered as need, strong and potent, raced through her. He pulled her into his arms, promising her a voyage into ecstasy and she knew that he was right—there would never be a dull moment at their house. And that they would spend the rest of their lives together.

She might be his delicious craving, but he was definitely her most ardent chocolate delight.

Epilogue

Two months later,
Christmas Day

Jessica smiled at her sister who was asking questions a mile a minute. It was her wedding day and she couldn't wait to join her life with Chase's. They had decided that since all the Westmorelands came home for the holidays, today would be perfect. And it was.

"Slow down, Savannah, and let me answer your first question," she chuckled. "His name is Durango Westmoreland and he's Chase's cousin. He works as a park ranger in Montana."

She watched the interest in her sister's eyes. It had been there since the rehearsal dinner last night when Durango, whose plane had been late, had arrived at Chase's Place, proving without a doubt that all the Westmoreland men were sexy.

"Now are you going to help me put on my veil or are you going to continue to stand there in a daze?" Jessica asked her sister.

Savannah laughed as she stepped behind Jessica and tugged the veil in place. "You look beautiful, Jess."

Jessica smiled. She actually felt beautiful. She glanced at Savannah's reflection in the mirror. Her sister was beautiful too, with hazel eyes, skin the color of caramel and long, wavy black hair that flowed down her back.

Jessica had also noticed Durango checking her sister out last night, but he'd kept his distance.

"Durango doesn't like city women," she said, turning around to face her sister.

Savannah lifted a brow. "Why?"

Jessica shrugged. "Something to do with an old wound. And sister of mine, you're definitely city."

It was Savannah's turn to shrug. She then smiled. "I guess he'll have to learn to like us. Because after seeing him, I've decided I definitely have a thing for mountain men."

Jessica raised her eyes to the ceiling. She didn't know who would need her prayers more: Durango or Savannah. Deciding she didn't want to dwell on that, she smiled, knowing she only had a few moments left before she became Chase's wife.

She and Chase had wanted a small ceremony, but it seemed the Westmorelands didn't know the meaning of small—three hundred plus guests had been invited. With everyone's help they had pulled things off in two months. Savannah was her maid of honor and Chase's cousin Quade was his best man.

The two sisters hugged. "I'm happy for you, Jess," Savannah whispered brokenly.

"Thanks. Chase is a good man. I'm getting the best." She pulled back and gazed lovingly at her sister. "One day it will be your time."

Savannah chuckled and a mischievous glint appeared in her eyes. "Let's not hold our breath for that to happen."

Oh, God, she's beautiful, Chase thought as he watched Jessica walk down the aisle toward him on her brother's arm. He was filled with emotion and had to fight back the lump in his throat and the mistiness in his eyes.

When she reached his side he saw her tears of joy, lifted her hands to his lips and whispered, "I love you."

He saw her smile through her tears. She was making him the happiest man on earth today by becoming his wife. Together, they turned to face the minister. Before he started speaking, Chase spoke up and said, "I do."

The minister lifted a brow. "You do?"

Chase nodded. "Yes."

The minister, who had known Chase since birth smiled. "I haven't asked any questions yet, Chase."

"Doesn't matter. 'I do' to all of them." At his side, he heard a snort and knew it had come from Quade.

The minister's smile widened. "Nevertheless, we will go through the ceremony as planned."

A short while later the minister said, "I now pronounce you man and wife. You may kiss your bride, Chase."

And he did. He turned and gathered Jessica into his arms. There was nothing gentle about the kiss. He totally ignored the fact that he was standing before three hundred guests as he devoured his wife's mouth.

Durango…or maybe it was Storm…tugged on his tux tails and said, "Leave something for later, will you?"

Chase let go of Jessica's mouth and looked at her, then returned her smile and whispered, "I couldn't help it, sweetheart. You're simply delicious."

* * * * *

0111/05b

Live life to the full - give in to temptation

Four new sparkling and sassy romances every month!

Be the first to read this fabulous new series from 1st December 2010 at **millsandboon.co.uk** In shops from 1st January 2011

Tell us what you think!
Facebook.com/romancehq
Twitter.com/millsandboonuk

Don't miss out!

Available at WHSmith, Tesco, ASDA, Eason and all good bookshops

www.millsandboon.co.uk

Walk on the Wild Side
by Natalie Anderson

Jack Greene has Kelsi throwing caution to the wind—it's hard to stay grounded with a man who turns your world upside down! Until they crash with a bump—of the baby kind...

Do Not Disturb
by Anna Cleary

A preacher's daughter, Miranda was led deliciously astray by wild Joe... Now the tables have turned—he's her CEO! But Joe's polished exterior doesn't disguise his devilish side...

Three Weddings and a Baby
by Fiona Harper

Jennie's groom vanished on their wedding night. When he returns, he has his *toddler* in tow! Jennie can't resist Alex's appeal and, for a successful businesswoman, one kid should be easy...right?

The Last Summer of Being Single
by Nina Harrington

Sebastien Castellano, prodigal city playboy, has mysteriously returned home to his sleepy French village. Now he's reminding single mum Ella how much fun the *single* part can be!

On sale from 4th February 2011
Don't miss out!

Available at WHSmith, Tesco, ASDA, Eason and all good bookshops

www.millsandboon.co.uk